The Road To The Bridge

Laurence O'Bryan

Ardua Publishing
Argus House, Malpas Street
Dublin 8,
Ireland
http://arduapublishing.com

Ordering Information: Contact the publisher.

This novel is a work of fiction. Any resemblance to actual persons, living or long dead, is entirely deliberate.

Acknowledgements

I'd like to thank my editors, Sheryl Lee and Alex McGilvery, & early readers James Campbell, Marie Duff, Fichot Guillaume, Tanja Slijepčević, John Spencer and Susana Zabarskaya. All remaining errors are mine alone. Special thanks also to my wife, Zeynep, and my children, who've had a lot to put up with.

Historical Background & Recap
from The Sign of The Blood, the first novel in this series:

This new novel takes place between the years 307 A.D. and 312 A.D. The Roman Empire had numerous emperors in the preceding century. Constantine, the son of the Emperor Constantius Chlorus, had recently been proclaimed emperor by his troops in Eboracum (York in England) following the death of his father. Constantine had been helped to power by a slave, Juliana, and his friend Lucius, who had both traveled with him from the eastern provinces and were present when his father died. After his father's death Constantine headed for Treveris, the capital of the western Roman Empire at that time, where his mother also resided. Below are the real historical figures we encounter in this fictional retelling of a crucial period in world history.

Main Characters

The **Emperor Maxentius,** emperor of many Roman provinces, including Italy and much of Africa, and based in the city of Rome at this time.

Emperor Constantine, later to become Constantine the Great, thirty-five years old in 306 A.D., had recently proclaimed himself Augustus after the death of his father at Eboracum.

Helena, Constantine's mother, had separated from Constantine's father (now dead) the Emperor Chlorus, many years before this.

Theodora, a Roman aristocrat, and the **Emperor Chlorus'** widow.

Juliana, a fictional character I created to help tell the story of Constantine's bloody rise to power.

Place Names Used At The Time (307-312 A.D.)

Bithynia – A Roman province in what is now western Turkey.

Britannia – A Roman province now comprising England & Wales.

Caledonia – Much of Scotland, outside of Roman control.

Eboracum – The Roman city, now York, in the north of Britannia.

Gaul – A Roman province, now largely France.

Germania – Germany, most of which was outside the empire at this time.

Italia – Italy, the home province of the Roman Empire.

Londinium – The Roman city, now London, in southern Britannia.

Massilia – The Roman port city, now Marseilles, in southern Gaul.

Nicomedia –- The Roman city, capital of the Eastern Roman Empire at the time, now the city of Izmit in Turkey, on the Sea of Marmara.

Treveris – The Roman city, now Trier, in western Germany, on the River Moselle, inside the Roman Empire, capital of the western Roman Empire at that time. Also known as as Augusta Treverorum in official records of the period.

"When evil men advance against me to devour my flesh, when my enemies and my foes attack me, they will stumble and fall,"
Psalm 27:2.

Prologue

"Run, Juliana," shouted Missina. The light from the moon, filtered through layers of branches, was not enough to see clearly in the woods.

What Juliana could see was shadows approaching.

Missina, who'd brought her to the woods, promising to show her where the sweet herbs grew, faced the shadows. The thin herb-knife in her hand glistened as she raised it out to her side.

That was a wrong move.

A shriek split the air, followed by a gurgle. The arrow that pierced the slave's throat was almost as black as the shadows coming towards Juliana.

She turned and fled.

Branches whipped at her as she went, head down, leaping first one way, then another, tripping over a tree trunk, scrabbling to her feet, slipping on damp leaves as she listened for her pursuers.

Finally, chest aching, she stopped. The edge of the wood lay directly ahead. The sound of rushing water echoed. If this section of the river was similar to the section they'd passed on the road from Treveris, it would be as wide as a galley from end to end and as black as a pit.

She bent forward, struggling to slow her breathing, to stop her chest pounding. Bile rose in her throat. Her hands covered her mouth. They were trembling. Missina should not have tried to stop them. She should have put her knife down.

1

A rustling noise startled her. She spun around. Fear screamed inside her, tightening every muscle. Why had they been so willing to kill? Were they coming?

She strained to catch any sound.

An owl hooted. Then another.

She moved slowly, brushing against branches, holding them so they wouldn't snap back. Ahead lay the river. When she reached its bank, a bird flapped behind her. She looked up at the clouds.

No wings beat into the sky.

Water glistened ahead like black marble. The river reeked of moss and the marshes that lined its banks all the way downstream to where it joined the Rhine. She waded in. Her breathing quickened as the ice-cold water came up her body. When it reached her neck, she let the flow take her and half-floated half-walked downstream, shivering and shaking, her breath coming fast through bared teeth, her feet catching on weeds.

But she'd escaped.

When she got back to the palace she'd order Constantine to scour these woods and punish the bandits who'd done this. How could they? Anger rose fast inside her. She didn't deserve this. Missina didn't deserve to die like that. All they were doing was looking for healing herbs at night, at the best time to cut them.

She waded on, her hands out of the water. Soon she would pull herself back onto land and look for the road to Treveris.

Something flew through the air, wrapping itself around her head. She pulled at it but it was all around her, as if snakes had fallen on her. What evil was this?

She looked to the riverbank. Shadows were moving. She kicked out, but it was no good. A net had closed all around her. She was yanked to the side and her feet came out from under her.

As she lay on a slab of cold mud at the riverside, panting, one of the shadows bent down to her.

The man spoke in rough Latin. "We will keep you, but try no tricks or you will die as quickly as your friend did."

"I must go back for my child," she said softly.

He leaned near her. "You should not have come walking in the woods if you have a child to look after."

I

The Roman City of Treveris (Trier) - Northern Gaul, 307 A.D.

Constantine paced back and forth in the basilica. The three scouts he had sent looking for Juliana were standing with their hands in front of them, their heads down. He stopped at the one in the middle, the oldest man. His gray hair was pulled back into a ponytail and there were three bronze arm rings on each bare arm.

"What did you find?" He jabbed a finger into the man's chest.

The man looked at him, stony eyed. "We found tracks at the river, signs of a struggle. They can't have gone far. The tracks disappeared. Whoever took her knows how to hide. We need more men to look properly, and cavalry to hunt further east. That is why we came back." His accent was rough, Germanic.

Constantine took a step nearer him. He could smell the seediness of the man's breath. "Tell me what you don't want to say."

The man looked up, licked his lips. "A Saxon raiding party passed near here last summer. Maybe they came back." He shrugged. "You were not here last year. The governor sent a cohort after them, but we didn't catch them. We watched the roads. But they never use them. They only travel at night and across country."

Constantine pointed at the commander of the Alemanni cavalry standing to one side. "Get your men ready, Crocus. We are going on a hunt."

He left the basilica by the back door, almost at a run. It was early summer, and his father less than a year in the ground. His authority in Britannia, Gaul and Hispania, his provinces, the western provinces of the empire, had been confirmed and preparations were almost complete for him to go to Rome to be officially proclaimed co-emperor. He'd been exhorted to come without his legions. The messenger who had carried the invitation claimed he had nothing to fear from the other emperors.

Constantine had still not decided how many troops he would take as a personal guard or if he would go at all. Crocus wanted a cavalry unit to go with him. Juliana had pleaded with him to take at least one legion.

He had to find Juliana.

There was no reason for her not to return. Something must have happened. His hands became fists. Curses. She still acted like a slave. He should have warned her. This was not the east. The frontier was near. There were good reasons they needed so many watch towers along the river that separated them from the warring tribes of Germania.

Why had he let her go outside the palace so often? He should have stopped it. He took a turn to the left in the flag-stone corridor that led to their house at the back of the palace compound. The governor of the city had given them the building when he and Juliana, and their baby son, had moved back into the city at the start of winter.

The building was similar in layout to the villa of any prosperous merchant in Rome. At its center lay an atrium, where he and Juliana spent most of their time together. When he wasn't giving orders and listening to his officers at the legion command headquarters in the east of the city, by the parade ground, this was where he preferred to be.

Marcus, the master of the household slaves, stood waiting at the entrance to the atrium, his head down.

"Get my horse ready. And assemble ten of the best men of the imperial guard at the eastern gate at once, ready for a hunt."

"Yes, my lord. But there is someone waiting for you."

Constantine knew at once what the worried tone in Marcus' voice meant. There was only one person who could make him like this.

He pushed the door to the atrium open.

"Mother, you have come at the wrong time. Juliana is missing. I need to go and search for her now."

Helena sat upright on the cushion filled couch by the back wall, under a painting of Hercules battling with the Hydra.

She did not get up as he approached. Her stern look gave away her mood as she held out her hand for him to kiss.

"Juliana is why I am here to speak with you, Constantine."

"I must go, Mother. I have no time to debate Juliana's merits with you."

Helena bent forward until her face was hidden. A sob emanated from her. Constantine went toward her and put a hand on her shoulder.

"Do not despair of me, Mother." He glanced around to see if there were any slaves nearby. He hadn't seen any when he came in, but they could be very quiet and in the background, listening, ready to spread gossip.

"There is no need to do this. Juliana accepts that I must have an official marriage. She accepts her place. She will not stand in your way."

Helena looked up. "It is the right thing for you." A smile beamed from her face.

He could not smile back. "Juliana understands I will do whatever is needed to be proclaimed emperor in Rome and secure my position. So, you can stop your scheming. Now I must go and find her."

He turned and went to the chest near the door, opened it, and picked out the dark gray traveling cloak that lay inside, the one he used to disguise himself when he went out into the city. He called loudly for a house slave. When the boy arrived, he helped Constantine undo his leather breast plate adorned with medallions, and to fasten the simpler breast plate of a legionary.

There was no point in attracting too much attention on the roads east of the city. The frontier with the Germanic tribes lay two hundred and fifty leagues to the east, too far to travel in one night, or even three. If Saxon raiders had taken Juliana, there was a good chance they could be caught before they reached the Rhine and safety on the far side.

But if it had been raiders, what were they doing so far south? And what would they be doing to Juliana if they had captured her?

"Leave it," he said as the boy fidgeted with the last harness strap.

When he reached the imperial stables at the back of the palace compound, the men he'd asked for were mounting their horses.

All that day they searched for Juliana. They found the body of the slave Juliana went to the woods with, in a pool of blood, her limbs splayed out and flies buzzing around the arrow wound in her neck. Her head had been twisted too and her neck broken, probably after death, so that it faced almost behind her.

Constantine feared the worst when he saw that.

His heart pounded in his chest as they searched, forcing their way through every nearby thicket, expecting at any moment to find Juliana's body, but when they'd completed a wide circuit of the nearby area he was comforted by the thought that they'd taken her.

Helena would be happy if they had, but for Constantine the blow was devastating. Juliana had brought laughter and beauty to his household, and her warmth in his bed and by his side had helped him do all that he needed to do to secure his position in the past year.

They reached a narrow river, a tributary of the Rhine, by the afternoon. They searched first upriver, then down, until eventually they found fresh tracks leading to the water.

"Find the cavalry commander back in Treveris," he said to one of the guards. "He has ordered a troop of cavalry ahead towards the Rhine. Tell him to order two more cavalry troops to search north of here, and that they must split up and search the woods as they get near the river. Tell him there is a reward of a hundred gold coins for each man in the troop that finds Juliana."

The man smiled, then began his journey back to Treveris at a canter.

Constantine called the other men to him. Many were veterans who had fought with his father in campaigns against the Germanic tribes on the other side of the Rhine.

"We must find Juliana tonight. From the direction they took between this point and where they slew the slave, it looks like they are heading north, not east. It will take them longer to reach the river this way, but it will give us more time to find them. It is likely they rested all day and are only starting out again now, as the dusk falls. We will go on in pairs, within sight of each other and at a walk. If you see or hear anything, look for me. I will be in the center of the line. Make no sound. Let's find them."

But it wasn't to be.

They spent the whole night searching, and as the moon went down they reached a wide meadow one pair after the other. Not one of them had seen or heard anything unusual.

They needed a rest.

"Stand watch and when the sun rises above the trees, wake us," he said to one of the older legionaries. To another, he said, "Ride back now to Treveris as quickly as you can. Tell Crocus he must sweep the woods behind us in case the bastards are still hiding. You can sleep when you get back to Treveris and have given your message." The legionary saluted and hurried away.

Their horses were tied to trees and left to doze standing up. The men slept wrapped in their cloaks in an area of thin grass nearby

It wasn't long until dawn.

Constantine knew they could spend another day and another night at this, but they hadn't brought enough rations for a long hunt and would need to find a town or village soon. The only good news was that they hadn't found Juliana, with her neck broken and the last of her blood seeping into the ground to feed it.

That meant she'd either told them who she was, or whoever had taken her wanted her for another reason.

II

In the Woods, North East Gaul, 307 A.D.

Juliana's hands were tied tight together by a thin rope. A gag had been placed over her mouth. She'd fallen a few times as they led her through the woods by a narrow path, and each time they'd pulled her quickly to her feet and rubbed over the ground where she fell with a branch. All that had come from her each time was a muffled groan.

All night they'd walked.

At dawn, the men stopped as sunlight filtered through the trees. They found a bush filled clearing and pushed her under the bushes until they were all near the center, in a place with soft ground and a roof of brambles.

As she came to her knees there two of the men held her tight and removed the gag. They took a knife out and waved it at her as they put a finger to their lips, ordering her to be quiet.

She nodded in reply, imagining what they were planning for her. She trembled. She did not try to hide it. Better they thought she was weak for now. If a moment came when she might escape, they would be less watchful.

So far, she had focused on survival only, putting one foot in front of the other, praying to the mother god that she would dry out quickly from her time in the river, but now they'd stopped, anything could happen.

The only comforting thought was that if they wanted to kill her, they would have done so already.

They passed her a water skin and some hard, dark bread and after she had eaten, they grabbed her and put the gag back across her mouth. Then they waved her to lie down. She shivered almost uncontrollably at the thought of what they might do next.

But all they did was lie in a ring around her with one of them attached by his wrist to the thin rope around both her wrists. She tried picking the knot free, but every time she moved one of them looked at her and after a while, waiting for them to fall asleep, she put her own head down and fell into a deep slumber, filled with long-haired men in dirty tunics, their skin covered with swirling symbols.

She woke, despairing at where she was, wondering how her baby was. The thought of him came so strong into her mind she thought she could smell him, that he was somewhere close. She had such a strong urge to beg them to release her, her hands shook. But she resisted the urge, pressing her hands together under her chin.

The men from her dreams were around her on their knees or still lying down. It was light, but the sun was lowering fast. Her bones ached from the hard ground. One of the men shuffled toward her. He had thick black hair in a ponytail. The sides of his head were shaven well above his ear on each side and blue animal face symbols entwined around his skull.

"If you say you will not scream if we hear people looking for you I will let you speak, and we will agree not to cut your heart out and eat it for our next meal." His Latin was good, but his accent made it sound as if he growled instead of speaking.

She stared at him, then nodded.

He pulled her gag away. Then he reached forward and touched her chin. She tried to stop it, but her chin shook.

She waited patiently until his eyes lit with the pleasure of touching her, then she swiped at his hand, catching his skin with her nails, even though her hands were tied. She wasn't going to be easy. He pulled his hand back, his eyes wide. One of the other men around them laughed. Others joined in.

The man she'd struck reached for his belt and pulled a long knife out from a leather sheath. Its handle shone blackly. She stared at it, her trembling getting worse. He pointed it at her, then he held it, handle first, toward her.

She knew what he meant.

He was giving her a chance to try to kill him or to kill herself. But this was not the moment to seek freedom.

And she could never kill herself. She'd been through worse than this, even if it was a long time ago.

She could survive more than most, too. If a Roman matron had been captured, a woman used to slaves doing her bidding, she would probably have died of shock already.

Juliana shook her head. She would defend her virtue, but she would not start a knife fight she had no chance of winning with so many men around her.

The man put the blade away and motioned her to come closer.

"The only reason we do not take turns with you is that you must be pure for the selection. If you pass that test we will decide which of us will fill you up. And I promise you, we are hung bigger than your Roman friends, so you will enjoy any one of us a lot more than when they plowed you." He grinned. "But until we cross the great river you must be quiet, if you wish us not to feast on your beating heart. Do you so swear?"

Juliana nodded. "Who are you people?" She looked around at their faces. Many of them looked very different to the people in Treveris. Their foreheads were wider and half of them had dirty blond hair, with a wide sweep above their ears shaved and tattooed.

"My name is Athralar. That is all you need to know." He pointed at her. "What is your name."

"Juliana."

He made a sign to the men around them, his hand sweeping outward. They strapped on their swords and pulled on their cloaks. Athralar went first out from under the bush. The forest around them was gloomy as dusk fell. He led them at a fast walk, with Juliana in the middle, her hands tied and the rope leading to a man in front of her with a giant head and a bird's nest of red hair on the top of his head.

All that night they walked. When the moon disappeared behind clouds she thought they would stop, but they didn't. The path they followed was thin, but clear of all obstructions and ran mostly straight. When they came across a gully or stream they simply headed straight across and each time they picked up the path unerringly. Juliana wondered about Constantine. He would come after her, she was sure of that, but would he find her and what would happen if he did?

That could be the most dangerous moment for her.

And what was this selection Athralar had spoken about? She had heard tales of the German tribes sharing their slaves with all the young men of the tribe on one night. And not only slaves, but the wives of any man who died in battle too. It was considered a gift for the women, the old slave who'd told her the story had said. Then she'd giggled, showing the black stumps of her teeth.

They slept in an earthen mound the next day. There had been no need for her to even think about crying out as they walked, as they'd heard only owls all night and later the pre-dawn chorus of wood pigeons. The mound appeared dry and as the chamber inside was not big enough to stand up in, and there was not enough room inside for them all in any case, some of the men slept in the stone lined passage.

Once they were inside one of the men struck flint on a wall stone and lit a rush candle. He put it out soon after he'd passed her his water bottle and some more black bread. She stuffed it all in her mouth in case he changed his mind and lay down as the other men were doing. The bread tasted gritty but was welcome. Her stomach had been growling constantly and even her bones felt tired.

She could smell the bodies around her much stronger this night and their snuffling and snoring echoed so loudly from the stone walls and roof she did not sleep for long. The fact that she had not heard any pursuers all through the night told her that whoever was looking for her was looking in the wrong places.

Finally, she slept a little more and woke to a tug and a rough push that told her to leave the mound. The following night, after walking far again, they reached another river. From the position of the sun she knew they were still heading north. Worms of dread churned inside her as she remembered the stories she'd heard about what the tribes did to strangers in Germania.

"This is not the great river, but it shows us the way," said Athralar, who stood near her. "We will be out of Roman territory soon and into the lands of giants." He put both his hands up, palms forward, as if feeling the heat of a fire.

"That is what Roman farmer's wives call us, you know, when they see us after we have killed their husbands and when they are begging us not to cut their children's heads off." He laughed, pulled a dirty satchel from his shoulder and opened it for her to look inside.

She peered in and then pulled back. A human scalp lay inside. It was clearly a recent kill as the smell from the skin did not overpower, but she could still feel the stink of it tickling at her nostrils.

She looked around. All the other men had similar satchels. She'd assumed they were for food, but some of the men had a second, larger satchel, too. The smaller ones all looked full.

Her stomach turned as she wondered what her scalp would look like in a bag.

"It is an honor to lose your head to a Saxon raiding party, Juliana. These scalps will adorn the great tree. We have buried the heads they came from so we can collect them next year when they are whitened skulls. They will be protected by Frigg until then, and each will be brought back to life at the end of all things. Would you not want such an honor too?" He smiled. "I would be happy to end my life this way."

She didn't answer. She stared ahead. She could not show them her fear. They would despise her for it. The weak could not expect to live long in Germania.

III

The festival of Magna Mater was being celebrated that day at Maxentius' palace on the Via Appia, with a party so extravagant none of the other high-patrician families could hope to match it.

Which was why most of those families were here, in the flower bedecked, triple height marble-floored hall with a midnight blue painted ceiling covered with silver stars in astrological patterns.

Other parts of the palace had not been completed yet, but what had been finished gave a powerful signal for what Maxentius planned to do with his imperial power. It was also the first festival since the celebration of his victory over Emperor Severus and his assumption of the title, Augustus.

To be crowned with that title had been the goal of most of his life, but now it had been achieved, now that he was co-ruler of most of the known world, he had to prove that not only was he worthy, he was also blessed by the gods.

And he had rivals to watch.

Each of his co-emperors would have spies in Rome watching everything he did. In theory, they ruled the provinces they'd been allocated without enmity between them. But such aspirations had proved ever more difficult to adhere to.

He had decided, to ensure the word went out that he was prosperous and loved by the gods and by his people, that no expense would be spared for the celebrations in Rome of the festival of the great mother.

A troop of Gaulish druids, or at least men who claimed to be druids and looked the part, were parading naked, their members flailing around as they danced with their heads adorned with antlers down the center of the hall. Behind them a troop of Greek drummers beat loudly. Behind them a group of priestesses of the great mother, their bare breasts swinging as they danced, threw petals in the air, taken from red bags on each hip.

Maxentius lay on a couch at a long table at the top of the room, looking toward the procession passing through from the north entrance to the south. Beside him sat the high priestess of the cult of Magna Mater, the Great Mother. Her breasts were covered in gold leaf.

She leaned toward him. "You are planning a circus nearby, I am told."

He smiled. "Not just a circus, Great Mother, but the largest ever built in Rome."

"You will be remembered for all time, as is fitting for the greatest Augustus Rome has ever seen," she replied, her smile rigid on her face. She turned and waved one of the priestesses hovering behind her forward.

"This is Paulina. She will serve you in whatever secret arts you need performed."

Maxentius looked the priestess up and down. She had jet black hair down to her white breasts and was both muscular and well proportioned. Each of her bare upper arms had a wide gold band circling it.

"What arts does Paulina know?"

"She spent three years in the east studying medicines, and poisons. She is also trained in the Egyptian arts of seduction. You may try her and discover for yourself what that means." She waved Paulina to come even nearer. As Paulina did she opened her mouth, licked her lips slowly and stared straight into Maxentius' eyes.

He laughed and turned his head, looking for his wife, who was deep in conversation with a young senator. He turned back to Paulina, beckoned her to him.

When her head came close to his, he said, "Come back to my gate at dawn and we will celebrate a new year of the great mother together. My guards will be waiting for you." He put a hand to her cheek. It had the soft texture of silk. "I will be too."

She bowed, then stepped slowly backward, his gaze on her all the way until she turned and disappeared into a crowd of slaves carrying trays of sweet meats.

"You can depend on Paulina," said the high priestess, "she will not let you down. Tell her the name of the man or woman who must die, and it will happen as fast as you wish it. She has never failed to infiltrate a household, either by convincing the man that she loves him or a woman that she is her friend."

"And what does she do after a job is done?" Maxentius' attention was distracted by a group of young dancing girls, whose long hair flapped wildly around them.

"She comes back to us and is protected by us, my lord."

"Good."

The high priestess leaned closer to Maxentius. "What task can I tell her you need performed? Will she stay and help you here in Rome or do you have something else in mind?"

He looked at her, his gaze hardening. "If you speak of what I will tell you I will cut your heart out and feed it to my pigs, Great Mother. My praetorians will not respect the sanctity of any temple if I order it. Forget this and they will tear yours down until no two stones are piled upon each other."

She pulled back. "My lord, If I betray you, I would expect even worse."

He leaned close to her. "I have a task for Paulina in Treveris."

The high priestess leaned so close to him her breasts rubbed against Maxentius' bare arm. "You want her to kill your rival, the upstart Constantine?" She clapped her hands. "This is why I chose Paulina. No man has ever refused her."

Maxentius waved at his wife, who was staring at him from the next table, then shook his head slowly as he replied to the priestess. "Paulina must seduce Constantine and use any feminine wile to gain his confidence. And she must come to me when she has information that will damage him, no matter how long that takes." He jabbed a stubby finger at the priestess. "Make certain she knows what the consequences will be if she does not carry out every part of this task. Understood?"

The priestess nodded.

IV

The West Bank of the Rhine, North East Gaul, 307 A.D.

Constantine stroked his horse's neck as he looked across the river. Sweat glistened on his mount's flanks. The ride that had brought them here had been hard and fast. On the far side of the river, half a league away, the marshland that marked the start of Germania began. Beyond the marshes the dark line of the endless forest stood out clearly like a black rope.

If Juliana had already been taken across the river there would be little hope of getting her back without the cooperation of the tribes beyond. He dismounted and led his horse to the water's edge. The men with him did the same. The land sloped gently down to the water at this point. It was an ideal place to begin a crossing.

"Emperor," called out one of the men to Constantine's left, where the forest came close to the riverbank in a tangle of thick roots. "Look at the marks here. These could be from a raft."

Constantine looked down at where he was pointing. There were long, clear gouges in the mud leading to the water. He looked back up to the road and the forest behind it to where they had come. Whoever had chosen to place the Roman watch towers along the bank to warn of raiders had clearly missed this perfect spot for landing any craft. He looked around for footprints, a smaller one in particular, a sign that she had been here. There was nothing obvious. He shook his fist at the river. The endless frustration during their ride through the woods had worn him down.

Emotion rose inside him. He pushed it away, tightened his fist. No weakness was allowed. He had to be careful what his men saw in him. He'd had hardly any sleep during the past two days. It was an excuse for how he felt, but he could not use it. Only the weak use excuses.

"This means nothing," said a voice behind him. "There are a hundred places like this along the river."

"How do you know this?" said Constantine, turning.

"I patrolled here for two years."

Constantine put a hand on the man's thick leather shoulder pad. "Have you been across to the far side?"

The man nodded. "A few times. We went in pursuit of the thieving Alemanni who stole horses and the wives and daughters of farmers, the legionaries your father had settled here. We never had any luck finding them. They disappeared into the endless forest over there. We heard there are tribes beyond the Alemanni who use young women for their evil festivals where human brains are eaten, and the blood of young men and women is drunk until the warriors have had their fill. They claim it keeps them young."

Constantine stared into the man's sky-blue eyes. "Is this what you think will happen to Juliana?"

The man stared back. His eyes were bloodshot from lack of sleep and his beard looked haggard with bits of straw in it and clumps of hard biscuit around his mouth. "This is what I fear." His eyes searched Constantine's.

"Well, we must stop that happening." Constantine smiled and looked back up toward the road. It stretched away on each side, set well back from the riverbank. "Which way should we go to find a boat to take us across, or should we make our own raft? Which will get us across quicker?"

"A few leagues north of here there is a fort. Last time I passed they had two patrol barges pulled up on the shore."

"Let's find those patrol boats."

It was early afternoon before Constantine sat in a flat-bottomed patrol boat with four oarsmen pulling hard as it made its way across the river with him and three of his men. This was all the boat could carry without risking all their lives. Four horses were swimming behind the boat, tied separately to the back of it with hairy, ancient looking ropes. These were the strongest of the horses, but there was still a chance they would drown and that their rope would have to be cut to prevent them tipping the boat over.

The commander of the small wooden fort had told him the second boat was unusable and that no order had come to replace it, so a new one had not been made.

He also said that an Alemanni village lay on the far side of the river, opposite the Roman fort. It was why the fort had been established here. They could watch fishing skiffs coming and going on the far side and if groups of men were being carried over, they would see them.

"You would not see them at night, though, would you?" Constantine had said.

"No, they can come and go at night as they please, but mostly they stay on the far side," said the fort commander.

"Do you ever go across?"

"Yes," said the commander. "We trade with them. They bring us amber and furs. We give them wine and olive oil."

That was why there were two amphorae in the bottom of the boat. One had the dark red tinge of a Gaulish wine amphora. The other had the yellowish tinge of an olive oil amphora from Hispania.

The oarsmen bent to their task as they worked the oars to head across to the fishing village on the far shore. The pilot called a rhythm to them which must also have acted as a warning to the village they were heading for. As they came closer, Constantine could see smoke drifting into the air from three mud-brown roundhouses near the shore. The houses were surrounded by a woven wicker fence. He had seen villages like this across the northern parts of Gaul. The fence was mostly used to keep their pigs and chickens in. Its defensive uses were limited as it could be cut through by anyone with an axe or a well sharpened sword.

No one stood waiting for them on the muddy shore bank as they arrived, where two thin skiffs were pulled up on the mud bank, but at the gate to the wicker enclosure a group of three men stood waiting, knives on their belts and swords dangling from their hands. The men had long straggly hair, reaching below their shoulders, and parts of their heads were shaven at the sides or at their forehead. They wore animal skin tunics and one of them had a shiny neck ring. Their beards were long and plaited.

As Constantine's boat came toward the shore it slowed, at the command of its pilot. He turned and looked at Constantine. He was waiting for an order. This was the moment Constantine could decide to turn back and get more men and more boats, perhaps a fleet. He had been advised by the head of the imperial treasury, before he left Treveris, not to pursue a missing concubine, but to send his troops. It was not right, the man said, that he exposed himself to danger in this way. He would definitely not have approved of what Constantine was doing now.

The man had been appointed by Constantine's father. He was one of the many older officials Constantine had decided not to replace, yet.

He knew the man was right in his advice, but he could not just sit in Treveris when it came to looking for Juliana. The thought of doing that sickened him. What man would do that for a woman he loved? He owed her this, at least. Juliana had helped him achieve the purple. She brought joy to his life. She was the mother of his child.

He would not leave the search to others, whatever the dangers.

He waved for the pilot to go in and jumped out first into the shallow water and then strode up towards the village, his men scrambling to keep up.

It was a real risk looking for her on this side of the river, but he knew instinctively that he had to act quickly to have any hope of finding her. The biggest problem was that he had so few men with him if they did come across a large group of raiders.

The commander of the fort had told him that the peace treaty with the Alemanni tribe on the far side of the river was definitely still holding, and that there would be no immediate danger in a short trip across the river. He'd emphasized the word immediate.

These Alemanni villagers would be wary, as they didn't know who he was, but they would probably be hoping he would want to trade when they saw him approaching. The commander had also provided one auxiliary legionary as an interpreter, a man they usually used when they wanted to trade with the fishing villages along the river and beyond.

And Constantine did want to trade.

For information.

"One of you stay with the horses. The other two come with me and take an amphora each," he shouted over his shoulder.

When Constantine and the two legionaries beside him reached the entrance to the village the three men there were smiling broadly. The man with the neck ring had his fist up in a greeting.

Constantine and his men were led into the largest of the round houses. Inside, there were women at the back working at something in a group in a corner, and in the center of the house a fire flickered in a raised hearth. Beyond the hearth stood a tree stump carved into a seat. An old man with long gray hair sat there. At his feet were two young boys.

The interpreter bowed and went forward. He laid an amphora down in front of the man and started talking. Constantine waited. The interpreter turned and pointed at him. The young boys and the women stared, a look of wonder on their faces. News that the new emperor of the western provinces had come across the river himself in pursuit of raiders would travel fast. Hopefully, his appearance, boldness and youth would be good for his reputation.

But the old man laughed as he looked at Constantine.

"What's the joke," said Constantine, loudly.

The old man laughed again.

"He wonders what this woman has between her legs that you have to come here looking for her," said the interpreter, turning to Constantine. He had a bemused look on his face, as if he too wondered why Constantine was here.

Constantine put his hand to the hilt of his sword and rattled it hard in its scabbard.

"I know you don't value your women," he said, as he took a step forward. "But I believe you don't like things being stolen from you, do you? Well neither do I."

At the back of the hut two men appeared out of the shadows. They were both carrying spears, holding them on their shoulders, as if they were about to throw them.

Constantine put a leather boot on the amphora. "Perhaps our friend doesn't want our wine or our oil."

That was when he noticed the skulls around the bottom of the tree stump the old man sat on, and the necklace he wore with what looked like finger bones dangling from it.

The old man stood. For a moment Constantine thought they would have to fight their way out, but the man bowed and waved Constantine forward.

Then he spoke in a long stream of strange words. When he stopped the interpreter translated.

"The village chief wishes you well in your search for what was taken from you and thanks you for your gifts. He says he too had a woman who became lost in the forest many years ago. But she still gives him gifts every day." He smiled.

Constantine took his foot off the amphora.

"Ask him has a party of raiders crossed back to this side of the river in the last few days."

An exchange with the old man followed.

"They have seen no one and have kept to the treaty themselves, never landing on the far bank for any reason. He asks would you be interested in one of his daughters."

The old man barked. Two young women stood and came forward. Their breasts were bare and their hair wild and blonde. They giggled and bared their surprisingly white teeth.

Constantine shook his head.

"Ask him to send a message to all the other chieftains in the kingdom of the Alemanni. Tell them all that I will blame them if this slave who was stolen from me is not returned unharmed. Anyone who aids the thieves will lose their own slaves and their heads if they do not return what is mine." He shouted the last few words. The two men with spears came closer. They could skewer him in an instant.

He could kill them both.

The old man raised a hand. He spoke slowly, as if trying to calm things down. The interpreter translated.

"He will send a messenger to the other chieftains along the river and also get word to the Alemanni fortress deep in the forest where the council of elders meets. They have not approved any raids on Roman soil, and they will search for your woman. And they will find her."

The old man waved at someone behind Constantine. Constantine turned and called the other legionary who crossed the river with him forward. The man put his amphora down beside the other one.

As he did Constantine spoke. "Tell him we will be back before the next new moon if Juliana is not returned by then." He put a hand over his heart. "And tell him that peace with Rome depends on me getting back what was stolen."

Constantine left the round house. The horses were saddled and ready. He looked along the riverbank. A path led off each way along the bank.

"Wait for us until nightfall," he called out to the pilot. The pilot gave a thumbs up in reply.

All that day they rode. By the time they returned to the village their horses were about to die on their feet and rain had started. All they saw during the day, on the single horse track by the river, was the occasional small round house near the shore, all with an abandoned air, and some racks of fish drying near a second village.

Reaching that village was the point he decided to turn around. Six spear men stood near the entrance to it and skulls stood out in a long row, dangling from the branches of a tree nearby. He needed more men to do this properly.

He turned and headed back as behind him jeers rang out. He raised a fist. "I'll be back for you," he shouted.

V

The Alemanni Forrest, Germania, 307 A.D.

Juliana spat out what the man had forced into her mouth. It tasted like dirt. It looked like dirt too.

"If you do not eat, I will be forced to cut off one of your fingers every day until you change your mind. And believe me, you will, whether it's when you have nine fingers or only two left." Athralar held the piece of wet dark bread towards her. It had been raining all that night and still they had marched on. She had expected they would travel by day now they were in Germania, but they didn't. And they still kept the rope on her wrists.

She bit at the sodden bread, almost taking part of his finger. "When my master finds out I have been taken, he will come for me. And if he finds you he will skin you alive. Then he will salt your body until you scream yourself to death," she hissed at him.

Athralar leaned toward her, his face close to hers. "I do not fear your words. Where we are going no Roman master can reach us, no matter who they are. No Roman army has ever reached our territory and they never will. We are protected by Woden and Frigg and one hundred thousand warriors who could march on Rome and burn it to the ground if we wanted to, today," he hissed back at her.

Juliana stared at him.

The Persians she had met had the same arrogance. But they had been defeated by a Roman army soon after. She knew Constantine would come for her. The question was, would he bring enough men?

"Whose territory are we heading for? Who are you?" She looked at the brown markings on his arms and neck. They were unlike any she had seen in Treveris or Gaul. They were a mix of animal heads, all twisting and on top of each other. He had a wide wrist-guard above each hand, adorned with lumps of amber. She had never seen anyone wearing such a thing and she'd seen many different tribespeople in the market in Treveris.

"We are Saxons from a deep place in the great forest where it meets the white flecked sea. A Roman army would not dare come near us as they know their skulls would deck our halls, so know this, your master will not dare come after you. You are ours now."

She waited until he pulled his head back, then replied, "Is that where you are taking me, Saxon territory?"

He grunted.

"What will happen when I get there?"

He leaned toward her again. "Do not be concerned. You will do well at the selection. Women like you who are clever and…" He reached forward to cup her breast. She pulled back just in time. "…fertile always get selected."

"Selected for what?" She swallowed the last piece of bread in her mouth.

He shook his head. "You will see. All I can tell you is there are others brought to the selection from every direction for a thousand leagues and that you will enjoy the feasting."

She slept badly the following day. Thoughts of her son were so strong it felt as if she'd been poisoned. She started silently repeating a prayer to block his face out whenever it appeared in her mind. She had to survive this.

She had a nightmare in which Constantine, at the head of a Roman legion, lay dying, overwhelmed by a host of Saxon tribesmen like Athralar who filled a great white plain as far as the horizon. She felt an urge to warn Constantine not to come looking for her.

She closed her eyes, pressed her fists to her lips. She had to accept her fate. The great mother had taken him from her. But her time with him had been taken for a reason. She had to trust. Every part of her life had seemed cursed, a show of giving her things and taking them away, so now she would have to accept whatever came next.

"Get ready for another night of good hard marching," said Athralar, as he pushed at her with the toe of his hard leather shoe.

She got to her feet. Three days and nights she had worn the same clothes and had slept in them too. She had lived like this as a child, when she was working at the big estate in the east, but in the last year she had become used to having a different, lighter tunic at night and washing every day. And drinking watered down wine when she wanted. She'd even got a taste for the light wine and honey drink that Constantine favored.

The drink the Saxons shared with her had a sharper taste. She didn't like it, so she sipped only a little from the skin bag that Athralar passed her as they got ready to start walking again.

That night a half-moon filtered clearly through the trees, lighting the way. At one point they stopped when growls rose up behind them. The men all turned, looking toward the sound, and one took a bow from behind his back and notched an arrow. The growling went on, but no animal appeared.

"The bears around here like to fight," said Athralar, when they made their way onward. "If you ever think of running away you should know there are large wolf packs in this forest too. Traveling without companions to fight them off is a sure route to having your bones sucked clean."

She'd heard about children being taken by wolves in Gaul, but it happened so rarely people spoke about it in hushed tones. It was always assumed that in Germania such things were a regular occurrence.

She held her hands up. "Untie me. I will not run away." She smiled at him. She would need help to get back to Roman lands safely. If she could persuade this one to help her, she would.

Athralar cut the rope around her wrists. A few of the men made comments she didn't understand. He walked near her from that point. The forest grew thicker then, and they passed up and down steep hills with ravines appearing occasionally, where you could kill yourself if you took a wrong step.

"Give me a knife if the wolves come for us, Athralar," she said to him, as the moon went down and the first light of dawn could be seen in the sky, and distant howls echoed through the trees.

27

"You will not get a knife in your hand until you are back in our lands and we have decided what to do with you. You will just have to use your hands against them."

She snorted. "You want me to think you're protecting me, is that it?" She pressed her fist into his shoulder. "Is that it?"

"You will appreciate protection if the wolves come."

But they didn't come. And Juliana and the men slept in a large cave in a rock wall that marked the edge of the dense forest. The next night the forest thinned, and the land became flatter. They progressed faster now, but stopped halfway through the night as the moon went down and the forest around them became as black as a pit.

One man lit a small fire. She knew what it meant. They felt safer here.

She slept in her cloak again that day, with her shoes as a pillow. It was fortunate she had worn her thickest pair, as the house shoes she sometimes wore to the market would have fallen apart with the walking she had done in the last few days.

They heard a wolf pack later that day.

They started off in the afternoon this time, and at sunset howls could be heard, first from one direction, then another. The men picked up the pace and Athralar pushed her in the back if she slowed.

She turned to him after he pushed her especially hard one time.

"Are you so afraid of a few wolves?" she shouted at him.

"That's not a few wolves. Wolf packs here can have a hundred members," he said, before he pushed her again. "The she-wolves are the most dangerous. If their pups need food, they will attack bears and even break into villages."

She picked up her pace and was happy when they crossed over a wide heath with no trees anywhere for the wolves to hide behind. The heath seemed to go on forever, but when they rested, this time not long after sunset, they lit a fire again.

"We are in Saxon world now," said Athralar. "The journey will be easier. But you will only be able to rest properly when we reach the Firefort."

"What is a Firefort?"

"It is the fort of fire, where all things are cleansed and the selection takes place."

"What happens to the selected?" That thought had been gnawing at her. She'd heard that the tribes in Germania had women who fought alongside their men and that women could even lead a village or a war band. The idea was new and intriguing. Was there hope that the selected were being prepared for something good?

"The selected are treated with respect and given gifts," Athralar replied. "They pass through fire with the others who have been selected. That is all you need to know."

But it wasn't enough to stop the doubts. And each night as she went to sleep, she imagined waking to find Constantine had arrived with enough men to kill every one of these Saxons for daring to take her. It would only be a matter of time before he found her. He was looking for her, she knew it.

And he would find her.

And if he didn't, she would find a way back to him. One way or another.

VI

Treveris, Northern Gaul, 307 A.D.

"You must consider them dead," said Crocus. He shrugged, as if throwing off a weight. The atrium of Constantine's villa stood empty, but starlings could be heard from the trees on the nearby road.

"I cannot," shouted Constantine. "I won't give up on them." He closed his eyes. For two nights, since he'd arrived back in Treveris, he'd barely slept.

His baby son, Julius, had also disappeared. It was assumed by many that he'd been taken by the same people who'd taken Juliana or that perhaps she had come back herself to take the child.

People whispered behind their hands when they saw him. He had ordered the houses of everyone connected with the palace to be searched and any baby being taken out of the city to be stopped, but it had produced nothing except ill will and a stream of screaming parents being taken to the basilica to have their child looked at.

And now people were asking, when would it stop? Why did he not blame the gods and move on, sire another?

It was common for young children to die, and he'd hardened his heart to the child after it was born in case that happened, but having him taken like this sickened him. He could not let it go.

"A child born out of wedlock holds no sway on its father," repeated Crocus.

"That is not what I believe. Have you been talking to my mother?"

Crocus started straight ahead.

"I want a hundred of your Alemanni cavalry to be ready by tomorrow morning at dawn. I don't abandon people easily, Crocus." Constantine stabbed his finger in Crocus' direction.

"Yes, they will be ready. May I suggest you will need a lot more than a hundred if you intend to go far into the great forest."

"How many more?"

"Twenty-five thousand at least. Five legions, which you do not have here. Varus brought three legions with him with little combat experience, but about fifteen thousand of his men died on that campaign, strung out over the narrow paths through the forest, their bows useless in the wet once the rain started. They say in Germania that Frigg herself brought the rains that only ended with the death of Varus by his own sword and the loss of his legion's eagles."

"I know all about Varus' campaign," said Constantine. "It is taught to all officers in the east, as an example of the treachery of auxiliaries." He stood.

"I will not summon every legion in the west to look for Juliana and my son, but I must do more for them than cross over the Rhine for an afternoon. See that the men I asked for are ready for a five-day search, and I want you to come too. I know the tribes on the far side are Alemanni, as you are, and I will want you to spread the word that I will reward whoever brings Juliana back."

"A hundred Roman cavalry will not get far in the forest before they are attacked, my lord," said Crocus. "It does not matter that we have a treaty, Roman units are not accepted across the river and our treaty states that no campaigns will be carried out by either side on the other's territory."

"This is not a campaign. This is a search party." Constantine's voice was raised again. "We will not be raiding villages and killing everyone we meet. We will seek cooperation and extend the hand of friendship to those who will cooperate with our search. I do not plan to come back soaked in blood."

"And you are sure that your son has been taken there too?"

Constantine raised his hands. "What other explanation could there be? We have searched the city. No one has demanded a ransom. Tell me, Crocus." Constantine put both hands up, then groaned, turned, put his fists to the wall. Was it his fault? Should he have doubled the guards on their child when he'd heard Juliana had been taken? He put his head to the wall now, banged it against the stone.

"You are right." Crocus placed a hand on Constantine's shoulder. "We will find them."

It took four more days for the cavalry unit, with Constantine leading at a fast pace, to reach the river. It had been almost a week since his son had gone missing. Constantine hated the thought of what they were doing to her, to them, or had done. But he kept the mission focused. They were seeking raiders.

They found out that the fort on the Rhine at Rigomagus was the most likely one to have the number of large patrol vessels needed to carry the cavalry across fast without delaying for days.

When they reached the fort, they found that it too had neglected to maintain all its patrol vessels, but they did have five in working order and they were larger than the ones upstream.

The village on the far side here was bigger too and they'd heard that Constantine had come across pursuing a raiding party. None of his men spoke about him searching for a woman or a child. Most assumed that he wanted the culprits found and personal revenge for the raid and previous raids over the past few summers.

Two heavily bearded traders they met at the fort said that whoever was responsible for the raiding was probably not Alemanni, but from deep in the forest, from one of the tribes that did not have a treaty with Rome.

Crocus went across the river first, with a few of his personal guard, to speak with the headman of the village on the far side. They returned as the rest of the Roman cavalry were keeping themselves busy drying and polishing weapons in small groups on the shingle beach.

Constantine was told the news. The village chief knew nothing, would give away nothing.

"You have done enough," said Crocus. "Have a funeral pyre for Juliana and another for your son and find a new woman to warm your bed."

"Where does the council of elders of the Alemanni meet?"

"At Vadum Frankorum, upriver from here. But you do not want to go there. It is well defended with a much bigger force than we have, and they will not greet you with open arms with a force like this beside you. It'll be assumed you wish to take bloody revenge. And maybe you do. But we don't have enough men for anything more than a hit and run attack. They will summon men from villages far and wide and lay siege to us, with the aim of taking you prisoner and offering you back to the empire for a giant ransom."

Crocus pulled out his sword, knelt. "I am willing to die for you, but I will not keep my mouth shut if you are on a path to humiliation."

Constantine pulled his cloak tighter. It had started to drizzle.

"We are going to Vadum Frankorum. When we get there you will make them an offer."

It took three days to reach Vadum Frankorum. The path they took grew narrow, barely wide enough for two horses to pass. Constantine asked if there was a wider road, but Crocus shook his head. They slept huddled together around fires with men on watch in a ring around them.

They weren't attacked on the way and encountered only a few traders with sacks piled up on small ponies, and one with a string of beaten looking slaves behind his horse. All were wary and headed into the thick woods when they saw the Romans. Each night Constantine asked Crocus questions about the Alemanni elders, about how and why they made decisions. It was like extracting gold flecks from rocks. It took time. Crocus had become even less talkative than usual. Being back beyond the Rhine did not seem to suit him.

"You are in good standing here?" asked Constantine.

"Yes, for everyone but my brother," replied Crocus.

"What's the problem with your brother?"

"He wants to kill me."

Constantine groaned. "For what?"

"He says I'm betraying our traditions by fighting for Rome."

"But Alemanni have been fighting for Rome for hundreds of years. Even in the time of the great Augustus there were Alamanni auxiliaries on Rome's side."

"I know, but it's not what he really resents me for."

"What's that?"

"I took his wife. She hated him. He beat her almost every day."

Constantine punched Crocus' shoulder. "So, I am not the only one in trouble over a woman."

The following morning they reached the meeting place for the Alemanni elders. It was not like a Roman town. It was a wide circular clearing in the middle of a thinned area of the forest. They could probably have fitted a thousand men and women in the clearing, but when Constantine arrived there were only a dozen shaven headed men at the center of the clearing where a stone circle stood. They wore long black tunics and their heads were tattooed with a spider web of brown lines.

"Where is everyone?" said Constantine. "I thought this was your capital."

"We don't live all together, like you Romans do. There are villages spread out throughout this area. This way we do not destroy the forest, we are part of it." He pointed to the right, where the trees grew thin and the ground was flat and covered in lush grass. "We will camp there. It will be tomorrow, possibly the next day before the council meets. Messengers will have been sent that we are coming, but some have a long way to go."

They set up camp where Crocus instructed. His men put together a series of lean-tos with branches for a roof for them to sleep under. They made them quickly, using the axes that hung from their wide leather belts. They posted only four guards and kept a fire alight between the lean-tos, as they expected they would not be attacked before the meeting of the elders.

They were wrong.

Constantine was fortunate to be at the end of one of the lean-tos when the attack began. He woke to the shouts of one the guards, and the screams of the attackers as they rampaged into the camp, axes swinging.

Constantine always slept with his sword by his side and he was up and had it ready in front of him when the first long haired attacker came toward him, a howl on his lips and his axe raised high.

Constantine let the man come and watched his eyes, and as they narrowed he bent to the left. He heard the wind passing over the axe as it came close to his head. Too close, but his feint had opened the attacker's side for a killing strike. Without hesitation Constantine rammed his sword point into the side of the man's chest and ripped it upward, cutting him wide open.

The look on the man's face didn't change, but blood spurted across them both as he fell back. Constantine turned full circle. The scene around him was a blur of shapes, men swinging axes, the screams of the dying and the attackers drowning each other out.

"Ad aciem, form up," Constantine shouted, first in one direction, then another. As the words left his mouth an even larger tribesman raced toward him. This giant had an axe as big as any Constantine had seen. It looked as long as any Roman spear and glistened blackly, except for where blood smeared the blade. The man who swung it had blood splattered all over him and he wore a wide grin, showing off sharpened teeth.

His eyes were wild and red. *They are all drunk,* thought Constantine.

He held his sword far in front of him, pointing it at his attacker. The man laughed and swung at the sword. Constantine went to one knee as the axe flew and jabbed at the giant's genitals, launching himself forward and then turning on the ground as the axe swung again and headed toward his chest. His thrust had not connected, but the man's axe head was now buried in the ground. Constantine came up and raised his sword fast at his attacker, both hands holding it tight.

The man batted it aside with an arm, but Constantine swung it around with a well-practiced circular motion and swept it up so that his sword caught the man under the chin as he came close. The tip of the blade did not enter far, but the giant's axe hand came up to fend it off, which gave Constantine the freedom he needed to push the sword deep into the man's head. Blood flowed down the sword in a torrent.

The giant opened his mouth. The sword blade could be seen inside it, but he was not dead yet. Another hand held a dagger, and he swung it for Constantine's heart. At the last moment Constantine saw the danger and twisted his shoulder. He felt the dagger like a hot poker jabbing into him and in reply pushed his sword up with a jab and a twist until the tip emerged from the back of the giant's skull.

"Emperor, come with me." Crocus was at his side. Around him were a ring of his men, perhaps twenty, all bloodied, but with their weapons raised and swinging, while beyond them their attackers raged, killing off anyone they could with defiant shrieks. The attackers made one last charge against the men surrounding Constantine, but it was repulsed, and then the fighting was over.

Constantine put a hand to his shoulder, pulled it away and looked at it. It was slick with blood.

Crocus looked at the wound. "Wait here, sit."

"I do not need to sit," said Constantine. "I will stand, in case they come back in greater numbers. I will die on my feet, Crocus."

Crocus shook his head and headed toward the fire, which was still throwing low flames into the air.

He returned a little later. Only the groans of the dying could be heard now, and the whinnying of horses. Crocus' sword blade glowed red hot. He pulled Constantine's tunic off his shoulder – he hadn't even had time to put on his breast guard – and without asking permission pressed the hot blade hard against where the knife had sliced into Constantine.

The last thing Constantine remembered, as his flesh sizzled, was a cheer from the men around him. He later found out that the reason the men cheered was that Crocus had told them in their language that Constantine had clearly killed the leader of their attackers, and that was most likely the reason the others had run off.

Constantine didn't recover consciousness until near dawn. He was lying on a bed of leaves. Nearby, his men were mounting their horses.

"Crocus," he shouted.

Crocus appeared leading Constantine's horse, saddled and ready.

"You do not think we should stay?" said Constantine.

"They may elect another leader and come at us again. It is best we go. The elders will be told why you came and of your offer to reward anyone who brings Juliana back. I know my duty. I must get you back to Treveris. I do not wish to have the Alemanni blamed for your death."

"I will not die from a shoulder wound," said Constantine. Then he groaned. He had moved his shoulder and a stab of pain reached into his neck and down his back like a knife entering.

"I know, but the prospect of taking you prisoner, now that we are weakened, may inspire others to join the band that attacked us. They are probably right now touring the villages near here looking for young men in need of a share of the spoils from a ransom payment."

"They were Alemanni, then, who came for us? Was your brother among them?" He winced again. Even talking sent spears of pain through his shoulder and down his back.

"No, that was not my brother. They were Bructeri. I saw a woman directing them and their markings and torcs were all Bructeri." He handed Constantine a giant golden torc.

"Did you see this, when you were finishing off that giant?"

Constantine nodded. "It was tight around his neck. That was why I aimed for under his chin."

"It is yours now." He held it out to Constantine.

"Put it with any other torcs or good weapons you find. I also want that bastard's axe and his dagger."

They rode fast back toward the Rhine. They took Constantine across first and he changed back to the original horse he had used for the journey back to Treveris. Every step of the journey was painful, but he'd decided not to wait to recover anywhere else.

If he was unable to get to Treveris many would assume death had taken him and would start planning for who was to follow him. Word would reach Rome and Maxentius in ten days. He would then spread the word that Constantine needed replacing, whether he survived his injuries or not.

He had to get back to Treveris.

VII

The Alemanni Forrest, Germania, 307 A.D.

Seven nights passed before they reached the black river, which marked the entrance to the sacred forest. They rested at a bend in the river and sat under a canopy of tall oak trees that reached partly across the water. There was something magical about the place, a sense of peacefulness, which surprised Juliana after the many days in the dark forest, with the memory of hungry wolves howling behind them.

"You will wait here, while some of us hunt," said Athralar, when he came over to her.

Juliana looked from face to face at the men behind Athralar. These were the youngest and fittest of the group. The men left behind would all be older and less likely to be able to catch her if she ran off. And less likely to rape her.

She nodded in reply.

"And don't think about breaking your word and running away. You will be staked to the ground and sliced open for the wolves and bears to come and eat you alive if we catch you. And we will catch you. It's a bad way to go. I have seen it. You will wonder where the screaming is from, but it will be from you."

"I told you, I'm not going to run away, Athralar. You will not have to listen to my screams."

Athralar and his men returned as the sun went down. They were carrying a young deer, its legs looped on a branch. Blood dripped from the carcass. The arrows that had brought it down had been pulled out, but Juliana could see how expertly they had felled the animal. One had pierced its eye, now a bloody mess.

Athralar set the deer down and pulled a long knife from his belt. Then he waved Juliana to join them. Juliana stood with them in a circle around the dead animal lying on a bed of grass and the brown mulch that had been shed from the trees. The gurgle of the river was loud here and in the distance birds were singing.

Athralar said something in their language and two of the men picked up the deer by its front legs and held it up, its head sagging down and to one side.

Athralar raised his knife and began chanting. It sounded like repeated rhythmic growls to Juliana. The men around her took up the chant and as Athralar stuck his knife into the deer's belly and slit down the chant grew faster. Athralar opened the stomach of the beast wide and its intestines spilled out in a brown and red sludge.

Juliana wanted to look away, but she knew that would be seen as a sign of weakness. She knew the Roman elite were considered spoiled and soft by many, and that the tribes beyond the empire's frontiers prided themselves that they were closer to the cycle of life and death than any Roman, seeing it every day with their own eyes.

Steam rose from the pile of intestines and a stench of half made excrement filled Juliana's nostrils. Still she did not look away.

Athralar went close to the deer again and opened the slit high into its chest, pulling out its ribs and pushing the knife further in. He twisted the knife a few times and turned to her with the bloody heart of the deer in his hand, blood dripping from it. He raised it up and sucked at it briefly, blood and jelly like flesh dripping down his chin. He held it out to the man nearest him, who also sucked it.

When it came to Juliana's turn, she kept her mouth shut.

Athralar shook the glistening heart near her face.

"You cannot cross the sacred river until you have swallowed some of this blood and are part of our sacrifice to the river god. If you cross without doing this, you will be cursed with ill fortune until the day your own heart stops."

Juliana had swallowed warm blood before, when a sacrifice had been made on the estate she had been brought up on in the east, and each slave had been given a sip of a slaughtered bull's blood to drink to show they were all granted part of its strength, but that had been a small sip taken from a bowl. This was very different.

She closed her eyes, opened her mouth and sucked at the heart. It was still warm. It tasted salty. She wanted to retch. She swallowed. Athralar moved on. When all the men had swallowed, he went to the river and dropped the heart in the water while continuing chanting. Juliana wiped her mouth. Whatever happened, she did not want to be cursed by the river gods here, for they appeared strong and had a total hold over these men.

They crossed the river at a ford, where stones had been placed in the water allowing anyone agile to jump their way across. One of the stones was a little loose. Juliana almost went into the water, which flowed fast here, but she kept upright, just, to the cheers of the men ahead and behind her.

The far side of the river was thickly wooded. They followed a thin, barely visible path straight into it and into a green gloom that enveloped them as soon as they passed under the trees.

It was the afternoon now and hunger sapped at Juliana. Usually Athralar passed her black bread during the march each day, but this day he seemed to have forgotten.

Juliana wouldn't ask for food. She'd learnt to live with hunger a long time ago and to do so again would not be that difficult. They reached a large house made out of tree trunks, from which could be heard banging noises as they approached. There was no door in the front of the building and the back was open to the woods. Inside lay a fire, an oven, and a bronze block on which a sword was being beaten. A bellows nearby had a team of flaxen haired boys minding it. And all around stood men, some holding their weapons, waiting for their turn to have them beaten flat or repaired.

Athralar motioned for his men and Juliana to wait at the side of the building as he went inside to talk to the man at the center of it all. That man stood proud, naked to the waist, a giant red-haired man who, it appeared, could beat any of the men around him in a fight, and take on anyone else straight afterward.

As Juliana waited, a blond-haired warrior, with one side of his head shaven and covered in blue tattoos, stared at her. He had a large black leather shield dangling from his shoulder. At first, she didn't care, she was used to being stared at, but when he didn't look away, even after she turned her back on him, her skin began to crawl. She knew this would not end well if he persisted.

When Athralar returned with news that their weapons would be mended the following day, the man approached. Behind him were two companions. They could have been his brothers.

The man pointed at Juliana and started his claim by shouting and reaching for the pommel of the sword that hung from his belt. Athralar responded in kind. The men of his band came behind him, their hands on the pommels of their swords or their axes.

The man made a fist and pushed it toward Athralar's face.

Athralar shouted something, then turned to Juliana. Her heart thumped, almost coming out of her neck. She knew what the man wanted, but only Athralar knew if that meant sharing her with every one of them until she was half dead.

"Will you go with this man?" said Athralar. "That is what he wants me to ask you. But if you wish to, I will have to kill you first and then him and then his brothers, so if you know what is good for you, you will not." He glowered at her.

Juliana shook her head. "No, I will not go with him. I'd rather be a pig getting ready to be slaughtered."

Athralar laughed and turned back to the man, but the man had his sword out already and was swinging it up toward Athralar's chest.

Athralar was lucky he'd swung around so quickly, as the sword only nicked him in the arm as he twisted away from it.

The man who wanted Juliana was not so lucky. An arrow hit him in the eye. Athralar's bowman, standing behind them, had another arrow notched already when Juliana glanced behind her. The man was aiming his bow at the companions of the man who had just died for pushing his luck

Athralar raised his sword and spoke. The men looked at each other, then bent down and dragged their companion away. Athralar put his face up to Juliana's.

"One hero has died for you here already. I expect others have died for you in the past. Am I right?"

She narrowed her eyes. "The son of an emperor fell for me. He will be looking for me."

Athralar took a step back and bowed. "I knew we should not kill you. And your skull would have made for a small enough drinking bowl." He winked at her, then smiled.

It was the smile of someone who'd just been told some good news.

VIII

Maxentius gripped Lucius' arm. "You are very welcome, brave Lucius."

Lucius nodded like a dog. "I have news of many things which will interest you, my lord." He looked around, hoping Maxentius would pick up his need for a private audience.

Maxentius put a hand in the air and shouted. "Everyone, leave us." As the people who had been sitting in the large pink-marble floored atrium filed out, his hangers on and an assortment of slaves, he shouted again, "Paulina, you will stay."

Then he hugged Lucius.

"News of your arrival in Rome was most welcome." Maxentius waved at the couch he was sitting on. Its arm looked to be solid gold but was probably just gold leaf. The sofa was covered in golden silk with a purple edge. Maxentius wore a matching purple toga.

Lucius sat near Maxentius and smiled at him, trying to look delighted. Maxentius waved Paulina to come closer. "Sit beside me, cousin Paulina, this should interest you, though I know you want to spend your life deciding what face paint to use each day and who your betrothed should be."

Lucius looked at Paulina. She was richly dressed in a loose, long yellow gown with a thin band of pearls at its edge and a matching band of pearls running through her black hair, which had been pulled up into the type of bun a Roman matron twice her age would wear.

Paulina sat at Maxentius' knees, but with a distance between them, as if she did not want to give the impression that she was available to him.

Lucius wondered if there was some amorous battle going on between them.

"What is Gaul like, Lucius?" she said, in a soft, barely audible voice. *Someone should teach her to speak up*, he thought.

"It is a vast country, not just one place. There are many provinces, many parts to it."

"I would love to see it someday." Her eyes were wide as she looked up at him.

Maxentius laughed. "Paulina, you are ridiculous. Your wiles are too easy to see through." Maxentius poked her shoulder with a stubby finger.

She looked at him as if a poker had touched her. "Yes, Uncle." She put her head down, as if she had been beaten.

"Gaul is an interesting place. I'm sure your uncle will let you go there one day," Lucius said softly.

Maxentius shook his head. "I told you before, Paulina. You can only go to Gaul if someone I trust takes you there. I was entrusted with protecting your virginity, so I must ensure you are married to a suitable husband first."

Paulina looked up at Maxentius, a pleading expression on her face. "One trip to Gaul before I settle down would be good for me. It would allow me to help my future husband, as I would understand more about our world."

Lucius thought about offering his own services, as he would be heading back to Gaul soon, but he bit his tongue. He did not want to get involved with a relative of Maxentius. He had enough problems.

Paulina smiled up at him, leaned toward him. He could see the brown mound of one of her breasts through the thin slit down the middle of her gown. It bulged like a ripe pear ready to be plucked.

His mouth went dry. He looked away.

"You must leave us now, Paulina. I have introduced you, as I promised. Now we have important matters to discuss."

Paulina stood, bending conspicuously toward Lucius as she did so and smiling at him, as if he was the answer to her prayers.

When she was gone, Lucius said, "I will be traveling back to Treveris in a few days. She could come with me." His voice was firm, his tone nonchalant, as if he didn't care either way.

Maxentius shook his head. "No, impossible. How would she get back to Rome?"

Lucius put a hand up. "In the summer I can bring her back. I hope to come back again soon and act as a private messenger between you and Constantine."

"That's possible." Maxentius didn't look convinced. "But tell me first, what is the message you are here to convey."

Lucius looked around. There was no one nearby. He leaned toward Maxentius.

"You're following the edicts of persecution against the Christians, as Galerius does in the east, so I came to tell you that Constantine has shown a willingness to be lenient to Christians for reasons that you will find easy to understand." He stopped talking.

It was well known that Maxentius was not persecuting Christians with anything like the zeal that Galerius had been doing it in the east. Mentioning Constantine's support for Christianity was unlikely to cost Lucius his head, but with someone like Maxentius you could never be sure how he would react.

Maxentius nodded. "Yes, I heard Christians were not being pursued in the west, but I assumed Constantine had decided to follow in the weakness of his father. What other reason could there be?"

Lucius opened his hands wide. "I've heard a rumor that he received gold from Christians in the east, before he even came to power. That helped him pay off the commanders who supported his ascension to the purple."

"What Christians paid for this?"

"Christians from the east who wish to bring an end to the persecutions across the empire."

Maxentius slapped his knee, laughed. "Aaah, I see it all now. You are from the east, Lucius. Do you perhaps know who these Christians are, who were able to make such useful donations?"

Lucius looked him in the eye. "Perhaps I can find out who they are. Do you wish me to make contact with them for you?"

Maxentius slapped his knee again. "Let us not beat around the bush any longer, Lucius. I know you are something of an ambassador for these Christians. My question is a blunt one. What size donation did your Christian friends give Constantine, and could they match it for my treasury?"

Lucius lowered his head. "These are people who represent the poor and slaves, but they are, I hear, willing to contribute what each one can to any who will lessen their burdens."

Maxentius sat back. A belly laugh broke from him.

"Indeed, you are the bearer of glad tidings then, Lucius. I think my cousin will enjoy going to Gaul with you."

IX

Treveris, 307 A.D.

Helena, Constantine's mother, took a step back from him, as if she had been struck. "You must stop this obsession, Constantine. It has nearly cost you your life already."

Constantine stood perfectly still, one arm strapped to his body at his elbow, to ensure he moved his shoulder as little as possible. He hated the restriction to his movement and looked forward each night to the strap being taken off.

This was his first visit to his mother since he'd returned to Treveris a week before.

He would not let her intimidate him. "I cannot abandon Juliana to her fate. If you were kidnapped, I would do the same for you."

"But she is not your mother. And you are not even married to her." Helena shrieked every word. "She is no more than a concubine."

"Then you, of all people, must understand why I cannot forget what I have with Juliana and cast her aside like a dirty tunic." Constantine's hand came up as he spoke, as if to ward her off.

Helena walked away from him, her sandals clicking on the marble floor of the small atrium of the villa she occupied in the east of the city, where the breezes from the river were strongest.

She sat on the red silk couch near the life-sized bust of the emperor Diocletian she kept on the floor, presumably in order to kick it occasionally when she felt like it. Diocletian had ordered Constantine's father to leave Helena and marry another more suitable woman when Constantine was only sixteen, which led to her being banished for years.

"Things are different now, son. The only thing that matters is that you must ensure your grip on power here in the west, or we will all be slaughtered. The Alemanni and the other tribes had a treaty with your father. They can easily cast it aside if they think you are weak. And as for Maxentius, he would have all our heads on spikes and take control of all your father's lands, if he thought he had half a chance of succeeding."

"I know we are under threat, Mother. I have plans for strengthening our position."

She came close to him. Her tone sounded more like an appeal now. "The impact of your father's death has not fully played out, my son. Everything is in play now, including all our lives. I know you cared for her, but you have risked everything already to find her, and she is gone. You must think of her and your son as dead now." She stroked his injured shoulder through the folds of his red cape.

He turned away, bringing up the fist of his free hand. "I will not give up so easily. This is my son you are talking about."

His mother put her hands together, begging him. "You must marry someone else soon, Constantine, someone suitable, someone who will increase your legitimacy and bring a dowry. It is better for your son that he is gone. He will be in danger when you have sons with your new wife. He will be their bastard brother." She lowered her voice. "If you care for that baby's life you will forget him or you will bring death to him."

"Must you always talk about death, Mother?" He strode away from her, put his fist in the air again and winced, as his other shoulder moved. He'd been warned not to go far, but he couldn't stand being stuck between his atrium and his bedroom any longer.

"Can I not for once in my life, not live in fear of what will happen to others because of what I do?"

"You are the emperor of the west now, my son. You are not like normal people. You have been chosen for a task. You must bear the burdens along with the pleasures of your position." She waved at the world around them, as if everything he could see was a pleasure of his position.

"I can find a girl who looks like Juliana if you wish. After a few weeks with her you will barely remember Juliana's face." She walked to him, her arms wide. "Shall I do that, my son. I know how men need their comforts at night."

Constantine stared at the wall. It had a painting of Hercules triumphant on it. If he could not protect the woman he loved and their child, what kind of man was he, never mind what kind of an emperor?

X

Juliana lay awake that night in a clearing further into the woods. She stared up at the stars. She could almost see Constantine's face in front of her. He looked stern, as he mostly did, but a smile beckoned at the corner of his mouth, as if he was about to reach out for her.

A lump formed in her throat. She swallowed hard and pressed her hands together, fist into palm, as she been taught to do years before by a slave who saw her crying. "If the masters see you like this, they will think you weak," the old slave had told her. And it had been true. Another young slave girl who cried all the time for her family and was unable to work had got sick and had died and her body had been fed to the pigs.

Juliana would not let that happen to her. She would escape these people and find a way back to Constantine. He would not forget her. She knew his love was real and their son made their bond even stronger. She must be careful from now on. Telling Athralar that she was close to Constantine may have been a mistake, but it might also save her life. However, she must never tell them she had a child by him. That would expose her to threats against her baby, that they would find him and slit his throat or take him too. She could only pray, as she did every night to the great mother, to protect their boy.

As the stars dimmed she slept some more, not much, but enough to ensure she could walk the next day. This would be the day of the selection, Athralar had said, and a great coming together of all the Saxons from every part of their territories and beyond.

They ate black bread the following morning. Juliana washed her face and feet in a nearby stream. She didn't dare wash her body in case the men were watching. She knew how the sight of a naked woman could inflame a man enough to kill.

Athralar joined her by the stream.

"My men will not rape you if you need to wash," he said. He looked down at her as she ran her hands in the water.

She knew what he meant. Was she in his blood?

She shook her head.

"Are you with child?" he said.

"No." Her monthly blood was late, but she would not tell him that. She'd been late before when her life changed dramatically, and she did not want him waiting for a baby from Constantine to appear, which they could ransom to the highest bidder.

That would be a fate no baby should suffer. It was well known that Saxons ate the babies of villagers they conquered after boiling them alive.

He bent down to her. "Today is important not just for you, but for me. I will see my mother again. She is the chief of my clan. My raiding will be judged by her according to what we came back with."

"What did you come back with?"

He pointed at her, then at the dirty bag on his hip.

She stood. "What will happen to the scalps you have won?"

"They are treated with reverence. They will be hung in our long house behind my mother's throne. We need new ones every year or Woden will desert us. Everyone knows this is true."

"And what will happen to me? Will I be hung in the long house?" She stepped closer to him, looked up at him. If she had to play him, she would.

He put a hand on her shoulder. "You should know I am not capable of siring children, so your appeals to my flesh are not as powerful as you may think."

She stepped back, shrugging his hand away. "Why not?"

"My balls were crushed when I was seven summers. My mother did it as a gift to the gods, but mostly to ensure my sister will inherit her position."

Juliana let her breath out in a whoosh. "Can you still fuck? I heard of a eunuch who fucked every one of his master's friends."

"I can, yes." He smiled, wistfully, as if remembering something long ago. Then he raised his hand and waved it in a circle between them.

"I tell you this so you know that the men who will be doing the selection are like me, the sons of clan leaders, and we are not bound by the same level of desire for a woman's flesh as most men." He put his hands up, palm forward, as if holding the sky up.

"Know also that we consider ourselves blessed by the gods. It was my good fortune she did that to me. Her choice was either to crush my balls or cut my head off. No threat to my sister could be allowed to exist. I am lucky to be here, Juliana, on this side of death. And so are you. Everything will change for you today. I planned this raiding party to prove to my tribe that I am not cursed. You will be that proof."

"Who says you're cursed?"

"My sister does. That is all you need to know." He walked away.

Juliana stared at his back. Why had he told her all that? The only time men revealed things to her in the past was when they wanted something from her they wished her to give freely. Or was he just preparing her?

She made her way back to the other men. They were all standing now, brushing twigs off their clothes and getting ready to move on. Not one of them looked at Juliana, as if they knew what was coming for her.

That afternoon they came to a circular clearing. Inside it, families were gathering in strong sunlight. In the woods around it, lean-tos and leather double and single pole tents had been set up. In the center of the clearing a tall structure made of tree trunks and branches stood out against the blue sky and the wall of trees beyond.

They walked around the edge of the clearing. Juliana assumed they were looking for their clan. They found them almost on the far side. When Juliana looked at the structure in the center, as they made their way around, it became clear that the shape was a human. Wagons carrying more wood arrived. Men were piling the wood inside the structure.

She'd heard about giant human figures being burnt at ceremonies, with slaves inside, offerings to the gods, and she prayed to the great mother that this would not be her fate.

She was beside Athralar when they came to the group of his clan members. Athralar was greeted by an old woman with long gray hair with bones and beads and shiny stones tied into the rat's tails of hair that hung around her head.

Athralar pushed Juliana forward toward the woman, sitting stiff and upright on a low tree stump. Around her were maybe thirty men and women. He went down on his knees as he came close to her. Someone behind her pushed Juliana down too. The woman began talking fast, her voice raised angrily, her finger pointing at Athralar. Then she pointed at Juliana.

Juliana's mouth dried. A sickening smell filled the air. She was used to the smell of dirt and shit and death that hung around the raiders who'd captured her, probably why the wolves followed them for so long, but this was different, stronger. Then she saw where it came from.

In front of the woman, Athralar's mother presumably, lay a small mound of scalps in a pile, most with long hair. All presumably killed in the recent past. Athralar stood and emptied the contents of his bag into the pile. The men who had been with Athralar all emptied their bags after that. There must have been ten scalps in the pile now. Two were small, perhaps from children.

When they were finished the old woman pointed at Juliana. Athralar shook his head. A series of exchanges passed between him and his mother. Juliana listened intently, her skin crawling and her mind racing as she thought about the implications of what their conversation was about.

A woman behind Athralar's mother stood and came forward. She put a hand on Athralar's shoulder and tapped at it. He went quiet. This must be his sister, thought Juliana. Was she going to help him?

From the people watching came three men. One stood behind Athralar, the other two by his side. They grabbed him by the arms and took him away, without a word emerging from his mouth.

The younger woman came toward Juliana. She walked slowly. Her hair shone thick and black like Athralar's, but it was loose around her head and she had bones sewn into it, like her mother's, but not as many. The sides of her head were shaven above the ear on each side like his, and like him she had blue animal face symbols entwined around her skull.

Juliana looked up at her, said nothing. The woman spoke in a bark at Juliana. Then she put her head down and appeared to repeat what she'd said. When Juliana made no effort to reply the woman raised her hand and slapped Juliana hard across the face. The stinging blow sent Juliana's head cracking to one side. Then, from behind her, Juliana felt hands grabbing her, yanking her to her feet.

An opening appeared in the crowd and she was marched fast back into the woods and over to a wooden pen, designed for animals, and pushed inside. There was no one else in it. A thick mat of dead leaves covered the ground. She could probably have climbed out, as the walls were not that high, but two guards were watching her. She sat in a corner observing everything, holding her burning cheek. Not far away, she expected, someone was deciding her fate.

No one came with anything, no water or bread all that afternoon, but before the sun went down she was handed a bowl of a mushy black substance. She set it down, tasted it with her finger, then ate no more. It tasted like tree bark and water and the great mother only knew what else they had put in it. She lay down in the corner and started whispering Constantine's name over and over.

She needed him now more than ever. She had to get out of this place. She could see what was coming next.

XI

Rome, Porta Ostiensis, 307 A.D.

Lucius looked up toward the sun. It had climbed over the roof tops. Paulina was late, very late. She had agreed to meet him at the statue to Augustus inside the gate at dawn. The road beyond led to Ostia and the ship waiting to take him back to Gaul.

Already he was two days late because of her. And now she was even late to their meeting. He stamped his feet, looked around. A team of men were at work nearby. Their shouts and the sound of winches and pulleys echoed around the square. It wasn't hot yet, but spring was coming to an end and soon the summer heat of Rome would descend.

The three men who accompanied him were nearby. He had brought two slaves to help him with his horse and his baggage and a giant freeman to carry things and, more importantly, to use the cudgel hanging from his belt on any thieves who got ideas. It was unlikely they would meet any on the road to the coast, but inside Rome you had to be prepared for anything.

The slave who looked after the horses kept them quiet with words in their ears and strokes on their necks. They had hired the horses in Ostia and there would be a tough conversation when they were given back about how much extra he owed for them.

Lucius had already instructed the slave to hand over only one extra silver denarii per day per horse, though the man who they'd hired them from would probably demand ten and question the silver content of the denarii he was given. Lucius had only received the coins he would use in the past week. They were recently minted eastern coins, which would also see them get a bite by most who received them to check if they were real. Lucius had met with a friend of his father's in the market near the Circus Maximus soon after he'd arrived in Rome. As a result, the two grain sacks on one of the horses had only a little grain in them. The rest of the contents were bags of coins recently issued by the Emperor Diocletian. Some were gold aurei, but most were silver denarii from Nicomedia, where his father had arranged their collection.

The gold coins were for Constantine, to ensure his continued support for the cause of the Christians. The denarii were for payments to anyone else he saw fit. It was fortunate his father trusted him, but Lucius knew that eventually he would have to provide a full accounting of where all the coins had gone. His father knew all the ways to lighten a purse, so Lucius had been careful not to waste much on extra services at the tavern they'd stayed in or on anything else.

He'd enjoyed one indulgence though. One of the tavern girls had been so friendly he'd been unable to resist her. He'd promised her that he'd be back to visit the next time he was in Rome.

She probably heard that from all the men whose beds she warmed.

The stream of people heading into the city from the gate quickened as the sun moved higher. A smaller stream of travelers headed the other way, legionaries returning to their posts, officials heading for the port of Ostia and beyond and families heading home after visiting the city.

Rome was as busy as ever. If they didn't get going soon the road would be slow all the way to the fifth mile marker.

Lucius strode across the square to see if he could see Paulina on the far side, if she had misunderstood the very clear instructions he had given, but she wasn't there. As he strode back, he was delighted to see two horses by his own mounts and two women, their gray traveling capes over their heads, talking with his freeman.

As he came closer, they turned to him.

"Why are you keeping us waiting?" said Paulina loudly as he came near. "We have been here half the morning."

Lucius shook his head. "I've been across the square looking for you. Do not lie about how long you've been here."

Paulina slid off her horse, took hold of his arm and leaned close to his ear. "I brought this slave with me as my mother insisted I have another woman with me while I'm with you, to protect my honor. And then, this very morning she was not even ready on time. She had not packed half of the things I need for this journey."

She pointed to the right. Lucius looked at where she was pointing. A string of six sturdy looking horses shifted and whinnied, while being quieted by two slaves. Four of the horses were weighed down by polished oak traveling chests.

"We're not going to a festival, Paulina. Treveris is a border city and full of the most unsmiling people, as dour as only refugees from Germania can be."

"We will be going to Constantine's palace there, yes?" She looked at him expectantly.

"Constantine is not big on palaces. He entertained in a confiscated merchant's villa when I left."

Paulina looked disappointed, but she raised her nose and said, "Well, they will want to see what an heiress to a great estate in Rome dresses like, I am sure." She walked over to her horse and mounted.

"Is he married yet?" she asked, over her shoulder.

"Ask him yourself."

"Does he like boys? Is that why you don't want to tell me?"

"No, he doesn't like boys. He has a woman, as I am sure you know, but they are not married."

Lucius waved at his entourage to also mount up. Then he led the way toward the gate. Three legionaries were standing to attention at the gate with a door guard in a red tunic to one side, watching everyone. Above, on the ramparts, there were archers ready to act on command to stop a thief or a fight, if one started.

They were waved through the gate. Lucius could understand the lack of diligence in checking people. The city of Rome had not been attacked by any foreign power since the Gauls had sacked it seven hundred years before, though the Aurelian walls, which had been built forty years ago because of the threat of a barbarian army, gave an indication of the fear of tribal hordes and the need for strong leadership in the empire now that the hordes had grown in their audacity.

They had to move slowly with the crowd, and it took until almost noon before they were beyond the fifth mile marker and the traffic had thinned with people side tracking to walled villas and estates that could be seen on either side of the road. Soon after they reached a long stretch of straight road lined with tall pine trees with their branches all high up, like giant sea-green versions of the sunshades ladies in the eastern provinces used to protect their pale complexions.

So far Paulina had ridden behind Lucius, with her companion, as if intending to show to all that she had no interest in Lucius, no matter what his position.

Soon after, they ate in the garden of a roadside inn, at tables set up under trellises of vines which snaked on each side and above them. Lucius, Paulina and her companion sat at one table at the front of the building. The slaves and the freeman were all at the side of the building, in a less attractive area with only simple wooden tables and benches.

Paulina was still not talkative. She whispered with her companion so much, and looked around at the other guests that Lucius gave up trying to engage her and went inside the inn to discuss what he owed with the proprietor, and to see if there were any travelers from Ostia who knew what conditions at sea were like that morning.

He went outside soon after, only to discover that the giant he had employed at Ostia to guard them had gone missing. One of the other slaves told him that the man had gone to a large group of other men to talk, and that the group had since left. Lucius went out onto the roadway to see if they could be seen either way, but they couldn't. Whoever the man had gone with, they had clearly moved fast.

He was glad he hadn't paid for the man's time yet. He would complain bitterly to the horse trader who'd recommended him.

But it also meant they had limited resources to defend themselves. He looked around the inn to see if there were any men he could hire, but he was out of luck. They would just have to keep going. They would be in Ostia by nightfall.

His slaves brought the horses to the front, loaded them up with the pile of sacks and boxes that had been unloaded near their table earlier and they all set off again. It wasn't until they were passing through a wooded area, with a mixture of thin, elegant Cyprus and umbrella pine that he figured out the real reason the giant had left him.

Waiting by the side of the road, in an area where the trees were thick, was a group of what looked like ex-soldiers. They were lying down as Lucius' party approached and were almost invisible until they were close enough to shoot an arrow with accuracy through someone's eye. At that point they stood up out of the grass. The men wore some military equipment, dirty breast shields and arm greaves, but none of them had helmets, which might have helped him work out who they were.

Lucius rode at the head of their party, with his two slaves directly behind him. As they neared the group of ex-soldiers the men came into the road.

One of them, a man with a shaved head and bulging shoulder muscles, put his hand up high as Lucius approached.

"Stop, if you value your lives," he said, loudly. As he spoke, he unsheathed his sword and held it in front of him. Lucius looked to the side. The other men were spreading out along their line. He could try to race away on his horse, but he'd never live it down if anyone found out about him deserting Paulina. Maxentius would have him flayed alive.

He pulled his own sword out, let it fall to his side and leaned forward on his horse.

"Let us pass. You have no right to stop us," he shouted back.

The man took a step forward and said, "Look behind you. Your women are ours now and if you don't want all their throats cut you will drop your weapon."

Lucius turned. The man was right. Paulina and her companion had a sword held up to them. Paulina had her mouth open, as if about to scream. When her gaze locked with Lucius the scream came out. At the noise her horse reared up, and so did Lucius'.

Leaning forward fast to shift his weight, tightening his reins, and pushing to one side, he brought his horse under control.

The man who'd had a sword at Paulina's throat had brought her horse under control by pulling its head down. Paulina had come off it.

"Who are these men?" she shouted.

"No idea, but it seems they want something."

Paulina strode past him as he slid from his mare. She shouted at the man who had spoken to Lucius.

"Do you know who I am? My mother can have you castrated, and your eyes and balls fed to the dogs. Get out of our way, or you'll regret it for eternity."

The man laughed and shook his head.

"I have a good mind to take you with us, my lady. You seem like a woman with a bit of life in her."

Paulina went close to him, then fell to her knees. She put her head down and hands up in front of her and began intoning a prayer loudly.

"The trees will weep for you.

"The earth will weep for you.

"The birds will weep for you.

"The sky will weep for you.

"The gods will weep for. If you do not release us."

Everyone stared at her. The slaves each had a man beside them with a sword pointed at their chest, as did Paulina's companion.

The man she was appealing to threw back his head and laughed. "I have not heard that prayer in a very, very long time, but you have no need to fret, acolyte. You are all safe. I am only here to extract a tax on your friend and then you can all be on your way."

Lucius stood beside Paulina. "What tax? We have little enough, but I will pay anything that is rightfully claimed. Under whose guidance are you making this claim?"

"That is not your concern. And you must pay the tax because we know where you got the coin you are carrying, and if you do not do so, you risk the lives of everyone with you. Some experienced bone breakers are ready to do their duty." One of the men behind him growled at the mention of the term bone breaker.

Lucius sighed. It was not unheard of to have tax collectors confront you in the road, but that meant this man had received information. And that meant he probably knew about the coin they were transporting.

"One bag from every ten, that is all we can spare. Ask your master to write to me with any higher claim and we will discuss it," said Lucius.

The man took a step forward and pointed his sword at Lucius' throat.

"Half of everything. That is what we want."

He looked down the waiting line of people. Paulina did not have a sword at her throat anymore.

He feinted to the left and down, watching the sword tip follow him. He reached to the ground and grabbed a handful of the sandy earth by the side of the road and threw it quickly up and into the man's eyes.

A scream split the air. It was Paulina.

XII

Treveris, 307 A.D.

Constantine pointed at Crocus.

"I know how dangerous it can be in Germania, but I want spies sent to every corner, and every tribe in that treacherous country forsaken-by-the-gods. They are to warn everyone they meet that not a hair on Juliana is to be harmed. Is that clear?"

"Yes, it will be done straight away." Crocus began to walk out of the atrium of Constantine's villa, then turned back. "And if they find out where she is, what are they to do?"

"Tell them to come back as soon as they find out anything, and that they are not to come back without news of her."

Crocus headed for the door. After he left the head of the imperial household came in, bowing low, then attempting to prostrate himself on the marble tiled floor.

"Stop, get up," said Constantine. "I've told you this before, and I mean it. There is no need for you to prostrate yourself every time you see me. Now, what needs my attention?"

"I'm so sorry. Your father was very different." The man took a scroll from under his arm. "I have the names of the new house slaves for you to approve."

He handed the scroll to Constantine, who pulled it open and looked at the list. "These are all women. I didn't order six new female house slaves."

"Your mother ordered them. Now that Juliana is not supervising the cleaning and other duties, she wanted to make sure you had enough slaves to get everything done the way you want." He put his head to one side and smiled broadly.

Constantine handed back the list. "Pick one. Someone you think is the most capable in the kitchen. That is where Juliana excelled, and send the rest away."

Later that day the smell of roasting pork filled the villa. After his meetings with a magistrate and then the governors of two cities in southern Gaul, Constantine went into the kitchen.

As well as the usual crew of two chefs, two servers and a wine taster, all male, a young woman with straight black hair, like Juliana's, was hurrying around. This woman was taller than Juliana. When she saw Constantine in the doorway, she bent her head and then went to her knees. The other slaves did the same.

Constantine turned and went away, vowing to make sure that the new slave did not make an appearance in front of him in his bedroom in the middle of the night, stark naked. There was still plenty of time to find Juliana. He would not give up on her.

But that night as he lay awake, he listened for sounds in the villa and wondered where the new slave was and unbidden, as he drifted off to sleep, he thought about what it would be like to lie with her.

XIII

The Territory of the Saxons, Northern Germania, 307 A.D.

Juliana walked around her cage again. She had been in it now for five days, if her counting was correct. She had become confused that morning when she woke as to whether she had already been through day five or if it was day six.

Each day she received only one bowl of black gruel. The second day she had been so hungry she ate it all, even though it tasted foul, and she had no idea what plants or animal parts they'd put in it. She'd also been given a leather bottle with a foul fermented drink in it. She had no choice but to drink that as well, though it left her lightheaded and wanting to sleep afterward.

"How long will it be, Great Mother, until my fate is decided? How long will they keep me here?" She went down on her hunkers and hugged herself.

She spun around at the sound of a creaking noise. The side of the cage was opening, being pulled out. In the gap appeared Athralar. He came into the cage and looked up. Raindrops fell all around them. The ground, matted grass, became slick mud quickly.

But Juliana could not stop smiling. It was good to see him, a half friendly face.

"Your sister and your mother do not like me," she said.

"They do not like anyone from the Roman world. You are all demons sent to enslave us, as far as they are concerned."

"Tell them I was a slave for most of my life, captured in the east, and I had no choice of who I am since I was a child."

"You have a choice now."

She looked into his eyes. They were sea blue, flecked with silver. She looked away. He was the type of man she could easily admire.

"I've been given a choice, Juliana. I must either let you fight for your place at the selection or keep you as my slave, but cut off your nose and your ears to make sure you do not appeal to any other of our warriors and cause any more deaths." He leaned one hand against the branches that made up the wall of the cage.

Juliana took a step back. Her hands trembled as she raised them to rub against her nose, which had, weirdly, started tingling as if the gods were sending it a message.

She shrugged as if to throw off despair. "What is the alternative?"

"That you will fight to the death with one of the other captured female slaves who is also preparing for the selection."

"So, you came to let me decide my own fate?"

"No. I came to tell you what my decision is."

He paused, looked up, moved to an area in the cage where the rain fell less, then went on. "Are you really able to read the future, as you claimed?"

"What has that got to do with fighting?"

"Have you seen your fate?"

"I see many things in my dreams. I saw you fighting beside me in one dream and us sharing a table with a wolf in another."

"Can you change the weather, too, Juliana?" He looked afraid, as if she had said something more important than she knew.

"No, but I can change your future. And that is more important, isn't it?"

"My mother said you were a demon sent from the underworld to tempt me. She and my sister want to see you dead and your head on our table at our celebration of the new year starting as the growth returns to the forest."

Juliana went up close to him. "I want to fight, but who will I be fighting? Will it be a Saxon or a Roman?"

Athralar laughed. "It will not be a Saxon, they do not want it to be over too quickly."

Juliana sniffed. "I will not be easy prey."

He shook his head.

"You will be fighting a Bructeri shield maiden. She is dangerous." He put his hands up, as if to warn her off. "Have your nose and ears cut. They burn the wounds quickly so you will not die from them, and I am sure you will still be able to attract men." He smiled.

She spat on the ground between them. "I have no interest in attracting men, but I will not spend my life with the marks of a Saxon slave on my face."

"Bructeri shield maidens are trained to fight from an early age. You should think a little longer about this."

She took a deep breath. She was shaking inside. "I'd rather die than submit to your mother's knife."

He walked around the cage. "How did you know my mother will do the cutting?"

"I saw it in her eyes."

She went down on her haunches. What else could she do?

"The great mother will decide my fate."

"You are brave."

"No, I am not. This will be an easy way out."

"Do not expect it to be easy."

He went to the gate and rattled it. As it was pulled open, he said, "It is not the great mother who will decide your fate, it is the all father, Woden. You must say your prayers to him tonight." Then he disappeared.

She didn't pray to anyone but the great mother that night. She'd heard that the followers of the Christ god also prayed to the great mother. It was the religion of the slaves and the weak in the Roman world now, and she'd heard stories of how its followers embraced death, so convinced were they that they would awake in an afterlife, their heaven.

It sounded like a good way to go. Full of certainty.

She couldn't sleep that night. One of the guards passed in a hand's length of smoked sausage to her. A few bites of it had set her stomach twisting. Or it could have been the thought of a knife in eye the next day. She'd heard stories about shield maidens killing men that way. Men who got distracted by their jiggling breasts.

The guard also passed in an animal skin with fermented mare's milk in it. It tasted better than the milk they had used on the journey here, but she didn't drink much. Before she fell asleep, she pressed her hands into the earth beneath her, praying over and over.

"Great mother watch over me.

"Great mother make me strong.

"Favored are thou among women.

"Favored is the fruit of thy loins.

"At the hour of my death, protect me."

Her dreams were filled with memories of her first mother, her birth mother, calling to her, warning her about something, but she could not hear her properly and she could not move to get closer to her.

Juliana woke, sweating, though it was cold. She listened to the sounds of the trees creaking and far off, humming and slow drums beating.

She wanted the night to end. She wanted it all to be over. She lay awake until finally her despair turned to drowsiness, as if she no longer cared what happened to her.

She woke late in the morning. No one came to collect her. The day passed slowly, as if the demon of time had decided to make her suffer by dragging every moment out. The sun had lowered into the trees before the gate opened again.

By this time a smell of burning had seeped into the cage, filling her nostrils with a sweetness, like roasted pig, but which she knew could also be roasting human flesh.

In the part of the forest she was taken to, the trees were thick and spaced far apart. There were people everywhere, shadows all around. Some were sitting on the ground. Others were standing by tress. More were sitting up in the trees. They all watched her as she approached, her guard behind her with a blazing torch held up high.

Up ahead lay a circle of tree trunks on their side. Within the circle stood a single upright tree trunk, whitened by ash. It had only one branch.

Around the circle of fallen tree trunks stood a ring of men about a pace apart, each man naked except for a loin cloth and a spear held in front of him. The spear tips shone in the moonlight. Their bodies were smeared in ash. It gave them the look of the dead.

Her guard grabbed her shoulder as she neared the men. They turned to watch her. Juliana's gaze shifted to a woman fifty paces away who was also accompanied by a man with a torch.

She was a lot bigger than Juliana. She could have passed as a man. Her hair was short, and her arms were thickly muscled. She wore a short woolen tunic like the one Juliana had been given that morning, A hush fell over the people watching.

The woman she was to fight raised a hand and bowed at the circle of men. Then she looked toward Juliana, threw her head back and laughed as if the outcome of the fight was more than obvious. The laughter echoed as the people watching hushed to listen.

XIV

Via Ostiensis, outside Rome, 307 A.D.

Paulina's shout distracted the self-styled tax collectors.

Lucius lunged at the big man claiming to be a tax collector as he rubbed at his eyes. The man's sword had dipped as he rubbed away the dirt.

Lucius grabbed at the man's sword hand. He bent his hand up sharply. A grunt of pain followed. The man jerked his head back. Lucius had his other hand around the man's shoulder. He could smell the garlic on the man's breath.

"Tell your men to go, or your own sword will cut your tongue out from inside." Lucius pressed the tip of the man's sword into the side of his neck. One more slight push and it would go through the skin.

The tax collector shouted something in a Latin dialect Lucius was not familiar with. His men stepped back, then as one turned and headed into the woods.

"When we reach Ostia you will be released," said Lucius into the man's ear. He shouted at one of the slaves to come and tie the man's hands behind his back. He held the blade tight to the tax collector's skin until he was bound.

Paulina came beside him when it was done. He expected her to thank him. Instead, she slapped him hard across the face.

"Did you have to tell everyone in Rome you would be carrying gold?"

XV

Treveris, Northern Gaul, 307 A.D.

The following day the new slave brought Constantine fresh bread at the table in the atrium when he was having breakfast. Her tunic was short and her hair long and tied in a knot on her head.

After he'd eaten, he spoke to the slave master, found out the new slave's name and told him that Antonia must stay in the kitchens in future. If he wanted another woman to sleep with he would find one himself, not take the bait his mother had laid for him.

"If Antonia cannot stay in the kitchens, sell her," he shouted at the slave master as the man walked away, backward, as he left Constantine's presence, even though Constantine had told him not to. Force of habit was his excuse, though Constantine knew the man hoped Constantine would eventually come to appreciate the traditional way a slave should behave with their emperor.

"And leave me the way I told you," he shouted after the man.

He took a deep breath. The sight of Antonia's legs had stirred his desire. He stood and walked around the edge of the atrium. He would send for the pretty bath house slave whose massages had calmed his loins before. Now that he had his own bathhouse, he might even employ her permanently if Juliana didn't return. Better that, than to fall prey to one of his mother's spies.

Sunlight streamed through the opening in the roof at the center of the atrium. Dust mites swirled and he could hear chaffinches and blackbirds from the trees that lined the marshaling area nearby.

He swung his sword arm, exercising it the way he had been taught while serving in the legions. His shoulder was getting better. Soon the fighting season would be starting again, and he would have to decide whether to send a legion or three over the Rhine to look for Juliana. The problem was that even three legions could not get as far as he needed to go, to beyond the meeting place of the Alemanni tribes.

Three hundred years before, the Roman general Varus had lost three legions in the forests of Germania, and his life. It had been a defeat which shaped the Empire, even though it should never have happened. Varus had let his enemy pick the battleground and the time of battle.

He would not make that mistake.

He would not go down in history in the same way as Varus.

Two of his personal bodyguard helped him with his dress uniform in the room set aside for his armor. He had hand-picked the men from among the younger legionaries who served in his father's guard when he died, and who were stationed here in Treveris, far from Eboracum.

That helped to ensure the men were not close enough to his father to have been brought with him to Britannia on his last mission, but were trusted enough to stay behind in Treveris and guard the imperial villa.

When they were finished he stood to attention, weighed down with a gilded breast plate and a row of gold medals, gold arm greaves and leg greaves. They all put on their helmets and marched together the short distance from his villa to the giant basilica used for larger meetings.

The streets were filled with all types as they made their way in the spring sunshine. Everywhere he looked there were young women, though that was probably because their ambitious mothers pushed them forward when they saw his guard approaching.

When they reached the basilica, trumpets blew and a line of standard bearers on each side of the entrance roared his name as they went up the stairs at a run, two stairs at a time, to the double-height pillared entrance. At the top of the wide stone stairs he turned and addressed the crowd who had gathered to watch him. They were murmuring their approval.

They always noticed his vigor and that of the young guardsmen who accompanied him when he appeared in public. Grief had been expressed widely in the city after his father had died, and he'd heard reports that some of the patrician class were afraid he hadn't enough experience to govern or hadn't as many victories as his father, but he would make his own victories and until then they could be proud they had a young emperor again, of not even thirty-five summers.

He raised his fist high and held it there. "People of Treveris, I salute you." A roar of approval came from the onlookers. They were probably still hoping for a public donation.

"I know you are still grieving for my father, as we all do, and with that in mind there will be a games held in his name during the summer. We have asked all the cities in our provinces to provide beasts or gladiators for your entertainment." A whisper of approval rustled through the crowd.

Most of the people preferred to see well matched gladiators with complementary skills fighting each other, but a mix of beast hunts, executions and gladiatorial games would be less costly and with the treasury still low, it was the best option for keeping the city entertained that summer.

He would have other things to keep him busy.

Turning, he walked slowly into the basilica while adjusting his balteus, the wide ornamented belt that passed from his right shoulder down to the jeweled scabbard at his left side. While he preferred a short sword and a thinner belt when in the field, he knew what was expected of him at this type of event.

He knew too that he had a long way to go before the doubters would accept he'd come to power legitimately, so he had to play his part with care. His father had told him to always keep his enemies close. He intended to do that. Two guardsmen pushed open the doors of the basilica and he walked into the semi-darkness. He stopped, letting his eyes adjust. A crowd of men waited for him. On the left were men in togas and embroidered tunics, the administration officials and patrician families of the city, and representatives of the city guilds, as well as vineyard owners and the brightest schemers and deal makers from all the wealthiest families in the province. They were mostly here to seek positions for themselves or members of their family, or they were looking for contracts of one type or another for their family estates.

On the right stood military officers, first the legates, prefects and tribunes, appointed by his father, and behind them, the commanders of the auxiliaries and the cavalry units and the marshals of the river units and the navy which patrolled both the coast of Gaul and Britannia.

He'd called this meeting to ensure that any who'd heard he'd been wounded would see that all he'd suffered was a scratch, and would take that message out from the city to wherever they came from and beyond.

It was critical that these men see his power and feel his authority. He knew enemies could be far away and close by. His father's fate had taught him that.

"Augustus of the west, Valerius Aurelius Constantine," proclaimed a herald.

As the crowd hushed, he strode up the center passage toward the far end of the basilica. Standing there was the only woman in the room, Theodora. She had a pearl imperial diadem in her black hair and wore a purple stola similar to the togas many of the men wore, but with a band of gold embroidery at its edge. She too had put on her best for the meeting.

Theodora held her hand out, as if expecting Constantine to kneel at her feet and kiss her ring, as he might have done when her husband was alive.

He didn't. He went to stand near her and she pulled her hand away, as if her fingers had been burnt.

When he was younger he had feared speaking in front of big crowds, but now he'd got used to it, mainly because he had no choice. If he didn't speak up, he could die.

"Today is an auspicious day. We are gathered to celebrate Lemuria, when the spirits of our dead are exorcised and the virgins from the temples help us to ensure all ghosts are freed from this world."

He raised a hand and pointed it at Theodora.

She stared at him, her eyes wide. There had been nothing about Lemuria in the invitation Constantine had sent to her. She'd probably expected that he needed her influence with these men and had invited her here for her help.

"I wish to announce that Thoedora, the ex-Empress, has renounced all her titles and will be going into seclusion in the palace here in Treveris, to allow time for the ghost of my father to be fully exorcised. She will be accepting no visitors from this day forth."

A murmur passed through the crowd. It grew louder as he turned to Theodora and opened his arms to hug her. As she hugged him, he held her tight and for longer than usual and whispered in her ear as he did, "If you object to what I have announced, I will force you to watch your children have their necks sliced open."

She pushed away from him.

He held her tighter. "Speak against me and you will find out that I am a man of my word."

Theodora pushed him gently away, stepped back, went down on one knee and said, "Hail Caesar Augustus, our new emperor."

There was a little more emphasis on the word 'new' than he wanted, but there was no point in making an issue of it. Behind him the rows of men were cheering and raising their fists. Whatever else he did, this would make clear that Theodora was not available for scheming with, and if anyone wanted favor, they would have to come to him.

Theodora's smile was fixed on her face like a mask, but her eyes were staring like a wild dog's. He raised his hand for silence and when he got it, he said, "Now, we must wish Theodora well in her period of devotion to the memory of my father."

Injured pride and a burst of anger rose in Theodora's face and caused her to blush and her expression to harden. But she kept her mouth firmly shut as she passed out down the center of the room. Two of Constantine's guards waited for her there to escort her back to the palace. Constantine had already agreed which men would guard her rooms and that would leave no chance for her to have visitors or to escape.

The last look she gave him as she was about to exit the building held pure venom.

XVI

Woden's Cage, Territory of the Saxons, Northern Germania, 307 A.D.

Juliana stared back at her opponent. She would not lose this fight before it started. As she stared, she repeated a prayer to the great mother.

"Holy mother of God, as the hour of my death approaches, protect me."

She spoke it in the language of her birth, Aramaic, and each time she spoke she said it louder.

Some of the people near to her noticed her muttering. They turned and stared at her. One man laughed. She didn't care. She stood still at the edge of the fighting ring. She could see the center of it clearly now. A mound of branches was visible. It looked as if it extended down, perhaps into a circular pit, about the width of a man lying down. A burning arrow hit the mound of branches. The branches must have been dipped in tallow. Within moments the soft roar of fire silenced everyone watching.

Juliana kept praying as a man handed her a thin knife with a bone handle. She kept praying as they pushed her into the empty space between the ring of trees and the now roaring fire at its center. She kept praying, but louder, as she turned to face the Bructeri shield maiden.

The woman threw her knife up in the air and caught it with her other hand, as if juggling it was second nature to her. She smiled at Juliana, and when she caught Juliana's eye she put her head to one side and blinked, as if she sympathized with her.

Juliana mimicked her, putting her own head to the side. The hush from the crowd ended in shouts as a war horn rang out. The call echoed through the woods and on into the distance as if animals were calling to each other.

Juliana walked around the circle. The shield maiden followed her, slowly at first, but then faster. Juliana went faster too. The crowd whooped, expecting a quick kill.

Juliana had an urge to break through the ring of men and run for her life, but the men had their arms extended and they were watching her as she ran. She looked up at the largest tree around the circle as she passed it and saw Athralar on a thick lower branch, his mother and sister watching from higher up. Only Athralar looked concerned. The others appeared pleased.

Juliana stopped.

"Ooooh," screamed the crowd.

The shield maiden came rushing at her, her smile fixed now, her knife held up in front of her.

A primal fear rose within Juliana. Her stomach tightened as a half memory rose from early childhood, of hiding from someone dangerous where the family kept their chickens, and then a face looming. Her bowels wanted to open. Her mouth had gone as dry as dust.

She waited, transfixed.

A scream ripped from the shield maiden's mouth. It opened wide, as if she wanted to eat Juliana.

Juliana waited.

And then, at the last moment, as the knife came rushing toward her, she stepped to the side.

Her opponent must have been expecting the move as she lurched to the side too, and swung her knife back immediately, the tip catching Juliana's bare arm.

Whoops went up.

First blood to the shield maiden.

Juliana had not even swung her weapon. Whoops echoed all around her. More laughter came. Juliana was tempted to look up to the watchers in the tress, but she resisted. She kept moving now, one way, then the other, until she could feel the heat of the roaring fire behind her.

Was that where the loser ended up, burning to death?

She sidestepped again as the shield maiden ran at her, then took off toward the ring of men. When she reached them, she stopped. Her pursuer came slowly now, her smile gone, as if she wanted to get it all over with quickly. She pointed at the fire, as if Juliana should go there.

Juliana shook her head. No rush.

The shield maiden came near and swung her knife from side to side. It was a trap. The men behind her were shifting. The circle seemed smaller, the trees bigger, her body not part of her. She jabbed her weapon toward the shield maiden who, with surprising agility, grabbed at Juliana's wrist.

Juliana's knife fell as her wrist twisted. The shield maiden's weapon came fast toward her side. Juliana twisted away from the worst of it, but she still felt a sting at her waist. She didn't look, but the whoops from the crowd told it all.

Second blood.

It would be over soon.

Juliana slipped free and raced for the center of the ring, for the fire. Without thinking further she reached in, grabbed one of the longer burning branches and turned and headed back to her adversary, screaming in pain. The woman stared at Juliana, a proud hunter's look on her face.

Juliana's hands shook with the pain. Her skin was burning. Her hair was in danger of catching fire. The smell of burning flesh filled the air. Whoops turned to gasps around her.

She would have to drop the branch.

The shield maiden stepped back as Juliana came running at her and laughed, as the burning branch came up.

XVII

The Port of Ostia, near Rome, 307 A.D.

When they reached the port Lucius went ahead to the vessel waiting for them. He had to make sure the captain would keep his word and take his party back to Massilia on the next tide.

The ship was a large trading galley with two rows of oars on each side, one above the other, and a large center sail. A covered area for the rowers stood in the center of the deck and a large wooden cabin covered the back of the vessel, where the captain slept and kept any important cargo.

Lucius' three slaves had spent each night on the deck under a canvas awning on the way from Massilia. Lucius had slept in the captain's cabin on a thick rug on the floor, wrapped in his cloak. The journey back would have to be done differently. The captain would require extra payment for carrying Paulina too and for Lucius keeping him waiting a few extra days.

"Brave Lucius," shouted the captain, as he walked up the gangplank onto the galley. The ship looked deserted except for the captain and the bulging-muscled chief rower. Normally there were men swarming.

"Captain Macro, where is the crew?"

"Scattered, brave Lucius. When I told them we were waiting as long as it took for you to come back, they all headed off. My cargo is rotting, and my men are going back to being land lovers. We need to talk, now." He waved Lucius after him and headed for the cabin at the back of the ship.

Inside it was almost dark. Shafts of light streamed from thin gaps in the side planking and a small candle lit up the low box table where the captain ate while sitting on the floor. On the box lay a wineskin. The captain grabbed it, opened it and sat. He took a serious swallow from the wineskin and passed it to Lucius.

"You survived your visit to your family?" said the captain. "Are they all well?"

"I have no good news, Captain. I have been tasked with too many things and the money is low. I can pay you what we agreed, but no more, and I have another passenger who will come with us. I'm sure that will not affect our price as she is a small thing and will not cause any problems." Lucius passed back the wine skin.

"She, you say." The captain let out a sarcastic laugh. "That may not be a problem for you, but it is for us. Every man on my ship will want extra not to curse you, because Neptune may want to take our passenger down to his palace to seduce her." He raised a hand in a sweeping gesture, as if grabbing something from on high and pulling it down.

"Neptune will not come for this woman. She is a priestess and has the protection of Hecate and Ceres."

"A priestess. Worse still! Neptune will have to be paid to look aside." The captain swung around, taking in the space around them. It was low roofed and a blanket hung down one side, blocking part of the cabin off.

"I expect she will want my ample sleeping area as well." He grinned at Lucius. "Will you be sleeping beside her?"

Lucius shook his head.

"Will you be wanting to sleep near her?"

Lucius shook his head.

The captain laughed. "Well, my friend, I don't think she'll be wanting me to sleep anywhere near her." He leaned across the box.

"The passage fee is double if we take her." He spat on his hand and held it out.

Lucius stood. "We will find another ship."

A roar came from the captain. "No, you cannot do that. I have not been paid for my trouble so far, waiting here for you day after day."

A bang reverberated through the room.

The captain had smashed a dagger head into the tabletop. At that, as if on a signal, the thin wooden door to the deck burst open. The chief rower stood in the gap, his whip in his hand.

"Come, brave Lucius. Let us negotiate."

The sun was sinking fast when Paulina was shown on board. The captain had cleared the table in his cabin and scattered the crumbs from his last meal on the floor, but he had done nothing else to prepare for her arrival. As her three chests were hauled into the cabin she made her displeasure clear.

"I expected better than this, Lucius. How can you expect me to sleep there?" She pointed beyond the curtain. The end of the pile of rugs the captain slept on was visible.

"You may sleep where you will. What you can be sure of is that no one else will sleep in this room. It cost me a steep price to get this for you, so please, complain to someone else or make your way back to Rome."

Paulina looked at him. Her lower lip began to tremble. She lowered her eyes.

"I cannot go back to Rome." Her voice broke. She sobbed, softly, her head down. Lucius took a step toward her as an urge to comfort her rose up inside him.

Paulina raised her hand, as if she wanted him to stay away.

"Please, just say you will not leave me to the rats in this cabin all alone."

"You want me to sleep with you?"

"No," she replied, sharply. She looked up. Her eyes were red rimmed, and a tear sparkled on her cheek.

Lucius wanted to wipe it away.

"Can you sleep on the other side of the curtain and protect me?" Her gaze was steady. Her tone pleading.

"Happy to. You will not have to fear man or beast on this voyage." He turned to go outside to tell the captain to cast off, no matter the lateness of the hour.

As he left the cabin Paulina stared at his back, smiling.

XVIII

Treveris, Northern Gaul, 307 A.D.

"Yes, I was the last to see him." The old woman bent her head and began to cry. Her sobs were loud and piercing.

"I know this already," said Constantine. "What I want to know is who came to see the child?"

She sobbed as she spoke. "The day before he disappeared a man visited us. He asked for Juliana. I told him she'd gone missing. He asked after her child. I told him nothing. I ordered him to go. I did not let him into the house. Your mother warned me to be careful of who I let in. I did not know your son would be gone that very night." She started wailing.

Constantine felt a cold emptiness creeping up on him from his legs into his stomach.

"Who was this man?"

"He spoke like he was from Treveris, but I have never seen him. He was young, with a well-trimmed beard."

"Have you seen him since?"

"No."

"Sejanus," he roared.

The prefect of the imperial bodyguard came marching into the atrium, the pommel of his sword clanking against his side. Sejanus saluted.

"Yes, my lord."

"Take this woman back to her house. It is not far from here."

Constantine stopped, put his fist to his palm.

He pointed at the old woman, his finger shaking. "Say nothing about this to anyone or I will have your tongue cut out and fed to the fishes."

Her mouth opened. Her sobbing stopped abruptly. She stared at him, her eyes wide and her face paling visibly in front of him.

"Now go. Get out of my sight."

He walked the empty corridors of the villa, back and forth.

Could someone from Treveris have taken his child? Would they try to use the child against him? He had to be strong. He could not be seen as caring too much for the baby or the child's mother, no matter what his real feelings were.

As emperor, he was expected to be ruthless with concubines and their children, moving from one beauty to the next as he saw fit. He'd heard there was wild speculation about his journey beyond the Rhine, searching for a concubine and a baby. And that his failure had become the talk of the taverns. He made decisions for the empire with his cock was one of the charges against him being circulated by those who enjoyed dragging down anyone in power and exposing any weakness.

He had to show strength.

He would be overturned by his own officers if he didn't and end up skewered by a usurper's sword.

His enemies further afield would be looking for opportunities to depose him and kill anyone associated with him.

His hands were tied.

He had fallen hard for Juliana, and her son as well as soon as he'd been born. He'd felt the bond between them, and he'd promised her that their son would inherit his position as emperor.

He groaned. How stupid he'd been.

He could not be foolish any longer.

With luck, whoever had taken them would come forward with a demand, which he would pay.

And if they did not he would harden his heart. There was no other way.

He slept little that night, wracked with guilt over his decision. To make things worse, this was the second time he had lost contact with a son.

He'd had a better excuse the other time.

That son, Crispus, had been born when he was stationed with the legions in the east. The mother, a beguiling beauty named Minervina, had died in childbirth. Her family, wine merchants, had kept the boy and warned him not to come near them again.

That was ten years ago.

Minervina's father had told him to his face that it would be best for all if they took the baby as their own. Their grandchild, he'd said, could have his life snuffed out by anyone who wanted his father's imperial line destroyed or be kidnapped by someone who wanted to blackmail Constantine.

Minervina's family would look after the boy, but they could not do so if they needed to guard him night and day.

Constantine had agreed.

It had been a simple solution to the dilemma he'd faced when the baby was on its way. He'd contemplated asking for permission to marry Minervina, but he knew that would also put them all in danger. The Emperor Galerius, whose thumb he'd been under, had been so unpredictable he could have wiped them all out at a whim. That had been why he'd kept the pregnancy secret. Constantine had given the next allowance in gold his father had sent him to Minervina's father and had never talked about the child again.

The man had been right, too.

It was the best thing he could do for the boy. Seal his lips.

He'd loved Minervina as much as he loved Juliana now, and he'd only been with her a few months while he was stationed in Byzantion, and he and the men under him had been enjoying the taverns around the temple to Sophia on the hill overlooking the Bosporus one endless summer.

She'd pretended to be one of the priestesses of Sophia on the night they first met. That was a night to remember.

He walked the corridors on and on, wondering why memories he hadn't talked with anyone, ever, had all come back so clearly.

Why was it that even though he was now emperor, he still could not do what he wanted? He still had to think about how things would be seen by others.

He promised himself that when he'd consolidated his power and his position was secure, he would do exactly as he wanted and to Hades with anyone who disagreed.

The next few days passed in a blur. He spent the daytime on official business and the evenings discussing with Sejanus what next they could do to find Juliana and his son. Sejanus was from Britannia, from Londinium, and had a mixture of Roman and Brigantian blood. He stood tall and had a cool attitude, which Constantine appreciated.

They sat on carved chairs in the atrium of his villa with maps on the marble table between them each night. At the end of a week of searching Constantine decided to change the tactics.

"Stop the searches. We have done enough," he said, his voice raised. Then he forced himself to breathe slowly. Anger had bubbled up inside him at the news of more failures in the search, but he would not take it out on this man.

Sejanus leaned back. "I will not stop searching. I know people beyond the great river who can search for him again on that side too. That will be our next step."

Constantine pointed at Sejanus. "Tell no one who you do this for."

Sejanus nodded. "I am your servant, my lord."

"And take whatever gold you need from the treasury. I don't care what it takes."

"Yes, my lord. Perhaps we could send messages again to all the tribes on this side of the river. If you consider who came to see him before he disappeared, this could be wise."

"We will not do that."

A loud banging reverberated through the room. A shout went up from the door guards. There were four on at night, all well capable of handling themselves in a fight.

Answering shouts echoed into the atrium. "Who goes there?"

A muffled reply came.

"You must move into the main palace grounds," said Sejanus. "Security here is not good."

"Be quiet," said Constantine. He stood and went to the chest at the back of the room. Inside there were swords and daggers, enough for half a dozen skilled men to hold off a hundred in the entrance passage.

"Let's find out what's going on, Sejanus." But before they could leave Constantine's mother, Helena, entered the atrium, her green cloak still around her shoulders.

"Constantine, this is absurd. You cannot live here. Your concubine and her bastard son disappearing are an omen. You must forget your hope of being a normal man ever again. Everyone around you is in danger because of who you are. I hope you have learned your lesson with these kidnappings."

"Thank you, Mother. Now the lesson is over, goodbye. Let us not detain you."

Helena ignored him and sat, heavily, where he had been sitting.

"Prefect Sejanus, I am sure you agree with me, yes?"

"Yes," said Sejanus. "I do."

"And you must be married as soon as possible, Constantine. Then all these rumors of affairs and children you are fretting over will vanish. I promise you that. You were offered Fausta last year. You have no excuse to turn her down now. You must accept her."

"Don't try this again, Mother."

Her voice rose. "You will have to marry someone. You have no reason not to now. I will come here every night until you do."

He stared at her for a long time. She stared back. "Mother. I will consider it. But only if she is half the woman Juliana is, because if she is not, I will leave her as soon as Juliana reappears."

"She is more than good enough for you," said Helene. "Now you must see things clearly. An emperor cannot be open to being swayed by any passing pretty face. You must be sated of all desire when you venture out thanks to the powers of your wife in the bedchamber. Am I right, Sejanus?"

Sejanus nodded, smiling.

Constantine looked at them. They were right, but he hated it.

XIX

Woden's Cage, Territory of the Saxons, Northern Germania, 307 A.D.

"Marya!" Juliana screamed the great mother's name in Aramaic as she closed with the shield maiden.

"Woden!" the shield maiden screamed, as she tried to sweep the fiery pointed branch away.

Juliana's hands were blistering. A fierce, mind-numbing pain ran up each arm, making her shake.

But she would not drop the branch. She would not let the bitch kill her.

She plunged the branch straight toward the eye of the shield maiden.

The expression of surprise on the shield maiden's face was imprinted forever on Juliana's mind.

Juliana screamed as she pushed with the entire strength of her body behind the branch. She felt herself falling forward as the shield maiden gave way, stepping back. Juliana leaped after her.

The fiery spear went into the shield maiden's eye. Juliana ended up on top of her surrounded by a hissing noise as flames were doused in gore.

Juliana rolled away, shuddering, as cheers echoed until they faded and her mind became only one thing, pain.

XX

Treveris, Northern Gaul, 307 A.D.

One full moon later

"So, Paulina, you are a priestess." Constantine pushed himself up onto one arm as he leaned on the couch. Around him reclined the legates of his legions, their wives and concubines. They had been drinking wine since the early evening.

He didn't care that he was half drunk. He didn't care that Lucius had returned with a priestess. And he didn't care that his mother had sent a message to Fausta that he would marry her.

All he cared about was the drinking game he was taking part in, with each man around him taking it in turn to tell about the moment they came closest to death and how they saved themselves or if someone else had saved them.

"Is this how you all prepare for battle in the north, my lord?" said Paulina softly, before bowing low in front of him, so that almost all her breasts were visible because of the low front of her gown.

"It is, fair Paulina," said Constantine, staring at her. "Come, sit with me and try the local wine. It is not like the Greek muck everyone in Rome loves these days. It is far better, smoother and sweeter." He waved for a slave to bring forward another gold goblet and fill it. When it was done and Paulina put it to her mouth, he touched the base of the goblet, pushing it up so she had to drink more.

She gulped some down, then turned away from him and spilled the rest of her goblet on the floor, while coughing loudly.

"Yeuuch, that is vile," she shouted.

All the talking around them stopped.

Constantine tried to stand, but he needed the help of Sejanus to steady himself.

"Breach another amphora," he shouted. "Open one of the older ones for our guest."

Paulina stood too. "I will wait for you outside. The night air might be good for us both." She slipped away from the table and headed for the side door of the palace dining room.

Constantine stared after her. Her diaphanous green gown was almost see-through, but not quite. Her jet-black hair hung down her back in a snake-like ponytail. It had been some time since he'd seen such a Roman beauty. He remembered now why his father had warned him against going to the temples in Rome and telling them who he was.

"Man-traps," is how he'd described the priestesses in Rome.

And he'd been right. Sybellina had proved that already.

Would Paulina be different?

He stumbled after her, leaning on Sejanus' shoulder as he went.

He didn't care if he got trapped by Paulina. His father was dead. He had got what he wanted. And now it might all be turning to dust in his hands.

Another new moon had come and gone and still there was no word of Juliana or their child. It felt as if they'd never existed.

He could not even bring himself to speak about her anymore. It felt like itching at a scab, and at every mention of her name an ache ran right through him because of his abject failure in finding her. Far from feeling like the most powerful man in the western provinces, he felt like its weakest.

Which was why he didn't care what happened to his life or what happened to the provinces he'd inherited. Urgent messages from city governors and military prefects went unanswered, and events he should have attended he refused to go to.

They could all go to Hades in a hand cart for all he cared.

Beyond the wide doors lay a small garden. He stumbled into it. Paulina was sitting on a marble bench in front of the red brick wall at the back of the garden, framed by thick bunches of purple wisteria, which gave the scene such a magical quality he stopped and stared.

The sweet scent of wisteria came to him as he sat heavily beside her. She took his hand and pressed his palm to her cheek. Her skin felt cool, downy, as it brushed against him.

"Lucius told me everything on the way here. I am so sorry. Losing your partner must have cut you to the bone."

He pulled his hand away. "It is all in the past. Whatever does not kill you makes you stronger. Isn't that what Marcus Aurelius said?"

"I have a suggestion. May I speak freely?"

"Why not, who cares who listens to us."

She held his hand tighter.

"I'm but a messenger, and I will tell you my message soon, but first I must tell you that I hope you will take up the offer contained in the message, and that I will do whatever I can to help you find peace again. You cannot establish your rule like this." She waved her hand toward the dining room. A shout and the sound of laughter came through the open door. She moved a little away from him, as if he might be contagious.

"What is your message?" He glared at her.

She bowed. "I mean no criticism. You may rule as you will. I just want to tell you what I see. It is what I have been ordered to do. Please forgive me if I have offended you." She came off the bench and lowered herself to her knees directly in front of him.

"If I have offended you, please, you may take my life now. I have no more need of it." She looked up at him, her eyes wide with fear.

He breathed deeply. Her pleading and the mounds of her breasts, almost totally visible now as she looked up at him, were stirring him. A warm humming rose inside him.

He pushed her hands away. He would not be so easily hooked.

"Tell me your message. Tell it to me now."

She bowed low. "The Emperor Maximian offers his daughter, Fausta, to you in marriage."

"I know this already." Constantine folded his arms.

"The great Caesar Augustus, Maximian, is on his way to Arles at this moment. He wishes for you to come to him and that all of you together will celebrate the joining of two imperial families with great joy."

Constantine sighed. It was bad enough his mother pressing Fausta on him, now others were too.

"What do you make of Fausta, Paulina? The only time I saw her she was still a child, pale faced and scared looking."

"Fausta is a dutiful Roman woman as a member of the imperial family should be, and she is trained in the arts of love, as a woman should be. She will make you a fine wife and bear you many sons, if the gods so wish it." She peeked up at him, smiling.

"What about if I do not wish it?"

"A good wife will help soothe your mind from all your troubles. And you will need an heir to continue your family and your name. Fausta is a perfect match for you. Why would you refuse her? She brings you many things." Paulina pressed forward again, smiling up at him, her lips slightly parted, as if she wanted to be kissed.

"And you come with this package?"

"I am yours any time you wish. I cannot marry, as I have sworn not to, but I can take the pleasures of the flesh when I desire to. And I have been trained to make those pleasures last and to heighten as the gods allow." She took one of his hands and pressed it to her left breast.

She pressed it so tight into her that her heartbeat fluttered through the mound of her breast. He licked his lips. It would be hard to refuse her.

He made a fist with his other hand.

Juliana would laugh at him if he was so easily lured. If he wanted a woman, he should pick his own, perhaps two of them tonight, from among the young slave girls who the imperial slave master had crammed the imperial household with recently, without even asking for permission.

By picking his own women he would not fall into the trap of a spy.

"I will think about your master's offer. Go to Arles and tell the aging Maximian that next year may be better for this betrothal, if it takes place at all. I have not finished my campaign against the tribes of Germania. I must do my duty there first."

He stood, swayed, stepped away from her and pulled his hand free from her grip.

Paulina groaned and put her forehead to the red tile floor.

"I'm also instructed to tell you about a gift that Maximian will make to you, should you travel to Arles and follow the path he proposes."

Constantine looked down at her. They had made a mistake. There was no sack of gold or gift of a parcel of land that could sway him. He'd received gold from the Christians and if he needed more land, he would take it himself, not wait for someone else to gift it to him.

Keeping Maximian and Fausta dangling was his best option.

"Do not waste my time with any more of this. Take my message to Maximian. Tell him I will consider his offer next year, if he agrees to confer on me the title of Augustus."

Paulina stayed down. Her voice lowered as she replied, "I will do this, but you may wish to change your message after I tell you the gift that Maximian will bestow on you for coming to Arles."

He shook his head. "I can think of nothing that will make me change my mind on this."

XXI

Juliana raised herself on an elbow. Athralar had come into the windowless, rush floored timber hut she'd been treated in since her victory in Woden's cage.

"It is time for you to join me at my camp, Juliana. You have put it off as long as you could. There is no reason for you to lie here any longer. You must start using your hands properly again."

Juliana raised her hands. They were still painful, especially at night when they throbbed, depriving her of sleep. The healing woman had wrapped them in leaves covered with boar fat when she woke in the hut the day after the fight. She also made her drink a foul-tasting liquid, which sent her back to sleep. She'd fed Juliana by hand too, and shooed Athralar away. She'd also stopped Juliana when she tried to leave the hut by barring her way with a stick and beating her about the head when Juliana did try to slip out of the hut for some air late one night.

Since then, Juliana had decided to wait until her hands were healed. That was taking far longer than she anticipated. But she had little choice. She could not make it back to Constantine like this. And another thought dogged her.

Would he even want her back with her hands unable to carry things without her screams reaching the treetops? She did not want his love for her to turn to pity. She had been promised the pain would go in time, but it was taking too long, way too long.

"What will I be in your camp, Athralar? Will I be your possession, your slave?" She stared at him.

He'd tied his hair back into a ponytail and there were new marks on his cheek, blue circles she had seen on the cheeks of other men here in the last few days.

He shook his head, laughed.

"I'll not make you a slave. You have proved your worth. I want you to join me in a raid and to find out what it is like to be a shield maiden." He paused.

"You want me to be a shield maiden?" The idea repulsed her. She did not want to make a life out of killing people.

"You have the right to call yourself a shield maiden of the Bructeri, as you killed one of them, but you must earn the right to call yourself a Saxon shield maiden."

"And go around killing people? I have never wanted to do that."

"Saxon shield maidens are called upon to fight injustice, to punish criminals, free captives and avenge murders. Shield maidens are respected. Many women would love to be in your position, with this chance." He shrugged.

"It does not appeal." She could imagine kitchen slaves wanting something else to do, but not free born women. "Anyhow, I will not be much use with my hands like this." She raised her scarred hands. Her skin glistened deep purple across her palms and fingers and the fingers themselves had only half the movement they'd had before.

"They will get better. I will get you more ointments."

"They'd better work."

"When you are ready, you will come with us."

She could sense there was more he wanted to say.

"Where are we raiding? To Gaul?"

"No, we raid against the Bructeri. They destroyed a Saxon village and killed women and children. They must be punished."

"I will not kill for you." She closed her eyes.

Athralar shook his head. "You do not have to."

She used her elbow to push herself to her feet. She had to think more about his offer. It would be good to get out of this hut.

He stood. "Will you come with me freely and agree not to try to escape?"

What choice did she have?

XXII

Treveris, Northern Gaul, Summer, 307 A.D.

Paulina straightened the folds of her gown. It wrapped around her like a second skin.

"Spit it out," said Constantine, staring very deliberately at her face.

"I am aware you have a son."

Where was this going? Did she know something about his son's disappearance?

"Go on." His right hand fell to the handle of the ornamented dagger hanging from his belt. If he found out Maxentius was behind his son's disappearance he would be seriously angry.

"Emperor Maxentius discovered that your son Crispus is in Rome. He has offered him his protection."

"Crispus?" said Constantine. He stared at Paulina as if she was a ghost. He had expected that someday the child he left in Byzantion would come back to haunt him, but not yet. The child could be only nine summers old.

"What boy named Crispus do you speak about?" He had to be careful. There were those who would pretend to be the son of male members of the imperial family, born to slaves or tavern girls, who spent their entire lives trying to prove who they were to claim an inheritance.

"The Crispus I speak about has a birth mark on his knee in the shape of a helmet." She smiled.

He stepped back. That was the birth mark he had seen on the boy, the birth mark his mother, Minervina, had pointed out to him as the best way his son could be identified in future.

"Where is this Crispus?" He had to see him. The thought that he had a son in need of help filled him with hope.

"He will be in Arles soon, with your wife to be, Fausta."

Constantine put his hand to his mouth. Paulina was right. This was the news that could change everything.

"Have you seen him? How is he? How did he come to be in Rome?"

"Your son is in good health. He came to Rome with his uncle. They had a tale about the taverns in Byzantion all burning because of riots, started by followers of the crucified god."

He stared at her. It didn't surprise him that Maxentius would try to use Crispus to achieve his own ends.

Crispus' guardian must have heard about what happened to the boy's father. He probably took the boy to Rome in the hope of contacting him. And Maxentius had taken Crispus under his wing, most probably as a prisoner. Constantine's hand gripped the handle of his dagger.

Could Maxentius be persuaded to give up Crispus, if he married Fausta?

As if Paulina had read his mind, she said, "Maxentius said you must come to Arles with no more than fifty personal bodyguards to protect you on the road. If you bring a legion or even a century, he will withdraw his party to Rome and assume you do not wish your son restored to you."

Constantine stared down at her. He had lost one son. Could he afford to be careless with the life of another? "There will be one condition," he said.

XXIII

Territory of the Bructeri, Northern Germania, Late Summer, 307 A.D.

"Shields up," Athralar shouted. The Saxon raiding party crouched in a circle and raised their shields as one. To the attackers they would appear like a hedgehog with red patterned skin, from the red circles painted on their shields.

They had been resting on the bank of a wide but shallow river in the territory of the Bructeri. Two scouts had gone ahead to see if the way lay clear down-river. A Bructeri village was known to be not far off. They'd been told that this village was where the last raid on Saxon territory had come from.

Juliana crouched in the second row, behind the shield wall, as arrows came thumping and whistling in. The aim of the Bructeri warriors was good. The man in front of her fell back with a scream, his hands grasping at an arrow which had struck deep into his throat.

Juliana lifted the shield from the man's shaking hands and set it into the wall, closing the gap. The man beside her nodded, then motioned downward with his head, telling her to keep her head down.

More arrows flicked through the trees around them. Some slipped past the shield wall and went straight by her. Others thumped into a shield or flesh.

But no Saxon screamed again and the hail of arrows slowed.

"Forward," shouted Athralar.

Juliana had a short Bructeri axe in her other hand. She held it up and to the side, ready to strike or throw. She spent some time every day now throwing it, both to get her hands working again, and to become a useful member of the raiding party.

This would be the first time she would use it to draw blood.

They were near the edge of the glade. The tightly packed trees here could be pushed through, but the shield wall would have to break. A humming noise filled the air. She'd been told the Bructeri liked to hum when they were about to attack.

Her breath came fast. Her head felt light., the axe heavy in her hand. She gripped it. Sweat pricked on her face, down her back.

She could smell blood and something stronger. Was it her own fear?

"Hold," shouted Athralar. He was on the far side of the circle of Saxon men. To Juliana's left stood a Saxon giant, at least two heads taller than her and twice as wide. He also used an axe. The man had taught her over the past few days how to swing her axe so it could be more effective than a sword. To her right stood a wiry man with bright blue hair she'd never spoken to.

He nudged her in the side now. "Go, wait in the center," he hissed at her. "I'd rather a man to protect my side."

She swung her axe back a little. "Shut your face. I'm as willing to die to protect you as any man."

A roar cut her short. Her shield reverberated as if a bull had struck it. The tip of a spear appeared through the middle of the shield. The shield felt double the weight it had been. Her arm began to wilt.

The giant beside her elbowed her hard. "Ready your axe," he shouted. His own rested on his shoulder now.

Juliana followed his example, then peered through a gap in the shields just in time to see a long haired Bructeri warrior, as big as the giant beside her, come racing toward her. She gulped. Her shield shuddered.

"Throw it," came the command from the man beside her.

Juliana moved her shield to the left as she'd been taught and threw her smaller throwing axe into the face of the man running toward her.

It missed. Throwing it at him had required her to ignore the likely effect of it striking him.

And now her lesson came.

His sword came plunging toward her through the gap in the shields. The giant beside her was shouting something. Her ears seemed to be blocked. All around there were screams and shouts, a strange cacophony of noise, as if the fight was taking place in a cave.

She twisted to the side. The sword thrust missed her. The giant beside her slammed his shield up into the Bructeri warrior's face.

"Cut him." Now she understood what he was shouting.

Another blow landed on her shield. She went back at the strength of it. As she did, she pulled her short sword out of the scabbard on her belt and with one movement swung it.

This time the Bructeri face loomed on the other side of her shield. He had a sword in his hand and jabbed it at her. She let the sword in her hand flow forward this time, as if it had a mind of its own.

Her sword went into the man's side. She pulled it back, slicing further into him and across his stomach. He fell, scrabbling at his stomach, as if trying to hold his guts in.

"Good," shouted the giant beside her.

The shield wall moved forward. She stepped over the Bructeri warrior. He must have been handsome, once. He probably had a wife and children. He wasn't handsome anymore. Thick red blood flowed from his bubbling wound where his intestines were clearly visible. He was down, dying, but his mouth was still moving and his eyes flashing up and down. A rancid smell came to her nostrils, like two-week-old meat.

His eyes stared at her.

"Quicker!" shouted the giant.

She glanced to her right. The giant was using his short sword to stab at a Bructeri who stood, if anything, even bigger than him. The Bructeri fought naked except for an animal skin belt that barely covered his oversized genitals. In his hand he had a giant axe, which he swung back and forth as if it was a twig.

He chopped at the Saxon shield in front of him.

Juliana swung her sword fast into the man's thigh. He screamed as the blade connected. Blood poured down onto Juliana's hands. She was splattered all over with blood now.

The Bructeri giant looked down at Juliana as if he could pull out her heart with his gaze. The Saxon giant beside her chopped his axe into the man's head. He chopped just above the forehead which opened up like a mouth.

An explosion of blood and brains covered them both with pink mist. Then a horn blast sounded and as quickly as it had started the Bructeri attack on the Saxons ended.

Juliana wanted to run straight to the river and wash herself. She stared down at the two giant Bructeri warriors near her feet. She was shaking, almost uncontrollably. The warriors looked ugly in death. The smell of shit filled her nostrils. One of the dead had loosened his bowels already. She puked up bile. Then puked again. Then she straightened, wiping her mouth with her arm, her shaking slowly coming under control.

Around her cheering broke out.

The bodies of five Bructeri warriors and two Saxons who had also died were pulled into the center of the glade. The Saxons were covered in branches and as the sun went down the pile of branches was lit. The smell of burning flesh flowed over everything.

Juliana couldn't eat that night. She wanted Athralar to head back to Saxon territory, but he wouldn't.

He propped the Bructeri warriors back to back, sitting up, using more branches, and set guards in the woods to watch out as the rest of the troop slept.

Juliana didn't sleep.

Her mind raced from images of the dead warriors to thoughts of who was waiting for them in the woods to thoughts about what her body would look like with a wound like they'd suffered. She'd seen death before, often, but this was different. She'd been in the shield wall.

When Athralar sat by her side, she put a hand on his arm. "The gods smiled on us today."

He squeezed her hand. "The men are saying you are a good omen. We were outnumbered, yet we won."

She looked him in the eye. "Why did you not leave me behind with your sister and mother and all the rest of the women? Why did you bring me with you, to be your lucky charm?" She glared at him.

He glared back at her.

"Here is the truth, Juliana, shield maiden, good omen. My mother and my sister were arguing about which of them would kill you after I left you behind, and what parts of your skin would make a good purse, your belly or your thighs." He went to punch her shoulder. She leaned out of the way.

"When we get back to our territory, I will tell them you fought in the shield wall and proved yourself and that if they harm you, they will have our whole warrior class looking for their blood."

He gripped her knee. She was sitting cross legged on the flattened grass. "Do you know who you helped to kill today?"

She shook her head.

"The son of a Bructeri chieftain from these parts." He went quiet.

She shuddered. "Will this start a blood feud?"

Athralar shook his head. "We will decide on what tales of courage will come out of this encounter."

He put his hand on her thigh. "You will drink with me now, yes, so we can sleep before they come back for us tomorrow." He handed her a wineskin. She sipped from the opening. Whatever was in it tasted like fiery piss.

She swallowed, passed it back to him. They each drank three times.

When she woke in the morning a horn was blowing. Sunlight filled the glade and the men around were putting their shields up. Pain pulled at her arms where there were scratches, and from her side and her thighs, where there were purple bruises, though she had no idea what had caused any of them.

XXIV

Treveris, Northern Gaul, 307 A.D.

Constantine strode to the front of the cavalry unit waiting near the black gate at the river side of the city. It was dawn, before most of the city had woken. The giant stone gate dominated the marshaling square.

"Mount up," he shouted. "We have a long way to go."

Helena stood by his white charger. The horse shivered in the cool of the early morning. It had been a hot summer and the month of Augustus was getting hotter by the day.

"May I follow tomorrow, not in three days?" she asked, a smile lighting up her face.

"Mother, have I ever been able to stop you from doing what you want?" He settled on his horse. An attendant pulled his cloak until it spread neatly down from the back.

He pushed his cloak away from his side and motioned for the attendant to stay back.

"This will be a great year, Constantine. You will be married to a woman who can help you, a woman who can make you an heir quickly. The women in her family are famous for their ability to make babies. You must plow her every night after you wed. Mark my words, when you have a legitimate son the plots against you will be called off. An imperial family is much more stable than one man alone."

Constantine patted the neck of his horse and bent down to his mother.

"You have told me this a hundred times already. I will see you at the next moon. Do not rush after us. I have a lot to discuss with Fausta's father before the wedding is agreed."

She leaned up and squeezed his arm, still smiling. "Maximian is a wily fox, but he needs us. You will get what you want."

Constantine pressed at his mother's hand as it lay on his arm, then turned and waved at the troop behind to follow him.

Helena stood with a group of imperial slaves and staff, watching as the city gate was dragged open with a loud grating noise and Constantine's journey south began. After crossing the river and passing the traders on the far side of the bridge, waiting for the gate to open, they headed south along the bank of the river.

Paulina and Sextus rode directly behind him. Ten cavalry men rode ahead, the rest guarded a string of packhorses to the rear. Lucius wasn't with them. Neither was Crocus. He had tasked Lucius with another job and in any case, it was better he wasn't seen as being too close to Constantine.

Crocus had been sent to the Rhine with a cavalry cohort to patrol the Roman side of the river and prevent incursions while Constantine marched to the south.

The fifty handpicked men who rode with him were from the imperial cavalry. Most were men in their late twenties who had fought numerous engagements against the Germanic tribes. There were no Alemanni among them. He did not want Maximian and his officers mixing with the Alemanni.

Paulina moved her horse closer to Constantine's soon after they left the city. He was batting away flies.

"Rub this on your arms and legs," she said. She held a small earthenware pot toward him.

He looked at it. "What is it?"

"You are suspicious of everyone, aren't you? Don't worry. My mission is to get you in one piece to the meeting in Arles. I will lose my head if you die before you get there."

"Rub some on your arms first."

She sighed, balanced the pot in her crotch and spread some of the light brown paste inside it on her bare forearms. He noticed there were no flies around her.

"What's in the paste?"

"A little magic," she laughed. "And a bunch of cloves." She passed the pot to him.

He sniffed at it, then rubbed some on his arms, balancing the pot in the gap between the wolfskin covering his saddle and his crotch.

"Is there any other part of your bargain with Maximian I should be aware of?" He passed the container back to her.

She sighed. "I'm to test if you're a real man." She stuck her tongue out at him, licked her lips, smiled.

"Why in Hades name will you do that?"

"Maximian wants to be sure you prefer women, not boys, before passing his beloved daughter on to you."

Constantine looked at her. Her thin leather riding jacket had been fastened tightly around her. It showed the contours of her body clearly.

Her eyes were wide as he looked back up at her face.

"Come and see me in my bed tonight. I am sure we will find something to do on this journey to pass the evenings."

They stopped that night at a new garrison camp his father had established where the road forked to head deep into Gaul or to follow the river south. The imperial tent didn't need to be set up here; the commander of the garrison, the camp prefect, gave up his without comment.

Constantine ate with the officers of the camp. Sejanus joined them. Paulina stayed away. When Constantine got back to the commander's tent it was late. He'd been drinking wine and celebrating the success of the garrison against a Bructeri raiding party and discussing tactics, if any, of the Germanic tribes raiding the garrison while he was gone.

The food had been good too. Roast pork, stuffed chickens, stuffed pigeons. All crispy with honeyed sweetbread and different wines to wash it all down.

Paulina had dismissed the two imperial slaves who had brought Constantine's baggage to the wide, extra high tent of the camp commander. It was lit by a cluster of oil lamps on a stand in the center of the tent and a row of yellow candles at the back.

She lay on his bed, a giant wolfskin pulled over her. Her bare arm lay on top of the wolf skin. Her black hair flowed around her head in waves.

Constantine stood at the end of the bed taking in the sight. She looked up at him with a wide smile, her tongue poking out at him again. As he watched she moved the wolfskin. The honey brown skin of her naked body slowly emerged. A smell of roses hit him.

"Stand up," he said.

She did.

"You truly are a goddess. Come here."

She padded toward him.

XXV

Juliana grabbed her shield from where it lay beside her and joined the shield wall. No arrows were coming in. Just horns were sounding.

Then, where the thin path south opened into the glade, two Saxons they had set to watch duty emerged. They had their hands bound behind them and their feet hobbled by rope. Both their faces were bloodied, as if they had traded blows with whoever captured them during the night.

"Who is out there?" shouted Athralar.

"They want to talk," one of the watch men shouted back. Then the two men stopped. One of them stumbled. They were attached by their ankles to a rope leading back into the trees.

Juliana twisted her head to see what was happening. Athralar opened the shield wall by moving his shield to the side.

"Tell them to release you and I will come and talk to them."

"No," shouted the watchman who hadn't spoken yet. "It is not you they want to talk to. It is Juliana, the shield maiden. They think she is our leader."

Athralar turned, eyes blazing with anger. Some of the men in the shield wall guffawed.

"They say they will attack if Juliana does not come to speak to them."

Juliana's mouth hung open. She didn't want this. She had no idea what to say to a bunch of Bructeri warriors. She stepped back and into the center of the shield wall. Her place in the wall closed behind her.

Athralar motioned her over to him. Then he opened a gap in the shield wall.

She stood in the gap and shouted, "Athralar is our leader. If they want to talk, they will talk to him."

A small Bructeri warrior appeared behind the watchmen. He carried no weapons. He put both his hands up and walked toward Juliana. He began speaking as he came close. He spoke loudly. She had no idea what he was saying.

Athralar pushed Juliana through the gap in the shield wall and followed her. He put his axe down and walked toward the man. She went with him. The Bructeri warrior motioned for them to sit.

The three of them sat cross legged on the grass. Juliana listened to Athralar and the man talking in the Bructeri language. The talking went on endlessly. She looked into the woods. Faces peered at them. When the men stopped talking a chorus of bird song could be heard.

Athralar put his hand on her thigh. She smiled at him. The Bructeri would tell his people that she and Athralar were partners. She didn't mind that. It would stop men trying to force themselves on her. Athralar was a formidable warrior with arms as thick as her legs and a neck as thick as her body.

"They want to join us," he said. He smiled at her. "No, it is more than that. They want us to go raiding with them. They were planning a raid on the Alemanni and with their leader dead they want you to lead them." He put his head back and laughed.

Juliana reached over and put her hand on Athralar's chest. He stopped laughing.

"Tell them we will lead them together, you and I, but on one condition." She paused.

"What condition?"

"They do what you tell them. You know what needs to be done on a raid. I don't." She pressed her hand flat into his chest hard, then pulled it away. "And the first thing you'll do is to tell the Bructeri around us," she pointed toward the woods, swinging her arm around, "to come out and show themselves." She wasn't sure what his reaction would be, but this was an opportunity that had to be grasped.

Athralar translated what she had said. The Bructeri warrior stood and shouted into the woods.

A few moments later they began coming out. There were almost twenty Saxons left in Athralar's war band. About fifty Bructeri warriors emerged from the woods. They stood in a row around the edge of the trees, their weapons still in their hands as if they were waiting for a signal.

Juliana and Athralar stood still. There was a coolness to the way their leader spoke to his men and to their response.

A moment later Juliana understood why.

One of the Bructeri, an older and bald-headed warrior covered in blue tattoos, started shouting and waving his war axe. He remonstrated at the Bructeri around him and pointed at Juliana and Athralar as if disgusted at what had happened. From his gestures it seemed he thought the Bructeri should wipe out the Saxons while they had them outnumbered. Some Bructeri near the man started smiling and gesticulating along with him.

They clearly thought they would win any fight quickly.

Athralar shouted, raised his war axe, and shook it at the man.

A hush settled.

"What did you say?" Juliana looked up at Athralar.

"I challenged that bald bastard to a fight to the death. The winner will lead a combined war band."

"And get me as part of the prize?"

Athralar nodded. "Of course."

Juliana looked at the bald man. He leered at her.

She held out her axe to Athralar, held it as he took it, and then began reciting her hymn to the great mother in Aramaic, over and over, louder and louder. Soon everyone had gone quiet around them. The Saxon shield wall opened. She stood in the center of a ring of warriors, both Saxon and Bructeri.

Juliana kept reciting.

She put her head back now and shouted the hymn, as if appealing to the heavens.

None of the men around her would have any idea what she was saying, but it was clear what she was doing, giving power to Athralar.

A shout went up from the Saxons.

She turned. The Bructeri warrior was walking toward them swinging his giant axe from side to side. One blow from that and she would be cleaved in two. His shoulder muscles rippled as he came. He smiled at her. Juliana stepped back.

Athralar raised the axe Juliana had given him.

The Bructeri began running, his intention clear. He wanted the fight over quickly. He stood at least as tall as Athralar and appeared at least as confident. His axe swung as he came. It looked as if he could cut his way through a dense forest with it.

Athralar stood still, waiting.

"Do something, Athralar," Juliana hissed. She could feel the man pounding nearer through the earth under them. This could not happen. Getting handed from one war band leader to another would not be a way to survive even a summer with these people. The next man would most likely not treat her as well as Athralar had. He'd probably want to rape her every night. And later she'd be on her back to service a different warrior every month.

A shudder ran through her.

Athralar took a step forward as the Bructeri warrior took a final swing. He held his axe handle high with two hands. The Bructeri's axe handle cracked into it. It would have been the blade if they'd been further apart. Juliana was sure it would crack in two. It didn't.

Athralar stepped in closer to the Bructeri. One hand dropped to his belt. He pulled a dagger and stabbed it fast at the Bructeri warrior's throat.

The Bructeri would not be so easily taken. He swung his head and came around Athralar to his right. Athralar turned, but his foot got caught on something and he staggered as he came around. The Bructeri swung his axe back. Athralar was lucky he was falling. The axe head came around, touched his shoulder, a cut opened, blood flowed. The Bructeri cheered.

Juliana looked at them. Was this their plan all along? If they won in single combat none of them would die. Was this whole thing about wanting Juliana to lead them a trick?

Athralar had twisted so fast out of the way of the axe he had lost his footing completely. He lay on his back on the ground now and the Bructeri was raising his axe to finish him off when Juliana roared at him.

His gaze only shifted to Juliana for a moment, but it was enough for Athralar to stab upwards into the man's genitals with his knife. He forced the knife further up quickly and blood flowed down it fast and then down Athralar's arm as if he'd stabbed into a water pipe.

The Bructeri swung his axe at Athralar's arm.

Athralar got it out of the way just in time. The Bructeri staggered back, as if he'd just taken in that he'd been stabbed so deeply. Athralar rose quickly, swinging the axe in his other hand into the man's neck as he came up. It didn't go all the way through. It was a single handed effort. But it went far enough that the man's body went limp and he toppled like a felled tree.

A roar went up from the Saxons, followed by a low grumbling from the Bructeri, then the steady chink of their swords and axes landing in a pile near their champion.

Athralar looked as if he'd bathed in blood as he walked to Juliana.

When he reached her, he went down on one knee and held the axe she had given him toward her.

"You were right. This axe handle is stronger than ours. And I acknowledge you distracted that bald bastard long enough for me to land a good blow."

"You had him anyway," she said. Exhilaration at them having won the contest tingled through her. She raised both fists in the air.

"Athralar is our hero." She turned to the men around her. Some were nodding. Others were just staring at her. Something dripped from her chin. She rubbed at it, pulled her hand away.

Blood. No wonder they were staring.

Athralar came to his feet. "You will lead our combined war band, Juliana. It is clear to me that these men want you." He waved at all the men around them. "This is the normal way for us. If a shield maiden proves herself courageous and lucky in battle and wise with it, our men will always want to follow her before they follow any man. Frigg is the wise goddess who looks after us all. She helps men win victory when defeat is upon them, as you did this day."

Juliana came close to him. She could smell the blood all over them both now.

"You killed him."

"Anyone can kill. It's the one who can make victory happen who leads."

She stared up at him. Could he be serious? Could she lead a war band? The idea both exhilarated and terrified her.

"But before you take charge of our new combined war band you must be initiated as a Saxon leader."

She looked him in the eyes. Nothing was ever easy with these people.

"What does that mean?"

"Nine moons you will contemplate and learn what you need to. Then you will be reborn as a leader of our tribe."

"And if I don't want this?"

"Our men will not accept that. It would be an insult to them and to all Saxons if you turn your back on this, so you had better be good at running. We will give you until the moon rises before coming after you."

XXVI

Arles, Northern Gaul, the month of Augustus, 307 A.D.

Fausta peered into the polished metal mirror. "More around the eyes," she said to the slave holding it.

The slave girl took the thin horsehair brush, dabbed it in the pot of kohl and increased the dark outline around Fausta's eyes.

"You have spent long enough getting ready, daughter," said Maximian, who was drinking from the goblet he'd been handed on entering his daughter's room.

Fausta waved the slave girl away.

"I'm told Constantine has a partner and a child. Is it true?"

"Not anymore."

She looked at him. "What does that mean?"

Maximian looked around. They were in the prefect of the city's palace guest rooms on the bank of the Rhone, inside the city walls of Arles.

Maximian sat beside her on the wide limestone seat. It had been another hot day. Two Numidian slaves were waving fans in their direction. No one had taught them anything beyond basic Latin commands. If they showed any desire to learn more, they would be sent to the mines.

"It means that his concubine was kidnapped by a Germanic war band, and the baby son he had with her has disappeared too." He raised an eyebrow, as if he knew more than he was saying.

"That is terrible. Did he kill thousands in retaliation, as you would?" She kept her expression passive. She knew better than to show any weakness in front of her father. She'd been whipped often enough as a child.

"No, he did not. That is a flaw in his character I hope you will help him to address."

She couldn't help smiling, just a little, at the news. But then her expression stiffened again. She looked around.

"There are no slaves skulking?"

"No, I checked every corner. But we have only a few moments. Your betrothed has arrived in the palace and we must not keep him waiting any longer."

Fausta put her hands together and put them to her lips as if praying. She closed her eyes too. "I will not change my mind about what you asked, Father."

"Let me tell you again, then. I am not asking you to spy on Constantine."

"Asking me to report what he tells me is spying, Father."

"I am asking only for things related to your brother or our family to be reported. I do not expect you to reveal your marriage secrets, Fausta." He pointed a finger at her, his voice rising as he continued. "If you want to marry him, you must agree to this. I have warned you. I can make you a Sybelline priestess tomorrow, if that is what you want. You will live in their temple here under vows of silence and chastity until death."

Fausta's tone was pleading now. "He is not a stupid man, Father. Far from it. I have heard he is both capable and clever. I don't expect he will be talking to me about you or my brother."

"But if he does, you must send me a message if he's scheming against us. Your first duty is to your family. We were in the imperial line long before Constantine and his stupid father. And we will be in it long after his line is dust."

"I am sure Constantine will be your supporter now that you are giving me to him." She smiled. "I expect there will be no plots against you or my brother to report. I'm sure Constantine has enough to do in his own provinces."

Maximian squeezed Fausta's shoulder. "Your sacrifice has not gone unnoticed, daughter. When your brother is appointed senior Augustus, your husband will defer to our wishes or he will have every other province against him. That is the moment I will need you. I will call on you then."

Fausta turned to her father.

"Be careful, Father. My brother thinks only of himself. He will not be thinking of you, as you are of him."

"Say nothing against your brother."

She reached out, put a hand on his arm. "Father, I know you want to see our family do well and to extend your reign and see your son follow you. But you must accept that Maxentius is not half the man you are. And he never will be. You have earned respect. He has not."

"No, no more, Fausta. Stop, right now. You have no reason to say these things about your brother. He will be senior emperor, and nothing will stop him."

"I have good reasons." Her hands were shaking in front of her as she went on. "I never told you this, Father, but Maxentius forced himself on me when I was still a child. I was lucky I didn't bear him a baby nine moons later." Her shoulders shook with the effort it took to tell her father what she had hidden for years.

Maximian shook his head, fast. "Whatever has come between you and your brother, you will stand by him. You will put that incident behind you and never speak of it again. If it even happened." He spat out those last words, then stood and shouted down at her, "Respect your brother. I will not hear another word against him."

Fausta's hands were shaking. She wrung them together.

"But I hate him, Father, you cannot change that."

XXVII

Maxentius waved away the slave who had brought Lucius to him. They were in a double height pillared hall at the side of the Imperial Palace. Life size statues of previous emperors stood in two rows down the middle of the room. The largest statue at the top of the room was of Maxentius with a sword raised.

"Do you like my parade of great emperors, Lucius?"

Lucius walked to the statue of Maxentius and then around it. "This one should be bigger. It is you, but you are the greatest of all the emperors who have come. And you will be remembered above them all." He waved at the line of statues stretching back down the hall.

"You think so?"

"Without doubt. I have seen the baths you are constructing and the temples. No one will forget your name in all the centuries ahead of rule for your family."

"Come with me, brave Lucius. Tell me all that happened after Paulina met Constantine."

They sat in an alcove at the side of the hall. White marble benches lined each wall. The alcove was deep enough they could have a conversation without being overheard even from close by.

But the heat in the alcove weighed oppressively, even by Roman standards, though Maxentius did not appear to notice it.

Lucius sweated into his toga. He would have preferred to wear a short tunic, but the friends of his father, who had put him up since

8

his arrival back in the city, had insisted he dress properly to see the emperor.

Lucius told Maxentius everything he knew that had happened between Paulina and Constantine, even things he didn't know from personal experience, but had heard from others.

"Everyone assumes they are lovers, but I have no evidence of it. I expect the reason Constantine has agreed to marry your sister so quickly is because of the appearance of Crispus in your father's entourage."

Maxentius slapped his thigh. "That was my idea," he said. His chest swelled, and he smiled as he stared at Lucius.

"I am so, so glad we've finally found a use for that stupid sister of mine." He put his head back and laughed. "If I ever displease Constantine, he'll probably have her throat cut and good riddance. No one will be distraught when that happens." He put his hands out wide.

"You are a master strategist. A truly great emperor. That is why I offered my services to you long ago. I hope you see I have repaid your support with everything I am doing for you."

Maxentius reached behind the marble bench. He almost fell as he pulled something up. Lucius reached to the emperor's knee and steadied him. As Maxentius came back up his face was near Lucius'. The smell of sweet wine from Maxentius' breath was overpowering.

In his hand he held a dagger. He pointed it at Lucius' cheek and moved it closer until it almost touched his skin. The knife swayed back and forth in Maxentius' hand.

"I do like to do my own dirty work, Lucius. You have heard that, haven't you?"

Lucius nodded. The sweat on his brow streamed faster now. He gulped. He couldn't help it. He'd heard a story about Maxentius stabbing a messenger in one eye, then the other, because he'd seen something Maxentius did not want him to see.

"That is why, when the time comes, I will deal with Constantine myself. He will know who the better man is then."

"He deserves everything you will do to him."

Maxentius moved the dagger away from Lucius' face and laughed. "Do not think I'm stupid, Lucius. I know you say the same things to Constantine, and all so your Christian friends can have the persecutions against them reduced. I am right, yes?"

Lucius stared at the floor.

"You will be expected to prove your loyalty to me in a more real way than with bags of gold, dear Lucius. Is that clear?"

Lucius nodded. "You are not going to the wedding?" he asked.

"My father is building an alliance between our family and Constantine's. That is his plan. When the time is right, you will get Constantine to come back here to Rome and when that moment comes, we will work to my plan." Maxentius stopped. He stood, walked out of the alcove and clapped his hands.

The sound of marching feet echoed through the hall along with the noise of something being dragged.

Lucius imagined a troop of torturers on their way to show him the implements they would use on him if he betrayed Maxentius. He knew he was playing a dangerous game seemingly supporting both emperors, but he wasn't prepared for what happened next.

Four guards in black leather uniforms with short daggers on their wide leather belts appeared. They were dragging an old man with them. He looked around him wide eyed. For a few seconds Lucius didn't know who it was.

"Father," he shouted. He strode toward the man, now being held upright. The guards put their arms up to stop him getting close. Marcus, Lucius' father smiled faintly, but did not speak.

"Take him away," said Maxentius.

Lucius swung around, his hands raised. "What more do you want?" he cried. "You have our gold, you have my loyalty and you can have my life, but do not punish my father, please."

Maxentius still held the dagger in his hand. He stabbed it into the air around him, as if fighting invisible enemies.

"A moment will come when I need your total loyalty, Lucius. Until then your father will be my guest at my villa in Capri. I will treat him well. But if you hesitate when the moment comes when I need your loyalty, or if anything else unfortunate should happen to me, he will die with his eyes stabbed out and his ears cut off and his nose cut away and then a stake will be pushed up inside him, slowly. It is a horrible way to go. I have seen strong men beg for their throats to be cut when this is done." Maxentius swished the dagger through the air.

Lucius went down on one knee. "You have my word. I will do what you ask. Just tell me what to do."

XXVIII

Nine months later

Juliana lay totally still on the platform of branches. The island in the lake she had lived on with three priests of Woden since the previous summer was coming back to life after a hard winter.

One priest stood behind her head. He had a large wooden bowl in his hand. The other two were at her feet. They held torches. The night was dark and cloudless with only the twinkling stars to see by. Juliana was naked, except for a loin cloth.

The three priests were all like Athralar. They had had their testicles crushed at a young age, so they had taken little interest in her body in all the time she lived on the island with them.

The lessons she learned from them were about Woden and Frigg and all the magical powers she could call on to ensure victory in any campaign.

They'd also spent a good deal of time each day reciting stories of shield maidens who had gone before her and then making her repeat the stories, word for word, until she got them exactly right. Some days she was not allowed to eat for the smallest mistakes in her recitations.

"Juliana, your time to be reborn is here. Rise and face the moon."

She came to her knees first, bowed, then stood on the platform of branches. As they waited the priests recited the prayers of power to bind her to her warriors.

"In the name of Woden, you are bound to the tree of life.

"In the name of Frigg, you are bound to the earth.

"In the name of Woden you are bound to the tribe.

"In the name if Frigg you are bound to our tribe.

"You have the powers of the bear.

"You have the wisdom of the wolf.

"In the name of Woden, you are bound to the tree of life."

The recitation continued on and on as the moon rose through the trees. The island around her was filled with the warriors of the tribe who had been invited to watch her rebirth.

When her body seemed to glow from head to toe in the moonlight the chanting stopped.

"What weapon do you wish to be bound to, shield maiden," said the head priest.

Juliana bent down and picked up the axe she had won. She handed it with its blade hanging down to the priest.

He held it high above his head so the moonlight glistened along it. He chanted a prayer.

"In the names of Woden and Frigs I bring the speed of the wolf and the power of the bear into your axe. Kneel before me. We will see your spirit join with them."

She knelt. The priest placed the axe head to her chest. He swung it back as if he would split her chest in two. When he swung the axe forward, she trembled.

A shout rang out.

It was from Athralar's mother. "Stay the weapon. The shield maiden has proved her courage in battle."

The voice sounded right behind her. Juliana looked at the axe head. It had stopped a thumb length from her chest bone. The priest turned it to the side. Reflected in the axe head, Juliana could see the head of a wolf and then, when the priest turned it the other way, the head of a bear.

"Has the shield maiden learned the secrets of war?" asked Athralar's mother.

"Yes," replied the priest.

Juliana felt something heavy on her head. Claws hung down before her eyes. On one side were the wide, yellow tipped claws of a bear. On the other side were the black, thinner claws of a wolf.

"Have you learned the joy of bringing death upon our enemies?" asked Athralar's mother.

"Yes," said Juliana.

"Have you learned the joy of saving enemies' lives when they surrender?"

"Yes."

"Do you swear not to take the lives of women who are carrying a child or children who are not blooded?"

"Yes."

"Do you swear to give your life for the tribe whenever you are asked?"

Juliana hesitated for a moment, then replied, loudly, "Yes."

Athralar's mother did not seem to notice the hesitation.

"Do you swear to lead your warriors and kill all who stand in your way?"

"Yes."

"Rise up so, shield maiden. You have a raid to plan against the Romans who enslaved you."

XXIX

"Constantine, come here." Fausta crooked her finger, hooking him to her. Constantine stared out of the tiny window in their bedroom on the top floor of the imperial palace. The glass was thick, the pieces small, but he could see the guards changing in the courtyard below. The blazing torches they held illuminated the courtyard, but they were barely needed as the moon had risen and the sky was cloudless.

"No more rutting tonight, Fausta," said Constantine as he turned.

Fausta lay naked on their bed, on her side. She drank wine from a large gold-rimmed glass, one of the set the governor of Britannia had given them as a gift after their wedding.

"What else is there to do in this clammy province in this always wet city, my beloved, tell me?"

"I have a lot to do tomorrow and you are meeting the wives of the legates, if I remember right."

"Always, I am meeting with those low born women. I am tired of their gossip about their children and their fighting over next to nothing, what one slave said to another. Can you please arrange for some people of our level to visit us, so that I don't have to spend my time with people so far beneath me."

Constantine shook his head. "That is your duty, Fausta. We need everyone to work together, whatever their station, to make the provinces succeed."

"To succeed?" She laughed. "You cannot even keep your subjects safe. How can they hope to succeed in all the jobs you give

125

them, if they have to look over their shoulders for raiders every day and keep a sword by their side or armed men at their gate?"

Constantine snuffed out the two candles on the marble table near the bed and lay down beside Fausta.

"We will agree to a treaty with the Alemanni and the other tribes when they agree to a prisoner swap, and to cease raiding in our territory, and to stop all the other tribes' war bands who make their way through their territory to get to us."

"My brother would just cut all the prisoner's throats and send their heads back to their tribes as a warning."

"I am not your brother." He put his hand on her thigh. Her skin was soft, like a peach.

"My brother says that only fear keeps our imperial family in its place and that anyone who tries to rule with kindness ends up overthrown and with a blade in their heart."

Constantine had heard the argument many times.

"My father ruled with the sword and with words. He told me when I was young that the sword was not enough to rule by, that we had to rule with the words we use to get people to act for us and to believe in our plans."

"And if the prisoner swap sees that concubine stolen from you returned, where will you put her in this tiny palace?" She put her hand on his and pulled it across her thigh and up her body to her breast.

"You are jealous of a woman who is most likely dead, Fausta. I do not expect her to be returned in any prisoner swap."

"So, kill all their prisoners. They have no one important of ours, and then they will kill the prisoners they hold, and you can send our troops across the Rhine and burn their villages, so they know to fear us and to do what they are told."

Constantine stared into the darkness. Memories of Juliana and the way they used to laugh together at night, not bicker, filled his mind. Was she alive and with someone else, filling another man's life with happiness? Or was she dead, and should he be mourning her still? Every day he thought about her. Every day he faced the same sense of something unfinished hanging over him. When would it end?

"When is our child due?" he said.

"Do not change the subject, Constantine. If my brother hears you are unwilling to kill a few prisoners, he will know you are weak. Who knows what he will plan then? You do not want him sending an army up to our gates, Constantine, do you?"

"And this is what you are really afraid of Fausta, your brother."

"You do not know him as I do. He will do anything for power."

"How will Maxentius even know I refuse to execute a few prisoners."

"I am sure he has spies here."

"Not in this palace." He squeezed her breast. "Unless you are spying for him."

"I am not. I swear. I would rather die than spy for my brother."

XXX

Near the Circus Maximus, Rome, Aprilis, 308 A.D.

Lucius reached for his wine goblet. He put it to his lips and drank a large draught from it.

"You bring me no news."

"We were not allowed to land on Capri."

"You said they buy fish from passing boats. Were you lying?"

"That is what we heard, Lucius, but things have changed since your father was taken there as a prisoner."

Lucius slapped the table with his free hand. "Well, that is good news." He raised his goblet, drank again.

The man opposite drank too. His hands were calloused, his skin sun burnt and his beard scraggly. He looked out of place in the tavern. He downed his goblet of wine quickly, as if he wanted to get out of there as fast as he could.

"Why is this good news, Lucius?" the man said, wiping his hand across his mouth.

"It means my father is probably still alive. There are no reports of Maxentius sending other prisoners to his villa there recently."

A loud knock sounded from the door of the tavern. They had closed up a little earlier, when the last of the local drinkers finished. There was only Lucius, the fisherman and the owner of the tavern in the small, low ceilinged room. There were slaves in the upper floors preparing fish paste for the bread that would be delivered in the morning, and they could be called down to protect the tavern from thieves, but there'd been no warning that an attack was imminent. No drinkers that night had caused trouble.

The tavern owner put a finger to his lips.

Lucius didn't move. The fisherman swiveled his head, looking for another way out of the room. Only two oil lights on the wall and a candle burning on their table gave any light. Many parts of the room were in semi-darkness.

The banging came again, louder this time. Then the point of a sword appeared where the door met the frame. It moved upward, as if its owner was looking for a blocking post to move and get the door opened.

"I'm coming," shouted the tavern keeper. "Wait, I am busy with a serving girl. I will be there in a moment." He grunted, as if he'd been caught with his tunic off.

He waved at Lucius and the fisherman to go down the back. There was a way out through an alley, but before Lucius had even stood up a tramping noise echoed from the back of the tavern and a legionary appeared, a praetorian guard with a red tufted helmet and a distinctive black breastplate with an eagle embossed on it. Another followed. Then another. They had their swords drawn.

Lucius smiled at them. One of the praetorians went to the front door and removed the blocking post. Others swarmed in. In their midst strode a centurion with a silver breastplate. He marched up to the table Lucius and the fisherman were sitting at.

"We are here to arrest anyone conducting a ritual for the stupid god that died on the cross." He pointed at Lucius. "Are you leading this ritual?"

Lucius put his hands up. "We are drinking, that is all. Smell our cups, good centurion. We know nothing about these charges. They are total crap. Have you been fooled by one of this tavern keeper's competitors down the street? They hate him, I hear, because he charges lower prices and takes all their customers." He pointed at the tavern owner, who had appeared beside him.

"Centurion," said the tavern owner, bowing. "Please forgive me if I did anything wrong in charging lower prices."

"We will search this building," said the centurion. "And if we find a bunch of Christians hiding, we will confiscate this tavern and take all of you to the cells. You will be lucky to see the light of day again before the end of the year."

129

"Who sent you to this duty?" asked Lucius.

"I obey my commanders, no one else." The centurion turned and barked orders to his men. Some of them disappeared to search. Others waited in the room.

"Is Scipio still your tribune in the city?" said Lucius.

The centurion turned slowly. "You know Scipio?"

"We fought together in the east. I saved his life. He saved mine. Is he waiting nearby to see what you find out is going on here?" Lucius stood and walked to the door to the street, as if he would look for Scipio.

"Go and sit back down until we've finished our search. Then you can ask to see our commander."

"Scipio," shouted Lucius to the walls.

No one answered.

"Scipio," he shouted again.

The centurion pointed at the fisherman. "Was this man in the east with you?"

"No, we met tonight. He likes his wine, as I do. I may go fishing with him tomorrow. He says the fish are swarming in this weather."

The centurion grabbed the fisherman by the collar of his tunic. "Have you been filling this veteran with some stupid story you have made up about the abundance of fish in some special place only you know about?"

The fisherman shook his head.

"We will get the truth out of you outside." The centurion started dragging the fisherman toward the door.

"He did not try to trick me," said Lucius. "If you want to take him, you will have to take me too."

The centurion nodded at one of his men, who held some thick chains in his hands. "You can come too then."

Lucius and the fisherman were put to their knees in the street while the other praetorians finished searching the building. Two passers-by stood watching as the centurion wiped his sword on his arm band.

"I do not want to cut off parts of your friend's body, so tell me, quickly, before I begin all that, what happened to the followers of the crucified god who were supposed to be meeting here?"

"Scipio," shouted Lucius.

The centurion laughed.

"I forget to tell you, your friend Scipio retired to the country last year." He raised his sword and laughed.

"Put your hands out, fisherman. If your friend will not tell us the truth you will have to pay the price of it with your blood."

He looked down at Lucius. "If we take his left hand, and your right hand, I will have enough to show the emperor we are carrying out his orders to the letter."

He kicked at Lucius' thigh. "Or would you prefer we took his right hand and your cock?"

XXXI

Territory of the Bructeri, Northern Germania, Aprilis, 308 A.D.

Juliana looked around. Thirty Bructeri warriors were swinging their axes in the clearing by the wide river. The moon rode high and the breeze coming down from the lands of ice, where the gods lived, blew strong. She was glad she had accepted the wolf skin cloak Athralar's mother had given her.

Learning to fight at night and in a combined unit of axe wielding warriors were the two innovations she had brought to the war band.

A scream went up from the middle of the pack of men.

"I told you they would injure themselves practicing at night," said Athralar.

"Come forward if you've been injured," shouted Juliana.

One of the men shuffled toward her. Blood poured down his thigh. He was bending to the side, half crouching and had an arrogant look on his face. He stopped in front of Juliana.

"How did this injury happen?" said Juliana.

"Not my fault." The injured man looked around. "Doing this by moon light is a stupid idea. This is not the way of the Bructeri. This is a Roman thing, or worse, some stupid Brigantian moon-goddess trickery." He spat on the ground between them.

Juliana pulled her axe from her belt and put it on her shoulder. "This is the way you will learn. I am in charge now. You will speak not one word against my wishes. Do you understand?" She kept her voice low, but with a rock-hard tone. She would not publicly humiliate him, if she could avoid it.

The injured man spat between them again. "I will be leaving this war band and if the other men know what is right for them, they will leave it too. You do not have the right experience to lead a war band. This is all wrong." He shouted the last part.

Murmurs behind him made it clear he was not the only one with such thoughts.

"No one leaves this war band without my permission," she said, her tone still low, as she took a step toward him. She breathed slowly. Her body tingled all over, as if it knew she could make no mistakes at this moment. Everything depended on her getting this moment right.

A hush fell as the men gathered around as they sensed a confrontation approaching.

"I will not ask a slave's permission for anything." The man still had his axe in his hand. He held it up and toward her. "You should know your place like all good slave girls, on your knees."

Athralar raised his axe beside her. Juliana turned her head, spoke to him. "This is not your fight, Athralar. I will persuade this idiot to see the light. It seems he has only darkness between his ears now."

She turned back to the injured man.

"Get down on your knees now and beg forgiveness, or you will die."

The man laughed. "You are a stupid bitch if you think I will beg a slave for anything."

Juliana took her axe off her shoulder and passed it from hand to hand.

"One last chance."

The man laughed, straightened himself and looked around for support. He was about double her height when he stood up straight.

Without any further hesitation she swung her axe. The man moved his body, but her swing came in the direction of his knees. His nearest knee avoided her axe, and a grin formed on his face, and his own axe was coming up when her axe head struck his other knee with an ear jarring crack.

His eyes widened and both his knees buckled. His own axe ended up flying through the air between them as he screamed in anger and went back down, a look of shock on his face.

"Sometimes it is better to be short in stature," she said as she stood over him, her axe again on her shoulder.

"Shall I take his head off, Athralar?" she said, loudly. Her hand shook on her axe, but she put the other one over it so no one would see.

A cheer went up and she raised her axe with both hands gripped tightly on the handle.

The man stared up at her, his face twisting in pain, both his hands holding his shattered knee. The wound would have to be burnt quickly if he wanted to live, even as a cripple.

"Athralar?" She looked around.

Standing behind her were two large men who looked exactly like the man whose knee she had just shattered. Athralar stood between them. They had their axes in their hands. He shook his head. He knew there was trouble ahead.

XXXII

Treveris, Northern Gaul, 308 A.D.

Constantine was the first to the basilica that morning for the weekly meeting of his military tribunes, prefects and legates. His three legates were at the front of the hall. They greeted him as he came up the room. They commanded a legion each, though only one legion was located nearby, the other two were at their camps, one a little to the north, the other to the south.

He liked to have the camp prefects and the tribunes, who led the centurions, at the meetings as well, to ensure that his wishes were not mangled in the communication process.

The room was heated by three large braziers which were stoked by burly bare-armed slaves. Aprilis was a cold month this far north, he had come to discover, especially for someone used to the warm early springs in the eastern provinces. A row of oil lamps had been lit before his arrival as the sun came up, and they still burned, despite the light from the high windows being enough to see by.

On a wide oak table at the top of the hall lay a map painted onto the tanned hide of a bull. His father had ordered it to be created to show the legions and camps along the Rhine, and the opposing tribes on the far side.

An imperial slave, one of the new crew his wife had brought with her, carried a tray with watered down wine to them. The slave was a woman, sturdy and sour faced, unlikely to ever raise a lustful glance from Constantine or his men.

Sejanus, the prefect of the imperial bodyguard, was the next to arrive. He arrived in full military uniform, his red cloak flying behind him as he came into the room.

"You are up with the birds these days. How goes it?" he said as he joined Constantine and the three legates at the top of the room.

"I am glad you came early, Sejanus. I have a plan for what to do with the Germanic tribes this summer."

"Go on."

"Let's wait until the others are here." Constantine sipped at his watered wine, then walked to the back of the room where the head of the imperial household waited.

"The prefects and the legates will be staying to eat," he said. "But make sure there is enough to feed the tribunes too, as there will be twenty or more of them arriving. Any problems?" He looked at the older man, who shook his head and bowed in reply.

Constantine headed back to where the map was laid out. The low backed chairs they usually sat on had been moved away from the table. There was enough room for all the men expected to stand around, listen, and give their opinions if they thought they had something useful to say.

He'd made a point of continuing his father's tradition of listening to his military officers and provincial administrators, not just to go around ordering them what to do. The legate of the XXII Legion, the 22nd Primigenia, stood nearby. The two other legates were at the far end of the table, talking.

The legate of the 22nd was about to retire.

"We have good news legate," he said. "Come, let us speak by the brazier. I hope you don't mind me warming my hands."

It took only a few minutes to tell the man about the vineyard that would be allocated to him near the city and about Constantine's decision to make Sejanus legate of the 22nd after the man had retired. When the legate agreed that Sejanus was a wise choice, Constantine called Sejanus over to them.

"By the next moon you will be leading the 22nd, Sejanus. I expect our campaign into Germania this summer to be carried out quickly and forcefully. The 22nd is critical to this and must be managed well."

Sejanus bowed. "I am honored and will serve and die if needed for you."

"There will be no need to die, if you look after your legion properly as your predecessor has done." He slapped the older legate on the shoulder. "Now, the two of you are to spend the rest of the day discussing everything that needs to be done with the 22nd. I want a part of your legion ready to cross the Rhine by the new moon."

He left them and went to the other two legates.

"Sejanus will be taking over the 22nd," he said. He looked from one man to the other.

"What is your plan?" said the shorter legate, a man with thinning red hair and a slight paunch. Brightly polished campaign medals filled the upper part of his leather breastplate.

"We will drive a wedge through the Alemanni and the Franks and raid up toward the land of the Saxons. Our spies tell us the Saxons have been sending out war bands into the empire. They must be taught a lesson."

The legates looked at each other. "No Roman legion has ever gone that far north in a hundred years. There are three large rivers to cross and the forest provides endless opportunities for winnowing out our lines. The tribespeople are wily in Germania. They will keep falling back until our supply lines are thin, and they have us where they want us when the rains start and our bows become useless."

"We will not be running a normal campaign. We will adopt their tactics. We will send bands of men, a hundred strong, through their territory. They will move fast, foraging and raiding and paying for supplies from villages that submit. The Germanics tribes will not be able to focus their attacks on a long line of Roman legionaries and pick us off as they decide."

"Whatever you command, but this goes against all the tactics your father approved." The red-haired legate looked to the other legate for support, but none was forthcoming. "Overwhelming force is what our legions are good at. The Germanic tribes will be surprised if we show weakness in our numbers. They can overwhelm a hundred of our men easily."

"Surprise will be on our side. Five centuries of our men will set off along a different route through the woods each day for three days."

"That's almost half a legion," said the legate in a growling tone.

"Yes, and each of you will contribute your best men." Constantine paused. "If any of our troops are overwhelmed the loss will not be catastrophic."

"It's an unusual plan, I'll give it that," said the other legate. He was almost bald, but taller and slimmer than his colleague.

"And it will succeed," said Constantine. He stared from face to face.

For a few moments only the crackle from the braziers could be heard. Then the other legate, who had been quiet, spoke. "I agree. We have wasted many good men on full frontal assaults in Germania. It is time for new tactics."

The noise of men approaching up the room broke into their conversation.

"Will you both give your full support to this strategy?" Constantine looked from one legate to the other. He would have their vocal support, they had no choice in that, but he was also interested to see if either man would hesitate.

"I am honored and will serve and die if needed for you," said each man in turn, but the red-haired legate hesitated, and his tone sounded unconvincing.

"Only you will know the details of our campaign," said Constantine, stepping closer to the legates. "Do not act surprised at what I announce today. I do not want our real mission the subject of wine soaked arguments by midnight tonight."

When the room had filled with officers Constantine stood on a low wooden platform and addressed them.

"We will be campaigning this summer. You and your men will have a chance for glory, a chance for spoils and an opportunity to prove your skills in battle once again. This will be our first real campaign together and we will be victorious. Fortuna favors the bold."

A cheer started at the back, then quickly filled the room. Fists were raised. Every man wanted the opportunity to fight. Life in the camps grew dull quickly and the whores and wine merchants who made their time bearable all needed to be paid, and if a man wanted any hope of being granted land and a peaceful old age with children playing around his knees there was only one way to win it, by blood and the sword.

A voice called out. "Where are we going?"

"Hibernia," he replied, loudly.

"Hibernia," came an echoing succession of shouts. There were a few mutterings too, but not many. Hibernia was an island beyond Britannia. The average officer did not care where they went, as long as they got to use the skills they'd been honing all winter. There is no point in being good with a sword and a javelin if you don't get to use your skills in combat. They knew also that trust in their leaders was what kept their legions together.

"Call in the Haruspex," Constantine shouted. He pointed at the guard standing by the small door at the back of the hall.

The guard opened the door and in walked the auger, a priest in a traditional long white robe. He was bald, tall, and walked at a steady pace toward Constantine, his eyes glaring, as if out of his mind on something, perhaps some mushrooms he'd collected in the forest.

Constantine received regular visits from the small band of priests and priestesses who held traditional ceremonies in the temples of Jupiter and Vesta in Treveris. He only ever visited the new temple to Sol Invictus, the cult of the unconquered sun, as the priests there were mostly ex-officers from the legions who still had influence over many of their former comrades in arms.

They also had access to the best wine in the city.

The priest stopped to Constantine's right and bowed, perfunctorily.

Constantine turned to him.

"Are the augers propitious for our campaign this summer," he said.

139

"They are, my lord, they are the most doubly propitious I have seen in a long time."

Before the priest could continue, Constantine turned back to his officers. "The gods are with us, fear nothing."

The answering cheers echoed from every part of the room.

The next few days were filled with the problems of provisioning. Leather had to be brought in from Hispania for the new light-weight tents Constantine wanted. Grain had to be set aside from the grain stores, as well as olives, cheeses and the long, dark local sausages. Constantine wanted each unit to be well fed. Each centurion in command would be briefed about their real mission only on the day they would depart.

How many men would return was hard to assess, but most should and the trail of destruction and death they would bring to any who opposed them would be wide and unforgettable for a generation. It might even bring the Germanic tribes to agree to a wider treaty with Rome.

The tribes would not be expecting multiple raids and the use of their own tactics against them.

As the kalends of May approached, he decided to visit his mother without Fausta. The last few times they had been to see her together the conversation had been so frosty he had cut short the meetings each time, claiming he had urgent tasks to complete. Before he headed out campaigning he had to find out what the problem was with his mother.

"It is good to see you, Mother," he said, when ushered into the small garden at the back of Helena's rooms.

Helena didn't get up. "You were never a good liar," she replied.

He kissed her outstretched hand. "I mean it, it is good to see you are well."

"Thank you. I am blessed with a strong mind above all. I know you have inherited it too. I just hope it reaches your children." Her tone had an icy edge to it.

He sat beside her on a cushion on the wooden bench. He touched her arm and leaned toward her.

"Mother, you must tell me what I have done to displease you. I do not want to head to war without your blessing."

"What you have done? Why, you have done nothing. How could an emperor, less than one year in his position, do anything to disturb his mother?"

Her smile came thin. It didn't last long.

"No more games. What's going on, Mother." He deliberately hardened his tone. "I have a lot of crap to do and no time to sit here begging you to tell me what's wrong."

She studied him, then took a deep breath and pointed a finger at him. "Is this the type of crap you mean? Your wife visiting the temple of Vesta and giving them gifts. You know about this?"

He nodded. "Yes, I know about it. She says they will help her when she gives birth after the summer. There is nothing wrong in that. The high priestess of Vesta will know all the right women to make the birth run smoothly." He stared at her. Was this all she was concerned about?

"Fausta needs to escape all that, as I have done, Constantine. She certainly doesn't need them to help with the birth." Her voice rose. "This is not Rome. The people who helped you to power are not from the temples of the old gods.

"I know who helped us."

"Did you know that the followers of Christ are the only people in this city who have set up an infirmary for the sick who are too poor to pay?"

"You told me this before. I am sure they are doing a wonderful job. But you must also know they have the reputation for being part of a depraved superstition, so I have to be careful about what I am seen to encourage."

Helena took his hand. She looked into his eyes. "These people are not depraved. I've told you how they saved my life after the pestilence took my whole family when I was young. Is that depraved?"

He shook his head. "No, and do I know your story. You've told me it a dozen times. So, what is it you want me to do?"

"After your wife gives birth, I want you to call a Christian priest to bless the new baby, as well as an haruspex."

"Why?"

"It will show the followers of Christ in your province, and beyond, that you are one of us." She paused, gripped his hand tighter. "We must give them hope that the persecutions are coming to an end, that they will not be outcasts forever."

"I will think about it. If I get through this summer, we will talk about it again."

She hugged him and whispered in his ear. "It is in your gift to change everything and to save the empire."

"I have less power than you think, Mother. There are other emperors all around, waiting for me to slip."

"Someday soon you will have more power."

"I don't see much chance of that." Then he paused. He'd been wondering whether to tell her the next piece of news or not.

"There is something you want to tell me?"

She'd always been good at reading his mind.

He sighed. "One of our spies heard reports that a shield maiden named Juliana has been appointed to head a Saxon war band."

Helena cut in. "That's not likely to be your Juliana. I don't see how she could have won such a position so quickly. The Saxons are known for stealing Roman names, you know."

He looked at her. Since the spy had reported to him, thoughts of Juliana were hard to shake. He kept imagining her with a Saxon chief. A picture of her smiling face kept coming back to him many nights before he slept and after he woke. It annoyed him he couldn't stop thinking about her, but no amount of distractions stopped it happening.

"Spit it out, Constantine. You look like a dog that's lost its bone."

"I can't stop thinking about her." He raised his fist, pressed it to his head. "I imagine some Saxon chieftain laughing at me as he ruts her."

"I always thought that girl had placed some spell on you. It seems I was right." She put a hand on his arm. "I can have prayers said for you."

"I thought they only work for people who believe in them."

"And you don't believe in anything, do you?"

"I believe in taking action." He raised a fist. "That's why I'm going to Germania to find her. I want to see for myself who this shield maiden is."

"Just don't lose any legions as you pursue her." Her eyes widened. "You know there are conflicting rumors as to where you are headed. Most say you are going to Hibernia."

"I can't fart without someone reading something into it, Mother."

She smiled. "Will you agree now to allow the followers of Christ to build a temple here in Treveris?"

He shook his head. "It's one thing allowing them to hold their ceremonies in private. I see no reason to allow them to build temples. I have enough on my hands."

"But there are temples to every god in Treveris. Why not allow them what you allow everyone else?" She smiled. "That's what they say to me."

"We don't allow anyone to raise a temple, Mother, and especially not a cult that is unlikely to survive very much longer."

"Why do you say that?"

"Fausta tells me her brother is going to round up all the followers of Christ and send them to the mines. She looked pleased to report this news from her father."

Helena looked at him and shook her head. "If I had known Fausta was going to be like this, I would have let you marry Juliana."

XXXIII

Lucius pointed over the heads of the guards. "If you harm either of us you will have to answer to a high priestess of Magna Mater in the new temple the Emperor Maxentius is spending his every last coin on."

The praetorian stared at him. "Every dog claims to be in the pay of the great mother these days. What proof do you have of this?"

Lucius fumbled for the purse dangling from his belt, tucked inside his tunic. He pulled it out and opened the contents into his hand.

"You will find a red token for their temple here. I am due to be back at the temple later tonight. They will come looking for me if I don't. It will be bad news for you if they find out that you've stopped us doing our duty to the great mother." He took a step forward, as if convinced that the praetorians would now leave them in peace.

The leader of the troop stared at Lucius' outstretched hand, then at him, as if unsure what to do next. A round red token stood out among the gold and silver coins in Lucius' hand.

Lucius wondered if he should take the chance to lunge for a sword and try to fight their way out of the building.

The praetorian sniffed and put his hand on the hilt of his sword, as if he'd read Lucius' mind.

"Right, we'll take you to the great mother. She will confirm your story or we will cut your balls off and make them into a charm for pretending to be on her business."

The praetorians marched them to the other side of the Circus Maximus at double speed. The fisherman had trouble keeping up and ended up being held up by the elbows, almost being carried between two praetorians with his feet barely touching the ground.

The temple of Magna Mater filled the western slope of the Palatine, overlooking the valley of the Circus Maximus. It had a row of four massive white marble columns in its portico and a statue of the great mother at the top of the wide marble stairs leading up to the temple.

Behind the statue a light shone from within. It was late, the sky had blossomed with stars as a pale half-moon lit the way, but still men and some women were coming and going to the temple.

Most of these people would be the relatives of someone at death's door, looking for a sign or a word that would comfort them or their loved ones, or if they paid enough, a magical potion to help the ill relative.

The praetorians didn't slow as they made their way up the steps. At the top they went around the statue and walked straight past the line of people waiting to be allowed into the temple.

Two large shaven headed acolytes of the great mother stood in their path.

"We are here to see the priestess Paulina," said Lucius. "Please tell her it's a matter of urgency."

"Do you have a token?" said the older man.

Lucius took out the red coin he'd been given by Paulina when they returned to Rome the previous year.

The acolyte stood aside. "Just you can come inside," he said.

"I also need to see the priestess to find out if this man really does work for her," said the leader of the praetorians.

The acolyte looked him up and down. "You must leave your dagger and your sword with me," he said.

The man growled but did as he was asked. They were led inside the temple. Under an inner portico a line of people waited in front of a statue of the great mother, this time in black stone, and seated with stone lions on each side. They were led to a door on the right, guarded by two more shaven headed acolytes. These men wore only loincloths. Lucius assumed all the male acolytes were eunuchs.

The great mother demanded a harsh payment from those men who wanted to spend their lives adoring her.

The double height door opened. They followed into the dimly lit interior. Groans of ecstasy filled the air. A row of giant oil lamps lit the large hall. On either side stood marble pedestals, like beds, and on many of the pedestals couples and threesomes writhed on top of thick furs. There must have been twenty of these pedestals, half of them topped with debauchery.

At the top of the hall stood an even larger statue to the great mother, bedecked in flowers. It reached halfway up to the blackened roof of the hall far above.

The acolyte took them to a pedestal right at the top where a woman with a golden mask copulated on a thick fur covering with an older man with a barrel stomach. When the man saw them approaching he began to pump harder and harder between the woman's legs. Then he flopped exhausted on top of her.

The woman whispered something in the man's ear. He shuddered, pulled away from her, grabbed at a toga on the floor and fled.

Lucius still wasn't sure if this was Paulina, but when she came close and spoke to him, he knew it was her.

"Lucius, dear Lucius, you have brought a friend, how nice." She held her hand out. The praetorian kissed it. She stood proud and naked, except for a heavy gold necklace with a jeweled pendant. Her breasts were smeared in purple dust.

Lucius' blood quickened at the sight of her. The praetorian stumbled on his words as he spoke. He looked flushed.

"Is this man working for you, priestess?" he said. His eyes roamed up and down her body, as if trying to take it all in.

She put her hand to her lips, walked toward the praetorian and touched his lips. Then she pulled her mask away and smiled at him.

"You may stay with one of the lower priestesses if you wish, centurion. I can confirm that the brave Lucius you have brought back to me does indeed work for me." She looked at Lucius and winked.

The praetorian licked his lips. "We suspected him of being a Christian, priestess."

"Do the Christians have ceremonies like this," she said, waving at the pedestals around them. Then she went to Lucius and put her hand on his groin, rubbing him.

The praetorian shook his head.

"Please tell my fisherman friend to wait for me. I will be out soon," said Lucius.

Then he turned his eyes up to the roof as Paulina continued to rub at him.

"I just have a report to make," he said.

The praetorian stared until an acolyte approached and tapped his shoulder.

"Do you have a token?" he was asked.

The acolyte smiled when he saw it. "You are lucky," he said.

XXXIV

Juliana raised her axe again and held it in front of her. "Do either of you want to challenge me or do you both want to?" She stuck her chin forward and bared her teeth. She'd seen Athralar do it a couple of times and it seemed to work for him.

The two men looked at each other. "No, shield maiden. We simply want to ask if we can take our cousin away to have his wound burnt clean."

She nodded.

That night, she and Athralar lay together in one of the round earth-walled houses in the village nearby. It was a large village by Saxon standards, with twenty or more houses, a high earth rampart and a large hall made of tree trunk walls and a roof of thick branches leaning together to produce a high ridge with a row of blackened skulls on top.

Athralar knew the chief of the village and had been given the house set aside for visitors as soon as they arrived. The floor was covered in rushes and in the center a fire glowed, as the smoke rose up to a hole in the roof. The one roomed house had a large bed at one side and a low table on the other.

They lay on the bed, on top of a pile of wolf and bear skins. He had his arms around her. Occasionally he scratched at insect bites on his arms. "I had that dream again last night," he said, whispering.

"The same as before?" she replied, her tone low as well. It was possible that the chieftain had asked one of his men to listen beyond the wall for any little pieces of information that could be gleaned from their nighttime conversations.

"Yes, the same one, though it went further this time. The giant white palace by the river had its door open and inside there were tall statues, which came to life as I entered."

"And you still don't know what city you were in?"

He shook his head.

"And when I turn to you, I see you raising up a shield. And it's covered in blood. And there is a symbol in white on it I cannot understand. What does it mean, Juliana? Are you going to leave us?"

"No, I could not do that. We are shield brothers now. I am sworn to protect you."

"You are too sexy to be a brother, Juliana." He put a hand on her bare shoulder, but he went no further. It was what Juliana liked about him. He never took advantage.

"I have told you what the dream means, Athralar. I'm not going to go through it all again."

"So, you still think it means I'll go to Treveris and find my fate there?"

"Yes. You will find your answers in Treveris."

Athralar sat up. "Did Woden allow you to win two fights just to interpret this message for me?"

Juliana shook her head. "Woden did not send you this message. It was the great mother."

"Then we will raid to Treveris and see what the great mother has in store for us there." He pulled at Juliana's hand.

She scratched his back. A rustling noise from the wicker door made her sit up. Someone was out there.

"Who's there?" she called.

No one replied.

She went to the door, as quietly as she could, and threw it open. There was no one outside. An owl hooted from the nearby forest. The glimmer of a candle could be seen through the wicker door of the house opposite. Further away, the sound of laughter echoed, mingling with the barking of the wild dogs that lived around the village and fed from the rubbish pits.

"Come back to bed," said Athralar. He stood behind her. "You see dangers everywhere." He put his arms around her and tugged her backward.

She went with him. As they lay down she said, "Where has your mother gone? I haven't seen her in days."

"She went to a meet at Fabiranum, near the coast. The biggest meet for the Saxons is there every year. She will tell them our plans and get approval from the chiefs of all the other Saxons. They share what they are all planning to ensure that we have peace across all the Saxon lands. No Roman army has ever come this far north, and this is the reason why. We work together to beat our enemies. Rome tries to force people to do its will, to become its slaves. We live free."

She'd heard it all before and hadn't put much store in it, but the more she saw of how the Saxons lived, their slaves almost free, able to buy their freedom at any time, made her wonder if the way the Saxons lived was better than how the Romans did. She'd also heard that killing your slaves for any stupid reason was not allowed in Saxon lands, and that you'd have to answer to the chief of your tribe for killing a slave, as if they were a free person.

"So, what did they teach you when you were being prepared to lead?" He pulled her down beside him.

"I thought you went through the same thing."

"It's different each time. What they teach is related to who you are and what you bring with you to the preparation."

Juliana hesitated, but what harm could it do telling Athralar? "I learned to curse people."

He laughed, but stopped as she pushed back and away from him. "I'm sorry, yes, it can work. You are right. I saw a priestess do it. She stood in front of our war band and cursed the leader of the other band, saying how weak he looked, that his mother hated him, and how his wife rutted with his brother because he couldn't please her."

"Did it work?"

"It did. We won. Their leader had a faraway look in his eye when we cut him down."

"So, a curse can kill."

"Yes, most surely. I heard of other cases of people, of their wives and relatives dying after they were cursed. It seems some people just give up if they are cursed."

"Does it work on people who don't believe in the power of a curse?"

"Of course." Athralar laughed. "Everyone knows this. How could you doubt it?"

She shrugged. "What symbol did you see on the shield in your dream?"

"What does it matter? When I get to Treveris I will find it."

"It matters because I'd like to know which legion we will find when you get there. Some of them are loyal to Constantine, others are not."

"It's a rune symbol, the thundercross. Two lightning bolts intersecting."

"Does anyone still use that symbol?"

"Not sure. Saxons don't use it. It is a sacred symbol. Why do you care what symbol was on the shield?"

"I wondered if it was Constantine's."

He hugged her tight. "You still dream about him, yes?"

"Sometimes."

"He must have been good at rutting."

"Good enough."

"He will not be any good when we kill him."

"I hope we don't have to."

"He is weak now, having just taken over from his father. If we kill him, no Roman emperor will dare to strike into Germania again."

Juliana looked at the roof. She had wondered why she was allowed to become a war band leader so fast. Had it been done because she'd told Athralar she knew Constantine? She would have to tread carefully. She stared into the darkness.

151

Every day here was like walking a high rope ladder with spears waiting below. Every step meant deadly risks, but what choice did she have? She had to keep going.

XXXV

Treveris, Northern Gaul, Aprilis, 308 A.D.

Constantine nudged his heels into the flanks of his horse. The big black mare lifted its pace. It would be good to be back on campaign. Dealing with his court, the governors and all the estate owners from every province drained him. They all wanted something, though they hid it well behind flowery words.

He looked back along the line of cavalry. They looked good, their breastplates sparkling in the early morning sunshine. Behind him stood the prefect of the unit and a cavalry decurion. They all had polished gold campaign medals across their chests. The first cavalry section of the 22nd legion was among the most decorated in the empire. Sejanus had told the officers they were heading for Hispania, not Hibernia, and had even sent two optios ahead to Numantia, to tell the local governor there they would be arriving the following month after a slow ride south.

The Governor would likely be displeased at having so many cavalry to feed at short notice, but when they didn't arrive the sting would be taken out of the issue.

On leaving Treveris they crossed the Moselle and headed south on a warm late spring day. At his side rode Sejanus. Behind, the cavalry officers, and behind them fifty cavalry legionaries followed by the same number of pack horses led in strings by the baggage unit.

Ahead rode fifty forward cavalry, split in two, with part of each unit riding on either flank to ensure there were no surprises. Other cavalry units would head toward Germania later that day along different routes.

The morning passed slowly, until they reached the crossroads where they would turn east. Before they reached it, Sejanus called the forward unit officers to him and, with Constantine beside him, told them to head east when they reached the crossroads. The officer's eyes opened wide at that, but otherwise they betrayed no displeasure. Many of the men of the 22nd were from the border region with Germania. A campaign against an enemy they knew was preferable to an expedition far to the south.

It was assumed at once they were going to raid into Germania, but it was also assumed that any such raid would last days, perhaps a week or two at most, and they would be back at their base by the beginning of the following month.

They would be wrong.

They crossed the Moselle at the narrow wooden bridge crossing at Mediomatricia and headed north for Argentoratum on the Rhine. Each afternoon they stopped at one of the Roman forts or post stations on the road. When they crossed the Rhine they would set up small fortified camps with stakes each rider carried with him.

The German held territory they would pass through would be quickly emptied of its inhabitants as the tribespeople got word of their approach and melted into the forest. Those tribespeople would be looking for weaknesses in the Roman camps at night or in their line during the day, which would allow them to pick off horses or men within bow range and whittle down the Roman cavalry.

Setting up the fortified camps would reduce the interaction with people in the Roman border territory too and reduce the chances of information getting back to the tribes, such as who led them.

Sejanus didn't ask any questions. It was one of the reasons Constantine liked him. They spent the evenings together sharpening their swords and daggers. It was a task Constantine usually preferred to do himself, since his time at the front line in Persia. He liked to know that his weapons were capable of slicing flesh quickly. Relying on an orderly to do it was not good enough for him.

He'd met worried stares from the palace staff when he'd started doing this himself at night, and veiled complaints as to whether he had a problem with the slaves tasked with keeping his weapons right. His father hadn't sharpened his own weapons in a decade. He hadn't fought in the front line in that long, either.

Constantine wasn't going to give up the pleasure of fighting easily, as his father had done. Constantine had seen the effect of having a leader fight on the front line with his men. It meant they would give more of themselves when they saw their commander trading blows and killing the enemy, and then pushing forward with an attack.

It could make the difference between losing and winning a battle.

When they reached Argentoratum the river was almost bursting its banks nearby. The garrison commander, a fat and slow prefect, came out to see them. It appeared he had taken to eating too much of the local sausage and drinking way too much of the sweet wine they made in the area.

"Bring your men out on parade," said Constantine to the prefect. They waited in the prefect's quarters, a stone building that looked as if it went back to the period of Augustus, three hundred years before, when Argentoratum was far inland to the border with the Germanian tribes.

When the men from the garrison were standing to attention in the parade ground near the main gate Constantine went to speak to them. First though, he paced slowly along the lines of legionaries looking to see what kind of condition they were in. Aside from a few with unpolished breastplates, and two men with leg greaves falling off, the men looked good, hard faced and bright eyed.

When he was finished, he stood in front of them and spoke. "Legionaries, soldiers of Rome. I have come to avenge the raids into our lands. You are the swords of Rome and together we will push across the Rhine and into the hearts of those who would take from us what is ours. Take heart in our strength. Victory will be ours."

A ragged cheer went up.

"I didn't hear you," he said.

The cheer grew louder.

"Again."

The last cheer could probably be heard on the other side of the river.

After dining he was offered the prefect's room for the night.

"I sleep with my men while on campaign," said Constantine, waving the offer away. He and Sejanus left the prefect's dining room and went outside the fort to the fortified camp of tents his men had set up against the side wall of the fort.

His own tent was larger than the others, mainly so he could have meetings with his officers. When he got back that night, the optio who managed his personal belongings had everything ready for him to wash at the silver bowl he'd set up on the fold up table and then lie on the thick bedroll at the back and sleep.

He woke before dawn to the sound of horn blasts. Three together, then a gap, then three together. That meant an enemy had been sighted in numbers. Constantine called the optio from where he was waiting outside the tent and told him to rouse all officers and have the entire unit assemble, but not mounted, as quickly as possible by the gate of their stockade. He wasn't going to have horses and men all blundering around in the dark.

With the help of his optio he put on his breastplate, greaves and helmet. The only thing that distinguished him from a centurion was the purple cloak he wore, which he always discarded just before going into fight. It was not a good idea to provide the enemy with a way to cut the head off a Roman attack.

When he reached the gate of the stockade most of the men were there, some still tightening belts or wrapping their legionary scarves around the scabbards to muffle them. Nobody spoke. They all knew that voices traveled far at night and the best weapon they had would be surprise. If a Germanic raiding party was going to attack the fort they would get a real shock when a hundred cavalry men arrived at their flank.

Constantine spoke with Sejanus and the two centurions.

"I will take twenty men and investigate," said Constantine. "No horses. It will take too long to saddle them up."

"I'll come with you," said Sejanus.

"No, you will stay with the men here. If you hear three more blasts on a horn, you will know we are in danger and to come and help."

"Yes," said Sejanus. "May I suggest one of the decurions comes with you and a personal guard accompany you as well."

Constantine led the men out of the stockade. They were in formation, three-wide, behind him. Their noise was less than it would have been during the day, but the rustling and the sound of hob nailed sandals on dry ground was unmistakable.

As they went out a glow from the east signaled the dawn was near. The sight that met them in the pre-dawn gloom was one of the strangest Constantine had ever seen. The gap between the front of the fort and the river held a group of Roman officers in full uniform. On the far bank, a little more than an arrow's flight away, waited a large group of Germanic warriors.

Constantine led his men behind the Roman officers from the fort and called a halt. "Form a line," he shouted. The men wheeled until they lined up behind the officers, who had barely glanced in their direction. When Constantine went to the prefect the man bowed and pointed over the river.

"It seems they're putting on a dawn show for us. Must be time for one of their sick festivals. They do all manner of strange things over there." He pointed to where everyone was staring.

Constantine squinted toward where the prefect pointed. Three tall Germanic women with long blonde hair, dressed in flowing white tunics, were standing at the front of a mob of men. The men held battle axes and had large helmets, with horns of various sizes. Each man's helmet was different to the next.

The women gestured toward the Roman officers and then turned and gestured to someone behind them. Another, younger woman, led a man wearing only a loin cloth forward to the women. Constantine assumed these were priestesses.

"He's one of ours," said the prefect, leaning toward Constantine.

"Why don't we send men across to rescue him?" said Constantine, as he hunched forward to see more clearly.

"Look at the river," said the prefect. "It's in flood. There must have been a lot of rain upstream. We'd be lucky to get across without ending up in the water and making fools of ourselves."

"So, we do nothing?"

"If they start to torture our man, I have our best archer ready to finish him off quickly. A fast end will be better than the lingering death these savages enjoy inflicting. We have a good record with our new bows." He pointed toward a man standing at the edge of the line of officers, a long bow in his hands. The archer stood still, staring across the river, as if he were awaiting an order.

Where he was staring, a large black cauldron had been dragged forward. Then, as if the gods thought this scene required a more suitable backdrop, rain began to fall. Constantine looked up. Clouds were moving fast across the sky. The scene in front of them grew dim.

The Roman officers and men stood in the rain, unflinching, staring at the priestesses, their gowns now stuck to their bodies. They held the man in the loin cloth by the arms and led him to the cauldron near the riverbank. It was difficult to make out the man's expression, but his head lolled from side to side, making it clear that either he'd been drinking or was still recovering from a wound.

And then, when the man saw where he was being taken, he let out a scream intense enough to chill anyone's marrow before the scream stopped abruptly, turning to loud gurgling roars, as the priestess behind him stabbed over and over into his back, slicing down again and again.

The man slumped forward, blood pumping out of him. A last whimper carried through the rain to them. A murmur ran along the Roman ranks behind them, but Constantine turned and raised his hand for silence. They would not be easily dismayed.

Across the river two of the priestesses held the man forward so his head came over the cauldron. The other grabbed the man's hair, pulled his head back and sliced at his neck, letting another gush of blood fall into the cauldron. Constantine thought he could smell the blood but it was too far away, so he knew he must be remembering the smell, as he knew it so well.

The man's head came off. One priestess held the body up so that it still pumped blood into the cauldron, flowing out like an upturned amphora. The priestess who had cut off the head carried it to the riverbank and set it down facing the Romans. A shaft of early morning sunlight came from under the clouds and lit the scene, as if the Alemanni gods had willed it.

"One of my best scouts," said the prefect. He raised his hand, then dropped it.

An arrow flew through the air and ended in the soil at the priestess's feet. She looked at it, picked it up and broke the shaft over her knee. A roar went up from the tribesmen behind her.

"Where are your boats?" said Constantine.

"Tied up, that way." The prefect pointed upstream.

"Let's go there," said Constantine. He waved for his men to follow him.

XXXVI

Near the Circus Maximus, Rome, Aprilis, 308 A.D.

Lucius dropped to one knee as Paulina smiled down at him. "You saved my life," he said.

"You will repay me."

"I will." He rose up, stepped close to her. They were both naked and standing near the marble table they had just made love on. The session had lasted a long time, mainly because Paulina insisted he keep going until she too was sated.

"What would you consider a good form of payment for a life?" said Lucius.

"That you save mine when the moment comes that it needs saving," said Paulina. She bowed, turned and pulled the thick fur that covered the table they'd been on onto her shoulders. Then she strode off, waving at him to follow. The tables down the hall were mostly empty now.

He grabbed his tunic, cloak and belt and went after her. She waited at the back door of the temple as an acolyte pulled a black tunic over her head and wiped away the symbols painted on her cheeks and forehead. Lucius dressed as she took on the appearance of a slave in front of him.

A small door in one corner opened at her touch and they went down a low-roofed, brick-lined corridor. They emerged through another, smaller door at the edge of the fish market facing the Tiber. The sun had risen above the river. A throng of fishermen, their wives, and some slaves sent to buy fish filled the market.

No one gave Paulina and Lucius more than a glance. They looked like a master and the slave who had fallen in love with him, because she kept touching his arm and smiling up at him.

Lucius wasn't sure if it was all an act, but he didn't care. He enjoyed having her beside him. It had been years since his wife died in the fire at the church at Nicomedia. He'd blamed himself, then the church, then god, after it had happened.

He'd used women for his needs since then.

They stopped at a sweet wine shop in the middle of the market. The man at the counter seemed to know Paulina, as he poured wine into a red cup and passed it to her as soon as she arrived.

"Is the room free?" she asked the wine seller.

He looked from her to Lucius, his eyes widening.

"It is just for my friend here, Lucius. He needs a place of refuge where no one will ask questions."

The wine-seller brightened, put his hand out and gripped Lucius' forearm.

"A follower of Mithras is always welcome here." He grinned, tapped his forehead, making the sign of a horn with his hand.

"Lucius is not a follower of Mithras," said Paulina.

The wine-seller's face changed. He grimaced. "A Jew then. You are on the run from some family matter, no doubt?"

Lucius shook his head. The wine-seller smiled with his lips, his eyes examining Lucius. "Well, whatever strange cult you follow, I don't care. If you've cut your balls off or drank wine every day until you piss red and black, you are welcome here." He grinned. "Especially if you drink wine every day." He pushed his hand into the air between them. "One good silver denarii, please."

"Your prices have gone up," said Paulina.

"They were lower for you because I thought you liked me." He smiled wider, showing broken teeth.

"I do like you," said Paulina.

The wine-seller tapped the wooden bar in front of them. "Don't look around now. But there's a troop of the night-watch outside."

XXXVII

Saxon Territory, by the river Alara, Northern Germania, Maius, 308 A.D.

"What did your mother say," said Juliana. They were by the riverbank gutting fish they had caught earlier that morning.

"The feast of the cauldron is not the time to be asking questions."

"That's a great way to have a festival to Frigg. Make sure that no one asks questions, because what would the mother god do if anyone questioned things?" Juliana poked her knife so hard into the belly of the next brown trout it came out on the far side and nicked her.

"Give your blood to the water god or Frigg will get her revenge on you," said Athralar.

Juliana leaned into the river and let the water stream over her hand. The water almost froze her skin, but it was as clear as air and the bleeding soon stopped.

She took her hand out of the water, held it to the sun.

"See how she works. Frigg gave you time off from your duties," said Athralar.

Juliana put her other hand on his bare knee. "Do you not hate your mother sometimes, the way she rules over everything?"

Athralar shook his head. "No, I am happy to live and die the way my father did and every father before him did in the great forest. If men ruled over us we would spend our whole time fighting about who is in charge. This way, we get to fight our enemies, not kill our fathers and our brothers." He looked at her, his face serene, as if what he said was so obvious no one could argue with him.

"You want to talk about Constantine again?"

He shook his head.

"You're a bad liar."

"And you're a bad liar when you say you won't go back to him." He pressed his knife through the belly of a fish fast, then pushed the guts out to the side and into the pile they would offer to the god of the river before they left.

"I'm happy here, Athralar. I haven't tried to escape, have I?"

Athralar picked up another trout and threw it at her. "Not yet. And the river is more abundant then I have ever seen it. The gods must like you being with us." He pointed the knife at her. "But soon you will have to be abundant too, even if you do not like rutting, as you claim."

"I've made this clear. I want no children. They create a burden for all."

Athralar coughed, as if he wanted to say something but couldn't find the right words.

"Spit it out. Frigg wants her followers to be honest. Isn't that what they say?" Juliana had no problem praising Frigg as another manifestation of the great mother. It mattered little to her what she was called in different places.

Athralar coughed, then started speaking fast, as if he wanted to get something off his chest.

"Mother says that you must rut at the blood cauldron festival. She says your mind will be twisted if you do not rut."

Juliana had been wondering if someone would try to break the bond between her and Athralar. She'd been expecting one of the men from the war band to make a play for her. It was known that Athralar might be able to do certain things for her, but it was part of the tribe's life that all who were capable would copulate regularly for the production of new fighters.

"Who will be put to me?" Most of the men she'd met here were covered in a mass of body hair, and the smell of dead animals and long dried piss carried with them everywhere they went.

"I am not going to say."

"But it has been decided?"

She put her hands in the water. Best to have them in good shape as quickly as possible if she would have to fight her way out of this place.

He shook his head.

"Not good enough," she replied.

"You will find out tonight." Athralar pushed the fish entrails over the bank and into the water. They spread like a stain. He bowed his head and whispered to the river in a voice so low, what he said was impossible to decipher.

Before the sun went down a large cauldron had been set up in the center of the village. It hung on a thick branch set across a fire pit. The villagers arrived slowly until all around Juliana and Athralar a great crowd had gathered, all sitting cross legged, waiting for the ceremony to begin.

The humming started as the sun went down, spreading a golden light through the trees around them. The humming noise made the trees seem alive. The night birds, owls and night swifts and blood chests, which usually filled the air with their sounds as the sun went down, were all quiet.

Juliana rubbed at her brow. It pounded. All she wanted to do was lie down and drink some of the boiled bark the druidess of the tribe had given her to help with head pains.

A deeper hush descended. A young man was being led by two older men into the center of the group. He was naked and covered in blue tattoos so that his whole body shimmered as he walked. He stood proud, his head high.

Behind him came Athralar's mother and sister. They had antler horns on their heads and their faces smeared with white dust. It was clear from the way Athralar's sister walked behind her mother that she was in training to take over her position.

The boy stood near the cauldron. The other men stood beside him.

Athralar's mother walked around the edge of the gathering until she came to Juliana. She looked down at her.

"The chosen one is here for you. Are you ready to accept him?" Her tone was hard, expecting no argument.

Juliana looked up at her. If she had a knife, she would have driven it up under this evil woman's chin. But she hadn't, so instead she just looked away, while all around everyone waited to see the result of a confrontation they had all been expecting for some time.

Athralar was biting his lip. His mother had not served him well in all she had done to him. He looked broken by something it was impossible to mend.

"What do I get if I agree to be passed to this man?" She nodded toward the man near the cauldron.

He stared at her wide-eyed, clearly angry at her hesitancy.

"You get to live," said Athralar's mother.

Juliana turned her head away.

"You get to see the dawn tomorrow."

Still Juliana kept her head turned, expecting to be taken by force, but instead Athralar came to her and whispered in her ear, "Ask that you be given freedom to lead our war band as you wish."

Juliana raised her fists and shouted to the trees. "I will do as you ask, Great Mother, but I also ask to lead our warriors against our enemies."

Athralar's mother stared at her. She smiled, raised a hand, dropped it.

"I swear it," Athralar's mother said. "Now go with the chosen one."

Juliana and the chosen one were led to a hut at the far end of the village. Inside, candles had been lit. The man was obviously excited as he kept touching her from the moment they stepped inside. She didn't stop him. He was clearly in need of relief.

Soon they were on the fur on the floor and he was on top of her, grunting loudly as he pressed himself into her. She pretended to enjoy it, mainly to get it over with quickly, and she was right. He was spent fast.

As he finished, he yelled. At that, the two men who were outside came in and dragged him away from her. Juliana covered herself.

"Where are you taking him?" she demanded, as her lover was pushed from the house.

XXXVIII

Argentoratum, Northern Gaul, Maius, 308 A.D.

The four long river craft were hauled up at a bend in the river, where a narrow stream joined the main channel. The bank was muddy. Constantine took his dagger from his belt and turned to the officers around him. He ran the blade lightly across his palm.

"We are blood brothers from this moment. Shake my hand and be marked with my blood."

He held out his hand. A trickle of blood dripped from the palm. The centurion and his optio clasped his hand in turn.

The centurion coughed. "I know it is not my place, but I must speak." He looked around to see if anyone was listening. The rest of the men were doing as Constantine had ordered. They were lying down in the long patrol boats, almost on top of each other.

"Centurion, I know we will never get all the men on board these skiffs. If we get half across that will be enough for what I want to do."

"My lord," the centurion pressed on, "it's not that." He shuffled. His short sword clanged against its scabbard.

"It's you. You should not be crossing the river without a legion going ahead of you." He looked straight at Constantine.

"And let you lot have all the fun, centurion! No bloody way. I go where my legionaries go. I fight beside you. We live or die as one." He held his fist out. They put their hands on top of his.

"Begging your pardon," said the optio. His tone was confident. "I fought with your father many moons ago, when he was putting down the Alemanni revolt." He stopped.

"Go on, man."

The optio stumbled on. "But it's a long time since he fought with us. And I'm so glad you're here. The gods will be with us too, when we have you directing things." He put his fist to his chest.

Constantine put a hand on each of their shoulders. "Let's do this."

They managed to get six men into each of the craft. Constantine insisted on being on the lead craft. There would be a greater chance of danger, but he knew everything he was doing was being watched and that reports would go back to the entire legion about everything that happened tonight.

The rain had stopped, and clouds were scudding across the sky as the flat bottomed patrol boats were pushed out, caught by the current and headed off fast downstream. There was only a small paddle at the back to steer by and oars to push them forward through the current. Constantine helped the legionary steering the craft to send them sideways across the river.

They were moving fast now, the thin craft creaking and shivering as the stronger current in the middle of the river took hold. Already they were passing where the atrocity against the Roman scout had taken place. All Constantine could see as they went past were two guards by the cauldron and other men at the tree line engaged in something he could not make out. As most of the men were lying down it would look as if each Roman boat had only two men in it.

There wouldn't be much cause for alarm with only eight men crossing. The guards across the river might even think they were heading off downstream. But then a shout went up and Constantine watched as a group of tribesmen broke into a run, shadowing Constantine's craft.

One of the men lying down groaned in front of Constantine. Another one spoke. "Are we near?" he whispered to the man beside him.

Constantine nudged him with his sandal.

"Soon you will reclaim the honor of Rome, legionary." For the benefit of the legionary steering the craft he pointed at the shore on the Germanian side, a part where the riverbank was low, and trees grew close to the water.

"Head there," he said.

Shouts echoed from the tribesmen keeping track with them. There would not be much time for what he wanted to do, but having a small group follow them was good. It was exactly what he wanted.

XXXIX

The Fish Market, by the Tiber, Rome, 308 A.D.

Two weeks he stayed with the tavern owner, and each day Paulina left the temple and came to visit him in his room. The night they arrived, she'd gone out to the leader of the night watch and given him a token to use at the temple of the great mother, to enjoy any of the priestesses available.

The man had been so taken with Paulina he'd followed her to the temple.

"He's come every day looking for me," said Paulina, a bemused laugh in her voice. "He's even kept the token I gave him and not used it for any of the far more beautiful priestesses than me." She lay beside him on his bed, leaning on her elbow. A thin blanket covered them in case the tavern owner came in, which he did regularly when she visited Lucius.

"I don't blame him. None of the other priestesses are half as wicked as you," said Lucius.

Shouting echoed from below. The tavern was in full swing. Many freemen and the better class of slaves were out enjoying the warm, late spring weather, with not a cloud in the sky.

"You haven't seen the other priestesses." Paulina stretched, exposing her breasts.

"I don't have to," said Lucius. He kissed her shoulder. "Will you be able to keep him away?"

"I can pick and choose who I take," she said. "That is the rule for a chief priestess. There are five of us who can do this." She stroked his arm. "Anyway, sometimes it is better to keep a man waiting, no?"

"It worked with me," he said.

She smiled. "It did."

Lucius leaned closer to her, breathed her spicy perfume in. "Why do you risk everything to come and see me? I mean," he looked around, "I'm probably not the richest lover you have."

She rolled a little more toward him.

"You are the only follower of the nailed god that I know well enough to trust." She gripped his arm. "It must be exciting being part of something so different."

"Is that the only reason you come and see me?"

She turned her head away, sniffed. "There are too many of us who have suffered. If only you knew what abominable things we have to do every week."

"What abominable things?"

She shook her head and gazed away as if remembering something. "Almost every week we must dispose of a new baby. We send the priestesses out to the country when any of them start to show and when their babies are born, they bring them back to the temple." She took a deep breath.

It seemed to Lucius as if she wanted to say more, but something stopped her.

"And what do you do with them? Are they adopted?"

She shook her head.

"What then? You find a way to raise them and you need money to do it?" Again she shook her head.

XL

Saxon Territory, by the river Alara, Northern Germania, Maius, 308 A.D.

The crowd around the cauldron had grown bigger. Some were holding flaming torches. The young man who had coupled with Juliana walked confidently toward it, his arms swinging free of the men who went with him. He raised both fists as he entered the center of the crowd.

"Saxons," he roared. "I am Saxon. Saxons are above all."

"Saxons above all," the crowd roared back, again and again. Many fists punched the air.

"I offer myself to Frigg," the young man roared.

The crowd went silent.

Juliana stood at the edge of the crowd, staring. She could guess what was about to happen.

Athralar's mother came forward. She held a carved wooden beaker in front of her. She gave it to the young man. He swallowed everything in it and then threw the beaker high up and into the crowd.

There were whoops of delight. The young man roared at the sky, at the trees, at the people around him, turning one way, then the other. He started plucking at himself, as if he wanted to pull his own skin off.

Athralar's mother was in front of Juliana now. In her hand she held a dagger with a blade of shiny black stone. She held the dagger out, handle first, to Juliana. The crowd parted.

"You are the chosen one. You must do it. You will release him." Her eyes blazed wide. Blood vessels snaked from each corner.

"No, I cannot," said Juliana softly. "I can kill in combat, but not like this. You must do it."

Athralar's mother hissed. "Yes, you are not one of us. They are right. My son made a mistake about you."

Juliana stared into her eyes. They were dark pits of venom. Everything Athralar had said about her was true. She hated anyone weak. She hated anyone who wasn't Saxon. She hated Juliana.

The air around them stilled as the pressure of hundreds of eyes bore down on them. Juliana stood still, unblinking. She took the knife and held it to her chest.

"Will I be free to lead my war band where I want, if I do this?" she said.

Athralar's mother leaned closer to her and whispered, "Prove to me that you are as strong a woman as we need you to be and you will get your answer."

Juliana stepped around Athralar's mother.

The young man still had his fists in the air. He growled at her, baring his teeth, as if daring Juliana to strike him. The crowd hushed completely. The crackle from the torches filled the air. Red sparks drifted across the sky.

Juliana put the knife straight out in front of her. The young man pushed his chest to her, daring her, and as she came toward him he began shaking. First his arms. Then his legs. Sweat gleamed on him. She could smell the salt of his fear now. The two older men were behind him, their arms wide.

His chest shook as she put the tip of the knife below his nipple. She trembled. Part of her mind said *no, do not do this*. Another part urged her on. She had to do this.

"Do it," a voice called.

She pressed the tip of the knife into his skin. He stopped shaking. Blood trickled. The tip hit a rib.

She moved the knife, as you would when you finished off a deer, searching for a way in. The knife went in deeper.

The young man gasped, then gurgled, then stepped back, wincing, as if to get away from her. His eyes were filled with fear. The men behind him held him. Juliana tightened her jaw, dismissed all pity, stepped after him and pushed the knife further in, and then upward as blood cascaded out and down her arm. The smell of it, iron and salt, filled her nostrils.

The young man groaned, trembled again and again, until Juliana thought she would lose hold of the knife. Then he fell back, his eyes turning up. Piss flowed down his legs and a powerful stench came from the wound, which widened as his skin ripped open.

She pulled out the knife and turned full circle with it clutched in her hand. A ragged cheer rang out.

Athralar's mother was behind her.

"You are reborn, Juliana. Now you are fit to lead. Where will you take the war band?" she said.

Athralar walked toward them. Juliana waited until he was near before speaking. Her hands still shook and cold sweat ran down her back. But a strange exhilaration had come over her. A sense of power. Athralar looked worried.

Her voice croaked as she spoke.

"I will lead the war band back to Treveris. I know a secret way to get into the imperial palace. I wish to take my revenge." She raised her knife. A wild cheer rang out.

Athralar nodded. "Who will you take revenge on? Is this about your child?" he said.

"There are lots of reasons I want revenge. That is one of them. I am the leader now, Athralar, and I will make decisions, and take the blame too." She hit her chest with her fist. It was time to put a stop to his smirking.

That night, as she tried to sleep, she found she couldn't. The face of the young boy she had killed kept appearing, his eyes sad, accusing. Yes, he had volunteered to die and if not her someone else would have done it, but she kept thinking that his eyes were like her baby's.

Blue as the sky.

Was it right to do any evil deed, if that is the only way to get what you want? She tossed and turned as conflicting thoughts flowed through her.

XLI

Argentoratum, Northern Gaul, Maius, 308 A.D.

Constantine jumped ashore first. The trees and undergrowth had slowed down the tribesmen who were tracking them. By the time they appeared three of the Roman craft had pulled up to the riverbank and twenty-four Roman legionaries stood ready in a line, their short swords held in front of them.

The tribesmen halted.

Constantine turned to the man beside him. "Pass it on, I want three captives. And I want them alive." The man whispered to the man beside him. Constantine passed the word to the legionary on his other side. The tribesmen roared at them in their usual way, hoping to set fear in Roman hearts. Then Constantine gave the order.

"Forward!"

The moments before combat were moments Constantine had come to enjoy. Each time they came his body filled with purpose. Each time his mind quickened, thoughts flashing past, decisions forming as quick as they needed to be made. Each time fear and excitement battled each other inside him.

The years of practice with sword and spear all came back to him quickly, exactly as they should. He'd been commended in training often on his skill with weapons, but it was only in the moment of conflict that you proved what you could do, what kind of a man you were, and if you were a real leader, not one appointed, but a man who could lead men to their death and beyond.

A giant German with stringy blond hair came toward him. The man had an axe in his hand and from the look in his eye he was about to swing it.

Constantine could hear his men rushing to join battle on either side of him. But his focus fixed on the man in front of him. Only a few paces separated them. Constantine raised his sword, as if to strike it down into the man's neck. In doing so he exposed his left side.

His opponent saw the opening, swung his axe deftly and at the same time shifted his upper body back to avoid Constantine's thrust. But Constantine changed his sword swing, pulling his sword down fast and swiping it across the man's exposed lower legs.

The axe came hurtling toward him.

Constantine shifted his upper body away from its path as he'd done countless times in the drills he'd loved as a young officer when spears came fast toward him. The axe blade missed him by a finger's width, whistling by. The man grunted in disappointment, his eyes narrowing in rage.

Constantine's sword struck the man's leg at the knee and jolted to a stop.

The man bellowed and made to swing again at Constantine. But he fell as his leg collapsed.

Constantine stepped back, glanced around. The two legionaries nearest him were parrying blows. Beyond, all he could see was a melee. He had to finish this man.

His opponent swung his axe again as he fell, but Constantine expected it and stepped to his right to avoid it.

The man grunted as he hit the ground. Constantine smashed the pommel of his sword into the man's forehead. A crack sounded. The man groaned and his eye dimmed.

"How many are down?" he yelled.

"One here," came an answering shout. The clash of weapons filled the air, as well as the grunts and screams that are normal in combat. Every man fought alone when the legionaries didn't have a shield with them. But to bring the shields over the river would have made it impossible for so many to fit in the craft. He'd needed the appearance of only a few men crossing to spring his trap.

His opponent lay senseless at his feet. Constantine swung the pommel of his sword into the side of the head of a tribesman on his left. The man was not expecting it. He went down on his side fast too, his eyes turning up in his head, almost falling on his own sword until Constantine pushed it away.

"Retreat!" he shouted. "Bring the enemy bodies. Four legionaries to hold the ground until we are in the craft."

It took three men to lift the giant Constantine had defeated and throw him into a boat. One of the captured Germans was small, luckily. and it only took two men to get him into the boat with his hands tied behind his back.

It was not long before they were ready to push off from the shore and calling to the legionaries they had left behind. The last one battled like a mad man, swinging his sword wildly as the tribespeople tried to overcome him.

"Retreat," Constantine shouted.

The legionary did.

Constantine reached for his dagger, aimed it, then threw it. It didn't hit the face of the lead tribesman pursuing the last legionary, but it did hit his thigh and made him stall.

"Come on," he called.

The legionary reached the boat. Constantine pulled him in.

"Head downstream and across," he shouted. "Let the river take us." They moved quickly out into the current, shouts from the tribesmen echoing behind them.

When they reached the far side the men they had captured were waking. There was a struggle with each of them, especially the giant, who had to be knocked out again and carried back to the Roman river fort.

At dawn, Constantine assembled all the men from his unit and everyone from the fort at the patch of ground where they had watched the previous night's execution on the far side of the river. He'd received reports about the number of men who had been lost and the number who were injured and unable to parade from the brief raid.

The cost had been high. That was going to affect morale. He had to get his next steps right.

At the front of everyone he placed the three captives. They were on their knees, a Roman legionary at each of their shoulders pressing them down and another behind their back with the point of a sword between their shoulder blades. When a crowd had assembled across the river to watch the proceedings and the expected executions, Constantine had three peals blown on the fort's signal horn.

He stood in front of the captives. At his signal, each man was forced face down into the mud. At another signal the legionary behind each man raised his sword and pressed his other hand down onto the back of the man he was threatening. Each of the captives responded differently. The giant, who had been woken by cold water, struggled this way and that against the ropes binding him and the three men holding him, attempting to slip forward to the river, until a sword was stabbed into his path.

Another man shouted at the people across the river, his voice raised as if demanding something was done.

The third man remained quiet.

Constantine waved at the legionary with the signal horn. He sent one long, high peal of sound across the scene and then stopped. The only thing that could be heard now was the burbling of the river and the forlorn shouts of the captives and their kin across the river.

XLII

The Fish Market, by the Tiber, Rome, Maius, 308 A.D.

"We slaughter every baby, Lucius." Paulina didn't normally show much emotion on her face, but her expression had twisted now, as if she was in torment.

Lucius had heard that temple girls who had sex with any man often threw their babies into rubbish pits or latrines, but he'd assumed it was done by individual priestesses and not too often.

He put his hand on hers. "Did this happen to you?"

Tears welled in Paulina's eyes. She nodded and rocked back and forth, her eyes wide.

"Twice," she whispered. "Two beautiful boys. I cannot bear it. I cannot."

Lucius put his hand on her arm. "You will have more."

"They would be ten and nine now," she replied. "How could I have done this?" She rocked again.

"I'm sorry. This is not the way things should be."

Paulina sniffed. "I heard the followers of the nailed god do not agree with killing babies. And I heard they do not agree with priestesses offering themselves to any man who comes to their temple. Is this true?" She studied him, her expression quizzical.

"Yes, it is true. Many men hate us for this, but I know we must stop these things. Every life is sacred."

Paulina pulled him close to her. "Make me a follower of the nailed god. I will do whatever it takes. I will pay whatever it costs."

Lucius held her close. "All our priests are in hiding, Paulina. But perhaps I can arrange for you to meet one of them. He will help you understand what it is you are taking on."

"Should I leave the temple?"

Lucius shook his head. "No, not yet. We may need you there. We have to stop the persecutions. Our followers in the east are suffering terribly."

She nodded, blinked. "I am going to see Maxentius tomorrow. Do you want me to talk on him?"

Lucius glanced over his shoulder, as if concerned someone might be listening.

"We need something different," he said.

XLIII

Juliana and Athralar had been allocated one of the long houses in the village. The building had a roof of rough timber beams and a firepit in the center. A hole in the roof directly above it took most of the smoke away. The previous occupant had died on the last raid into Roman territory. His family had been moved to a small round house in the past few days.

They were also allocated slaves. Juliana didn't mind most of them, but one of them was a young girl who spent most of her time staring greedily at Athralar. Athralar was able to have sex if he was massaged correctly, Juliana had discovered, but they had only done it twice in the year she had been with him.

She denied him often. If this slave girl was going to offer herself to him, a way would have to be found to get rid of her.

Juliana also needed to get the war band prepared. She had managed to hide her longing to see her baby for a year, but thoughts of her son greeted her every morning after she woke these days and stayed with her through the day no matter what happened. She'd thought her memories might lessen over time, but they hadn't.

She had to get back to Treveris.

By the next full moon they were ready. The war band was small, twenty men, two shield maidens, and her. They were all sleeping in the long house now, all down one wall on a carpet of wolf skins. She understood why they had allocated the house to her and Athralar.

The shield maidens had picked a man each they would have sex with, and the rest of the men had accepted it, some more easily than others. Juliana had warned them to be quiet when they were doing it, to avoid arousing the other men and causing fights.

The night before they set off the two shield maidens changed the men they would have sex with on the raid. A fight had broken out and one man ended up badly beaten.

"This is the right of a shield maiden," said Athralar early the following morning, as they were washing at the river after Juliana asked about what he thought about what had happened.

"We can't have fights all the time. This is not good."

"No, it is good. The winners will get to live, and the shield maidens will enjoy having men fight over them. What is wrong with that?" said Athralar. "It is the way of the stag and the bear. We must not forget where we come from." He stood still and naked in the water, which came up only to his knees.

"Should I and your little slave girl fight over you?" said Juliana.

She walked into the water and embraced him. She loved his muscles and the obvious strength in his body.

"She is not nearly as good as you," said Athralar.

"You've tried her?" Juliana pushed him away.

"Of course. She insisted on it."

Juliana stepped out of the river, picked up the new goat skin tunic she had acquired and put it on, her back to him, saying nothing, her lips pressed tight. Inside she was angry but pleased too.

He put a hand on her shoulder. She shrugged it off.

"It is the right of any man in our tribe to have sex with any slave, man or woman, who offers themselves freely. No one has ever dared question this. Why do you, Juliana? You think you know better than the law?"

Juliana sat on the thick grass and pulled her bear skin boots on. She kept her back to him.

"We have to leave. We have a long way to go, Athralar. And I don't claim to know better than the law or to own you." She turned to him. "But don't you claim to own me, either."

He put a hand toward her. From the look on his face she knew what he wanted. She turned and stalked away.

XLIV

Argentoratum, Northern Gaul, 308 A.D.

As the crowd watched, a brazier with flames leaping from it was carried from the fort on long metal poles and placed behind the captives.

"One hand from each," shouted Constantine. "Their right hand. Let the Alemanni know Roman justice." The short swords of the legionaries holding the men flashed through the air. The giant roared mightily when his hand came off and blood spurted. Then he fainted.

That made it easier for other legionaries to carry him to the brazier. He woke when they pushed the bleeding stump of his wrist into the burning embers and held it there. His mighty screams sent birds into the air for leagues around and saw shouts and curses raining at them from across the river.

The other two men roared and whimpered, but only the giant brought the curses raining down.

Constantine turned to the centurion in charge of the fort's defenders. "Carry the giant to the edge of the river and tie him by his neck to a stake in the ground."

They did as Constantine asked, and when it was done Constantine dismissed everyone and went back into the fort. The crowd on the other side of the river had grown by this time. As Constantine watched from the wooden ramparts of the fort it was clear that a lot of arguing was going on across the river. The giant had come alive again. He tried to pull the rope away from his neck but he couldn't, probably because of how much his hand pained him. That was clear from the way his face became animated by an occasional roar, which he let out from time to time.

"Fifty men are to wait near the gate. The best men with a bow you have," said Constantine to the prefect, who had come to stand beside him. A bad smell came from the man. It reminded Constantine of the smell from the tents of the injured when he was with Galerius in the east. The men who had such a smell around them never survived for long with whatever had gone bad inside them.

"The brazier is back in the kitchens," said the prefect. "There will be wild pig roasting for us tonight."

Constantine didn't reply. He stared across the river. A group of the Alemanni, two of them as tall as the giant whose hand he had cut off, were standing at the water's edge.

Two large fishing currachs had arrived near them. The currachs looked as if they could carry only a few people in each. The men, who looked like relatives of the giant, were pointing at Constantine. Then they took the currachs and put them in the water and paddled with wide oars toward the fort.

They ended up much further downstream, beyond the next bend in the river.

"Shall I send some cavalry to intercept them and kill them?" asked the prefect.

"No," said Constantine. "But get ready the fifty men I asked you to collect."

The prefect saluted. "Yes. And the other prisoners?"

"Put them in the back of the fort, we may need them," said Constantine. He went to put his helmet back on. "And you stay here, in case something goes wrong." He slapped the prefect's back. "Don't send any more men out if I don't ask for them."

He went down the ladder, skirted around a squealing black pig being led to the kitchens and called the fifty legionaries to attention.

"Attention," he shouted. "Listen up. We are heading out to guard a prisoner. I want no sword unsheathed, unless I specifically command it. Do you understand?" A ragged "yes" followed. "Are you sure you all understand?" A much larger assent came back at him.

"Good, now follow me, fast step."

The gate of the fort lay open. Constantine led the men at a brisk pace out toward the riverbank. It was only a hundred paces away, but already the Alemanni who'd come across the river could be seen moving fast to get to the captive. It would be a proper race to see who reached the man first.

"Full pace," Constantine shouted.

In a moment they were moving as fast as a man in armor carrying a long shield and a bow could move.

Ahead, only one guard had been left with the prisoner, as Constantine had ordered. Now he was about to find out if he'd judged the distance correctly.

XLV

The Fish Market, by the Tiber, Rome, 308 A.D.

"What do you need?" asked Paulina. "If not a spy, what? Someone to start fires or find jabs for followers of the nailed god?" She looked desperate to please.

"No, nothing as obvious as that," replied Lucius. He stood. The room was small, the yellow ceiling plaster peeling in places. He went to the door, a set of rough wooden planks nailed together with overlapping pieces at the top and bottom. He listened with an ear to the wood.

The only sounds he could hear were shouts and laughter from the tavern below and the crying of a baby from the tenement directly behind the building, and further away the barking of dogs.

He pulled open the door fast. A scampering of feet echoed as he peered out into the dark corridor. The light from the oil lamps and the two candles in his room did not illuminate it far.

"That will be one of the trainee priestesses," said Paulina. "I asked her to wait outside, but she may have taken that to heart. She loves to know everything I get up to." She smiled up at Lucius. "Would you like her to join us?" She blew a kiss toward him. "She is very flexible at love making."

Lucius shook his head, his expression downcast as he turned to her, after closing the door.

"A betrayal is what is expected of you, Paulina," he said. He stood with his feet apart at the end of the low wooden bed, his breathing heavy.

Paulina sat upright. The blanket fell from her, exposing her breasts. She raised a hand to him. "I know it looks bad having someone listening at the door."

"Yes, it looks bad, Paulina," said Lucius.

Paulina went to her knees in front of him and put her hands together, as if in prayer to him.

"I didn't think you would mind, Lucius." Her hands trembled as she held them toward him.

"Who is waiting for news about us? Is it Maxentius?"

Paulina stared at him, then nodded, put a hand to her brow, bent her head. "You have every right to hate me, Lucius." She sniffed. "But you have no right to harm me." Her hands came up again, pleadingly. "Nothing has been said to him that could put you in danger. We say only good things about you, believe me, please."

Lucius began pacing. "I do believe you, Paulina." He stopped, pointed at her. "I hope I've not been a fool."

"You have not."

He began pacing again. "I half expected this, so I am not overly surprised."

"You shouldn't be. I'm obliged in my position to report everything of note to Maxentius. That is why I see him every few days. He likes to know all about the senators and praetorians who frequent the temple. And what they like." She stopped.

"So he can blackmail them?" Lucius stopped walking and stood in front of her.

Paulina's eyes were wide. "I'm not involved in anything like that. What he does with the information is not my business."

Lucius leaned closer to her and stared at her, examining her. "What does he ask about me?"

Both her hands were up in front of her, as if she held a sack of wheat up. "Only the usual, do you speak against him, is your master plotting against him, who are you meeting."

"My master, do you mean he asks about Constantine?"

Paulina nodded.

Lucius laughed. "And does he like what you tell him?"

She shook her head. "I told him you never speak about Constantine and that you only meet with one man, that Marcellus character who works in the stables for the post horses."

"How do you know about him?"

Paulina pointed at the floor.

"But he only came here twice."

Paulina shrugged. "I get reports on everything you do, Lucius. If Maxentius found out that I helped you and you were conspiring against him it would be bad for me. Very, very bad." She made her hands into fists, wrung them. "A priestess who hid things from him had her nose and ears cut off and ended up impaled on a spike in his garden." She trembled. "Through the anus, slowly, for his entertainment!"

"We can't have that happening to your beautiful ass."

"That's what a lot of people think."

"Who else knows about us?"

"The tavern owner, of course. One or two of his friends." She paused. "One or two priestesses." She paused again.

"Half Rome knows then."

"A few friends advised me to stop coming to you."

"Why don't you?"

"I told you, I want to be forgiven my sins. Isn't that why everyone follows the nailed god?"

"We follow Christ, not the nailed god." Lucius sighed heavily. "Do you know when Marcellus is coming back?"

"He is expected here before the tavern closes tonight."

"You know as much as me then." Lucius went out of the room and down the stairs. A young girl at the bottom, she couldn't have been more than thirteen, scampered into the crowd as he came down. He went to the long counter the tavern owner stood behind serving jugs of wine to whoever had the coin to pay for it.

"Another jug of wine," he shouted.

When the man brought it over Lucius beckoned him forward. The man came close with his hand out for a coin. Lucius grabbed him by the neck of his tunic, scrunching it up in his fist and pulled him close until their noses were almost touching. He could smell garlic on the man's breath, old garlic.

"If I find you spreading rumors about me and my friends to the city watch I will pluck those bloodshot eyes out of your head and boil them in that bird dropping soup you sell us at lunchtime."

"Lucius," a voice called out sweetly behind him. He knew who it was. He'd heard her coming down the stairs.

A hush descended on the room. Lucius had to look. All eyes were on Paulina. She had appeared on the stairs, wearing only her wolfskin cloak. Her long, bare, golden-skinned legs were visible beneath it.

As he turned back to the tavern owner, he felt something sharp prick into his side, just below his rib cage.

The tavern owner grunted into his face. "Unhand me, or you can eat your own liver for dinner tonight."

XLVI

Saxon Territory, by the river Visurgis, Northern Germania, 308 A.D.

They had made good progress that day, and had even killed a doe, which had been slow to get away when the forward man, the eagle, walked into a glade by the river's edge.

"A gift from Frigg," said Athralar, loudly, when they set up camp further up the river's course. Birds squawked into the air as a cheer rose up around him.

They started a fire. Juliana had the animal skinned and roasting slowly on a thick stick above the fire in the same time Athralar spent polishing his axe. Then he started trying to get her to explain her plan once they reached Treveris.

"Trust me, I know how to get us in!" said Juliana, angrily.

"I trust you, yes, I do, yes, but I also need to know how we are going to get out again. It's not what we're all good at, breaking into a Roman town, while thousands of their legionaries are waiting for action." He waved around him. "There are twenty of us. We will be offering ourselves on a plate for them to gobble us up."

"There are twenty-three of us, Athralar. I know you don't usually count us female warriors, but when I'm leading the war band you will." She took out her knife and scored the flesh of the doe so that the juices would flow more easily. They'd hung the carcass until the blood had stopped flowing from it, and this would help it to cook quicker.

"That won't make any difference to getting us out of there." He sat heavily beside her. The others were lying in the tents or on guard duty in the trees around the camp.

She put her hand on his arm. "Stop, Athralar, I've measured the days to when we arrive. We should get there a few days before the feast of the great mother. There will be processions of young women. Half the legionaries will be drunk from the night before. And there will be tribespeople from every province filling the taverns of Treveris."

"So, we will sneak in as revelers?"

"Yes."

"All of us?"

"No. Some of you will wait in the woods. I will go into the city with the other shield maidens."

He inhaled quickly. "This is not much of a raid, sitting in the woods, twiddling our thumbs while you have a look for your family."

"Our raiding will be on the way back through Roman territory. The shield maidens will find out what villages the men drinking and whoring in Treveris are from. They are the villages we will attack on the way back."

"You will be spying for us too?"

"Yes."

"And you don't intend to abandon us, once you are back inside the walls of Treveris?"

She pursed her lips, shook her head.

Athralar stared at her.

XLVII

Argentoratum, Northern Gaul, Maius, 308 A.D.

Constantine blinked. The Alemanni from across the river had reached the captive.

"Halt," he called out. The legionaries stopped quickly behind him.

A shuffling and clanking filled the air as armor and swords came to rest. The only noise now was the giant grunting in pain. The Alemanni had already hacked through the rope binding him and now they had him between two of their number and were heading back to the river.

"Notch," Constantine called out. The shuffling behind him made it clear that his men were readying an arrow.

"Shoot ahead of the Alemanni, unleash." The twang of bow strings filled the air. Fifty arrows whistled into the sky. They fell hard with resounding thuds into the low, half flattened grass in front of the Alemanni.

The Alemanni stopped. In their path were the protruding arrows that showed they were about to enter a killing zone.

"Wait here," said Constantine. "And notch again, and if they attack me kill them all." He walked forward on his own.

There were four Alemanni. Two had their axes up in front of them. The other two, who were holding the giant between them, had their axes on their belts. They all turned to face him as he came forward, his sword sheathed.

When he reached about ten paces from them, he stopped. All the men in front of him looked like brothers. The giant, whose hand he had cut off, looked to be the oldest.

Constantine spoke slowly in Latin. "I cut your hand off because I want to bring peace between us. It is easier done when you cannot raise a weapon."

The giant grunted, coughed, coughed again. The coughing was soon broken by a loud grunt of pain. "Alles we want is for you to die today," said the giant, in heavily accented Latin.

"Attack me and that may happen," said Constantine. "But you and your brothers will all die too." He looked behind him and raised his hand in the usual signal for an archer to raise his bow.

The archers were in two rows behind him. In a moment each man had an arrow pointing high.

"My archers know the distance after that first volley. I expect each of you will have a dozen holes in him soon, if you decide you want to die."

The giant spoke fast in his own language. The two brothers with the axes started walking toward Constantine. One, then the other, started swinging his axe from side to side in front of him. One blow from either axe would cut Constantine deep, though it would probably take a blow from both axes to cut him in half.

Constantine unsheathed his sword, swished it out in front of him. He would not run. It would be better to be dead than to have a watching Roman fort view any cowardice.

XLVIII

The Fish Market, by the Tiber, Rome, 308 A.D.

"Lucius, your friend has arrived. Stop fooling around." Paulina brushed her fingers against the bare skin of Lucius' arm.

Lucius let go of the tavern keeper, shrugged his body so that his tunic sat better on him and followed Paulina toward a table at the back of the tavern.

One man sat at the table, alone, with a large jug of wine in front of him. It was Marcellus, the most senior priest of Christ in the city. He looked as if he'd already drunk a jug of wine, but Lucius knew that was how he normally looked, droopy eyed and nodding slowly, as if he'd heard some good news and was about to tell you all about it.

Lucius sat. "May I introduce the high priestess, Paulina," he said, pointing to Paulina who was arranging herself onto the chair beside him.

"I know Paulina well," said Marcellus. He held his hand out, took Paulina's when she offered it and kissed her large amber ring.

"You have not been to see us in many years, Marcellus. When I heard you were visiting with this man," she pointed at Lucius with her thumb, "I worked out what had happened to you." She leaned forward, conspiratorially. "You are a follower of the nailed god now." She tilted her head, as if pleased with herself.

"Lucius, what has you two hooked up?" said Marcellus. His expression had hardened. Lucius knew he was angry.

"Paulina wants to join us," he said.

Marcellus looked at him as if he had no idea what he was talking about. "She can join us for our regular drinking sessions any time." He waved at the tavern keeper. "More beakers, please."

Paulina looked from Marcellus to Lucius and back again.

The tavern owner dropped two more rough-edged earthenware beakers on the table.

"I want to follow the nailed god," said Paulina, after he had gone, her eyes wide.

Marcellus leaned close to her. "Lucius knows all about that stuff, not me. I went to one meeting. That's all. Ask Lucius about it."

"I can vouch for Paulina," said Lucius.

Marcellus raised his beaker, drank the wine in it and stood. "I must go. The stable master is expecting me." He bowed to Paulina. "I will visit you in the temple again. Now that I am working, I have coin for your services. That is why I didn't come to visit you all." He said the last part forcefully. Then he beckoned Lucius and walked out of the tavern.

"Wait here," said Lucius to Paulina. He headed out after Marcellus.

Marcellus walked fast along the colonnade of taverns. He glanced behind him as he crossed the street, heading for an alley. Lucius caught up with him in the alley, where he waited, his back against a wall, his gaze going one way, then the other.

When Lucius came close, he grabbed the front of Lucius' tunic, held it. Lucius put his hands up.

"Paulina can be trusted. She wants forgiveness for her sins."

"You are a fool, Lucius." Marcellus gripped the tunic tighter. "You are thinking with your cock. Everyone knows that Paulina reports to the emperor, to Maxentius directly. Paaah!"

He looked over Lucius' shoulder. "You didn't lose your family in the persecution, Lucius. I know that." Marcellus pointed at himself. "My wife and my brother died in the lower cells of the Tulianum when they refused, day after day, to name our leader. I will not die there too."

Lucius put his hands on Marcellus' shoulders. "Hold me responsible if anything happens."

"Much good that will do. I won't be able find you from the grave."

"I know she is a spy for Maxentius, but I also think we can use her. She can help us."

"How?" Marcellus' tone was dismissive. He released his grip on Lucius' tunic.

"By telling us of Maxentius' plans for us. By whispering our loyalty into his ear. By helping us in many other ways." Shouts echoed from the street. It sounded as if a fight had started.

"Yes, I know what her many ways are like."

Lucius moaned in frustration.

Marcellus pointed at him. "You said Constantine was our hope. I trusted you, Lucius. We helped raise funds for your stay here." He pointed back toward the tavern, then raised his hand in frustration. "There are not many of us left in Rome, Lucius. You know that. We've been hunted and we've died for our faith. We are the last of the followers in Rome. We could be wiped out soon, Lucius." He crossed his arms across his chest.

"You do what you have to do, Lucius, but don't involve me anymore. The risk is too high. And Lucius, you must deny that I lead us in Rome. Unto death."

Lucius shook his head. "It won't come to that. I trust Paulina."

XLIX

*Saxon Territory, by the river Visurgis, Northern Germania, 308
A.D.*

"I will not abandon you, Athralar," said Juliana. "You do live in fear,
don't you? I thought Saxon warriors were a tougher bunch."

"We are. I don't care what you do. I need to know your
intentions, so we can plan for what to do after you leave us." Athralar
stood, walked away.

Juliana let him go. She said some prayers to the great mother
by the water and then went back to the fire.

"Cut the meat into strips and give seven small pieces to each
of us. Make sure it's cooked hard. We may not find anything like this
between now and the River Rhenus," she said to the shield maiden
watching over the fire and the doe roasting above it.

She was right too. What they encountered as Maius became
Junius and the summer approached, were long days with rain and most
animals in hiding or if they were out, difficult to see and hear in the
downpour. And this was no ordinary rain. It was sheets of it so fierce
they were soaked constantly and almost everyone was soon
complaining that the king of the moss folk had heard of their raid and
was out to stop them.

Juliana kept her meat close to her body, but it was still ready
to turn into worms by the time she ate the last of it. They had reached
the river separating the Germanic tribes from the empire and were
traveling upstream, slowly.

At a bend in the river, where the two banks approached, a
fisherman took them across two at a time. They paid him with a
dagger. When they were on the other side they moved only at night.

The rain kept going, though mistily, but it kept them all in ill temper, though it also meant there were very few travelers out at night. Their journey to the woods north of Treveris, not far from where she was taken, took another six nights.

At last, as the dawn broke that final morning, she saw the high gray gates of the city in the distance from a perch on a ridge at the edge of the forest. Behind the gates the smoke from a few early morning cooking pots curled into the air from villas or from one of the many imperial buildings.

They stopped so they could take in the sight.

"You are home, Juliana. You can run away now," said Athralar, as he stood close beside her.

"You run home first," said Juliana.

"When do we go into the town?"

"Right now. You will wait in the woods. If we are not back by dawn tomorrow, assume I'm dead or captured and move away from here. I may have to kill some legionaries to find the people I want, so torture is not unlikely if I fail. I do not know how much torture I will be able to endure."

Athralar punched her shoulder. "Your lover, Constantine, would not allow you to be tortured, I'm sure of that. He wouldn't want to spoil your ass." He ran his hand all the way down her back.

She shrugged his hand away. "See you tomorrow," she said. She waved the two shield maidens to her side. She'd told them most of her plan. Now came the rest.

"Give your axes to your men. We go in with nothing but a dagger each. We are wayward daughters looking for a good time before returning back to Germania." She looked from one smiling face to the other. They nodded together. Perhaps there was some truth in what she'd said.

By the time the sun rode above the trees they were waiting in a short line at the magnificent gray sandstone northern gate of the city. Ahead of them stood a man with a large black pig. Behind them was a woman with two chickens, one under each arm. Their heads were facing behind and their legs facing forward. One of them looked as if she would lay an egg soon. There was a round protuberance in her behind.

"Can I go ahead of you?" said the woman in the Alemanni dialect that a lot of the slaves used in Treveris. "This one is about to lay."

"Yes," said Juliana. "But why the rush to sell these if they are laying good eggs?"

"My master thinks he will get a good price. I don't give a toss, but he may beat me less if he does get it."

"Give me one chicken," said Juliana. "They will charge you a tax if you bring in two. Everyone is allowed to bring in one, to feed themselves, so I heard." She'd heard that from the man who'd agreed to the law, she was going to add, but she didn't.

They went through the city gate with the shield maidens guiding the pig in front and with Juliana with a chicken under one arm behind.

None of them were stopped. They were waved through with a smile, as clanking city guards moved back and forth looking along the line of traders waiting to get in. No doubt they didn't expect trouble from a few women.

The farmer wanted them all to come to the market so he could buy them a drink in a tavern his brother ran. His pig had become reluctant as she'd seen the dark entranceway and it had taken three of them to get the animal through to the other side.

They all shook their heads at his offer. Then he insisted they come to his brother's tavern when their business was finished. They said they might.

They headed into the city along the main wide street leading to the forum. Twice they were stopped by groups of young men asking if they were in the festival parade at mid-day and would they join them for some wine before it.

They kept walking, brushing them all off. The second group were half drunk, pawing at them like dogs. Two of that lot had to be slapped hard in the face before they let them go. They moved faster after that, heading down smelly side streets with dung, piss and rotting vegetables clogging the middle channel, lying about decomposing waiting for a rainstorm to wash them away. It was fortunate that Juliana had spent many afternoons exploring the city.

She knew exactly which way to go and soon after they were at the side door of the imperial villa, where she had been living up until a year before. The villa looked quiet. No smoke came from its bath house or kitchens. Where was Constantine, Juliana wondered, and where is my baby?

She tingled with anticipation. A deep longing for her baby, which she'd suppressed since she'd been captured, filled her up completely, compelling her to knock hard on the small wooden door that the household slaves mostly used, and to knock again, even harder, when no one came. But it didn't make any difference how hard she knocked. No one answered.

Then they walked around the villa to the front door. It had a pile of dust in one corner, as if it hadn't been opened in a long time. After more fruitless knocking, she turned to the two shield maidens.

"Ask in these other houses what happened to the people living here," she said, pointing up and down the street. "Mention my name and see what they say. If they speak Latin, not Germanic, come and get me."

She walked up and down, looking at the villa. Everything looked almost the same as a year ago, but different, like finding that someone who you thought loved you, didn't.

One of the shield maidens returned first, shaking her head. "Nobody knows anything. I spoke to three house slaves, they all speak some Germanic, and they all claim never to see anything. Are all the slaves blind in Treveris?"

Juliana looked in the other direction. The other shield maiden was walking fast toward her. She arrived breathless.

"Frigg is with us. The slave who opened the second door speaks Latin. She was totally shocked when I said your name."

Behind her, walking toward them, was a young girl. Juliana recognized her instantly. She'd been a house slave in their villa when Juliana lived here with Constantine. Juliana ran to her, her ears ringing, her mouth dry. She would find her baby. This slave would know where he was.

"Where is my baby?" she shouted, as they came together.

The slave paused. Her face went visibly pale. She began shaking her head. Juliana grabbed her arms.

"What is it? What's wrong?" Dread crept up inside her like a giant dark worm.

"Your baby was stolen."

Juliana let her go. Her hopes died in that moment. She bent her head, a great shock flowing up through her, threatening her with tears.

She pushed them away. She could not cry. Not now. "What happened?"

The slave's mouth opened. Then it closed. She shrugged, turned on her heel and walked away.

Juliana stared after her. Hot bile filled her throat. She spat it out, put her hand to her mouth. Her hopes had turned to dust.

She contemplated killing the slave, then killing anyone else who didn't answer her. Killing everyone she could until she too was dead. Other thoughts crowded in. Memories of the baby. His smile. His blue eyes. His small nose. Where was Constantine. Did he know about this? What was he doing?

L

The two brothers stopped three feet from Constantine. Each of them held their axe high. Constantine adopted a fighting stance, his sword in front, his other hand on the hilt of his dagger, ready to pull it and fight with both hands. He smiled. There was a real possibility he would be dead in moments.

His training came back to him. Never show fear, unless you want to die. Focus on their eyes. A shout went up.

The two men looked at each other. They nodded at Constantine then dropped their axes. The giant, their brother presumably, shouted. The two men in front of Constantine went to their knees.

A shout went up from across the river. Constantine glanced there. A big crowd had gathered, pressing close to the water. He raised his sword, as if greeting them, or maybe he was about to kill both men who'd dropped down in front of him.

But instead, he lowered the flat of the blade on each of their shoulders in turn. The men nodded. He went past them to the giant. He was on his knees too. He touched the flat of his blade on each of the man's shoulders.

"Send your brothers to our fort in two days for a feast to celebrate our new alliance. Come yourself if you can. I have need of men like you and we will pay you more than any Roman auxiliaries have ever been paid before. You will not regret making peace with us." He held his hand out. The giant used his working hand and gripped it.

"We want spoils, Emperor. Provide those and we will fight beside you to ends of the world."

Two days later, with his right arm in a sling and stumbling a little, as if he was drunk, the giant came to the feast, to Constantine's surprise. There were not many men who could go feasting after such an injury. And from the way he ate with his left hand, Constantine was sure he could probably fight with it too. But his days of fighting would certainly be numbered if he went to battle like this.

His two brothers came with the giant and were introduced as Baldr and Bragi.

"My brothers will collect our warriors and be available by the next moon. If you want a hundred more men with you and want us to help you for more than one moon you must provision us for the time you want us to go with you. It will take three moons to raise a larger force."

"You will be coming?"

"No," said the giant, "just my brothers. What you have done to me has had the blessing of Woden. The runes were read for our clan and they are good, the best they have been in years. All our arguments about who will lead our clan after our father dies are over. I will lead in their name and they will fight for us and bring spoils back for us all to enjoy." He winced and sat back further on the wooden chair.

It was clear he was in severe pain, but he forced his expression to become neutral again.

"I will be back here in three moons for your brothers," said Constantine. "Tell them to bring as many men as are interested in fighting with us and against the tribes along the river who oppose us. Will they do that?"

"They will, if I tell them to. Their women and children are with me. They will not argue."

Baldr and Bragi sat beyond him. They raised their silver goblets when the imperial slave filled them and sniffed at her clean cotton clothing as she went past them.

Bragi turned to Constantine. "Have you given up looking for the woman who ran away from you?" His Latin wasn't as good as his brother's, but it was better than the Latin a lot of the traders you could meet on market day in Treveris had.

Constantine put his goblet down carefully. "I never give up on a friend, Bragi. My loyalty is absolute."

"But women are fickle, Emperor," said Bragi, leaning closer and grinning, as if he knew something. Half his teeth were blackened stumps.

"Some are, yes," said Constantine. "But not this one."

Bragi shook his head, slowly. Golden curls swirled. "So why is this Juliana of yours leading a Saxon war band?"

Constantine stared. How did he know Juliana's name?

"Are you sure of this?" he said.

"Half of our women are talking about it, Emperor. The other half are asking how they can lead a war band too." Bragi shook his head. "I thought it meant you were weak when I heard you lost your woman, but now I admit I was wrong. You sent her to the Saxons to become their leader, that is clear to me." He slapped Constantine's back. "You are as clever as your father. Maybe more."

"He is," said the giant. "He won us over to fight with him, didn't he?"

Constantine didn't answer. He stared into the distance, an image of Juliana smiling coming to him. He'd pushed her and their child out of his mind, as he'd been taught in the legions to push the faces of comrades and injuries and family out of his mind and to think only of training for the next battle.

But her warm smile and her presence had never fully left him, creeping in at night when he was tired or in the early morning, unbidden. Where was she? He shook his head. He had to stop these thoughts. He could not be distracted. He had to focus on what he had, and what he could do, the way his father had taught him.

It was clear now that he could go further than his father too. He wasn't dependent on a senior emperor the way his father had been. And his success leading his men meant his legionaries would follow him wherever he wanted to go.

He might even consider overthrowing Maxentius. From what Fausta had told him, her brother was incapable of ruling well. Arrogance and incompetence were the qualities she ascribed to him. But how long would it be before Maxentius could be taken down?

LI

The Fish Market, by the Tiber, Rome, 308 A.D.

Laughter echoed up the street as Lucius returned to the tavern. It crossed his mind not to go back in, but where would he stay, and they needed Paulina. He had to have someone inside Maxentius' entourage to have any hope of helping Constantine, and by doing so helping his family and his people.

The rough door of the tavern was closed when he reached it. He pushed it open, went inside. The first thing he noticed was the quiet. Most of the people who'd been drinking there were gone. But Paulina was still there. She'd been joined by a man in a dark gray cloak with his back to the door. His hair was gray stubble, as if he'd just left the legions.

Paulina looked at him. The man turned. He had a scar down one side of his face. He blinked when he saw Lucius. A smile curled his lips. Lucius hesitated. Every sense told him to turn on his heels and leave, but he looked at Paulina again. Her dress was half open and the curve of her breasts were hard not to stare at. Her smiled widened as he stared, and she put a hand out to him.

"Lucius, meet Felix, the head of the city watch. He asked about you." She put her head to one side, as if troubled by something.

Felix stood.

"Lucius Aurelius Armenius, I arrest you in the name of Maxentius, Caesar Augustus of Rome. Come freely, my men are here to enforce this order. You or your friends can appeal this through the courts."

A bolt of cold fear ran through Lucius' stomach. He looked around. Five men, with cudgels, had appeared out of the shadows. His bowels felt suddenly loose.

"What is the charge?"

"Spying and promoting a proscribed religion. You will be able to defend yourself in front of the emperor."

Lucius gripped the pommel of his sword. He could fight. It might be better to die now than to suffer the famed torturers of Maxentius.

Paulina stood. "Go with them. Don't start anything, Lucius. They've told me they will not charge me or arrest me, but only if you go with them without a fight." She put a hand to her mouth. It shook at her lips. Behind her stood the tavern owner. He looked pleased, as if he'd just won a prize.

Lucius pulled his sword. A hissing sound from behind him told that other weapons had also been drawn.

He passed his sword, hilt first, to the head of the city watch. "Paulina knows nothing about what I do."

Felix shrugged, as if he knew that already.

Lucius' arms were pulled behind him. Rough braids of a rope burned into his skin.

"Where are you taking me."

"The Tullianum."

LII

Juliana ran after the slave. She caught her as she was about to go back into her villa. Her desperation for more details about what had happened made her grip the slave tight by the shoulders of her tunic, as her chest heaved from running. She held the slave even tighter as her breathing slowed.

"I remember you, Juliana," whispered the slave. "But we were told you were dead. Seeing you is like seeing a ghost." The girl stared at her, wide eyed. "Are you a ghost?"

"No, I am not a ghost. I was kidnapped and taken to northern Germania. Now I am back. What happened to my baby?"

The slave groaned. "You really do not know?"

Juliana's anger made her grip the girl even harder, until she squealed.

"Tell me everything. Tell me now," she shouted. A dog barked somewhere. The girl put a hand to her mouth.

"Your baby disappeared soon after you did. Some of us thought you must have arranged it. Others said no, that the emperor or his mother arranged for the baby to disappear. They said the emperor was the father. That's why the baby had to go. I did not believe it."

"Where is my baby now?" Juliana's grip on the slave's tunic tightened again. Her head pounded. Could this be true about Constantine? Had he something to do with this?

"You're hurting me," said the slave. Her eyes were filled with fear.

210

"I don't care. Tell me everything you know, or these Saxon shield maidens will carve your heart out and I will eat it in front of you." She pressed her face close, so close to the girl she could see the rash on her forehead clearly and smell her sweat. "That's what Saxon shield maidens do. I'm sure you've heard that. Well I can tell you it is all true."

The girl let out a low wail.

Juliana was within licking distance of the girl's face.

"Do you want to see your heart?" she hissed.

The girl shook her head.

"Tell me everything."

The girl spoke quickly. "Soon after your baby disappeared, I was told to watch for men looking to gain entry to our villa. My master and mistress have two young children." She hesitated. "Please let me go."

"Come on. There is more. What else did they say?"

"Just that the followers of the nailed god were looking for babies. They use their blood in their ceremonies."

Juliana let go of the tunic, growled loudly, turned her head. A stabbing pain hit her stomach.

"Where do they have these ceremonies?"

"I don't know." The slave studied Julian's face. "Is the emperor the father?"

"Where is Constantine?"

"He is across the river, fighting in Germania." The slave girl smiled. "Do you know he is married?"

Juliana blinked. She hadn't expected Constantine to pine for her for a year and stay in his room, but she had not expected him to get married.

"To who?" Her mouth had dried.

"To Fausta, a member of the imperial family, sister to Maxentius no less, emperor of all the central provinces."

Juliana looked away, made her hand into a fist, held it rigid at her side, then said, "What else can you tell me about him?"

"Not much has changed. Constantine is still obsessed with striking fear into the heart of Germania. He helps this city with a weekly bread donation for the poor and there will be games at the end of the summer, like in the old days."

Juliana unlocked her fist. "Tell no one you saw me. If I find out anyone knows I was in Treveris, I will know it was you who spoke about this, and I will come looking for you with my friends and each of us will take a bite from your still beating heart. Do you understand?"

The girl backed away, nodding.

"Where to now?" said one of her companions.

"Back to the main street with those taverns. Then, we find out what village those men who tried to grab us were from."

When they walked back through the main street it had become rowdier than before. Many men were standing outside taverns with wine jugs in their hands. Almost all invited them to stop and try some wine. A few went further, including the men who had pawed them before. They stopped talking with these men when they found out the name of the village they had come from, and in what direction the village lay and how long it had taken them to reach Treveris.

Not all the directions were good enough to be useful, but they got enough. Getting away from each group of men was not easy, but they managed it. The best way to do it was for one of them to slip away as if seeking the latrine, only to find another group of men who could be persuaded to go back and rescue her friend. All it took was a few friendly words in a man's ear to get that done.

Twice they did this, after which they decided to head back into the side streets. They found a small taverna run by a woman and ate bread and cheese. Juliana was unable to eat. She just sat quietly, taking it all in as waves of guilt swept through her. Why had she gone to that stupid wood a year ago? Why had it been her who had been kidnapped? Why had it all happened?

Athralar and the men were literally lying low when they arrived back. It was dusk and they hadn't even started a fire. They were all on their sides in pairs, talking quietly, while three were on guard as a perimeter.

Athralar stood as she approached.

"What news?"

"My baby was taken." Her voice shook as the words came out. "A slave says the followers of the nailed god did it, but I don't believe it." She raised a fist to her mouth to stop her lips trembling. She was supposed to be their leader. She pressed her lips together, breathed in deeply.

"Constantine should have protected his baby with his life," said Athralar. "That is what any good Saxon warrior would do, protect his children first."

"There are a lot of people who would want my child dead."

"You must find them all and one by one we will beat them and cut them until they tell us what has happened."

Juliana shook her head. "It's not that easy. Constantine is not even here."

"What will we do then? Go home empty handed!" he demanded.

"I've found out the names of some villages where the men folk are enjoying a good time in Treveris. If we're careful, we can raid these villages with their men gone."

"What else did you find out?" He stared at her. "There is something you're not telling me."

She spun around to make sure no one was listening. "My blood time is late. Very late. This only happened once before, when I was pregnant." She regretted telling him for a moment, then dismissed the thought. This was the perfect time to tell him.

Athralar sighed. "So be it. There is new life coming." He put a hand on her stomach. "Soon we will feel it kicking, calling for the goddess to let it out. One thing is certain. You cannot lead the war band any longer. It is a rule that shield maidens must give up fighting while they are pregnant and while the baby is small."

Juliana felt relieved. He was right. Every day that had passed since her blood hadn't come had made her more convinced. Early morning sickness a few days before had sealed it.

"How long will it be before I can lead a war band again?"

"Long enough."

LIII

Four years later

Constantine paced up and down in the large tent set up at the center of the marching camp he'd established three days before. Outside, snow fell. It lay thick in every part of the camp.

"What use is a soothsayer, when everything he says is wrong?" shouted Constantine. Then he growled.

"It is not my fault," said the imperial slave, quickly. "These are the people you asked for."

Constantine shook his fist at the roof of the tent. It sagged in the center from the weight of the snow.

"Our whole campaign against Maxentius depends on this stupid snow stopping. If he gets word that we are at his border he will have time to get fresh troops from Africa."

The slave stared at him, an anguished expression on his face. "We can pray to the household gods. We should make an offering, a goat perhaps."

"A bloody goat is not going to save us. If Lucius was here, he would know what to do."

The slave bowed. "Shall I tell Sejanus you are ready?"

Constantine tightened the strap on his breastplate. "Yes, tell all the officers they can come in. The briefing will start."

"Sejanus wants to see you alone, my lord, before the others."

"Tell him to come." Constantine went to the brazier at the back of the tent. Its glowing coals gave off a heat that would warm any room. He heard Sejanus approaching and heard him bow, the segments of his armor creaking and scratching as they came together.

"Someone has arrived to see you, but I am not sure if you should see her."

"Who has come to this god forsaken place to find me?" He pointed at the sagging roof. "Don't they know we will all be buried under snow in the next few days?"

"It is Paulina, the priestess from Rome."

"Aaah," said Constantine. "I will see her."

A few moments later two women in heavy brown cloaks with their hoods still half over their faces pushed through the leather door of the tent. A gust of snow came in with them, settling on their shoulders.

"My lord, Constantine!" Paulina cried out as she rushed to him and the brazier he stood by. The other woman waited near the door. Paulina went down on one knee.

"Arise, Paulina. You made it. I wasn't sure you would."

"Of course I made it. I keep my word."

They hugged briefly. Paulina seemed more interested in the warm coals of the brazier than anything else.

"I knew you would come if I asked, Paulina. But messages have a troubling way of getting lost."

"Why have you stopped here?" She looked around.

"The pass cannot be done in this weather. As soon as the snowstorm is over and the road opens, we will be across and into Maxentius' territory."

"You must get through quickly, Constantine." She put her hand on his and squeezed it. He didn't react. She took her hand away.

"How is Lucius?"

"The last time I saw him, before the mid-winter, he seemed in good form. He has got used to being under house arrest. He reads a lot, mainly about old battles."

"He'd be long dead if he'd stayed in the Tullianum. You did well to get him moved out of there, Paulina."

"Maxentius trusts me, completely. He is grateful that I gave Lucius and Marcellus to him. He has two leaders of the nailed god cult in his grasp."

"He doesn't intend to kill them?"

"I've heard him say nothing about that. Anyway, he likes to delay things, string people along."

"Come, sit. You must be tired after your journey." Constantine pointed at a pair of gold rimmed wooden chairs.

Paulina dropped into one. Constantine stayed standing.

"Have you heard Maxentius talk about me?"

Paulina spoke with her hands waving about. "Maxentius is convinced you're planning a campaign in Germania. He's hoping you will waste your auxiliaries and deplete your legions."

"My letters to the senate explaining our plans helped then."

"What helped was your insistence that Maxentius not be told of your letters. It looks as if you are afraid of being attacked by him."

"So, now the moment of truth is upon us. This Alpine pass is my Rubicon. Once I am across my intentions will be clear." Constantine's tone had hardened. He made his right hand into a fist in front of him. "He will know what waits for him if he does not agree to my terms."

A noise, an inhuman groan, echoed through the tent. He looked up at the sloping leather roof. A large chunk of snow was moving down, sending the roof sagging.

He let out his breath in a whoosh. The one thing that was always outside his control right now was the weather. As he'd left Treveris for their fast march south, spring sunshine had followed them. Now they were facing the last grip of a winter that could be lethal for his troops up here in the Alpine passes.

"The weather will change tonight," said Paulina. "Give the order to strike camp and for the legions to prepare to march at first light."

Constantine stared at her, unmoving. "What makes you so sure this snow storm is coming to an end?"

"I've read your future. This moment is crucial. Give the order and you will get across the Alps before anyone knows you are coming. You will look like a winner. It will be enough to convince others not to back Maxentius. He will accede to your terms."

"Or it could be the moment I destroy my best legions." He paused. "I could doom many of the forty thousand legionaries who came into this storm with me."

"Believe me." She stepped closer to him. "The road to Segusio is open. It was not snowing in Segusio yesterday morning. Your legions will be better off there than they are here. One long night march and you can be at the gates of the city. They are not expecting you there. Your destiny is waiting for you, with one bold move."

Constantine looked down the tent at the woman Paulina had come with.

"Does this one know why you came here to meet me?"

Paulina shook her head. "She knows nothing. She is a slave."

"Slaves usually know more than we think they do."

"I trust her."

"I want you back in Maxentius' palace as soon as possible, Paulina. But she must stay here when you leave. Do you understand?"

Paulina nodded.

LIV

Lucius waved the slave away. He did not want his room cleaned. It was only an excuse for the head of the imperial slaves to check on him.

"When can I clean your rooms?" The slaves who came to his rooms, both male and female, were pushier and more direct in their speech with him than they should be to a guest of the emperor, but they knew he was really a prisoner.

Imperial slaves, he had discovered, knew what their position in the emperor's house meant and exactly how arrogant they could be. Almost all of them were young and well-proportioned with physiques a Greek sculptor could admire. And they could go anywhere they wanted in the extensive palace grounds.

Lucius wasn't allowed to go anywhere. He spent most of his time in the small courtyard his bedroom faced into, in a distant corner of the palace. And he had seen Maxentius only once since the Saturnalia mid-winter festivities.

He was tired of his rooms too, tired of the scrolls and the manuscripts that were sent to him and tired of the slave girl who came to entertain him at night once a month. The last time she had come he had sent her away.

Which was probably why they wanted to clean his room. The slaves had most likely been told they would be rewarded for any letter or notes they found, expecting he'd started a relationship with one of their own, but he wasn't that stupid.

He didn't have any letters. He didn't send any or get any.

His family sent him nothing, which fitted well with his story that he'd left the cult that his family adhered to in the east and was now a follower of the old gods.

Maxentius had never indicated how long Lucius would stay like this. Lucius could only assume that keeping him waiting was an intended part of his ordeal. And the thought that on any morning a praetorian with a hard face and a sharp blade might arrive for him did ensure that he slept badly and mostly in the afternoons.

But at least that end would be quick.

His last meeting with a friendly face had been when he'd met Paulina at a Saturnalia party, when he was allowed wander the emperor's quarters, but even then a slave had followed him constantly, within earshot, so he hadn't been able to speak to her properly, only exchange greetings and good wishes.

For entertainment Lucius had taken up writing poetry. He had hand copied every one of Ovid's poems of exile, twice, in the hope that the great master's patterns of thought would penetrate his mind and help him construct something to show for his time under house arrest.

It hadn't worked. Even he knew that. But there were many uses of poetry. He took the parchment in front of him and made a correction. Now it read:

> Either he was foul, or his attire was bad,
> Or he was not the man I wished t'have.
> Idly I lay with him, as if I loved,
> And like a burden grieved the nailed bed that moved not.
> And now I face the daemon inside.
> Yet though both of us performed to our true intent,
> I now cast anchor to what I meant.

He called for a slave. The young boy came quickly.

"Ask the head of the emperor's household to have this read out at the feast tonight."

The slave nodded and took the parchment. At the door he turned and said. "Who will I say composed this?"

"Tell them it is my composition. I want my name read out." He pointed at the slave, then waved at him to be gone. He was a long way from getting messages to Constantine, but at least he had hope now.

LV

Juliana listened to the sound of the Roman trumpet. The note was clear, which meant that Constantine's camp was not far away. She'd been looking forward to this moment for many moons, but now it was here the moment seemed empty, as if all her expectation had robbed it of meaning.

It had been a big risk coming here, and she still had doubts, but the tug of her missing child and her urge to see Constantine could not be dismissed now that she, at last, had the freedom to act as she wanted.

"We move slow now. No killing Roman scouts, Athralar."

"But why, we are near a Roman army and this snowstorm means we can kill their rear scouts, cut their supply lines and they'll never come out to fight us while this snow falls." He waved at the snow falling around them. "This is our chance, Juliana. Let's take it."

They were gathered around a fire at the edge of a wood. The branches above protected them from the worst of the snow. Four war bands had combined for a spring campaign. On Juliana's orders they were following the tracks of the army Constantine had led through the Alps.

"There is more glory for us all in waiting. That is the end of it, Athralar. Bring me some roast pig as soon as it is cooked. We need some." Juliana pointed at the two shield maidens who accompanied her everywhere since she had been placed as leader of the war bands.

Three summers she'd lived and trained in the arts of war in Athralar's village, while her baby was born and sucked and grew until now, when he was able to walk, it was decreed that she could take her rightful place again leading the war bands.

Athralar's mother and sister had helped her in many ways. They looked after her child for part of each day, soothed her when she was ill and whispered many words of advice on how to deal with the men all around them.

The children of the Saxons were brought up together from a young age, so that if a parent died there would be plenty of other adults to support the child. Parents were also warned to be cool to their children, as much as they could, as the risk of any child dying was high, with almost half failing to reach maturity. Investing too many hopes in each child would only see that adult in never ending pain if the natural order of the gods was carried out and half their children were taken quickly to the great forest in the sky.

The shield maidens looked at Athralar with expectant faces. When he turned on his heel and headed away they giggled.

"You have him wrapped around your thumb," said Frigg, the oldest of the shield maidens, named after the goddess, and as powerful looking with long flaxen hair as any would expect the real Frigg to be.

"He needs someone to explain things to him, that's all," said Juliana. "Like most men."

The shield maiden smiled.

Juliana pulled her wolf skin cloak tighter around herself. She sat on the bottom of the cloak, but even though it was the thickest she had ever worn, she could still feel the cold of the ground under her.

"What is your plan?" said Frigg.

"We are going to visit the Roman camp."

The three shield maidens stared at her, then looked at each other and made surprised faces.

"Why? We don't talk to Romans. They speak with forked tongues."

"I know this Roman commander. If you want glory you will do as I say." She watched as Athralar returned with a willow basket piled with slabs of pork and black bread. He passed the basket to Juliana.

223

"I only fetched food for our leader," he said, looking around, his expression hard, as if suppressing something.

"Soon you will get to prove your manly prowess with all my shield maidens, Athralar. The time of your glory is coming, but you must follow my orders. This is what your mother said. We have a mighty task ahead to win glory and spoils. It can only be done with cunning and courage."

Athralar chewed on a thick strip of pork. Hot juices streamed from his mouth into his beard. He raised his hand in a thumbs up gesture and looked from Juliana to the faces of the other shield maidens. His eye twinkled as he looked at them. Each of them stared back at him, hard eyed.

"Go on, pass the food around," he said.

LVI

East of Brigantio, Cottian Alps, Southern Gaul, 312 A.D.

Constantine woke at dawn. The troops had already been wakened and were even now pulling apart the palisade wall of the camp, strapping the best tree trunks to mules and pulling down tents. The mule train was one of the biggest he had ever seen. He wondered again if he should have gone to the expense of getting strings of pack horses, instead of mules. They would be able to manage deeper snow drifts. Hopefully Paulina was right, and they wouldn't have to deal with snow drifts much longer.

Paulina slept on. She would have to be wakened soon.

A warning horn sounded from the gate facing back to Gaul. It was a long note, signaling the arrival of someone at the gate, but not immediate danger. Who would be crossing the alps in this weather, he wondered?

His optio and two of the imperial family slaves were packing up the last items from his tent. All that remained untouched was the large, double sized camp bed, in which Paulina slept, and the thick carpet underneath it. As he looked down at her, her black hair around her like a wing, a voice called out hesitantly behind him.

"My lord, visitors asking for you."

He turned to the messenger, a legionary with a wolf skin cloak. "Who is it?"

"Three women. They were armed." He paused. "With axes. We took their weapons. They are waiting at the west gate."

"Bring them to me," he said. He went to the end of the bed where his breastplate and sword were waiting on a dark wooden trunk. He motioned his optio forward. Together they strapped his breastplate on. He put his sword and sheath and the wide belt that held it on the end of the bed, told the optio to have his last trunk taken and went to the double flap at the front of the tent.

It shouldn't take long to deal with an embassy from a local tribe. He would see what they had to say, and if they were peaceful they would be met with peace. If not, they would be sent away with a warning to match any insolence.

He watched as the figures approached. All around, legionaries were busy in the gloom, lit only by spluttering torches in stands along the camp paths and in front of each tent. Men hurried across the path the visitors were approaching on. The three women were surrounded by six guards. The head of the gate house watch was clearly exaggerating the possibility that these women could be a danger although they were tall, all of them. And the one in the center walked the way Juliana used to walk, with a slight swagger, as if she knew everyone was watching her.

The snow fell thicker now. He put his hand out. Definitely thicker.

Constantine stepped back into the tent. He couldn't talk to them outside. He didn't care if Paulina was visible in the bed at the back. There would normally have been a purple curtain shielding his private quarters from the main part of his tent, where there was usually a large table and a lot of chairs and braziers, but all that was packed away already.

The centurion of the watch entered first.

"My lord," he shouted, "three Saxon shield maidens." He had a bemused expression, which Constantine put down to the fact that any Saxons had come so far to find him.

Two giant blonde shield maidens entered first. They looked like the type who wouldn't need weapons to kill you.

They stood one on each side of the flap. It had closed behind them. A hand gripped the flap from outside and pulled it open slowly. There was something weirdly familiar about the hand. His stomach tightened as if it knew something his conscious mind didn't.

A woman's head came into view. A jumble of thoughts swarmed like bees in his head. He let out a roar.

"Juliana, back from the dead!"

He raised his arms and took a step toward her. She shook her head. It was only a tiny movement, but it was clear to him that she didn't want to be hugged.

He gripped her shoulders, then let her go. It was Juliana, but she was different. She never wore her hair braided like this when she was with him.

"Where have you been hiding? Come in. The last brazier has yet to be taken. We are about to march. You are lucky you caught us."

They walked side by side to the brazier in front of the bed, their arms touching occasionally. Every time he touched her the hairs on his arm stood up and something warm stirred inside him.

Paulina still hadn't moved. Only her black hair was visible from where they stood, warming their hands at the brazier.

"Who is this?" said Juliana, nodding toward the bed.

Constantine held a hand up for silence, looked around, and waved away an optio and a slave.

"Leave us alone," he said.

He stared at Juliana. This was the woman he'd lived with up until a few years ago. Mixed feelings rose up inside him; anger, relief, surprise. He looked her up and down. Until a few moments before he'd believed she was dead. Crocus and others had told him she was probably sacrificed at some tribal ceremony. Every month for the first year he'd sent our more messengers to look for her, but none had returned with good news and after a year he'd stopped.

He took a step back. Then another. It felt as if the ground had moved underneath his feet.

"You couldn't have escaped?"

"I couldn't at the beginning. Then I heard you'd remarried, and I had a child. I did not think you would want me with a Saxon's baby on my arm. I prayed to the great mother and she helped me, but I had to put many things aside." Her hand shook as she raised it to her mouth.

Constantine pointed at the back of the tent.

"That's Paulina. She's a priestess from Rome. She came here late last night. That is why she is in my bed." He groaned, waved a hand through the air in exasperation. "And yes, I am married now, to Fausta, the sister of Maxentius, the emperor in Rome." He kept staring at Juliana. She was older, her skin paler, her brow furrowed in a way he'd never seen before, as if she'd been marked by something. He looked at her hands. One had a leather covering.

"What happened to your hand?"

"It was burnt, but it is good now. Fausta is not here?" asked Juliana, turning on her heel.

She seemed pent up, as if she wanted to say something.

"No, she will join us later in the campaign."

"When you have taken Rome?"

He gave her a half smile.

She let out her breath fast. "We need to talk about Julius." She raised her fist, pressed it to her lips. Her eyes blazed. "Every night I pray for him. That the great mother helps me find him." Her voice cracked with emotion. She had to stop speaking for a few moments. She closed her eyes, turned away from him.

"I am sorry." Constantine touched her arm. "He was kidnapped while I was looking for you." He threw his hands in the air, then made two fists and shook them at her. "We searched everywhere. Crocus tortured two slaves. We found out nothing. There was no ransom demand. We expected one. Then I thought he would be used as a bargaining coin when some Germanic tribe wanted something. We raided Germania twice looking for you both. I almost died. Many legionaries did." He raised his hands high.

"We formed alliances too, and the messengers went out far and wide. Some never came back." He groaned as he remembered.

"I did not abandon you to your fate. I did everything I could. And more. What in Hades name happened to you?" He placed a hand on her upper arm, squeezed it, and pulled her to him.

She shrugged his hand away.

"I was kidnapped." She was angry. "I'm lucky to be alive. I challenged my kidnappers, joined a war band and now I lead them. I was blessed by our great mother. My war band is now ten leagues behind your army with three others who follow my command. Four hundred Saxons waiting on my word as to when to attack you as you make your way over this pass." She pushed her jaw forward. Her lips were trembling.

Constantine took in the leather breastplate and arm protectors she wore and the ornamental belt with small skulls in bronze decorating it around her middle.

"Four hundred Saxons." He paused. "Following you?"

"I am not your little slave anymore."

"You never were little, Juliana. And you were always full of fire." He laughed. "I should not be surprised."

"I paid a price in blood to lead these men."

"Are there many more like these guards in your war band?" he said, pointing at the entrance to the tent where the shield maidens waited.

"There are more like these scattered through our number."

"Our number. You are a Saxon now?" Constantine raised his hand, as if he would push her away. "How did you come to this in a few short years?" He pointed at her. "You were sworn to me."

"I was your slave and then your concubine, yes. But I also helped you. And I am from a royal line myself. All this was not an accident." Her voice rose. "This was predicted for me. I have my child back in Germania. Many things have changed." She pushed her jaw forward.

He stared at her, his mouth open. Things would never be the same between them.

"When will your war band attack us?"

Juliana looked over Constantine's shoulder at Paulina, then moved closer to him.

He could sense her presence all over his body, as if she had touched him.

Juliana looked in his eyes.

She was still beautiful, but there was a hardness there he hadn't seen before.

"A slave in Treveris told me Maxentius arranged for our son to be kidnapped. That he's being brought up at the emperor's palace

229

in Rome. I expect they wait for him to be old enough to be appointed as your blood heir." Her voice was steady now.

"What?" said Constantine. The force of the news sent his head back. Was this why Maxentius had given up Crispus so easily when he'd married Fausta? He turned. Paulina was sitting up in the bed and leaning forward, listening.

"Did you know this?" he shouted at her.

"No, I swear," said Paulina. "Maxentius never spoke about a son of yours. This is a lie. This woman wants to get inside your head. Do not believe this." She almost spat the last word out.

Constantine raised a hand, as if to ward away the news.

"What proof do you have of this, Juliana?"

"It is why I came here." Her tone was hard. "I heard you were marching on Rome. The slave in Treveris will swear that Julius is there. Do you think I'm so weak-kneed for you I would bring all these Saxon warriors here just to help you?"

"What about your plan to attack us?"

Her lips parted in a most inviting way. "We will not attack. Let us join forces with you as auxiliaries for your campaign."

A flowery smell filled his nostrils. Constantine breathed her in. "Now you make me happy."

Paulina stood. Her thin cotton night gown left little to the imagination. She came to Constantine's side and glared at Juliana.

Juliana raised her hand, as if she would swot Paulina away.

"Stop this," said Constantine. He looked from Juliana to Paulina. "Both of you. There will be no cat fights in my tent." He took Paulina's arm and pulled her to the bed. "Get dressed for the road. I will talk to you later." Then he returned to Juliana.

"I will not rest until our son is back in our arms. You have come at the right moment. I welcome you and your warriors. We will head for Rome together." He closed his eyes and shook his head as his thoughts raced. "It is far better that I confront Maxentius. He sees any weakness as an opportunity." He raised his hands, spread them wide. "I must force him to give up our son. Maxentius only responds to force. I have learnt this the hard way." He pointed at Juliana.

A jug of watered wine stood on a table at the side of the tent. Some silver mugs were upturned beside it. He went to the table and poured the wine into two of the mugs. He could feel her standing behind him. He turned, handed her a mug.

"We have another problem," said Juliana.

"What?"

"Not all my commanders know about this plan."

"How many do?" He felt his anger coming back.

She looked at the floor of the tent.

He groaned. "You haven't told any of them about your plan."

"No, not yet."

Juliana put her head to one side and opened her mouth, as if something had dawned on her. "I am sure you will pay handsomely for auxiliaries."

LVII

Maxentius' Palace, Rome, 312 A.D.

Lucius stood by the door leading out of his rooms. Dawn approached. He had a marble statuette in his hand. This was the appointed time when a new slave would replace the one who had been assigned to watch over him during the night.

The night slave was in a deep sleep, brought on by the herbs Lucius had saved up, which the physician had given him after he complained bitterly of back pain for a month.

The door opened. The day slave that came in was a young woman. She went to close the door and saw him standing with the marble statuette up. Her mouth opened, as if she would scream. He quickly motioned her to be quiet, held the statuette higher, then put a hand over her mouth and pulled her to him. He could not smash her skull.

If it had been a big Illyrian he would have had to and the man would have only had a headache after, but if he hit this girl her skull would cave in.

He'd seen it happen. The smell of brains was not something he wanted in his rooms.

"Be quiet, and I will not kill you."

She muffled a reply through his fingers. He pushed the door closed behind her. Someone was walking in the corridor outside.

He let his grip loosen on her mouth.

"Not a sound," he said.

"I have to lock the door, master, or the guards outside will know something is wrong," she said. One of her hands came up. In it was a long door key.

"Do it," he said, "but if you call the guard you will not live much longer." He raised the statuette.

"What is this about, master. What do you want?"

He looked her up and down. "Come to my room."

She followed him. The other slave lay sleeping in the atrium, at the back, where two chairs sat. He couldn't be seen. This slave he took to his bedroom.

As soon as he reached the room, he turned to her and said. "Take your tunic off."

She looked around, then smiled and undid her tunic so it fell to the floor. "You did not have to threaten violence for this, master." She raised her hands and twirled. Her breasts were small but perfectly formed. Lucius picked up the cups of wine he had laid out and passed one to her.

"Drink to our new friendship," he said, passing her the red cup.

She hesitated. "We are not supposed to drink with our masters," she said.

"I am ordering you to." He drank from his, then downed the rest. "Come on. You will enjoy it." He rubbed his fingers along her bare shoulder.

She downed the wine.

It was some time before she fell asleep, long enough for them to consummate properly and for her to show him everything she liked. She was the best he'd had in a long time. It would be a shame to see her punished for what was about to happen.

He left her sleeping deeply in his bed, checked the other slave was still snoring in the atrium and went to the door out to the corridor. He wouldn't have long. One of them could wake up, but they'd probably spend time looking for him before calling the guard. They would be the first ones to suffer if he had escaped.

But he didn't intend to escape. It was one thing getting out of his room. It would something else entirely to escape the palace. Maxentius often boasted about the number of guards posted on every wall and gate to his palace. Only those with a password would be allowed through and torches would be burning at this hour by the gates and walls. No, he had something else in mind. One of the other slaves who visited him had told him something.

He opened the door a crack. No sound came from the corridor outside. He opened the door a little wider. The sound of hob nails on marble echoed from far away. He closed the door gently and waited, listening at the wood for the guard on his rounds to pass.

When the corridor was quiet again, he opened the door, put his head out a little and looked one way, then the other. He knew from going to visit the emperor that there were three other doors on this corridor. He also knew that the same key would work in each door, he had seen a slave use the same key to lock another half open door and then to open his.

He slipped silently out in his bare feet and went straight to the nearest door and put the key in. He turned it slowly. If anyone called out, he would scarper back to his room, lock the door and wake the night slave. Neither of the slaves would admit that he might have left his room. They had seen too many other slaves being punished in bizarre ways to be honest about any mistake they made.

He turned the key, pushed the door open a little and listened. No voice shouted out. He pushed the door open some more. He could see into the gloom inside. This was a storeroom. Blankets and twig brooms filled the tiny room. He went to the next door. His heart pounded.

He turned the key, stopped. A voice called out from beyond the door. His hand was on the key. He pulled it out slowly. He looked up the corridor and was about to run when an answering voice told him immediately what was going on behind the door. A child was up early and playing.

LVIII

Juliana put her hand on Athralar's shoulder. "You will get what you dreamed. You will be part of an attack on Rome itself, the city that represents everything that the Saxons hate. That you hate. Why would you not want to be part of that? Think of the spoils."

Athralar stood under a tree apart from the others. His wolf skin cloak was stiff with ice and snow. He stamped his feet, then pulled his cloak tighter.

"You want us to fight alongside a Roman emperor!" he shouted. He made fists with his hands and grimaced, so his yellow teeth stood out in his mouth like an angry bear's.

Juliana put a hand up to placate him. The snow fell thinly now.

"Many other war bands fight for the Romans. We will be paid every four months and we will get a share of the spoils in every victory." She leaned close to him. "We are marching to Rome to sack it. Imagine that. What riches that must be there, waiting for us? This is our lucky day. Frigg has smiled on us and so has Woden." She slapped his shoulder. Snow and ice fell around their feet.

"But you are doing this for him." His eyes narrowed and he pointed at the Roman camp. "You are doing this for Constantine." He paused, shook his head. "It feels as if you tricked me."

"This is not a trick. Do you want us to attack this Roman army now, here, or attack Rome. You will be among the first Saxons to do this." She pushed her face toward him, the sinews on her neck stretching.

"Because I will order this, with or without your support. It's the best thing for all our people. Remember too, that my son is back in our village. I do not want him to find out that we are both dead on this pass."

"You are assuming again that I am the father."

"Frigg's priestess confirmed it for me before we came here, Athralar. You cannot deny it because I had one night with someone else. It is clear from the boy's markings and mannerisms that he is yours. That is what the priestess said and what will be in his story whenever it is spoken."

"What about the others? Have you told them about your plan?"

Juliana shook her head. She reached into the leather satchel that hung from her shoulder. She pulled out a large leather coin bag and passed it to Athralar. "For you, from him."

Athralar looked inside the bag. He pulled out a gold coin, examined it, tested it with his teeth.

"He pays well."

"That is because I told him you were the best warrior between here and the frozen seas."

"But I am." Athralar stood taller, pushed his shoulders out.

"They may argue with that." She pointed along the tree line. The pine trees were heavy with snow, as if caps had been placed on them. Two of the other raiding party leaders were trudging toward them, their axes hanging from their belts.

"Will you help me persuade them?"

"On one condition," said Athralar.

"What is it?"

"That you do not go rutting with Constantine."

Juliana looked up at him. "He wants it, yes, I can tell, but he will not be getting it."

Athralar laughed. "You play us all, don't you, shield-maiden, Juliana."

LVIX

Athralar looked down from the hill overlooking Segusio. Behind the fortified town the Alps, snow-capped all the way down their sides, loomed. The snow was still visible in patches on the road heading back up toward the pass, but it had stopped snowing for long enough to give hope that winter was over early in the Alps.

"It will take a month, maybe two, to get inside those walls." Athralar pointed at the giant, cliff-life, dark stone walls of the town. "I hear they are double the height of any one of our ladders."

Juliana continued polishing the sharp edge of her axe with a small shiny whetstone. It was the best one the war band had. They passed it each day to the next person in line. And every time you got it you had to make sure you used it for as long as possible during your day.

The ability of an axe, sword or dagger to cut through flesh was obvious, what concerned the warriors more was the ability of a blade to cut through a shield, breastplate or helmet.

"I told you before, Juliana, longer strokes make for a sharper blade. You like longer strokes, don't you?" He grinned.

Juliana walked away, down the hill to the palisade around the Roman army camp. She had been given a gold imperial token, which allowed her, with the right password, to get in and out of the Roman camp without too many questions.

The camp buzzed with early morning activity. Lines of legionaries were marching toward the far camp gate, probably to relieve the men who had been up all night manning the stockade perimeter fence that had been set up around the town. Gaps had been left in the stockade in the hope that the town's defenders would make a run for it straight into a killing zone, but that hadn't happened, so far.

They had laid siege to the town for four days now and the ultimatum to the town's leaders to surrender or face the consequences had passed two days before. Constantine's artillery and sling shooters were practicing on the defenders every time one showed his head, getting their range and testing the stones they had picked up on the narrow mountain road which had brought them here.

They would keep their iron pellets until a proper assault was mounted. As Juliana neared the imperial tent, she saw three of the senior officers, older looking legates with their scarlet cloaks flying and their red helmet plumes nodding, signifying their senior status, as they marched away from Constantine's tent.

The leather door of the tent opened as she neared. Constantine looked out. He smiled when he saw her and waved Juliana forward. Then he whispered something to one of the guards outside. They waited with spears crossed to prevent anyone entering.

"Come in, you are just in time. The ceremony is about to begin." Constantine pointed up the tent to where another group of officers, a mix of tribunes and legates, stood in rows around a large table. On the table, purple wooden blocks were set out around a green square.

"Juliana is the leader of the Saxon war band that has joined with us. Give her room," shouted Constantine, as he reached the table. "Your presence begins a new era for us, Juliana. Women leading auxiliary units hasn't been tried in a long time." He looked around, daring anyone to make a comment. No one did.

"I think Marcus Aurelius tried it last," someone said. "To some good effect."

At the head of the table stood Paulina. She had a wide engraved silver band running through her hair and her gown, which was also silver, had an opening cut to down to her belly button. She raised her hands high when Juliana came near the table.

"A Saxon shield-maiden, a follower of Woden, no doubt, is here to add her spirt to our proceedings. It is a good omen."

A mumble went through the crowd.

Seeing the crowd of officers gave Juliana a sense of the size of the army. Her own war band would have done no more damage against them than a horsefly attacking a bear.

"Silence," shouted Paulina. She was clearly used to being in command of a large group of men.

The officers fell silent around them. Only the clinking of armor could be heard in the large tent.

Paulina bent down and picked up a polished wooden bowl and placed it on the table in front of her.

Juliana's nose wrinkled. The smell of human blood and organs is not something you easily forget.

From the back of the tent hand-cymbals made a prolonged jangling noise. When they stopped all that could be heard was Paulina mumbling. Everyone else had gone quiet.

Paulina raised a hand. In it was an oddly shaped piece of meat.

A heart.

Dripping blood.

Juliana had seen human hearts after they were cut out of an enemy's chest before.

A jangling from the back of the tent started, as if a fever of expectation had come upon whoever was ringing the hand bells.

Paulina motioned with her free hand for Constantine to come to her. When he was beside her at the top of the room the jangling stopped. Paulina held the heart toward him.

"In the name of the gods of Rome, for Jupiter, and Juno, Minerva, Neptune and Mars, Diana and Venus, I offer to share in this blood sacrifice with you so you receive the strength of this great warrior and you are filled with his courage for the battle ahead." She bit into the heart then held it toward Constantine.

He bit into it. Red trails of blood and heart muscle covered his chin. Constantine stared at the heart, as if wondering what to do next.

Then he looked down the tent at Juliana and with a side movement of his head he called her to him.

Juliana had no choice. She went to stand beside Constantine. He motioned with his hand for Juliana to bite the heart. She could smell it now. It was at least a day old and would be stinking to the heavens soon.

She tightened her stomach, put her mouth forward and took a bite. A taste of iron and salt filled her mouth. This heart was hard. She bit off only a tiny bit, but it felt as if it would catch in her throat. She coughed.

Constantine laughed. "She is one of us now. Come, the most senior officers of my legions, follow the example of the shield maiden."

Juliana was pushed to one side as the officers came up and bit into the heart.

Each man let out a roar as he did so. Many raised their fists. After ten men had taken a bite the heart was a mess and blood from it had splattered all over Paulina's dress and on the table.

Paulina raised her hand to speak. "Each of the men who partakes will be protected by all our gods."

At the other end of the tent a sudden commotion broke out. Shouts came from outside.

"I'll be back," said Constantine. He headed for the front of the tent, leaving the crowd of officers around Paulina.

Juliana followed him.

He stopped at the tent flap and gripped her arm. "This was the best way to get my officers to trust you. You can wipe your mouth and clean up over there." He pointed at a table with glass pitchers of water on it and small yellow drying cloths.

She shook her head. "I want to find out what's going on," she said. She wiped at her mouth, taking away everything but a red stain.

Constantine stepped outside the tent, followed by Juliana. A runner, a legionary with no heavy armor, was arguing with one of the imperial guards.

"I need to see him," said the runner, loudly.

"Who?" shouted Constantine.

The runner turned. He went pale and his mouth opened.

"Speak, man," said Constantine.

"I, I have a message for you." He bowed low.

"Get on with it."

The messenger looked up and smiled. "The battering ram is ready."

Constantine made a fist and shouted, "Now it begins." He turned to Juliana. "Let's see if your axe men can help. Can you find me ten who will come with me to the town gate?"

"Yes," said Juliana. "Right away." She turned and headed back out through the Roman camp.

LV

Maxentius' Palace, Rome, 312 A.D.

Lucius felt for the key in his pocket. It was still there. He sighed. It was a week since his adventure in the corridor. Neither of the slaves had said anything when they woke. The night slave had been fearful he'd slept too long. The day slave had been fearful she'd slept at all.

The night slave had also come back the following day, looking for her key. She didn't find it. Lucius had hidden it well. And now was his opportunity to use it. The night slave slept again, with her key tied around her neck this time.

Lucius smoothed down his toga. It was the best clothing he had. He slipped the key in the lock, turned it and cracked the door open.

No one could be seen in the corridor outside. He walked out. His legs were trembling. If they decided to punish him, they could do anything they wanted, break his bones at each section, burn his eyes out or cut his tongue or his nose off.

He put those thoughts from his mind. He had to. He had no choice. He couldn't languish here without hope any longer. He needed hope. Hope that a friendly person would speak up for him with Maxentius. Hope that he had a chance of escaping all this. Paulina clearly didn't have much influence over Maxentius, but he knew someone who did.

She was his hope now.

He couldn't expect Constantine to come and free him. Valeria, the empress, Maxentius' wife, was who he had to see. And her rooms were not far away. Past the guards beyond the next door, then across a courtyard and past the guards at the entrance to her rooms.

It couldn't be that hard.

He had the password. He'd threatened his day slave with revealing her many unforgivable errors to get it. The woman clearly knew that a slave who was unreliable would be lucky to see the next dawn or to see it only for the purpose of prolonging the agony of torture.

The head of this imperial household liked making examples of slaves who broke rules.

The door at the end of the corridor was close. It looked as if it never opened, but he knew as soon as he knocked on it the door would open, and there'd be surprise on the face of the guard who looked at him. Lucius' lips moved as he practiced what he was going to say one last time.

He stood with his hand up ready to knock for a long moment. A part of him said, go back, don't risk it. Another part said, no, knock now, quickly. His hand hung in front of the door.

He did it. He knocked hard.

The response took longer than he'd imagined, and the door opened slowly, but finally a hard face looked at him.

The guard shouted at the other guards behind him. "Prisoner in the corridor." A rustling and a clanking of men in armor moving could be heard.

Then the door opened.

A wide faced older man, with pock marks down one side of his face and hair cut as short as was humanly possible stared at him, his right hand on the pommel of his sword, an angry expression on his face.

"What in Hades name are you doing in the corridor and knocking on this door. I will have that slave's guts for a bow string."

They stared into each other's eyes for a long moment. It seemed as if Lucius would be unable to speak. A grunt sounded from one of the other guards.

"Empress Valeria Maximilla has summoned me. I am to go straight to her rooms. She gave me the password." His voice sounded like someone else's.

"Go on."

"Juno," he said, confidently. He wanted to turn and run. There was a good chance the slave had tricked him. Perhaps that was the word that got you arrested. He stared straight ahead, waiting for the punch to his gut, signifying it was all about to begin.

The leader of the guards stared at him, his eyes bulging. Then a smile blossomed on his lips.

"Why didn't you say so. I will have two of my best men escort you there right away." He turned to his men, pointed at two of them and then with his thumb, back at Lucius.

"Make sure our guest doesn't get lost," he said. "And wait for him and escort him straight back. No messing. Understood?" Two wide shouldered guards saluted and stared grim faced at Lucius. The door opened wide.

The first part of his plan had worked. The more dangerous part was now approaching. The empress was the key to everything.

LVI

Outside the Walls of Segusio, Cottian Alps, 312 A.D.

All day and all night the fighting raged. The walls of Segusio had the reputation of being unconquerable, and perhaps they would be, but Constantine had a plan. He ordered attack ladders to be strapped together to make them almost double height, and that they be used in the area of the gate, concentrating them, and his archers, and his infantry and sling shooters at this, the most vulnerable part of the town walls.

The battering ram had been sharpened too and brought up to near the gate, just outside the reach of the enemy arrows. Dawn was hours away. This was their chance. The rest of the army could rest while a cohort, five hundred men, from the II Augusta Legio took the attack to the main city gate. The legion had proved itself in the far north of Britannia, against any number of impenetrable-looking mountain forts.

"I'm going in with them," he said, looking at the legates of the two legions who would be involved in the early morning attack.

Both men had their brightest breastplates on with the gold medallions they'd won on major campaigns shining on them. Their slaves were clearly good at polishing. The legate from the II Augusta was a tall, bony faced man with a hard Gaulish accent. He'd been dropped into his position when the previous legate had expressed surprise at Constantine's strategy of taking his legion this far south.

That meant one important thing. This man would be loyal to Constantine, the man who had raised him up.

Constantine pointed at the legate from II Augusta. "Your men will support the battering ram. I want legionaries in a tortoise on either side."

The legate stiffened and saluted.

"Yes, sir."

Constantine turned to the other legate. "As soon as we start moving all torches are to be extinguished on the road. We know where the gate is. I want fire arrows raining down on the wall above the gate, and iron sling shots raining down in a constant fury, and every ballista and scorpion you have firing non-stop. This is our moment. We take this stupid village this morning." He raised his fist. The officers around him did the same. A cheer went up.

Constantine waved at Sejanus and headed down the hill to where the road into the town turned and headed to the gate. Torches at regular intervals lit the path. On the roadway stood the battering ram, a tree trunk shaped into an iron shod point, hanging inside a long, roofed cart. The cart had been covered in red tiles.

The centurion leading the team of thirty brawny legionaries saluted as Constantine and Sejanus approached.

"I will be coming up to the gate with you," said Constantine. He looked around. Legionaries from other units were staring at him. It wasn't that unusual for senior officers to be part of the front line. It was unusual for an emperor to do so.

And it was well known that Maxentius was not a fighter. Constantine had heard that some thought it foolhardy for him to do this, that his life was worth more than any one victory, but he knew not to listen to such voices. The will and determination of a legion were the critical reasons for its victory, especially if it was going to face larger forces.

The will and determination of a legion could be lifted by its men seeing that the man they were fighting for was willing to stand with them, to endure the same dangers and revel in the same victories.

The legionaries under the roof of the battering ram had all stripped off their breastplates and were standing bare chested, with their helmets on, waiting for the signal to start pushing the wheeled carriage to the gate.

Sejanus strode a step behind Constantine as they came up to the cart.

Constantine turned to him. "You will wait here. Take command if I don't make it and fight on to Rome. Juliana will tell you why."

"Yes, sir," said Sejanus.

That was what Constantine liked about him. He didn't argue. He carried out his tasks without a word or a look that showed he disagreed.

Constantine went to the front of the cart. Two burly legionaries helped him remove his breastplate. With the sides of the cart covered over he would be protected until the gate broke open. At that point, the men at the side and coming up behind would pour into the town. What mattered was getting the gate open.

Constantine went to the first place in the cart. The man there went to the back.

"Let's do this together," he shouted. "Fast forward."

It took a few slow paces before the wheels of the cart started turning properly. A slight incline slowed the pace, but as the town had been built on the floor of the valley it was not as difficult as pushing the battering ram up a steep hill, which these men would have done.

A thin slit in the wooden front of the cart allowed him to see the gate ahead. It was made of thick tree trunks with iron bands holding it together. A lot would depend on the momentum of their first strike. A whistling sound filled the air and a noise like hail falling followed moments later. Groans sounded from the ramparts above. Another whoosh and a rain of fire arrows descended on the walls.

Before going into battle Constantine always felt exhilaration. His training and planning were about to be put to the test. Victory would be sweet. He knew its taste. But there was always a hint of fear too. He had to face the reality that if he made a mistake, thousands of his men might die, with him among them. Had he thought of everything?

"Faster," he roared, pushing harder. "Faster than you have ever pushed before. Let's break this gate on the first blow." The cart rumbled along now, bobbing up and down as it moved along the stone paved road. A bigger bump came and went, knocking some of the men's hands from the wooden beams they were pushing, but they all got their hold again, except one legionary who ended up being run over by a wheel and left groaning in the road in their wake.

A rain of fire arrows pelted down on top of them. He could see the glow of them as they splattered into the felt of the battering ram's covering.

"Where are the archers?" he shouted.

As if in reply a thumping sounded from the walls now looming above them. The ballistas had been loosened. Long iron-tipped missiles were striking the walls. Then a sound like hail filled the air as arrows from his side hissed over the walls far above them.

"Faster," he shouted, as he pushed with all his might on the beam of wood on his side of the cart. This was the moment to build speed up. A roar like the wind in a storm came from his left. He turned his head. A big red glow became visible through cracks in the wood.

His shoulders ached, muscles bunching as he pushed on, bending into his task. If they didn't break through, they could all burn alive. It would have been better to have tiles on the sides as well as the roof, but the weight would have been too much for the cart to move fast and be pushed up a hill. More roars went up on either side of the cart as fire arrows took hold. He looked through the slit. The gate neared. Rocks that had strewn the road, thrown down by the defenders, had been pushed aside by teams of legionaries working under upraised shields through the night. The path ahead was clear.

"Faster, men. Faster. We're nearly there," he shouted. The rumbling from the wheels came up through his bones. A crashing noise from above and then a trembling ran through the cart. Something had hit the roof.

They kept going.

He looked through the slit. "A little to the left," he shouted. "Push!"

With a bone jarring crash the cart hit the gate, sending many of the men pushing it to the ground.

Constantine was among them.

He tasted grit. He stood, looked through the slit. He could have touched the gate if he reached out his hand to it. He didn't. A clattering of arrows and spears and the gods only knew what else, rained down. The gate had not broken.

LVII

Juliana stood with Athralar and the ten men he had picked to join the attack on the gate. The hillock they were on was the same one Constantine and his officers had met on a little while before. Sejanus stood nearby talking to the lead trumpeter and four senior centurions.

"We go there now," said Athralar. He pointed at the main gate. The cart carrying the battering ram had just hit it.

"No, we wait for the signal," said Juliana. "I told you."

Athralar passed his axe from hand to hand. "We can help now," he said.

"They know what they're doing," said Juliana.

Sejanus waved at Juliana. His thumb went up.

"Let's go," said Juliana.

"No, you wait here," said Athralar.

"And let you have all the glory, no, I am with you." She shouted out the last word. She didn't want to show how scared she felt. And that the fear made her breath come fast. This was the first large scale attack she had ever been part of. Doubts gnawed at her.

But she knew she had to be part of this attack. The Romans, officers and men, were watching. They would assume she was simply Athralar's concubine if all she did was watch him take the lead. And he would see her differently too if she didn't join him.

But if she did this right, if she helped achieve victory, she wouldn't have to be at the front line next time. Anyway, what could go wrong with Athralar and the best men from their war bands beside her? Constantine fought in the thick of any engagement. He would see her. She would not be the slave girl he only wanted to keep his bed warm anymore. She had to do this.

They were beside Sejanus.

"As soon as you see the gate on fire, take your men to it and use your axes to open it up," said Sejanus. "Let's see what you can do."

Athralar lifted his axe and swung it from side to side as if he wanted to lop Sejanus' head off. Two of the centurions behind Sejanus put their hands on the pommels of their swords.

"My friend is getting himself ready," said Juliana. "Come, Athralar, let's do this."

They made their way past long lines of legionaries waiting for the gate to be opened, to go through it and spread out through the town.

The legionaries made humming noises hmmm…hmmm…hmmm as they passed, imitating the noises Germanic tribes made as they went to war.

Athralar and the other men raised their axes and roared back. Juliana walked in the middle of them all. Shield maidens were not protected in large open engagements. They were expected to fight as well as anyone else.

The torches on the last part of the road had been moved so they walked in a deep gloom. Up ahead the top of the wall was lit by fires inside the town and by the red glow coming from flames licking at the side of the battering ram, sitting at the gate. A regular thud sounded from the ram, as it attacked the gate.

"Up shields," she said.

They raised their round shields. They weren't as big as Roman shields, but they could be overlapped to make a roof. And that is what they did, so they looked like a large beetle scurrying toward the battering ram. A cheer went up from the legionaries watching. From the walls of the town a flurry of arrows rained down. Many of them were fire arrows.

Another, louder cheer went up. Juliana looked around. Beyond the gate Roman legionaries were rushing the walls. They were throwing long ladders up all along the next section. She saw men racing up the ladders, shields raised. Some fell. Others fought at the top of their ladders. Some disappeared over the wall.

At last they reached the battering ram.

LVIII

"The Empress Valeria is expecting me," said Lucius. "I am here to soothe her and say prayers for her." He smiled, put his head to one side, as if the guards at the empress' door would understand.

The lead guard, his helmet with a purple band of cloth tied around it, looked at him with suspicion.

"I've seen you before, have I not? You are a guest of the emperor?" His eyes flicked to the guards with Lucius. He was clearly unsure whether to be polite or not.

"I am a guest here, so do not waste any more time. Tell the empress Katerina sent me and be quick." Lucius looked away, hiding his nervousness behind an arrogant shrug.

"Wait over there," said the guard, pointing at a marble bench near the door. Then he went inside. The door closed with a resounding bang.

Lucius sat down. His guards stood nearby, their hands on the pommels of their swords ready to cut him down if he ran. But he wasn't going to run. If Valeria had heard his poem, if she remembered Katerina, a friend of hers who Lucius had met and who had been tortured to death for being a Christian, she might let him in.

But if she didn't remember or chose not to, she could send him away and report him to Maxentius. Who knew what he'd do, if he heard Lucius roamed around the place at night?

He stood up and walked to the far side of the corridor and back. And then again. All while his guards watched him. Occasionally a slave or a messenger came hurrying down the corridor. He got a sudden urge to stop one messenger who looked disheveled, as if he'd

LP O'Bryan

come from far away, and ask what was going on that he needed to rush, but he didn't. He had to curb his desire for news of the outside world, though it wasn't easy.

He lived in a marble cage. The slaves who watched him and served him seemed to have no interest in the outside world, or whether Constantine was dead or alive or anything else truly important.

Or were they just talking about things they were allowed talk about with him? He kept walking.

There were no windows in the corridor, but the oil lamps along the walls seemed to be getting dim. Or was it his eyes?

A creaking noise sounded as the door to the empresses' rooms opened.

A different guard stood in the opening. He looked Lucius up and down, the way you might appraise a slave at the market. "Take him back to his rooms. He has not been called for," he said to the guard waiting with Lucius.

Lucius' heart fell, as if a weight had been placed on his chest. The two guards from his rooms took a step toward him. Each put a hand on his shoulder and pushed him back down the corridor. He had failed. His stomach knotted as he imagined what would come next. His head went down.

This was the moment he should contemplate killing himself. Better that than to wait for the torturers to appear. They were men who enjoyed suffering and reveled in the screams of those unlucky enough to fall into their hands.

All he had to work out was how to do it.

The sleeping draught might help but did he have enough? They turned the corner in the corridor. Lucius felt numb, in a daze. How quickly would he have to do it? Could word be got to his father that he was dead? Perhaps he could bribe a slave to do that.

"Stop," a distant voice called out.

Lucius kept walking. No one would be shouting for him. They turned another corner. A clatter of footsteps echoed behind. Ahead lay his rooms and the guardsman who hadn't believed him, smiling broadly.

"Stop," the voice called again, nearer now.

Lucius turned, to see what was going on. The head of the guard unit at Valeria's door was running toward him. The man held his chest as if his humors were about to explode.

Lucius waited. Was he about to be arrested and taken to the torture rooms?

The man stopped, then pounded his chest with his fist, as if he needed to relieve some pain. Then he spoke. The two guards with Lucius still had a hand each on his shoulders.

"The empress will see you." The wheezing guard spoke the words softly.

Lucius stared at him. Then he shrugged away the hands on his shoulders.

"Take me back at once," he said. "How is the empress?"

The man looked down. "She has been better." Then he looked back along the corridor. When he looked at Lucius again, he said, in a soft voice, "Her father died."

Lucius' mind raced. That meant the empress would be less respected here in the imperial court. Like many emperors in the past, Maxentius had married the daughter of another emperor. But with Galerius now dead, the benefits Valeria brought were greatly diminished, especially as her father was known to despise Maxentius.

LIX

"Strike again," Constantine shouted. The men around him pushed the battering ram pole back on its ropes and then pushed it forward so that it crashed with a resounding thud into the gate.

The gate shook. It did not break.

"Again," shouted Constantine. The battering ram swung again. The thud when it struck the gate this time was louder, but still the gate didn't give. He could imagine the men on the other side piling sacks of earth at it, to keep it from breaking. How many had they put there already?

"Again," he shouted. The ram fell against the gate with a resounding thud. To his right the covering over the battering ram was alight. It wasn't blazing enough for them to abandon their position, but he could feel the heat and he knew what it meant. They didn't have much time.

"Where's the bloody pitch?" he said, turning. A stone had hit his foot. It had come through a split in the side of the battering ram. He had to get this done.

"Marcus, you're up," someone said.

"Ram again," Constantine shouted. The thuds of arrows and stones and rocks grew louder, or was it just in his mind?

A small man with a bucket of black tar-like substance came pushing up beside him. He had a pitch covered ladle in his hand. He opened a door in the front wall of the ram and used his ladle to throw tar from his bucket at the gate. A shout rang out behind. He looked back. The fire on one side of the ram had taken hold. The men near it had moved away, but they were still pushing at the ram. Their bodies were covered in sweat and gleamed in the flickering light from the fire. Soon the whole cart would be ablaze.

Then he glimpsed something that lifted his spirits. A Saxon shield wall coming toward them.

"The Saxons are here, men, let's get a crack in this gate they can open up for us. Ram again! Harder. Let's do this!"

The battering ram hit the gate. From above he heard laughter and insults. "Pigs, you will all die down there," someone shouted over and over.

"Light the pitch, Marcus," he said, as Marcus splattered the rest of his bucket either on the gate or just below it.

Marcus put a finger near his eye and grinned, showing blackened teeth stumps. The pitch on the gate was seeping down so that it almost covered the entire crack where the gate opened, as if they wanted to seal the gate, not breach it.

"We have come," a voice called. Behind it was getting busy. Saxons were standing beside Romans.

"Ram with us," he called out.

The ram went back and plunged forward. The gate rocked and for a moment he saw the wooden bars inside through the enter crack.

"Light it," he said to Marcus. Marcus picked some long rushes from a side pocket in his tunic. They looked oiled.

The battering ram hit again. Then some water flowed down the gate. They'd seen his plan. He pointed at the water. Marcus shook his head.

He had a flame on one of the rushes now. He leaned forward and jammed it into the pitch. Then another. For a long moment, punctuated by thuds and jeers, Constantine thought the fire wasn't going to hold and they'd have to go back and accept this attempt had failed, with who knew how many more losses as they pulled the battering ram back.

Then a different, stronger smell, hit his nostrils. The pitch was alight.

"Come up, Saxons," he shouted.

A string of thuds hit the roof of the battering ram. One cracked it. Another gush of water ran down the gate. It hit the pitch, making some of the fire fizzle out but missed most of it. Pitch spluttered in other places but didn't go out. And then, beside him, with a Saxon helmet on and an axe in her hand, crouched Juliana.

Red faced and grinning, a giant Saxon crouched beside her.

"Welcome! Hit the gate now," he shouted.

The giant Saxon went to the door in the front of the ram and hit the city gate right in the center. Chips of wood flew. Cries of anguish came from above. A sound like hail stones filled the air. More arrows fell.

"More axe men," he shouted.

Two axe men on either side of the ram were soon striking hard at the gate. Two other Saxons held shields up to protect the men striking the gate. One Saxon holding a shield went down, an arrow through his thigh. But then he stood up again, leaning on one leg, grimacing.

Most of the arrows and spears from above struck into the roof of the battering ram.

When chunks of the gate were cut out and the fire was spreading up and across, he shouted again. "Stand away, Saxons. Join the ram men. Let's do this."

Two more blows from the ram, then with a crash, like a wave breaking, the gate split open. An opening had been created, enough for two men to squeeze through. They could see the men beyond it.

They had wide eyes and swords at the ready.

"Shields up." He turned. "Pass me a shield." It came quickly.

Arrows flew toward them. A Roman went down, screaming, then another. And then the hail stopped. Had they used up their reserve?

He had his sword out. Side by side with the giant Saxon, shields up in front of them, they pushed through the breach in the gate, heads down, screaming for victory.

There were fewer men on the other side of the gate than he'd imagined. Arrows fell on them as they went through, as if they'd been waiting for them to come and one nicked his shoulder, but he kept going.

"Surrender or die," he shouted.

No one replied. The defenders were falling back already. Now they stood in a line at the other end of the gateway. He looked around. His men were clambering in after him. They had to keep the momentum going. They had to charge. With his shield up he ran forward and crashed into the shields of the defenders. Beside him ran the leader of his rammers and a centurion. Behind came a great roar. That meant his men were pouring in.

His sword jabbed deep into yielding flesh. He pulled it back with a familiar sucking feeling passing through his fingers and the iron smell of blood in his nostrils. A man screamed.

Then everything went black.

LX

Inside the Walls of Segusio, Cottian Alps, 312 A.D.

Juliana grabbed Athralar's arm. He'd just finished killing one of the town guards in the market square with an axe blow to the chest. Athralar had an exultant expression, as if he wanted to spend the rest of the day killing anyone who stood against him.

"We will stop now, Athralar. No pillaging. No rape. Those were Constantine's orders. Anyone breaking them is subject to immediate death and their bones to be crushed to dust."

Athralar groaned.

"We need to teach anyone who stands against us a lesson, Juliana," he roared, leaning down to her. "We need every city to be afraid and to open their gates. Go and tell him that."

"No, you are wrong. We must show everyone that Constantine is fair, and that if a city surrenders everyone inside will be spared from that moment."

"Constantine is a weakling. I saw him fall. We will regret this if we don't keep killing. Uurrrrghhh." Athralar roared at the stone buildings around them. Legionaries were forming up into units, waiting for orders.

"Where is he?" Juliana looked around.

"Back at the gate."

"Can I not even have them?" shouted Athralar, pointing his axe in the direction of some fleeing town defenders. "Who will notice?"

Juliana made a calming gesture and went close to Athralar. "We must look for Constantine."

Athralar nodded. He raised his empty hand, circled it in the air and shouted, "We've done our job. Let's go."

LXI

Maxentius' Palace, Rome, 312 A.D.

Valeria's rooms were very different to his. Beyond the door he'd been waiting outside was an indoor garden. A covered colonnade ran around four sides of an open area with white-gravel paths and a statue of a mother with a child in her arms at the center. Rose bushes, low shrubs and a bubbling fountain sat in each section of the garden. The garden was open to the sky and lit by moonlight and a row of glimmering oil lamps set in the walls under the colonnade.

A slave boy in a short yellow tunic led the way across the garden to a double height door with gold medallions and gold handles. He rapped a code of knocks on the door, three, then one, then three again. The door swung open. A golden haze of light flooded out. In front of them lay a dining room with gold painted couches and tables and full size, realistically painted statues of naked athletes, their skin creamy and hair black or yellow.

At the dining tables sat a party of a dozen people, mostly women. In front of them two naked male dancers were rushing into and out of each other's arms to the sound of plucking lyres. A cheer went up from the women as he entered, as if they'd been waiting for more male entertainment.

Valeria reclined at the top table with a younger woman on each side of her. Her hair was piled high in the patrician style and a gold band ran through it. Slave boys, in short tunics, were filling up the sparkling blue glasses of the guests.

Lucius bowed. Valeria stared at him, as if trying to work out who he was. She motioned him forward. He went around the dancers and behind the tables to approach her from the side. Two bald eunuchs stood in his way. Their uniforms were gold cloth and at their belts hung large ornamented daggers.

"Lucius, join us," said Valeria, loudly. The eunuchs stood aside.

Lucius went down on one knee as he got near her couch and bowed deeply.

"I am here with a message from Katerina, great Empress," said Lucius, his head still down.

"Arise. I heard your poem, Lucius, and I know who you are. What is it you come for?" Valeria shifted her position to face him. The other women were watching the entertainment. Shouts rang out. The spectacle was nearing a climax. One of the other women screamed, "Valeria, he's ready."

Valeria kept staring at Lucius.

"I heard your father died, great Empress. I want to extend my condolences. He was a good man. He deserved better at the end. I want to thank your family for the patronage your father gave to my family. I know my father would want me to say all this." He placed his hand over his heart and bowed again.

Before he could look up, he felt a hand on his shoulder. "Let us find somewhere quiet to talk, brave Lucius." Valeria bent down over him. As he rose, she took his hand and led him to a door at the back of the room.

"Valeria, look," someone shouted, but she didn't even turn her head.

The room she led him to was at the far end of a corridor and up a series of steps. It had a wide marble balcony overlooking the city. An array of stars shone above and streets below were lit by torches at the entrances to buildings.

A low rumble could be heard. Thousands of carts moved at night through the city, when fewer people were about. Night soil was collected, amphoras of wine and oil delivered and cart loads of grain and vegetable and fresh meat were taken to the early morning markets.

The sight of the city almost brought him to tears. It had been a long time since he'd been outside his rooms.

"Sit," said Valeria. She clapped her hands. Two slaves who had been invisible, standing in a corner, sprang forward. One held a gold jug. The other had gold goblets, which he placed in front of Lucius and Valeria.

"I'm honored that you would see me," said Lucius.

Valeria was sitting on a sofa covered with giant silk cushions. She patted the spot beside her.

"You are lucky my husband is locked in with the high priests from all the temples. He is looking, as always, for advice on what he should do next." She leaned toward him. "My father was so different. He knew his own mind." She raised an eyebrow. "Now, tell me, what is the purpose of your visit, brave Lucius?"

"I will not beat far from the bush, Empress. I need your help."

She raised a hand. "You must know that my influence over my husband has waned since my father died."

"Your influence with me will never wane, Empress."

"And are you now the leader of all the Christians in this city, Lucius, as they say?"

"No, that is absurd. How could I lead thousands of followers from a cell?"

Valeria shuffled closer to him and whispered in his ear. "Katerina was my best friend, brave Lucius, before my husband decided to make an example of her. What do you really want?"

Lucius looked around, as if he'd heard something. "Is there a child imprisoned near me?" he said. "I thought I heard one." He said it in an off-hand way, as if the question was of little importance.

Valeria shrugged. "No, there is not." She stared at him. "Is that all you want to know?"

A chill had descended between them.

LXII

Constantine put his hand to his forehead. Pain thudded inside. A centurion stood on either side of him. Sejanus was in front of him. He put a hand against the wall of the tavern, where he had been dragged by the centurions.

"Was I out long?" he asked. Feeling around his head, he discovered his helmet was gone.

"Your helmet is on the way back to your tent, my lord," said one of the centurions. "There is a proper big dent in it. You were lucky. How is your head?"

Constantine stretched his arms out and moved his shoulders. "I'm good," he lied. "Let's finish this job."

"We're collecting prisoners. Do you want them executed?" The centurion pointed toward the far side of the square inside the main gate of Segusio. A large group of the town's defenders were standing together, unarmed and without breastplates, surrounded by Constantine's legionaries.

"No. I will talk to them."

The centurion stared at him as if he had grown an extra head. Constantine groaned lightly, then put his hand on the pommel of his sword. Almost every eye in the square watched as he strode toward the captives.

There was no way he could tell them that his head throbbed so hard it seemed some daemon had got inside it. The truth is how things look, that was one of his father's sayings, and it was right.

265

"Stand aside," he said to the legionaries guarding the captives. They moved aside but kept their hands near their swords.

Constantine stood in front of the captives. He could smell blood and shit and piss. He saw faces he'd seen in his first rush to enter the town. Now they looked downcast, pinched, as if those men expected to die at any moment.

He waited until the captives had gone quiet. Many were looking at the cobblestones under them.

"You will live, if you join my cause. And today you will be released. Serve with me in the cause of justice and unity in our empire. I am here to bring peace to the empire. If you agree with my purpose, you will swear to it and be free to leave this place and travel wherever you want and tell all you meet of what happened here. There will be no retribution for any city, town or village dweller who joins with us. But if any stand against me after this offer there will be no mercy."

Without waiting for a reply, he turned and headed for the gate. Two centurions went with him, at his back. Sejanus was at the gate.

"Make sure the town is protected. Have all the fires put out," he said, to Sejanus. "And remember, no rape, no pillage. What we do today is the message we send to every town and city in our path."

Sejanus saluted him. "Understood." He coughed.

"Yes, what is it?"

"You have blood on your face and all down your arm." Sejanus smiled. "It is good to see you are still standing. Would you like some water?" He held out a water skin.

Constantine looked around, Legionaries on their way into the town were staring at him.

"I'm alive," he shouted to the legionaries, his fist raised. "We have the gods on our side. We cannot be stopped by blood or injury. Our victory has just begun."

A cheer echoed from the men and spread along the line. Many smiled like babes. The chance of death that day was gone.

When he got to his tent Paulina was at the opening flap.

"My lord, you are hurt," she said, rushing to him.

He put his hand up. "Praise the gods our victory came quickly, Paulina. I have a few scratches, that is all." He headed for the bed at the back of the tent and sat down heavily. He closed his eyes. His head thumped even worse now.

He'd been hit on his helmet with a spear before, a glancing blow, but that hadn't felt like this. He looked at his arm. Dried blood covered it. His stomach felt strange now too.

"No visitors," he said to Paulina. She had a silver bowl of water with lemon slices in it.

"I don't feel right." His vision darkened.

LXIII

Maxentius' Palace, Rome, 312 A.D.

"News, that is what I want," said Lucius. "My slaves won't tell me anything." He looked around, suddenly nervous. Was he making a bad mistake trusting her?

"What news? From your home, your family?" said Valeria. She put a hand out to him and touched his bare knee. The tunic he'd been given was cut differently than what he liked. This hung short, like a slave's.

He looked in her eyes. What choice did he have, he had to take his chance. "News of Constantine would be wonderful. He was my patron, you know that, I am sure."

"Is that all?" she said

"A new, longer tunic would be good."

"But you look so well in this one." She smiled at him, pushed her hand up his bare leg.

He stared at her hand. She stopped moving it.

"I don't need you, Lucius." Valeria took her hand away, looked around to see if any of the slaves were nearby. "You need me." She reached for him again, squeezed his thigh, hard, as if she enjoyed inflicting pain.

"What can I do for the woman who has everything and everyone?" said Lucius. He bowed. "But I am yours to command."

She slapped his shoulder.

He looked up.

"My husband has declared war on your patron. You'd better be careful, brave Lucius."

"I am as careful as I can be in this place. Has there been any military engagements between Maxentius and Constantine?"

"Not yet, but my husband is gathering troops. He plans to invade Gaul while your master is busy on the frontier with Germania this summer."

"So, it has finally happened." He shook his head. "You know I was tasked to stop this war."

"No one can stop Maxentius when he wants something," she said. She had a far-away look in her eyes.

"Do you still have sway with the followers of the nailed god, Lucius?"

He shrugged. "I'll only have influence if I am released." His heart began beating faster. He could see a possibility now of getting out of his gilded prison.

Valeria sniggered. "I cannot have you released. Don't be ridiculous. The emperor will never agree to that. He knows you are a spy for Constantine. Be grateful he didn't have you roasted on a spit for his entertainment." She pouted. "But you can send a message to someone through me. Just tell me who it should go to." She looked at him with no hint of guile in her face.

She was a good actress. But he didn't trust her motives for one moment.

He nodded, kept his face straight, trying not to let his suspicions show. "Let me compose something. May I come back tomorrow night?"

"Please do." She leaned toward him. "I think you can help me, Lucius." Then she stood and walked out of the room. He followed in her wake. On his way back to his rooms he tried to work out what sort of help she wanted.

Did she believe that the followers of Christ were strong enough to help her in some way? Was she in fear of her life now that her father was dead? Surely a man like Maxentius could easily throw a wife aside if she was no longer useful. But was it all a trick to find out who his associates were? It was impossible to know unless she told him more.

That evening he lay awake wondering what was happening to Constantine. Were his efforts in vain? Did Constantine even need him still? If only he had a way of knowing. For now, all he could do was stick to their plan.

The following evening, he prepared himself at the same time. When he reached the door of his corridor the guard outside laughed when he heard where Lucius wanted to go.

"You are a bit late, prisoner," said the guard.

"Why?" A chill grew fast inside Lucius' gut.

"Your empress friend was arrested, prisoner."

"The empress?"

"Yes, not the Queen of Egypt."

Lucius sighed. Was this the end of his only hope?

"That's absurd," he said. "She not a criminal. What are the charges?"

"The likes of us don't get told such things, especially the likes of you." The guard poked his finger into Lucius' chest.

"We have been talking about you, prisoner. You see, I reckon," he pointed over his shoulder, "that your balls will be cut off first, for daring to visit the empress, and that you'll have to carry them back to your room and eat them before they burn your eyes out the next day. I've seen it done. It involves a lot of screaming." He grinned and made a poking gesture at Lucius' eyes with two fingers. He was enjoying his moment.

Lucius' testicles moved, as if they knew what was to come.

LXIV

Inside the Walls of Segusio, Cottian Alps, 312 A.D.

"I must see him," said Juliana. She stood, chin up, near the entrance to Constantine's tent. Two legionaries, tent guards, had their spears crossed in her path.

"He is not seeing anyone," the older of the two men said. His hair was tightly cropped and gray.

"He will see me."

The guard looked her up and down. "Are you the shield maiden who helped break open the gate?"

She nodded. "My war band are part of your auxiliaries."

"Your war band, eh." He looked her up and down as if appraising her. "Every century in the army is talking about you. I imagined you'd be a giantess, but you're not, are you?"

"No, I am not. Now please, tell Constantine I am here." She shivered. A breeze had come up as the sun lowered to the horizon. She pulled her cloak tighter around her shoulders and looked away.

The Roman camp was ablaze with activity. Their easy victory had put a purpose in every step. Men were bustling about, carrying amphora or marching to a duty or running on an errand, doing everything with glee. Not many were going to have to die on this campaign, was the thought she imagined was going through a lot of heads.

But was it true?

They were still far from Rome. And one victory did not win a war. Maxentius had a large army at Rome. So far, they had only faced a frontier fort.

The guardsman reappeared.

"You are not to be admitted," he said. He waved her away dismissively.

Her jaw dropped. "My lord, how are you?" she shouted.

The guard went to put a hand on her shoulder, to turn her and push her away, no doubt.

She slipped back a step and out of his clutch.

"You must go, now," he said, forcefully.

"Why won't you see me?" she shouted.

The guard had her by the arm now. Men all around were staring at her. Some had stopped in their tracks and were pointing at her and laughing. She didn't care. If she wasn't allowed to see him now, she might be barred from the Roman camp the next time she came. She might never get this near him again.

Had he just wanted to use her men to break down the gate? A pulse of anger flowed inside her.

"It is me, Juliana," she screamed at the top of her voice. "Why won't you see me?"

The guard looked back at the flap of the tent to see if anything happened. "You are gutsy. I'll give you that. Stay quiet, and I'll count to ten. If no one comes for you by the time I am finished you must go, agreed?" He pointed a stubby finger at her.

She nodded.

He started counting out loud.

LXV

Inside the Roman Camp, near Segusio, Cottian Alps, Southern Gaul

Aprilis, 312 A.D.

Constantine leaned up in his bed. Someone was calling his name. A voice he knew. Who? He tried to remember. Then he fell back. The poppy juice Paulina had been plying him with made his head fuzzy, as if he was dreaming. Was this a dream?

Paulina sat beside him. "Are you well?"

"I heard someone call my name."

"It is no matter. You must get better first, before you see anyone."

Constantine shook his head. "Optio," he roared. He let his head fall back.

His youngest optio appeared. Had she sent the others away?

"Yes," said the optio. He sounded nervous, pliable. He stared, open-mouthed, down at Constantine.

"See who calls for me outside."

Paulina put a hand up. "Surely you must not see anyone when you are like this?" She waved at his prone form.

Constantine put his hand out to her. She took it. He squeezed it, hard. She squealed.

"I will decide who I see, not you." He let go of her hand. "If they have been in my tent before, let them in," he shouted. The orderly had already gone.

A few moments later a rush of cold air filled the room. He pushed himself up on his elbow. Juliana, wrapped in a wolf skin cloak, was marching up through the tent.

"I should have known you were guarding him," said Juliana, staring at Paulina. Then she turned to Constantine and went down on one knee.

"It is good to see you are recovering. We were concerned."

"Your emperor is in good hands," said Paulina.

Constantine pushed himself higher on his elbow and shifted so that his back was supported against the wooden back of the bed. It had an eagle carved into it. He raised his hand.

"I need the two of you. There will be no back biting. Do you understand, both of you?" He looked from one to the other.

Paulina nodded. It took a few more moments for Juliana to.

"To win this war I need you both."

"What are Paulina's talents?" said Juliana. "Aside from the art of keeping you warm at night."

"Paulina is not my concubine," said Constantine.

"I am helping in ways you do not know," said Paulina. She gave Juliana a half smile.

"And I can help him win battles," said Juliana, returning the smile.

"What I really want is for each of you to stay quiet and let me sleep." He closed his eyes. "If I awake to find you fighting, you will both be banished from my presence. I have more than one reason for wanting Juliana to stay with me, Paulina and, Juliana," he looked up at her, "Paulina is going to help us win this war, so you had better learn to get on with her." He rolled to his side and closed his eyes.

The two of them stared at him, then at each other. Paulina walked to a wooden side table with jugs of wine and blue glasses on it.

"Let's sit," she said. She poured two glasses of watered-down wine and carried them to the table where Constantine met with his officers.

They sat opposite each other.

"I heard you were a slave," said Paulina. "How did you become a shield maiden?"

Juliana wondered how much to say. If Constantine was right and Paulina could help them win this war, she should tell her everything. Well, almost everything.

It was dark when she'd finished and two optios had lit oil lamps, so the tent filled with light.

One of them asked Paulina if the emperor was ready to feast that night, as many officers were asking when they would celebrate.

"Your emperor will have a victory celebration when the war is won and Rome is liberated," said Paulina. The optio disappeared.

"Is that what Constantine said?" asked Juliana.

"It is exactly what he said," replied Paulina. "When I came here, I thought he was just trying to send a message to Maxentius marching toward Rome, to get him to agree a truce, but now he wants to take Rome as quickly as possible." She looked in Juliana's eyes and put her head to one side. "I believe he changed his mind after seeing you."

"I'm sure he has his reasons, things he's not telling us," said Juliana. "What is it like to be a priestess of Rome?" she asked, changing the subject.

"Pure misery." Paulina slammed her glass down on the table, spilling some of the contents. "For the first year you might enjoy different men pawing at you, but after a few years it is hell. They all stink. And the worst ones lie about how they care for you, and all until they get what they want. The fools believe they interest you. Ha! Pretending to enjoy them gets harder and harder while the men get softer and softer each time you see you. I would not wish it on anyone. It is a curse on the empire, forcing women to serve this way."

"Someday it will change, I'm sure." Juliana finished her wine. "Perhaps you can get Constantine to change things if he defeats Maxentius."

"There is no if, Juliana. There can be no if. You have to believe in something to make it happen. That is what we are taught to tell all our patrician clients when they doubt themselves, and they do come back and thank us, as if we magically made them stronger." She shook her head and smiled.

"So, when Constantine defeats Maxentius you can ask him to change things in the temples, yes?"

"Yes," said Paulina with a shrug. "He's agreed already. Maxentius may have a bigger army and be able to hide behind city walls that are called unbreachable, but Constantine has the faith of his soldiers, their belief that he is a just ruler, which I know to be true, and much more importantly," she leaned forward, conspiratorially, "he has us."

"True, but what more can we do?" said Juliana.

"Plenty." Paulina put her hand on Juliana's. "I know Maxentius' plans for defending the city."

LXVI

Maxentius' Palace, Rome, 312 A.D.

Lucius waited in his room all that day. He could barely drink anything, never mind eat. That night he only slept fitfully, expecting at any moment to hear the trudge of hob nailed sandals and to be dragged to the torture rooms. He looked for a knife to have ready to cut his wrists or his neck but didn't find one. The tiny bit of sleeping milk he had left didn't even make him yawn.

As the sky brightened over the open roof of his small atrium, he contemplated bashing his head against the walls to stop the endless fearful dread that filled his mind. As the sun rose and the gloom lifted on the tiled floor and the wall paintings under the colonnade came back into view he wondered if running as fast as he could and bashing his head into the wall would be enough to kill him. Or would his body prevent him doing it by slowing at the end?

He stood, went to the far end of the atrium and began to pray to whatever god would listen, Roman or the one god of Christ, to finish this, one way or another, to bring him peace. He sat again, drank some diluted wine, stood and stared at the sky.

Perhaps the torture would not be so bad? Perhaps he would survive it. Perhaps Maxentius would only want to punish him or main him, not kill him. Would he be able to survive blinded?

A loud slam broke through the atmosphere in the atrium, followed by the thud of sandals marching, and before they came into view he knew he should have rammed the wall head first as he wanted to, and that only cowardice had stopped him and that soon, very soon, he would regret it.

"Lucius Aurelius Armenius, come with us," a voice boomed.

Lucius stood still and stared up at the sky. A thin cloud, like a veil, drifted far away. Was that the breath of the one god, as he'd heard some claim, or a whisper of smoke from Jupiter's cauldron?

"You are summoned by the empress. Leave what you are doing and come at once." The guards were among the youngest he had ever seen. Lucius stepped back, a wave of relief shuddering through him.

Was this some trick?

"The empress has been arrested. How can she summon me, or is this to her cell?"

"No, this is not to her cell. The empress was released last night. Her arrest was a mistake. The emperor has had one of his advisers hanged. The empress has summoned you to celebrate her freedom with her."

Lucius' knees almost buckled. He sniffed, wiped at his nose. It was running. Tears streamed.

"Take me to her at once," he said, wiping his face.

"You do not want to put on a good toga?" the man's tone was friendly but accompanied by a sneering expression.

"I have nothing better." Lucius pushed past the man and headed for the corridor.

When he reached the empress' rooms a crowd had gathered outside. It appeared as if every lackey who wanted to stay in with her had heard the news. Lucius was escorted through the group. The door to her rooms opened to let him in and closed quickly behind them as voices were raised with pleas.

Valeria waited in the dining hall, a glass of wine in hand and two men sitting with her.

"Lucius, you came, wonderful," she said. "And without even putting on a good toga." She opened her arms. They hugged.

He shivered at the thought of how close he had come to bashing his own head in.

"These are two advisers my father valued most," she said, pointing at the two men. "They came to see the emperor yesterday." She gripped Lucius' arm, as if it was a rope she needed to pull herself up with.

"They advised him to ensure the followers of the nailed god are on his side if Constantine is to be stopped." She turned to Lucius, her eyes haunted by something.

"I told my husband you lead these people in this city and can promise their allegiance to him and that I can arrange all this with you."

Lucius felt his stomach lurch. What Maxentius expected was not going to be easy to arrange.

"What does all that mean?"

"He wants you to recruit your followers to fight in a new legion, the Defenders of the Palatina. That will be your first duty. We need spearmen, he says, as many as possible. Can you do this?"

Lucius stared at her, blinked, blinked again.

"Lucius, you must do this," said Valeria. She patted her neckline. "For me."

"Yes, yes, of course I will, I will recruit whatever number he wants," said Lucius, smiling.

"And first, you must promise your loyalty to the true emperor," said Valeria.

The two men stood. Lucius noticed that both of them had daggers at their belts.

"I swear allegiance to the true emperor," said Lucius, loudly. "To Maxentius. I have always supported Maxentius." He looked at Valeria.

Her grin widened. "Will you need gold to help you with recruitment?" she asked, softly.

He noticed her nodding, very slightly. "Yes, yes, of course. Not to pay the men. They will follow me, but to pay for swords and shields, the new kind, and for other provisions."

"We will take you to the treasury after we have all eaten," said the thinner of the two men. His face looked like a weasel's.

Valeria clapped her hands. "Is the breakfast ready?" she called out.

Two slaves appeared, a young boy and a young girl. Both had short tunics and long, beautiful golden-brown legs.

"Yes, my lady. Everything you asked for is ready."

It was half-way through the morning before Lucius was taken by the two men to the treasury. He'd collected his cloak and nothing else from the rooms he had been in for so long. Everything else he was glad to see the back of.

The two men accompanied him to a tavern he knew near the Circus Maximus. It was part-owned by a Christian the last time he had been there. When they arrived, the door was barred.

"What happened to the tavern that stood here?" he asked a man outside a leather goods shop next door.

The man pointed across the street.

The new tavern was much smaller than the original one. Its sign hung sloppily, and no one sat outside at the low tables near the door. Lucius pushed back the bead curtain that blocked the doorway and went inside. The man behind the counter had the appearance of a north African with a thick beard. The man smiled as he saw the new customers.

Lucius called out, "Where is brother Paul?" He looked around. No one else was in the small airless room and no one came in response to his call.

"Brother Paul was arrested a long time ago, over a year if I remember right. I bought the remains of his amphoras and his stocks from his widow. We have no more to do with followers of the nailed god. They did nothing but bring us bad luck." His eyes kept darting to the two quiet men standing behind Lucius.

LXVII

Augustus Taurinorum (Rivoli), 312 A.D.

With the alps to their back, Constantine's army had reached the plains of northern Italia. They were camped by the side of the road in a large field, lying fallow that year. Grass grew already in all unplowed fields. The snows of the Alpine passes were a distant memory. It was early morning. Swifts were darting among the brown leather tents and sparrows chirped from the line of tall, spear shaped cypress trees that lined the edge of the road into town. A decision had to be made soon what to do that day.

Late the previous afternoon the camp defenses had been dug and the perimeter stockade finished. The legion which had stood guard overnight were waiting for their orders. Outside the camp, the auxiliaries waited in their tents strung back along the road, including the two Alemanni cavalry units which had accompanied them from Gaul and the Saxon war bands, which had joined later. They all received provisions daily, a sack or two of grain, depending on their number, and amphora of wine each night, to ensure they were fed and did not start raiding in the countryside around.

Constantine had enough gold in his treasure chests to buy provisions until mid-summer. After that, they needed major victories or to start raiding the countryside.

Constantine paced in his tent at the center of his camp. Sejanus and his two senior legates, each one commanding a large legion, were having a meeting before the rest of his officers arrived. His plan for capturing Augustus Taurinorum in a similar way to Segusio had been disturbed by news from scouts, sent out at dawn, that an army had assembled on a low hill directly in their path.

"We must split our legions and attack him from two sides at once," said the older legate.

Constantine looked at the table on which lay a large map painted onto a thick, dark parchment. He motioned the scout who had brought the news closer. The man was half covered in mud. His hair gleamed white from dust.

"Tell me again what formation they are drawn up in."

"A bird formation. A bird with a long beak."

"A wedge?" said Constantine.

"Yes, that would be it."

Constantine slammed his fist down. "This was foreseen," he shouted. He turned to the older legate. "Are the clubs ready?"

"Yes, my lord. We have five hundred ready for distribution, but why will we need them?"

"You will see. Tell the officers to come in. We are ready." He looked at the scout. "Say nothing about what you have seen out there or what you have heard here on pain of death. You are dismissed."

The scout nodded.

As the other officers came in a ripple of excitement ran through them at the sight of the scout leaving.

Questions came fast. Constantine issued a string of orders. The camp was to be left as it was with a small guard. When the battle was over, they would return to it.

"We'll return with victory laurels. We have every god on our side. I've made sure of that." He raised his fist. The men around him cheered.

He leaned forward, as if taking them into his confidence. "The gods of Rome, the old gods and the new, are all with us, so we are doubly blessed." He turned, pointed at Paulina. She was holding a large golden goblet up in front of her at the back of the tent.

He waved her forward. She came slowly, as if she didn't want to spill a drop of whatever she carried.

"Legates and prefects of the legions about to fight, stand forward," said Paulina.

"Is there a blessing for the followers of the Christ?" said a voice, almost apologetically.

Paulina smiled. "I have also become a sworn follower of the Christ god. This blessed wine will be a sharing of his love for our cause." She bowed.

"Both the old gods and the new share in one blessing for us all," said Constantine. "This battle today will decide how every town and city between here and Rome falls, either for us or against us. We must move fast today, and we will move with all the gods on our side."

The legates and prefects sipped from the goblet. There was enough left after they were done for her to go around and tip a little of the wine into other waiting mouths. Every officer at least got his lips wet from it and more than a few offered her thanks for allowing them to be included, as they too were followers of Christ.

And then they were all gone.

Soon after, Constantine and Sejanus issued a string of orders to the waiting messengers. No horns rang out to mark their departure from the camp, but the dust they kicked up would have been enough to warn Maxentius' army blocking their path that they were coming.

When they reached a long abandoned-looking olive grove below the hill the enemy sat on, Constantine gave orders for his men to enter it and split into three arms. The arms on each side were to go forward at a faster pace, as if they wanted to flank the enemy.

Juliana had been allowed to ride with Constantine and Sejanus at the head of the second legion in their marching order. Paulina had been ordered to wait at the camp. Each person with him had to be capable of fighting.

Constantine led his horse to the far edge of the olive grove, where the land rose up to meet the hill. The opposing legions arrayed above were so numerous they spread back over the hill and down its sides, like great wings. Constantine could not see the enemy general leading them, but he had a good idea of who it would be.

A large heavy-cavalry unit stood, clearly visible, in the center of the massed ranks of enemy troops.

"We advance against their center," said Constantine, pointing straight up the hill.

Juliana looked at him, a puzzled expression on her face.

"Yes, we are taking on his oven men," said Constantine. "They are just lucky the sun has little power today, but with you and your men with us, I'm sure we'll have victory."

Juliana patted her horse's neck. "I will pull my axe men forward to drive up the hill with you."

Constantine raised his hand. "No. This is where we part company. You and your men are to wait here, in the trees." He pointed to the side. "Listen to the birds and be happy. You cannot be in the front line every time." He reached over, grabbed her arm, pulled so that their horses came together. "I will not lose you again. You will do as I say."

Juliana moved her arm, dislodging his. "We are here to fight. You are making a mistake." Her face was red.

"I have a plan for you, Juliana. Do as I say, and your moment will come." He pointed at her forcefully.

"What is your plan, to get me on my back when you tire of Paulina?"

Juliana's horse stepped sideways. She struggled to control it, then dug her heels in and went away without another word, wheeling her horse back to where she'd seen the war bands marching into the woods.

"All our heavy cavalry are here?" Constantine asked, turning to Sejanus.

"Yes," Sejanus replied.

Constantine adjusted the large helmet he wore and pulled down the visor. The helmet had a purple strip of cloth tied around it. As he made his way with the other cavalry officers up the hill again every eye was on him.

Every man knew that he had been injured at Segussio, but here he was, again, leading his troops into battle. Many of the men had not seen such leadership before, mainly the younger ones, and some of them had their mouths wide as they watched Constantine move up the hill in the front rank of the heavy cavalry.

Constantine's horse shifted its haunches under its chain mail blanket as it moved. He was also clad in chain mail, the Celtic type, with smaller hooks, which he preferred. He whispered to his horse as it clambered up the side of the hill. The hill wasn't steep yet, and the mare wasn't struggling, but he wanted the horse to know him, to remember the previous time they'd been together. When the time came for combat, he would need the animal to act in unison with him.

The line of cavalry moved with him, fifty horses wide and three deep. Anyone watching would have assumed they were not about to attack the forces arrayed above them. Perhaps they were going to join those forces, they moved so slowly.

And then a hissing noise sounded from the hill above.

"Up shields," shouted Constantine. The call echoed and spread along the line, carried by each decurion leading his troop of thirty cavalry.

The shields they had been carrying on their left side were raised quickly overhead. The spears that the men on the hill had unleashed rained down. Horses shrieked and whinnied, and men roared as they were struck. A spear whistled by close to Constantine. His cavalry kept to their steady upward movement.

Over the lip of the hill a much larger force of enemy heavy cavalry appeared. They were at least three times the number of Constantine's cavalry.

"Halt," he called out. The cavalry to his left and right came to a halt.

The enemy cavalry coming down toward them began to cheer, as if they were about to win an easy victory.

It would be a heavy price to pay, having faced the spears, for them to turn and retreat. Constantine waited until he could see the teeth of the men coming toward them, their smiles of imminent victory flashing.

And then, feeling the impending chill of a one-sided engagement about to befall his men, he turned his horse and shouted, "Steady retreat!"

Jeering followed them.

He looked back and saw not only were the enemy heavy cavalry following them, but behind them lighter cavalry were also streaming down the hill. His men had only fifty paces advantage, and the gap was closing. The pounding in his ears from the horses all around shook his bones and filled the air as if a daemon had taken over the world.

He rocked back and forward as he went on down the hill, his horse cantering dangerously, almost out of control now. He had to hold the reins tight, his sword clattering against his thigh and his chain mail jumping.

He didn't like retreating.

But they had to do it.

He turned. The Maxentian cavalry were closing the gap. Many of their men had swords up, ready to skewer any laggards from Constantine's cavalry.

One of his men pitched down off his horse, it had buckled under him. He rolled down the hill.

Constantine didn't see what happened to him next. The unlucky man was not likely to survive for long. Then the whistling sound came again. His gut grew tighter, as did his chest, as he waited to be pitted. The cavalry pursuing them had unleashed their light javelins.

Was it time to turn and fight? He looked back. A javelin hit the ground where he had just been.

No, not yet.

Roars and the screeching of horses came from behind. Their retreat had extracted a heavy price. Many would pay dearly for his decision to attack up the hill into the heaviest concentration of the enemy cavalry.

He bounced along faster now as his horse moved better with the ground flattening.

His shoulder ached deeply where his breastplate straps cut into his old wound. They would have to fight hard, fight for their lives, soon.

"Halt," he roared. The call was taken up along what was now a ragged cavalry line.

A few steps more with his horse resisting against the reins, but he managed to get it to stop and turn.

The enemy were closing. He unsheathed his sword and moved his shield in front of him. On either side between the trees ragged bushes offered little protection to large horses.

LXVIII

Via Circus Maximus, Rome, 312 A.D.

Lucius headed out onto the street. Valeria's two men went with him.
It was almost lunchtime. The taverns were starting to fill up with
people enjoying the warmer weather now that the winter was gone.

"Where to now?" said the older of the two men. He had a
beaked nose.

"To the Palatine." Lucius started walking. The two men fell
into step with him. He needed to lose them.

"The next people I have to meet will not see me if I bring you
two with me," he said.

Beak-nose nudged him. "Don't worry, we'll follow you at a
distance. We want to keep our eyes, brave Lucius. We've been told
they'll be fed to the pigs if we can't tell Valeria everywhere you go
and everyone you meet on this mission."

Lucius stopped. A blind beggar was in their path, rattling a red
bowl.

"Do any of you have a coin?"

Beak-nose put a small coin in the blind man's bowl.

"Pray for us," said Lucius, softly. The blind man had a blue
fish tattoo on his forehead. They walked on.

"I need to do this alone," said Lucius. "You must trust me.
When I finish what I have to do in this next house I will come back to
where we part company." He stopped walking. "There are thousands
of followers of Christ in this city, but nearly all of them are like that
beggar. The family I am going to see are of the highest class, an
equestrian family. I risk all their lives by bringing you near them.
When I leave you now, you must not follow me to their door or they

288

will not let me in. I will fail in the task set for me if you do. You will see where I'm going, and…" he pointed at each of them, "I will tell her you were warned about this and would not listen to me if you follow me."

He began walking again, faster this time. When they reached the Via Palatina Superior, a wide avenue of villas behind high walls, he pointed at a small tavern at the corner of the street where house slaves from the area met. Some were outside on wooden stools. But these were not just ordinary house slaves. Many of this class of slave would be wealthier than free men in the rest of the city.

"I'm going to the second house up the street, on the left," he said. "You can watch me knocking on the door and being let in." He pointed at the tavern. "Have a long lunch and wait for me."

The two men looked at each other.

Beak-nose nodded. "If you don't return by nightfall, we will be knocking on that door with these." He raised his heavy walking stick.

"Agreed." Lucius walked fast to the door he'd pointed out. All the windows of this house were shuttered except one, directly above the door. There, the thin center leaf of the shutter lay half open. Nothing could be seen in the gap except darkness.

Lucius gripped the small bronze lion head on the door and banged it down. He didn't bother looking back. He knew they would be watching him and ready to race after him if he ran away.

No one came.

He waited.

The sun warmed his skin as he looked up. He turned his face into it. In the distance birds cooed. It wasn't a noise you would hear in most other parts of the city. It gave the impression there were gardens behind the high walls and people relaxing in luxury, without a care in the world.

"Who goes there?" came a voice from above. A round woman's face appeared at the window. A house slave.

"Lucius Armenius. I am a friend of your master. Please tell him I'm here."

"The master is not at home."

"I am also a friend of the mistress of the house. She will see me," said Lucius.

The window above closed. He leaned against the wall.

The two men down the street were at a table now. They had red beakers of wine in their hands. Lucius licked his lips.

The door swung open. A tall slave with an angry, pinched face stood in the opening. He looked down the street, then up it as he spoke.

"How can we help you, Lucius Armenius?"

"I need to see your mistress."

"But you must know she is not here. You must know she was arrested years ago. Have you forgotten?"

The slave looked puzzled.

Lucius took a step forward. "Then I must leave a note for the master of the house. You have papyrus and ink?"

The slave looked at Lucius as if he was mad.

"Come in. I remember you. But you cannot stay long."

Lucius sighed in relief as the door closed behind him. They were in a long corridor, at the end of which stood a narrow door.

"Follow me." The slave led Lucius down the corridor, through a small atrium open to the sky and into a tiny room with shelves of papyrus, a desk and a chair. He moved aside some things on the table and unrolled a blank papyrus scroll.

"You can sit here," he said, handing the scroll to Lucius. "And when you are finished call me and I will seal your message with wax."

Lucius wrote a simple how-are-you message on the scroll and called the slave back. The slave made a great show of sealing the message and putting it in a box stuffed with similar scrolls, both large and small.

"If you can, please let me leave by the back door, I'd appreciate it," said Lucius as the slave finished pushing the scroll into the box.

Without looking up the slave said, "Are you running away from someone?"

"Not at all," said Lucius. "I just need to get to the next house I am visiting quickly." One of his fingers twitched as he replied, betraying him.

"So, the two men you came here with, who are at the end of the street, are not waiting for you?" said the slave. "They don't think you are visiting our master?"

LXIX

Augustus Taurinorum (Rivoli), 312 A.D.

Constantine held his sword in front of him. A Maxentian heavy cavalry man was bearing down on him with a spear in his hand.

Constantine gripped the reins of his horse. This was the moment he enjoyed most, and hated most. It held the promise of victory and the smell of death. Every sense was alive. He could feel the sweat from his horse on his thighs, hear the thundering of hooves and taste the dust thrown up by the horses. Sword blades were shining, scything the air.

One wrong move would mean a painful death.

And it was better than sex. It was living on the cusp between life and death, holding the power of life over other men and having your own death whisk past you as if it was fated not to ever find you.

He twisted to the side, almost falling from his horse. The spear shaft whistled by him.

"Arise," he shouted. The signalman riding to his side swung a red flag high in front of him.

As if by magic, the five hundred men who had been lying in the grass near the trees on each side rose up. And as he clashed swords with the cavalry man, his men ran in to disable the enemy cavalry's horses. Each of these men had a giant, iron capped club and they swung their clubs wildly. The enemy horsemen laughed at this, and kept engaging Constantine's men, but then, a wall of spears appeared through the trees on both sides and came toward Maxentius' men.

The enemy heavy cavalry managed to kill or unseat a dozen, maybe more of Constantine's cavalry before they saw the danger they were in. A unit of Constantine's light cavalry was holding enemy reinforcements from arriving and the men with clubs were now bringing down horses fast and moving on from one to the next, each followed by a spearman to finish off the downed cavalry men. Other legionaries were behind the spearmen, darting in and out to disrupt any attempt to kill their comrades.

Constantine took a blow to his chain mail. He focused on the man attacking him. The man's eyes glinted, flickered. Constantine swung way back in his saddle.

The man's sword swished in front of him.

But instead of retreating in the face of a rapidly swinging opponent he stepped his horse closer, soothing it with words.

"It will all be over soon," he said.

His eyes were watching his enemy. He came forward another step, put his left hand up in greeting. The man's sword swung fast. This time Constantine didn't try to avoid the blow. He clashed swords with the man, then angled his own sword up a little and jabbed it fast into the eye slit in the man's face mask.

A gush of blood spurted out.

Constantine pulled his sword back. The blade was slicked with the remains of an eyeball. The man fell back, his final sword thrust ending in mid-air, his horse spinning away out of control, and before Constantine could enjoy the moment a spear flew toward him.

It glanced off his shield. A sword swung at him. He parried, swung his sword tip up and jabbed it at this man's throat.

The man was quicker than the first, but he leaned back too much so when Constantine swung his arm into the man's shield and pushed, the man fell back. One of the club men was waiting as the man hit the ground. His club smashed into the man's visor, crushing it and his face.

The man jerked like a horse that had been gutted. Constantine's cavalry men gathered around him. A moment passed as the enemy held back attacking them. Riderless horses were wheeling about. One, nearby, reared up on its hind legs.

"Finish them all," shouted Constantine. With a mighty roar the blood splattered cavalry men around him surged forward. In the distance, up the hill, he saw his light cavalry fighting hard. They needed his support.

"Up the hill," he shouted. He kicked his horse in the ribs and urged the mare on.

LXX

Via Palatine, Rome, 312 A.D.

"You are right, and if they knock on your door you must tell them the truth, but if I am quick and return to them soon, there will be no need for them to disturb you."

The slave looked pensive. "I cannot stop you, if you want to go that way. But if you have brought bad luck on us, I curse you and your line to the end of the world."

"That's a bit harsh," said Lucius. His right hand twitched, as if a daemon had taken it over. He gripped it with his other hand. This was his chance.

"You will take the men waiting for you away when you are finished?" said the slave.

"I will, definitely. Now, lead on to the back way out."

The alley at the back of the villa was wide enough for only a single cart. He turned right, up the hill, picked up his pace and headed for the next corner. The house he headed for was even larger than the one he'd just come from. Whether they would let him in through the slaves' entrance was another question.

The back door of the house he wanted was easy to identify, though. It was the only door in a long stretch of high red brick wall. He banged his fist on it, as if the Harpies were on his tail.

A small viewing door opened and he was cross examined, but a few moments later he was being ushered into the garden of the villa. It had a shallow green marble pond filled with water lilies and statues of a nymph at each corner.

He'd spent many evenings in this house talking about religion and drinking his fill. The daughter of the senator who owned the house had been a good friend. He sat on a white marble bench near the pond.

"Lucius Armenius, I thought you were under house arrest," said a familiar voice. Claudia Calpurnia, his friend, came toward him. She was dressed in a thick dark-gray cotton gown with a rough rope as a belt.

Lucius put his arms wide. She didn't hug him. She looked around, as if looking to see who he'd come with.

"No one is with me," said Lucius. I did not come to betray you."

"I know you would not do so deliberately, Lucius, but I have to be careful these days, the emperor is a man of many faces."

They stared at each other. Her eyes moved over him.

"You came here from the palace. What is it you want?"

"To see your father." He bowed his head. He needed this to work to have any chance of earning his freedom.

"Things have changed here, Lucius. My father is dead. His estate was confiscated by Maxentius. We were lucky to escape with our lives.

"Then you will be interested to hear what I have to say."

LXXI

Augustus Taurinorum (Rivoli), Aprilis, 312 A.D.

The city walls of Augustus Taurinorum stood out like broken teeth in the distance, with the backdrop of the sun rising. It was the day after the battle in which Constantine had lured Maxentius' heavy cavalry to their death.

The retreating remainder of Maxentius' army were camped outside the city, which had closed its gates to them the night before and had refused to open them that morning.

Constantine, accompanied by Sejanus and four legates, stood on the top of a hill to the west of the city. Their horses were nearby. Maxentius' legionaries were visible, drawn up in fighting order, in front of the city walls.

"They have refused our offer of clemency. Aurelius Ienarius, their commanding officer, threatened our delegation with death if they reappeared. He said that you should surrender, as he'd heard you were wounded."

Constantine touched his shoulder. It hurt and the pain grew worse at night if he refused the juice of the poppy, but it was not enough to stop him fighting on.

"How many men has he?"

"About three thousand."

"Draw up our legions, but only one will attack. Tell the II Augusta to show us all what the men of Britannia can do. Tell them that only the enemy legionaries who beg on their knees are to be allowed live."

Sejanus smiled. "They will relish the opportunity," he said.

"I will not be with you today, Sejanus. You must extinguish the last of Maxentius' support here without me."

Sejanus saluted. "Victory is ours."

Constantine returned to his tent. Early that evening Sejanus arrived in a rush. He was ushered into Constantine's presence. Constantine was resting on his bed while Paulina changed the honey-soaked bandage on his shoulder.

"Is it done?" said Constantine.

"Yes, only a few hundred begged to live. The rest died beneath the city walls. The II Augusta legion lost fifty-six men and there are many more wounded." He paused. "The city will be sending a delegation tonight with gifts and the keys of the city. What shall we do with them?"

Paulina stepped back, taking her silver bowls with her.

"You must deal with them, Sejanus. The city is to be offered clemency, but demand they prove their support with carts of grain and wine. Make sure they supply enough to get us to Verona."

"Yes."

"Tell them we will strike camp in two days, and that we must receive the first part of their pledge by then." He put his feet out of the bed and stood. He was naked. Sejanus stared at the purple bruises, long red nicks and the white marks of old wounds on every part of Constantine's body. Constantine winced, put a hand to the bandage on his shoulder.

"Which road are we taking from here? South?"

"No, that old fox Zenas, you know they say he is Maxentius' best general, is holed up in Verona. We cannot leave him free to attack us in the rear. He would love that."

Sejanus nodded. "I do not know where you get your information, my lord, but whoever is feeding you, long may they continue." He hurried out of the tent.

Paulina pointed at Constantine. "I hope he doesn't guess who is feeding you with information. I don't want to find priestesses strung up when we enter Verona."

"No one knows about your secret messengers and no one will, Paulina. Take my word for it."

He picked up his parade sword from the table and swung it, practicing repeated jab and return movements at different heights, the staple of a legionary's sword practice. His jabs were not as fast as they should be because of the damage to his shoulder, but they were getting better.

"You must not fight again in the next few weeks," said Paulina.

"Is it that obvious?"

"Yes, it is, and as you like to lead from the front, you must pick your moments from now. You have done enough already to inspire your men."

"Send a new message to Rome, Paulina." He took a sip from his watered-down wine. "Tell them my injury prevents me from leading my men in battle."

"Are you sure you want Maxentius to know about this?" She pointed at his shoulder.

"Yes, the more you tell him the truth and the more he finds out about us, the more he will believe us."

She bit her lip. "I hope you are right." She put a hand on his arm. "Juliana isn't following you around these days. Has she been injured?" She looked hopeful.

"No, I don't think so. I asked her to take her Saxons and flank us."

Paulina stared at him. "Do you trust her that much?"

LXXII

Via Palatine, Rome, Aprilis, 312 A.D.

"What do you have to tell me, Lucius?" Claudia Calpurnia smiled, but not with her eyes. They held suspicion.

"We have a chance to end all the persecutions of the followers of Christ."

"How do we do that?" She didn't sound convinced.

"We must recruit our people to a new legion, the Defenders of the Palatina."

Claudia snorted. "How many men are you hoping for?"

"A thousand, maybe two."

"There is no possibility of that number."

"What number could you raise?' asked Lucius. "I know you have freedmen on your estates to the south. There must be hundreds of them available."

"You are well informed."

"How many Christians can you raise?"

"First, I must ask you why they should fight, Lucius?" Claudia threw her hands in the air. Her tone was sharp.

Lucius walked close to her and lowered his voice when he spoke. "Maxentius has promised that he'll remove all the edicts of persecution, that he will return all lands and property confiscated, and he will donate new land here in Rome to us as a thank you from a grateful emperor when he defeats Constantine."

She looked at him. Her mouth opened, closed. For a moment he saw her smile. Then the smile disappeared.

"What about all our followers who are imprisoned?"

300

Lucius pointed at her. "Every follower of Christ imprisoned will be released when he defeats Constantine. He pledged this to me himself. I have his word."

Claudia's mouth twisted. She shook her head from side to side. "It is a good offer. But will he keep these promises?"

"He swore it in the presence of witnesses. You cannot tell our people all over the empire that you turned down this opportunity to get their relatives freed and their lands returned."

She stared at him. He could almost see her thinking. He gripped his right hand. It had stopped shaking, but he did not want it to start again.

LXXIII

Verona, 312 A.D.

Constantine had finished eating. He watched a lyre player, a young woman from Macedonia with bells on her ankles and wrists and wearing little else. Paulina sat to his left, Sejanus to his right. Music filled the tent. They were reclining on cushions on a raised wooden platform, which could also be used outside in the open for addressing his men.

Imperial slaves were hovering around like mayflies.

"She is nothing special," said Paulina. She turned toward Constantine and leaned forward so he could see more easily down the front of her gown.

But Constantine's eyes were on the lyre player. She moved with the music, throwing her heels back and smiling at him.

Raised voices at the entrance to the tent distracted him.

"I thought I made it clear I was not to be disturbed," he shouted.

Sejanus stood. "I will find out what's happening."

Constantine went back to watching the lyre player. Her song had reached a climax. Her head swung wildly from side to side.

"Sejanus, what is it?" Constantine shouted irritably, as Sejanus came back from the entrance.

"A delegation from Numidia has arrived. They say it is urgent they see you."

Constantine shook his head. "How many delegations from Maxentius' territories have we received?"

"Six, my lord."

"And what do they all say?"

"They will give you the freedom of their cities and shower you with honors when you defeat Maxentius."

"So why should I see this lot quickly?"

Paulina moved beside him, like a snake rising from the grass. She put a hand on his arm.

"Numidia is one of Maxentius' most loyal territories. This is good news. Please, send this silly lyre player away and see them."

Constantine put his hand to his chest, nodded. "Do as she says, Sejanus."

He waved at the lyre player. "I will call for you later," he shouted. "Do not go far." The lyre player smiled and ran away, her feet barely touching the carpet.

Moments later three men came into the tent. Two of them were large bald men with overgrown beards, but at the front strode a smaller man with a neatly trimmed beard with white strands running through it and hands that flew through the air like flapping birds as he approached.

All three men prostrated fully, lying down and touching their foreheads to the carpet.

"Arise," said Constantine. "We do not require all this. Come forward."

The smaller man looked up and spoke. "My lord, oh wonderful son of a great emperor and a valiant warrior of great renown, praised by all who meet him on the field of combat and in his palace, we are come to lay our loyalty at your feet and beg that you look kindly on us when you achieve the final victory you so richly deserve." The man rose slowly. His companions helped him up.

"Who do you represent?" said Sejanus.

"The lords of Siga, Quixa and Cartena instructed me to find the emperor. We traveled through Hispania and Gaul as fast as we could." The man took a step forward. "May we speak in private?"

"I trust all the people you see here with my life. Speak openly. What name do they call you?"

"Berber Aquilus. But please, let me speak to you alone." He had a wounded expression on his face now.

"You have one last chance. Tell us all what you want to say or go back at once to your desert hole." Constantine pointed at the entrance to the tent. "It is that way."

"My lord, please forgive me, please, please." Berber Aquilus looked crestfallen. He took another step forward.

"I have come to tell you that the Christians in Rome and to the south of the city have taken up arms for Maxentius."

"That is nothing new," said Paulina.

"There is more," said Berber Aquilus. "They are being trained by someone you know."

"Who?" said Constantine.

"Armenius Lucius."

Constantine growled. He swung his hand across the table in front of him, knocking over both his blue wine glass and Paulina's.

"You didn't tell me this," he said, turning to Paulina.

"I didn't know," said Paulina, quickly.

"This may be true," said Berber Aquilus. "We met traders from Rome in Gaul only a week ago. This news is the very latest from Rome."

"Thank you for bringing this to us," said Constantine. "We will look at your petition when we have secured our victory." He sighed. "I assume it is about differences between you and your fellow tribesmen to the east of you."

Berber Aquilus lowered his head. "You are very well informed."

"Where are you heading next, Berber Aquilus?" said Constantine.

The man's mouth opened. He looked down. "We will travel in your entourage, if you permit it."

"I do not. You can come and see me after I have Maxentius' head off his shoulders and I can piss in his mouth." Constantine waved them away.

After they were gone, he smiled as if he'd won another victory. He called for the lyre player.

"And the rest of you begone too. It will be a day for fighting tomorrow. Sejanus, wake me at dawn. We need to move our men to make sure we are not trapped if Zenas appears with a relief force."

They had encircled Verona a week before, but General Zenas had escaped to the east. Most likely in search of additional forces to break the siege. He could be back any day.

The following morning the lyre player was not there when Sejanus arrived. She had been disappointed when he'd not sought to take her to his bed. But the small bag of gold coins he'd given her soon put a smile on her face and when Constantine explained that his injuries were more serious than anyone knew, she became sympathetic. He asked her not to tell anyone and smiled when she nodded. After she was gone he called in his most trusted optio. He has another message that needed delivering.

He and Sejanus spent most of the next day circling the city on horseback, crossing the river that surrounded it on three sides twice, looking for weaknesses in their siege line. By mid-afternoon they were back at their main camp to the west of the city

"Why not attack the gates again?" said Sejanus.

"Because Zenas is coming back and we will need our men ready for him," replied Constantine, as he got down from his horse. He handed the reins to one of the decurions.

"You are sure he hasn't just disappeared with his tail between his legs?" said Sejanus.

"Maxentius will see this as an opportunity. He'd love to catch us with our forces strung out around this city. It's too good a chance for him to miss."

"Do you think our reserve will be enough to deal with him?"

The blast of a distant trumpet interrupted them. The signal meant that a messenger had arrived. Constantine went into his tent and unbuckled his sword.

Sejanus was still with him.

"I will go and find out what news the messenger brings," said Sejanus.

"No, wait here with me." Constantine pointed at the table where he met with his senior officers.

They sat back in the foldable camp chairs and waited. Watered down wine was served in glass goblets with some of the bread and cheese they had received from Augusta Taurinorum. They sipped at the wine and ate chunks of the bread. A rush of pounding hooves told them the messenger had arrived outside. The flaps of the tent opened, and he came in. He was soaked, as if he had been swimming.

"Come forward," said Constantine.

The messenger shivered as he spoke, his voice full of tension.

"A large force under Maxentius' banners are approaching from the east. I took the shortest way here and swam the river."

"Their number."

"Three legions, I would say."

"You did well," said Constantine. "Go and find warmth now."

The messenger departed.

He turned to Sejanus, flexed his arms and swung them, as if in training. He looked pleased. "Now is our moment of reckoning. I will be fighting in the front line again. We must punch through their lines with a cavalry charge. They will not expect an assault as soon as they arrive. They will be tired after a forced march to get here. We have the advantage, if we move quickly."

The legates of two legions, the VIII Augusta and the I Martia were summoned.

"Your men have been held in reserve since this campaign season started," said Constantine to the two legates and nine tribunes, the senior command structure of the two legions. They were gathered around the map table. The winding river, which protected Verona, was visible as a dark wavy line in the center of the papyrus map. The legions were marked by carved wooden legionaries sitting on the map.

"You will both head north to the ford where the drovers cross and make haste to cut off Zenas before he makes camp. Hold outside of arrow distance. I will join you when you are ready."

"You will be fighting today?" said the legate of the VIII Augusta.

"This is an important day in our campaign to bring peace to the empire. Everything depends on this day. I will not only fight, I will address your men before I do, so arrange them ready to see me and to hear me." Constantine pointed at the officers one after the other. "I will be leading the first charge. We will not retreat today. Not one step. We will defeat them totally. I expect every officer here to have the enemy's blood all over them when we come back here tonight." He turned to Sejanus. "The Saxons are still foraging to the west?"

"Yes," said Sejanus. "I will send some scouts to look for them, if you want."

Constantine shook his head. "No need."

The sky turned sea blue that day and the birds sang wildly. But when the first charge came, with Constantine in the lead with a new red shield one of the blacksmiths had made for him, the birds stopped. Perhaps it was the drumming of war horses on the thin grass or perhaps it was the rolling battle cry of "Victory!" which stilled them. Or perhaps it was the squeals of the dying and the despairing cries of "Mother."

Whatever it was, Constantine blocked it all out. He was in his stride now, fighting again and again, getting better, fearing nothing, stabbing some men in the eye and others in the groin and then finishing them, fast. He lost count of the men he killed that day, but he knew at the end of it that he had been very lucky on a few occasions, when blades came close enough that he felt the wind of them passing. And he knew such luck does not last forever. No matter who you are.

It was early the following morning, with the dawn, when they reassembled in his tent. Three of the tribunes didn't make it back. Every other officer was covered in blood, many of them almost completely.

"Break out the best Valerian wine," shouted Constantine, as they rushed as one into the tent. Paulina waited for them with some female slaves and hangers-on, many of them concubines of the officers.

Constantine turned to his men. Some of them were holding bandages tight to their sides or arms. Others had lost their helmets and were sporting giant bruises. Two men were being held up between other officers.

"We have a famous victory, men. We have Zenas' head and it may have taken all night, but we beat them. You are the best of my legions. This day you will remember all of your life. This is a great victory. Be proud."

He turned to the women. "Come, join us."

Paulina came toward him slowly. She held out her hands, then hugged him. "Shall I call your lyre player?" she whispered.

"She will be long gone," he said. He winced, moved his shoulder.

"You have been injured again?"

"I cannot fight and be careful at the same time, Paulina. Unless you want my corpse to come back to you."

Quiet descended. He looked around. Had he been shouting? He pushed past the slave carrying a wine goblet for him and headed for the back of the tent and his bed.

LXXIV

Maxentius' Palace, Rome, 312 A.D.

"Come forward, Lucius," said Maxentius. He rose up a little from the reclining position, then flopped back down again. Valeria sat to his left. To his right reclined the legate of the praetorian guard. Other guests filled half a dozen couches set around three long green-marble tables.

Lucius came forward, bowed. "I'm grateful for this opportunity to show you what the followers of Christ can do when we are led by a just emperor," he said.

"How many men do you have now?"

"Four hundred and sixty. And there are more arriving from the south and from Ostia every day."

"Not enough, Lucius, not enough at all, and from what I hear your men will not even be needed. I expect our commanders in the field to bring Constantine's head to me any day now."

"That is wonderful news. I will await your orders." Lucius bowed.

"Train your men, Lucius. Do that for me and I may have another use for them. I will let you know by the end of summer." He turned to Valeria. "I suppose I must thank you for coming up with this idea of testing Lucius." He grabbed her arm, pulled her to him and licked it from wrist to elbow. He swayed then, as if he'd had too much wine.

"You taste good enough to eat, my empress." He looked at Lucius. "Would you like to eat the empress, Lucius?"

Lucius smiled. "No man's appetites can compare to yours. I would not dare to take your place."

Maxentius laughed. He pointed down the table. "You must talk to Berber Aquilus. He was with your one-time friend and soon to be ex-emperor a few weeks ago." He waved Lucius closer. "He tells me Constantine has been severely wounded, but he still insists on fighting in the front rank!" He laughed. "His injuries are the talk of his camp."

"The man does not behave like an emperor," said Lucius. "The way you do." He swung his arm around as if including the purple curtains, painted marble statues and golden plates all around in how an emperor should behave.

Maxentius grinned. "Did you know I send the men I want to die to the front line, if I fancy their wives." He laughed. "My rival will be dead by the middle of summer if he keeps this up. He cannot survive what we will throw at him."

A man with a well-trimmed beard waved at Lucius and shouted. "The emperor is right. Our enemy will be feeding the worms soon." He raised his glass. "Rejoice in our coming victory!"

"Our coming victory," repeated the emperor. The shout was taken up by everyone at the table.

Maxentius waved Lucius forward again until Lucius had his face down near him.

"And you will be made a tribune then, my loyal friend, as soon as Constantine's head is delivered to me. What do you say to that?"

Lucius raised his eyebrows. "I look forward to that day." He kept a hold on his cloak and smiled as widely as he dared.

LXXV

The Furlo Pass, seventy leagues north of Rome

Three months later, 312 A.D.

"How many victories do we have so far, Sejanus?" Constantine looked back along the line of men snaking back along the narrow road between the sheer gray cliffs of rock.

"I count seven."

"Are you including larger skirmishes, like the one this morning?"

"I am," said Sejanus.

"I make it five, including Ariminu." Constantine stared straight ahead.

"Ariminu surrendered, my lord."

"But there was a skirmish on the seaward side before the city fathers opened the gates."

"Foolish followers of Maxentius. I believe a cousin of his led that attack on our baggage train."

"And how many more will die before we have Maxentius' head?"

"That depends if he comes out of Rome and meets us in the field."

Constantine nudged his horse to move faster. Sejanus did too. The sky was gray with piling clouds. It looked like another rainstorm was on the way.

"I'm sure Maxentius is expecting us to fail before the walls like Galerius did," said Constantine.

"You know he has improved the walls in the last five years," said Sejanus.

"Everyone knows this. I want to fight this afternoon," said Constantine. "I need to test my sword arm in action again, not just swinging at it at friendly centurions." There would be nothing worse than going down in battle with Maxentius as he stormed Rome. He had to see some action before that moment came. He had to be confident of his prowess when he fought in front of his men. It was his mastery in combat that gave his legionaries their total faith in him.

Sejanus hesitated before answering. When he did his eyes looked down. "My lord, we need you to lead us to victory, not to personally dispatch everyone who stands in our way."

Constantine turned. "If I cannot fight, I cannot be sure of victory, Sejanus. This campaign has been built on my personal interventions." He waved toward the men on horseback around them and the much larger group marching in a long line stretching back into the dust behind them.

"I know it makes a difference when the men see me fighting with them. I've led them here. I have to fight with them to the end of this campaign. Whatever the risks, and there are many, this is my path."

Sejanus smiled. "If you want to fight, our scouts were attacked last night while we built our camp. We lost two men. I have a feeling we will be attacked every night now until we reach Rome."

"Shorten the daily march from today to half the normal rate."

Sejanus raised his eyebrows. "You don't want to keep up the momentum, now we are so close?"

"I want the men to be eager for battle, Sejanus, when we storm the walls of Rome, not tired out from long marches. That was Gallienus' mistake. And there is no possibility of surprise for us."

"We will be outside the gates of Rome in eight days, then, not four, as you command."

"I am going to find the decurion in charge of the scouts."

Constantine pulled the reins of his horse to the side and nudged his large black stallion in the ribs. The horse broke into a canter along the line of trudging legionaries. Each time he passed a century the men broke into cheering so that his passage along the line was marked by a rolling acclaim.

When he reached the forward marching units two lines of cavalry rode on each side of the line of legionaries. These were his Gaulish scouts. Some of their number would be riding ahead. They would return before nightfall and the men he now rode with would take their place riding out in the darkness, watching with just the light of the stars, the moon, or some nights no light at all.

These men were all from the southern provinces of Gaul, bordering the Pyrenaei. They hunted in the mountains at night and guided travelers lost in the deep woods bordering the mountains. They were the best scouts in all his provinces, even better than the renegade Picts who scouted for his legions in the northern reaches of Britannia.

He hailed the decurion, a man with a lopsided smile and deep grooves in his face, as if a chisel had been taken to it.

"How many men will you send out tonight, decurion?"

The decurion touched his dented grey helmet and bowed before replying. "Twenty-five tonight. Five more than last night. The road passes through a tunnel tomorrow, so we need to be sure to check places where rock falls can be arranged."

"I will go out with your men tonight."

The decurion stared at Constantine as if he had gone mad. "Most men would not want to be in this unit. We lose men every week, if not every night. Are you sure?"

"Don't ever ask me that again."

The decurion saluted stiffly. "Yes, my lord."

As the sun set the army completed setting up camp for the night. The rampart and ditch were finished quickly. The marching camp, in a square pattern, as such camps had been laid out since Rome was a republic, filled a large part of a long meadow bordering the road to Rome in the shadow of the Apenninus mountains. The ground below the road rolled away at a shallow angle with low, wooded hills in the distance.

The four gates were up quickly. The rows of tents soon looked neat as the smell of cooking, dust and horse shit drifted through the camp.

Near the southern gate Constantine, without his distinguishing purple plumed helmet and gold breastplate, looked like just another scout about to head out for the night. The only thing that set him apart was the size of his horse and his own bulk. That alone would not be enough for anyone who didn't know him to know who he was, but it would be enough to put off any but the most skilled warrior from taking him on.

If they could see him clearly.

They rode out in near darkness with only the last light from the sun setting beyond the mountains and a few early stars, to help them see the road.

"The moon should help us on our way back. It will be out by the midnight watch," said the decurion, who had decided to accompany them.

A chill night-wind rattled their scabbards and stole under their cloaks as they rode. Goose bumps ran up Constantine's arms.

"Vespasian's tunnel is not far ahead," said the decurion. "If they want to attack us tomorrow, that will be a good place to do it. We'll check through the tunnel and take a measure of what's waiting for us on the far side."

They dismounted and walked the last half league before the tunnel. Whispered conversations came back from two other scouts who had come this way during the day, but had not been through the tunnel, simply waiting and watching the road until that night's scouting unit arrived.

A whistle that sounded like a nightingale echoed through the cold night air. Constantine squinted, trying to make out the entrance to the tunnel ahead. The clouds shifted. A mass of stars appeared above them. But seeing beyond a spear throw was still impossible and anything beyond that was just grays and dark purples piled on top of each other.

The sweat from riding had cooled fast on his back.

The sound of the men around him moving slowly forward was as loud to him as if they were bears trampling through undergrowth. He was sure any enemy guards listening would hear them.

And then he smelled the enemy.

It was the smell of rank sweat, from men who had probably been waiting many days for their enemy to arrive, and each day in fear of their coming death.

The sounds from his own men stopped completely moments later when the echoing noise of a man clearing his throat came clearly through the air ahead.

The decurion touched Constantine's side and whispered in his ear, "I go ahead, see what waits."

Constantine grabbed the man's arm. "I'm with you." He pulled his sword free from its scabbard slowly.

He sensed rather than saw the other men creeping forward with him. The steep bulk of rock above them closed them all in and cut off the breeze that had been with them earlier.

The smell of sweat and fear grew.

And then, in front of him, a helmet stood out as a darker shape against the slightly lighter wall of rock they were approaching. He stopped and stared at it, trying to work out if the man had his back to him.

He did.

Maybe he did.

Stepping closer, slowly, he lifted his sword and got ready to strike it into the man's neck. There would be no warnings. The only men out here at this hour would be the enemy. Shepherds would have their flocks off the mountains by this time of year and there was no other reason for a man to be up here except defending the road.

Constantine stepped forward.

A twig snapped. The helmet turned.

Constantine swung his sword up fast and pushed it forward into what should be the man's neck. He felt it glance off a neck guard. He turned the sword tip, scraping it along, looking for a gap. The satisfying jarring sensation as the tip penetrated flesh was followed by a scream almost in his ear and then in quick succession, the shouts of men all around.

The decurion fought at his shoulder, swinging at another dark shape.

Constantine jabbed again into the darkness, to the left, then to the right and stepped forward, jabbing fast and furiously. And then he stumbled. Someone or something lay at his feet. Screams filled the air from all sides. His stomach tightened. He was glad he hadn't eaten a big dinner.

He squinted beneath him. The near darkness made it almost impossible to work out what was there. He wasn't afraid of fighting at night. He trusted his skills with a sword, but he knew the best advice for night fighting was to hit and run.

"Fall back," he shouted. Answering calls echoed around him.

And then he felt it. A searing pain in his thigh. He fell to his side, mainly to avoid the blow, and landed in a thicket of branches. He rolled and came to his feet, disoriented, trees above, shouts all around, the crashing of men moving through undergrowth and then the sound of a warning trumpet. The enemy was aware they were under attack. More men would be on their way.

He listened, heard another call to fall back and stumbled after it to where they'd left the horses. It was unlikely they'd be followed. The defenders of the pass would most likely fear a trap and prefer to stay on ground they knew.

"How many did we lose?" he said to the decurion as they rode back to camp.

"We'll know for sure at dawn, but you are injured, that is all that matters. I hope..." His voice trailed off.

Constantine knew what the man meant. "You will not be blamed."

A warning trumpet blared as they rode into camp. There were two large torches above the gate. As they rode through Constantine looked down at his leg. It glistened with blood.

LXXVI

North of the Furlo Pass, 80 leagues from Rome, early October, 312 A.D.

The next day

Athralar put his hand up to stop Juliana talking. "I have heard enough. Our leader is injured, again, and this time he may not recover. That is what all the men at the quartermaster's tent are saying. I asked would we have our rations cut if we go back the way we came. They said yes."

"What exactly did you hear about the emperor?" asked Juliana. She was sitting beside a neatly arranged pyramid of axes near her tent. The axe heads gleamed. They had expected to hear the horn announcing they were to break camp since sunrise, but it hadn't come.

Now she knew why.

"I say we strike out on our own if the army retreats. We raid and make our way back to Germania with our bags full of booty."

Juliana shook her head. "Wait here. Do nothing until I return."

It took longer than she expected to reach Constantine's camp. They had flanked the main army only part of the way, following tracks that a guide they had been allocated led them along, but sometimes they had been forced to follow the main army's dust cloud, due to the nature of the terrain.

Not many of the Saxons were happy with eating Roman dust.

She was stopped and questioned at the gate to Constantine's marching camp, but her password proved enough to get her through. She was also stopped by a guard not far from Constantine's tent, but was let through by an optio who had seen her with him before.

"How is he?" she asked, as she walked with the optio.

"He has a deep cut." He leaned close to her. "The priestess Paulina has gone to the woods to fetch healing herbs. He is alone right now." The man looked at Juliana. She couldn't work out if he meant that it was a good thing he was alone when Juliana arrived, or a bad thing.

When she entered the tent, silence filled it. At the back of the tent, behind a curtain, a few candles sent a thin yellow light through the gloom. The leather tent roof let in some other light, at the corners, so there wasn't complete darkness, but it was dark enough to make out that the bundle on the bed could be Constantine.

"My lord," she said, rushing to him. She took his hand, which lay outside the covers.

Constantine gripped her hand in reply. "It is good to see you," he said.

"We heard you were dying."

"A pack of lies," he said. He gripped her hand tighter.

"How long is Paulina gone?" said Juliana, looking around. "Did she give you the poppy juice?"

Constantine shook his head. "I hate that juice."

"Have you had the wound bound? Where is it?"

He pointed at his thigh. "Yes, it was bound, but she said not to put any weight on it until she came back."

Juliana looked in his eyes and bit her lip.

LXXVII

Maxentius' Palace, Rome, 312 A.D.

One week later

Maxentius paced back and forward. "If he is days away from Rome, why does he advance so slowly? Tell me that."

Paulina, dressed in a flowing green tunic with a split from neck to navel, opened both her arms.

"Total victory awaits you. He is mortally injured and hiding it from his troops. He cannot travel far each day. I saw his injury. You must take advantage of this and finish his army off quickly." Her tone was happy, exultant.

"I heard reports that he has a cohort of Saxon axe maidens." Maxentius stepped closer to her. The nymphaeum he had arranged to meet her in had a monumental fountain and was normally used for dining. The columns around its walls were of white marble. Gold busts stood between these columns on smaller quarter-height columns.

Paulina shook her head. "Fantasy and fear mongering, my lord. He has three shield maidens. One used to be a Roman slave. Your massed praetorians will cut them to pieces."

"You are sure of his injury?"

"I saw his leg covered in blood and his thigh wide open to the bone with my own eyes, my fortunate emperor, blessed by the gods." She pressed her hand to her forehead and went down on one knee, as if in prayer.

"The anniversary of your succession is in three days, my lord. That is the day you will finish him. Your victory has been predicted for that day for many years. You will grasp the opportunity and take his head before he can regain his strength."

"And what of the child of his we captured? Should we bring him with us to the battle and show him there, to let Constantine know what we will do if he gets close to us?"

"Keep the child safe, that is my advice. The boy will be good proof of your total victory over Constantine's blood line when you win. You could also show him his bastard son and extinguish the boy's life in front of him. He can watch his son's blood flowing, like the blood of all the Romans he's killed in his crazy invasion of your territory. Then you can burn out Constantine's eyes and cut off his hands and stuff his cock down his throat for daring to come to Rome against you." She raised her fist, held it in the air.

Maxentius threw back his head and laughed. "You paint a happy picture, priestess Paulina." He touched her arm. "You have done well. You will be paid well too when this all comes to pass, as I have promised you."

She gave him a deep bow. He stared at her exposed breasts.

"The gods are on your side, my lord." She stayed deep in her bow.

"What signs have you seen from the gods, Paulina?"

She straightened. "I see everything, my lord." She opened her mouth, then closed it, as if she was going to say more, but decided not to.

"Tell me what you saw."

Paulina pulled her cloak over her head, reached into a small bag on her hip and took a leather pouch from it.

"I will tell you, but first I must ask the great mother for permission." She pointed at Maxentius. "Do not move. Await the words that will come."

She walked in a circle around Maxentius, while dribbling salt from her pouch around him. Then she took a vial of oil out and sprinkled a little over him. Finally, she put her cupped hands to her face.

A bird called somewhere far off above the palace.

"The goddess had granted me permission to reveal what I have seen," whispered Paulina.

"Go on then, tell me," said Maxentius, his tone impatient.

"The rival will die within three days. You will be free of Constantine and all your enemies."

Maxentius clapped. "Your predictions have never failed me, priestess. They had better not fail me this time."

LXXVIII

Constantine's Marching Camp
Via Flaminia, the 11th Milestone North of Rome, 312 A.D.

Two days later

"I will not desert you," said Juliana. Constantine lay on his bed at the back of his tent.

"Your Saxons want to defect, so I heard." Constantine pushed aside the plate of gruel, flat bread and a slice of boar meat, his evening meal.

"Tell me again how we can win, if Maxentius marches out to meet us." He put his legs outside the bed and attempted to stand. His right leg had a winding bandage all up his thigh.

"Why do you need it told again?" Juliana put a hand out and steadied him as he stood.

"Because every morning since you told me, we have defeated all those who try to stop our advance. Your story brings me good luck."

"You defeat your enemies because of your schemes."

Constantine shrugged. "We start earlier each day. It's a simple marching trick."

"But tomorrow our march will be over, we will face the walls of Rome."

"We won't be scaling any walls. Maxentius will come out and fight us. His men are preparing tonight."

"How do you know this? A little bird told you?" Juliana moved her fingers through the air and made a plaintive bird call.

"No, not birds. They have spies watching us. We have people watching them. These men are called scouts." He smiled. "Maxentius believes the gods are on his side. He has been offering sacrifices."

"He has followers of the nailed god fighting for him, I heard."

Constantine shrugged. "Your one-time master, Lucius, has raised a legion of the followers of Christ. They are all sworn to him and Maxentius."

Juliana made a fist, raised it. "What? You're very relaxed about this. Lucius was your man. He found me in that slave market. I'm surprised you're not cursing him for the dog he has become."

Constantine paused, sighed. "It won't help our cause if I do."

She touched her forehead, looked down. "Years ago, I saw you in a dream with a golden laurel on your head and cheering crowds all around. I'm sure this means you will be victorious."

He leaned toward his sword, lying on the table near them. He touched the scabbard, as if for luck.

"You will keep to our plan?" He stared at her.

"Of course."

"Anything else you'd like tonight?" He held his groin, smiled, winked at her.

"You need your strength tomorrow. We can celebrate when we have Lucius' head on a plate."

"You are more vicious than I took you for, Juliana, when I met you all those years ago."

She raised a finger "There is one thing you might do for me."

"Go on." He sounded wary.

"You told me once that you had a dream about Lucius. That he was leading an army of Christians and they all had a cross on their shields, that symbol they use."

"Yes," said Constantine. "So?"

"Paint that symbol on the shields of your legions. Send the order out now and say that you saw an army with this sign winning the battle tomorrow. It will cheer every legionary up. A sign from the gods is what all men want."

Constantine stared at her for a long moment. "I will, if you promise me you will follow the plan we agreed."

LXXIX

The next morning

South of The Milvian Bridge, on the outskirts of Rome, Three Days Before The Kalends of November, 312 A.D.

Maxentius rode slowly on a giant black stallion. All around him were prefects, tribunes and legates. His legions had been streaming north along the Via Flaminia since the middle of the previous night.

"The pontoon bridge will be ready by the time we get there?"

"Yes, my lord," said the legate of the praetorians. "My engineers have been working since early yesterday. There will be two bridges for us to cross. Constantine will not be able to restrict our flow over the river."

"Good, and what news of the Saxons defecting?"

"Our spies tell us their war band is waiting near the Milvian Bridge. They will join us when you appear, so they say."

"Good. You'll need to watch them carefully. Put them in the front line, and the Christians too. I want Constantine to know he has lost them all."

Maxentius kicked the ribs of his horse. It picked up speed. He veered off the road onto the wet grass verge and cantered along the line of his legionaries marching to battle. He wanted to be seen, his purple cloak flapping behind him, his jeweled helmet sparking. The men looked to him and cheered as he passed. But the faces were mostly grim, as each man contemplated that their death could arrive soon for them.

He passed rows of archers, their bows so tight in their hands their knuckles were white. He passed four trumpeters, the signalmen of that cohort of archers, and ahead of them four cavalrymen bearing the fluttering standards of their legion, and in front of them a lone giant, golden helmeted centurion, the bearer of that legion's eagle.

In front of him rode that legion's cavalry section and further forward another legion began.

Maxentius, with a troop of his personal praetorians around him, reached the head of his army as the Milvian bridge came into view. It was clearly occupied by his own troops, as his she-wolf and twins – Romulus and Remus – standard flew at either end of the bridge, and cohorts with that standard were already arrayed in battle order beyond the bridge on the flat ground where the Via Cassia and Via Flaminia meet.

No one would doubt that his men, his legions, were defenders of Rome with that standard flying. Each of his legionaries would know they must fight to the death defending their city, their comrades, their wives and their children.

The old Milvian bridge stretched across four high stone arches. Below it the Tiber flowed wide and strong. Further upstream floated the wooden pontoon bridge his praetorians had constructed. Constantine would be surprised when he saw that. It meant Maxentius could deploy troops on either side of the battle line. Lucius had been right to recommend it.

Maxentius looked back toward Rome. The red roof tiles of the Temple of Jupiter Maximus were visible above the gray walls of the city and near them the yellow tiled roof of the imperial palace on the Palatine. Rome looked far away.

He tightened his grip on his reins, hardened his expression, pushed away his doubts. He would win today, as had been predicted.

His wife, the Empress Valeria, had moved out of the imperial palace two nights before with their son. She'd claimed it was for the purpose of praying for his victory. He assumed she was preparing for any outcome. He should care, but he didn't. After this day he would be done with her. He would divorce her fast and have his pick of the youngest daughters of the senatorial class. He had already invited every senator with a daughter under sixteen to his victory feast tonight.

Each had been instructed to bring their daughters.

He laughed. What senator would refuse a victorious emperor whatever he wanted.

He leaned forward. A cloud of dust bloomed far off on the Via Flaminia.

LXXX

North of The Milvian Bridge, on the outskirts of Rome, 312 A.D.

Constantine rode near the front of his men, his dark purple cloak flapping behind. His thigh burned as if a fire raged inside it, but he was able to ride, and that was enough. Sejanus rode behind him with a century of the imperial bodyguard in tow. They had been instructed to ensure Constantine stayed in his saddle, whatever happened that day.

"They are all ready for us," said Sejanus. He pointed ahead, beyond their marching legionaries, to the enemy legionaries formed up already in two large squares and waiting for them in front of the bridge.

"I expect they've been told not to let us across, to save their city," said Constantine. "Maxentius wants to prove he could stop us before we even got to the walls of Rome."

"What are your orders, my lord?"

Constantine pointed ahead. "The Saxons will lead the wedge with our best heavy cavalry, your oven men, behind them. We will use speed to break the enemy will."

"I have bad news about the Saxons."

Constantine kept riding, his pace unchanged.

"They slipped away during the night. I expect they are making their way back to Germania, like the cowards they are."

"No, they are not. I expect we will see them again soon."

Sejanus turned to him. His helmet had a red plume on top. It looked worn and damaged. "I will kill them all with my own sword if they have defected."

"You will stay with me, Sejanus. If they are to be killed, I will give the order when I see them in battle."

He looked back along the line. Many of his men had battered helmets. Some centurions helmet plumes were missing tufts or were missing altogether. Many of the shields his men carried were battered and had chunks broken out of them. His men also carried heavy packs balanced on long poles laid across one shoulder.

Maxentius' men would not be carrying any kit. They would be expecting to be back in Rome that night, their enemy defeated.

"Send the order to drop the packs now where the men stand and to form one wedge quickly," said Constantine.

Sejanus wheeled his horse and rode back to where three trumpeters waited. A series of trumpet blasts followed.

As Constantine's legions marched onto the grassy, open area in front of the river they formed quickly into a long wedge facing the enemy. The benefit of such a formation was the possibility of a knock-out blow against an enemy army. The danger was that they would be surrounded by the larger Maxentian force. But it was a danger he was willing to take. He needed a quick victory. His men would not last an all day battle.

LXXXI

North of The Milvian Bridge, on the outskirts of Rome, 312 A.D.

Maxentius leaned forward in his saddle, his legs holding tight. "I'm honored you have come to join us," he said. "But I thought there were more of you." He looked along the line of Saxons standing with their axes over their shoulders.

Juliana stamped the foot of her axe into the flattened grass by the edge of the river. The pontoon bridge was nearby. Legionaries were still crossing over it.

"I am Juliana, shield maiden and leader of this band. We are enough for many tasks, Emperor. We can help you achieve victory today, despite our depleted number."

Maxentius stared at her, suppressing a smile. This would be easier than he'd imagined. He didn't trust any Saxon, but he had no need to. They could hack away at Constantine's men until they were overwhelmed. And now he would have every god fighting with him, even Woden, as Paulina had predicted. Perhaps she did deserve the new palace, which she'd asked for on this side of the river. He could pay for it from the taxes he would be getting soon from just one of Constantine's provinces.

Sending Paulina into Constantine's entourage to lure him here, with a tired army, was a master stroke he could be proud of.

Juliana stared up at him.

"You will be in the front line, Saxons. I expect you to show no mercy. We will be watching you," he said.

Juliana bowed. "We will be pleased to strike down those who are about to lose this battle. But before we fight it is our tradition to wash our faces in the nearest river and seek the blessing of the river gods."

He shook his head. "There is no time."

"Emperor, my men will fight with added vigor, if you allow them this small act. We will be back before the armies strike each other."

She had a pleading expression.

"Go with them to the river, make sure they are quick," he said to one of his praetorians. "Take five men with you."

Juliana and the eighteen Saxons who had wanted to come with her, walked down to the Tiber.

Maxentius watched from his horse. Juliana knelt, reached out and touched the flowing water as if stroking a cat.

A horn blew. He looked away and moved his horse to higher ground nearby so he could see better.

It was clear the Saxons knew which way this battle would end and intended to be on the right side when it did.

The leading section of Constantine's army, heavy cavalry with multiple centuries of legionaries following behind, were heading straight for the center of his formations, as if they wanted the battle to start early.

He waved at a tribune to come to him. "I want all those heavy cavalry of Constantine's dead before the sun is any higher. Do you understand?"

The man nodded, then raced away.

Maxentius looked back toward the river. He couldn't see any of the Saxons or the praetorians that had been sent to watch over them. Good. They were finished whatever ritual they'd wanted to perform. Now they would reach his front line just as Constantine's troops engaged with it.

He remembered then what he'd heard about a slave called Juliana. Constantine had a concubine once with that name in Treveris. He licked his lips. If this Saxon Juliana still lived after the battle, he would order her to come to him to celebrate his victory.

He'd enjoy breaking that one to his will.

LXXXII

North of The Milvian Bridge, on the outskirts of Rome, 312 A.D.

Constantine pushed with his knees to get a better view by rising higher on his horse.

"Our attack is faltering," said Sejanus.

"I'm going in," said Constantine

"Are you sure?"

Constantine reached toward Sejanus. "I know you bring a wine sack with you to battle, Sejanus, pass it over."

Sejanus pulled the wine sack from where it hung from his belt. He passed it to Constantine.

"This is the battle that will end the war. It may be the last battle I fight too. I want to enjoy it." He drank from the wine sack.

Constantine, Sejanus and his imperial bodyguard rode fast to where the head of his army was engaging in close combat with Maxentius' forces. His cavalry were hacking into Maxentius' front line. They were making little progress.

Familiar noises echoed in his ears. The clash of weapons, shouts, cries, the thundering of hooves and the beat of his own heart filled him with anticipation for the fight ahead. His hands were clammy gripping the reins. He wanted to scream. He did.

"Victory!"

His shout was echoed from his men. He whooped, raised his fist.

But inside he felt hollow.

Today, everything could change. Today, everything would change.

He would win or he would die.

Sweat trickled down his back, but his mind was calm, clear. Only one thing counted now. Bringing death to as many of his enemies as possible, as quickly as possible. If they got an early break-through, Maxentius' superior strength would not grind them down. They needed momentum to win this battle.

He veered toward Sejanus. "Signal all cavalry units to join us," he shouted, grabbing at Sejanus' arm, nearly falling into flattened grass as he did so.

Sejanus gave him the thumbs up and waved his hand high in the air in a circle pointing forward.

The cavalry units from other legions, still waiting to engage, some still coming onto the field of battle, streamed behind them in a long line. Soon there were five hundred cavalry, every last one of their cavalry units, thundering behind them.

It wasn't ideal, but with Maxentius' back to the river they had to take this chance.

As he raced across the thin grass, he heard cheering. Then a cart came into view. It was high-sided, the wood stained red on almost every part. They swerved around it. Constantine got a glimpse of its contents. Legionaries helmets were piled up at the back of the cart. Each helmet represented a legionary who had died on the campaign. Each was a life that had been closed and its owner sent over the river to the underworld because of him.

He tightened his grip on the reins, his body bouncing in rhythm. He would gamble everything today. This campaign had to end in total victory. Nothing else would do.

He remembered Fausta, his wife. Though they were not as close as he had been with Juliana, she was still the mother of his children.

He heard again the words she'd told him before he set out on this campaign.

"My brother, Maxentius, your enemy, raped me when I was twelve years old. He deserves whatever you do to him."

A shout went up from his own men ahead, fighting in a line in front of him. They had seen him coming and were disengaging, waiting for his unit to strike.

This was like a dream he'd had.

They were racing toward a line of enemy legionaries who had their shields up and their spears pointed out. The risk of being impaled was high. As they neared the spears Constantine was in the lead. He pointed to the left with his gloved fist and veered that way just before he crashed right into the spears.

As he turned, he pulled a short throwing spear from where it hung on the side of his horse. He threw it hard into Maxentius' shield wall. Behind him five hundred of his cavalry men did the same as they swerved to follow him. Many of the spears stuck in the shields, weighing them down.

Screams ripped through the air.

And again he turned, signaled with his hand and all along the line his men knew what to do. Gaps had appeared in Maxentius' line. His men closed with the gaps, and the bending line of shields. The weight of shields with two of three spears in them was too much for some men. The gaps were few, but they were there.

Constantine kicked his horse and pointed it at a gap in the line, urging it on. His horse would be at risk of impaling itself on enemy spears, but if he succeeded, he would be on the other side of their line. His men would follow.

Spear heads glistened menacingly. And then a shout came. Some cavalry were rushing to support him. Their screams must have been heard in the palaces of Rome.

He pulled the horse up to jump over a fallen enemy legionary and landed with a jolt that almost unseated him but he was alone and through the enemy shields and swinging his sword wildly, catching one man in the neck and another straight into his back and grating against bone.

Then spears were poking toward him and the grinning faces of Maxentius' legionaries had surrounded him. This was their opportunity to end the battle quickly.

LXXXIII

North of The Milvian Bridge, on the outskirts of Rome, 312 A.D.

Maxentius watched, smiling, as Constantine led a cavalry charge directly into his front line. Constantine was stupid to risk everything. All they had to do was stop his charge and then grind Constantine's forces down. If it took all day and thousands had to die, so be it.

"Stop," a shout rang out behind him. He pulled on his horse's reins and wheeled around in a stamping of hooves.

A tribune from the praetorian guard was racing back to the river, on foot.

"Go and see what that's about," he said, to one of the junior officers who were crowding around him.

Then he turned his horse back to the main event. He was just in time to see a swirling mass of confusion around where Constantine had been. Helmets were bobbing, swords flashing in the air, blood spurting. Shouts from that confrontation were mixed with noises from all across the battlefield. Units had engaged to the left and multiple skirmishes were happening as Maxentius' archers sought to take up positions at the edge of the trees where the via Cassia came into view heading for the Milvian Bridge.

Another engagement, this time an assault by his light cavalry on a legion of Constantine's men setting up on the right of the battlefield was also taking place. Shouts and the sharp noise of clashing swords and the whistles of arrows came from all sides.

"Both flanks to move forward," he shouted at the senior signalman. Moments later trumpets blared.

He gripped the jeweled pommel of his sword. He didn't expect to use it. From all the reports he'd received he knew he had about twice the men than Constantine commanded, and his troops were fresher, not having had to march every day for weeks. And Constantine was fighting right in the middle of the most dangerous part of the battle. All it would take would be one lucky thrust.

This was the moment when Constantine's luck would run out.

"Stop now!" This time the shout came fainter, barely audible above the din. He didn't look around. If someone had disobeyed orders, he would deal with them after the battle.

He remembered the battles he'd fought with his father in Germania and Hispania. Both times they had won. Both times they had had a larger force. Both times they had worn the enemy down. It would be the same this time.

Might would win again.

LXXXIV

North of The Milvian Bridge, on the outskirts of Rome, 312 A.D.

Constantine rubbed a gloved hand across his eyes. Blood had splattered into them, making him blink repeatedly. The salty smell of it filled the air.

"Close up," he shouted.

All around were enemy faces. Some were grinning. Others bared their broken teeth. Swords were raised.

He spun around, sword up. Some of his own cavalry were not far off, but they were too far away to help him. He stared into the faces of his enemies. Why weren't they finishing him?

Were they savoring the moment?

His legs ached. His side throbbed. His breathing came heavily. Was it over?

No, it couldn't be. He would fight them all.

And then he knew. This was that moment in a battle when opposing men stopped striking at each other, as each surveyed the scene and caught their breath for the next round of flesh-cutting blows.

"Pull back," someone shouted.

The men around him grinned wider.

Their enemy was retreating.

"Pull back, Christians," the voice shouted again.

Constantine held his sword up high, ready to strike. Why weren't they closing on him?

A familiar face appeared in the crowd around him.

"Lucius, what in Hades name are you doing here?" A loud gasp broke from his lips. He shook his head, blinked.

Lucius, blood splattered, carrying a round wooden shield with a cross on it, stared up at him, his mouth open in exultation, his hand held toward him. And then he went down on one knee.

"These are all your men to command."

And all around them men kept grinning and then, as one, they turned their backs on him as if they were his personal guard. Row after row in front of him the men, who had apparently been fighting for Maxentius, turned and faced back toward the Milvian Bridge.

Lucius opened his arms to reach up and hug Constantine. "And what in Hades took you so long to get to Rome?"

LXXXV

North of The Milvian Bridge, on the outskirts of Rome, 312 A.D.

Juliana looked at her hands. The skin had recovered a good deal since they were burnt, thanks to the ointments she'd been given with strict instructions to rub the salve into her skin four times a day, but her palms were still hard and the pain still came when she gripped something tight, though the cold didn't affect her hands as much now.

Which was a good thing that day as the ropes attaching the pontoons together were connected below the water line of the river.

She'd volunteered to go into the water as any of Maxentius' men watching would never assume she would be intent on doing any damage to the bridge. They would most likely assume she had waded into the water up to her chest to avoid being spied on while she evacuated herself.

Cutting through ropes as thick as a giant's wrist underwater was not an easy task.

She pulled herself under the bridge while smiling at Maxentius' guard, as if embarrassed to be watched over.

He'd obligingly looked away.

When he looked back, she was gone. He looked along the bank, then went to the other side of the pontoon bridge. That took him a long time as men were still crossing it and he was shouted at three times by centurions to get out of the way.

Juliana was on the other side by this time. One of the ropes connecting the barges used for the bridge was almost cut through. Now she had had to cut another, despite her chattering teeth and the fact that she'd had to tie her dagger to her wrist to prevent it slipping away.

A few of Maxentius' men on the far side spotted her, but again, as she was a lone head in the water no one seemed to think she would be capable of doing any damage to the bridge.

She kept going, slicing at a new rope underwater, her mind focused only on the task, and on surviving the water around her, which tugged and pulled at her like a crowd of hungry slaves looking for food.

LXXXVI

North of The Milvian Bridge, on the outskirts of Rome, 312 A.D.

"Emperor," someone shouted behind him.

He turned. The junior officer he had sent to investigate the disturbance had arrived back, red faced and sweating heavily under his helmet.

"What is it, man?" shouted Maxentius.

"They've cut the pontoon bridge." He pointed behind him. One of the long wooden pontoon sections had indeed broken free. It was sailing down the river to the Milvian bridge.

"Who did this?"

"Saxons."

"We'll deal with them after." He turned to the legate of the praetorians. The man's lip curled, as if he wanted to say something. Maxentius pointed at him. "I want those Saxons captured and skinned alive after the battle." He pointed at the Milvian Bridge. "I'm moving to the Milvian."

He leaned toward the legate. "Get me Constantine's head or fall on your sword. That is an order." He kicked his horse in the ribs and cantered toward the Milvian Bridge. His men were still streaming over from Rome. Three of his legates were with him as well as a dozen other officers and signalers.

"The flanks are to come in. Signal again," he shouted at a tribune. Trumpets blared. Maxentius' stomach knotted. Losing the pontoon bridge had been an unexpected blow, but it was not enough for him to lose the battle. It couldn't be. He still had the larger force.

And Constantine could have fallen by now. What they had to do was grind down Constantine's men until they retreated.

And he needed a safe place to command from.

A sudden sharp clashing of massed swords on shield bosses filled the air. He leaned up on his horse but couldn't see where the noise was coming from. Did it mean Constantine had fallen? Yes, that had to be it. His men were celebrating.

He leaned up, looked again over the heads of the men in front of him. He narrowed his eyes. The center of the battle was near, a line of helmets coming steadily toward him, as if they were cutting through the legion in front of them.

"Why is that cohort retreating?" he shouted. "Tell then to turn back."

And then it dawned on him.

They must be Constantine's men advancing toward him.

He sucked in his breath. Fighting raged to the left and to the right. His men were winning. But in the center his line was folding.

And then, he could see the fighting clearly, about fifty paces away, stabbing, stabbing, blood spewing, piercing shouts, swords swinging.

"I'll go back over the bridge and command from there," he shouted. His officers stared at him, blank faced. He didn't care what they thought.

He turned his horse and headed onto the bridge.

He shouted at the men coming toward him. "Out of the way, make a passage for your emperor."

Most of the men did, and he was onto the wooden planks of the bridge quickly. But there were more legionaries coming toward him. And then he saw a face he knew. It was the face of a centurion he'd moved to the praetorians as his wife had thrown herself at him. Successfully.

He leaned down. He was too near one side of the bridge. To his left he could see over to the rushing waters of the Tiber. The river flowed fast below, white flecked. It hadn't seemed so angry when he passed over it earlier.

"Make way for your emperor," he shouted at the centurion, who had stopped with all his men around him, staring up at him, their faces perplexed.

"I will command from the south side. Help me get over there." He leaned down. "Cut through your own men if you have to. I must be allowed to pass."

There were more men crowding forward, heading to the battle. They had grim faces. Many knew they would die. And then the press of men around him grew tighter, like at the colosseum when the fights were over, and everyone wanted to leave the arena at the same time.

This centurion had to help him.

He leaned down. "I never touched your wife," he lied. The man stared up at him as if he wanted to spit at him.

"I'll make you a legate. I'll give you a palace and an estate south of Rome. Get me across the river now!" He looked around. The fighting sounded close. The clash of swords and the despairing wails of injured men filled his ears. He had to get across the river.

"I will help you, Emperor," shouted the centurion, leering up at him. "Come, men, let us do our duty." Men crowded around.

Maxentius put his hand up. "No, no closer. The river is just here." He pointed to his left. He could hear the water thundering below the bridge now.

And then it started to rain.

Not just any rain. Sheets of it, as if the heavens had turned into a waterfall from the dark pools of the River Styx.

Maxentius tightened his knees, kicked softly, his boots slipping against the side of his horse. Surely the mare could push its way forward through the men.

"Emperor!" someone shouted. Hands were reaching for him. Some were holding his legs. Rain flew into his face and then, with a lurch, he knew he was going to fall into the river.

His horse went first, and he hung in the air for a moment as he pushed away from the ornamental saddle and turned, hoping the hands of his men would hold him, but they didn't, or they couldn't, and with a ragged shout he went down and into the raging torrent and down deep, his breastplate and cloak pulling him like weights into the cold and dark, his mind numbing as he turned and turned, reaching for the light. He needed air. He had to breathe.

And he did. And water filled him up.

LXXXVII

Constantine sheathed his sword. "Have his head put on a spike and bring it to me."

Sejanus saluted. They were a hundred paces from the bridge. All around Maxentius' men were laying down their arms. Word has passed like a fire from the men who had seen Maxentius fall with his horse into the raging Tiber.

But Maxentius' legions further away would need more to convince them.

"Take the surrender of as many officers as you can and disarm all his men. Tell them to wait on this side of the Tiber. My personal guard is to come with me over the bridge as soon as we have that bastard Maxentius' head. Send a cavalry unit to the city now to spread the word that their new emperor is coming to Rome. All resistance must cease." He bit his lip. Could it be true? Had he won?

He looked around. The giant black mare he rode had been wandering riderless. No one knew whose it was, so he'd claimed it. All around, men were staring, looking up at him as if he was a god. Some were even cheering as word spread and the noises of conflict died down. Most were staring, wide eyed, haunted by the death they'd seen or inflicted.

"Maxentius is dead. The war is over," was the shout that spread from one side of the battlefield to the other, like a wave, drowning out all other calls.

He crossed the bridge, stopped on the far side, drew his breath in hard, held his reins tight.

345

Many of Maxentius' men had run away, but a few were still standing nearby, staring at him, some sullen, many looking relieved.

Three of his cavalry men, all quiet, blood-splattered and grim faced were beside him.

"There will no reprisals," he shouted, leaning forward. "Spread the word. All of you are invited to join with me in bringing peace back to our Roman world. The war is over. Our provinces are united." He raised his fist.

A loud cheer went up. It echoed down the river.

He rode on. No man tried to stop him. And soon, at the next turn, the walls of Rome were visible as a gray wave ahead. Trumpets were blaring far off now, probably from the city walls. Did they think Maxentius had won?

He let his breath out, looked around. There were about a hundred men with him now, a mix of cavalry and legionaries on foot. A sudden wariness came over him. Was all this a trick? Would Maxentius appear with a thousand men to cut them all down?

His thigh throbbed fiercely and his left side ached. His head, too. Sticky blood covered his hand when he put it to his forehead.

He needed Juliana's touch.

He reined in his horse.

On each side of the road ahead stood a line of crosses with crucified men hanging from them, stretching into the distance. Hanging as a warning, probably meant to frighten captives after Maxentius' victory. Most of the corpses were only days old. The stench of rotting flesh came to him. Birds could be seen pecking at eye sockets. It was a stark reminder of how Maxentius ruled.

He looked around. Lucius was on a horse right behind him. Sejanus was on the other side. Both were grim faced and smeared with blood. Sejanus' helmet had a big dent in it. His cloak was ripped. Constantine had lost his. He had no idea where.

"Sejanus, remind me to ban crucifixion in my first speech to the Senate." He pointed at the nearest crucified man. "This is the way Lucius' friend Christ was killed. I want an end to this practice in every province I govern."

Lucius cheered in a low voice, as if he'd lost his energy in the battle. "That's real good news. Every Christian will be pleased, but," Lucius stuck his tongue out at Constantine, "you still only rule half the empire."

Constantine laughed. "I am still only forty years old, brave Lucius. My father was older when he won his greatest laurels. I expect the same to be true of me."

He turned his horse. All doubts were gone. The crosses and the discarded swords and spears and shields and the expectant faces of Maxentius' legionaries staring from a distance were enough. He knew the taste of victory and the smell of it.

It was the taste and smell of blood.

"Find Juliana and her Saxons, Sejanus. Bring her to me, I will not enter Rome today."

Epilogue

The citizens of Rome welcomed their new Emperor with an Adventus, a ceremonial parade usually only given to emperors returning from a victorious campaign. It was likely that the parade had been prepared for Maxentius, but the citizens did not care about that.

The war was over, no more of their men would die fighting against Constantine. A new emperor would have games to celebrate his victory, and he'd shower coin on every one of his supporters, old and new.

Constantine entered the city in a golden four-wheeled carriage, pulled by four giant black mares with wide eyes, in the middle of the day. He had a golden laurel on his head. Lines of his legionaries, who had entered the city soon after dawn, kept back the populace. In front of him the standards and eagles of the legions who fought with him led the way. They were all on their way to the Forum, where the Senate would be addressed, and bread and wine distributed to the people.

Maxentius' big battered head, his hair smeared on his skull, sat on a spear for all to see straight in front of Constantine. It, and the man carrying it, a Maxentian legate, were showered with abuse, spittle and rotten vegetables. At the Forum Constantine had to listen to speeches extolling his virtues in Latin and then translated versions in Greek. The speeches went on for so long he wondered if they'd been designed as a punishment for him for winning the battle of the bridge.

After the speeches Constantine did not go to the Temple of Jupiter to sacrifice to the old gods, as he was expected to do. It was a clear sign to all the people of Rome that things would change under Constantine.

He'd already distributed awards, gold medallions to his officers and torques to his Gallic and Saxon auxiliaries. Juliana had been brought to his tent and had helped him bind his wounds again in the morning and get ready for this day.

She would not be seen in public often after this, but as an officer in his auxiliaries she could come and go to his palaces whenever she wanted.

Fausta, his empress, would resent this, but at that moment she was hurrying to Rome with Helena, his mother, and Crispus, who, because he was only fourteen, it had been decided that he should remain in Gaul.

Fausta's appearance at his side had been long delayed and Constantine had wondered if she'd been expecting her brother to defeat him.

Constantine ordered that Maxentius' head be pickled in sweet Greek wine, so that not only could Fausta enjoy seeing him impotent and lifeless, but he could also send the head to all Maxentius' previous provinces so they would know he was definitely dead.

Constantine had been awarded the title Augustus, senior emperor of Maxentius' provinces and his own, by the senate.

There was still another emperor in the east, but there would be time enough to deal with that threat. For now, all Constantine wanted was to consolidate and to reward those who had helped him.

Chief among those were the Christians, followers of Lucius. To them he granted a title of the land on the west of the Tiber, where the Circus of Nero had been used for centuries to sacrifice Christians who refused to give up their one god.

The Christians and their talk of a life after death also provided solace for Constantine when he found out that the son, Julius, he'd had with Juliana, who had been captured and taken to Rome, had been executed as Constantine neared the city. His body could not be found, despite multiple search parties being sent out to look for him.

Juliana pulled her hair and screamed at everyone when she heard the news that an order had been given to execute the boy. She'd spent every day since she'd arrived asking after him in all the palaces Maxentius used.

She covered herself in ashes soon after she heard the news.

The imperial slave who came forward to reveal what had happened said that Valeria, Maxentius' widow, had looked after the boy in her rooms near the end, but had handed him to Maxentius the morning he left for the battle.

In a fit of rage on hearing that news Constantine ordered Valeria, Maxentius' widow, and their son to be both executed.

The price of victory is high.

Even when Constantine heard that Valeria and her son were dead his grief did not diminish. All further victory celebrations were canceled.

When asked by Lucius days later if he would agree to be baptized a Christian, as faith in Christ would help him and all his sins would be washed away, Constantine replied, "I'll do it later. I am sure there will be many sins I'll need washed away in the future."

He stared at his hands for a long time before continuing, "There is a lot of blood on my hands, Lucius, but I'm sure there is a reason my life was spared, when I could easily have died a dozen times. There must be a reason we won. That is what I live for now. To find out the reason. The reason you dreamed about me with a golden laurel on my head and it became true."

"Yes, it was strange seeing that dream come true."

Constantine wrapped his arms around Lucius and hugged him.

"Have you seen Paulina?" Lucius asked.

"I have. She told me she is working with you, making plans for Nero's circus."

"You don't plan to punish her for running back to Maxentius?"

Constantine shook his head. "Paulina didn't tell you why she really came back to Rome?"

"No."

"She lured Maxentius out of Rome, Lucius. She told him that Saxons would join him and help him win. He was convinced he would win the battle because of her." He spoke slowly as he continued. "She'd been his spy for years, helping him with information on all his enemies in Rome. My problem is not how to punish her. It is how to reward her. That is why your plans for Nero's circus have my full support. I promised her there will be a new temple there, and no more priestesses will have to do what she had to do ever again in our empire."

Before You Go – Two Things

I hope you have enjoyed this book. If you can be persuaded **to write a reader review on Amazon, I'd really appreciate it.**

Reviews on Amazon are critical to the success of an author these days.

To join the mailing list and receive news of the next book in the series, put this link in your browser: **http://bit.ly/TSOTBseries**

Made in the USA
Middletown, DE
18 May 2021